I0461026

Truth or Dare

A Novel

by

Anne Denmark

Stapleton Press
©Copyright 2017

Truth or Dare
Copyright: Anne Denmark
Published: December 2017
ISBN: 978-0-692-93229-2
Publisher: Stapleton Press

ALL RIGHTS RESERVED. No part of this book may be reproduced or transmitted for resale or use by any party other than the individual purchaser, who is the sole authorized user of this information. Purchaser is authorized to use any of the information in this publication for his or her own use ONLY. All other reproduction or transmission, in any form or by any means, electronic or mechanical, including photocopying, recording, or by any information storage or retrieval system, is prohibited without express written permission from Anne Denmark.

DISCLAIMER: This is a work of fiction. Names, characters, businesses, places, events and incidents are either the products of the author's imagination or used in a fictitious manner. Any resemblance to actual persons, living or dead, or actual events is purely coincidental.

This book was published with the assistance of Self-Publishing Relief, a division of Writer's Relief.

Published by Stapleton Press

© Anne Denmark, 2017

For My Mother, Ruby Nell,
My Daughter, Adrienne,
& My Granddaughter, Amelia.

1

When Doris arrived at the hospital, it started raining. A heavy soaking downpour permeated her lightweight sweater, and water seeped into her spring green pumps. She splashed her way from the parking lot to the front entrance; a chill took over her body, but she didn't even feel it. "My mother, Avis Peechum, was admitted tonight. Can you please tell me what room she's in?" The woman behind the desk was busy on the computer, the phone receiver cradled precariously between her shoulder and ear. Pleasingly plump, with a line of dark roots in her parted blonde hair, she tilted around in her chair and nodded to Doris but then turned back to the computer screen. "I'm sorry," Doris raised her voice slightly, "I don't mean to be rude, but I found out my mother had a stroke, and I must see her immediately."

"Can you hold for a moment?" The woman asked the phone, staring at Doris like she was a raving lunatic who might pull out an Uzi at any moment. "What was the name?"

Doris took a breath, wiping water from her face and absentmindedly wringing out her sweater on the tile floor. "Peechum, Avis. P-E-E-C-H-U-M. I think she had a stroke." The woman typed a series of numbers and letters into the computer, and a blue screen came up with a list. Doris pulled tissues from her purse and dabbed at her face and hair, trying to regain her composure. Tears welled up in her eyes, but she was out of tissues, so she wiped them away with her hands.

"Peechum, here she is," the woman sounded triumphant, which Doris found inappropriate for some reason. "She's in intensive care. You take the elevator to the third floor, go down the hall following a blue line to another set of elevators, and then take that elevator to the seventh floor. This will take you right to the Intensive Care Unit and you can speak to the nurse there about seeing your mother."

"Thank you," Doris muttered and rushed off toward the elevator.

Martin came through the front door as Doris's elevator door was opening. She entered, turned around, and looked in his direction but didn't see him. All she could focus on was her mother and remembering the insane instructions she needed to follow in order to find her. The woman at the desk resumed her phone call as Martin tapped on the desk and asked where he could find Avis Peechum. The woman opened her mouth slightly, released a heavy sigh, and asked the caller to hold on once again.

The elevator seemed excruciatingly slow to Doris. Finally, the doors opened on the seventh floor and the nurses' station was in plain sight. "My mother," Doris said, out of breath now from worry, not exertion, "The receptionist said she was here."

This nurse looked sympathetic and concerned. "Her name?"

"Peechum, Avis. My name is Doris Peechum. May I see her please?"

Nurse Cindy, according to her nametag, looked at Doris with a serious expression. It alarmed Doris, but she kept silent. "Ms. Peechum, your mother has experienced a very serious stroke and is unconscious." The nurse looked at her watch and sighed. "We normally don't let anyone visit patients in Intensive Care after nine, but I can see you are upset."

"I would appreciate any time you can give me," Doris said, a tear escaping the corner of her eye and her breath catching in little gasps.

"It will have to be brief." Doris nodded desperately. Nurse Cindy hesitated for a moment then smiled. "Okay, follow me."

Martin emerged from the elevator in time to see Doris turn the corner, but he possessed the good sense not to yell at her. He took a seat in the waiting room, knowing she might need some company when she came back.

The nurse stood outside Avis' room and opened the door for Doris. "Five minutes, okay?" Doris nodded and tiptoed into the room. Avis lay perfectly still on the white bed linens in the white room with one long fluorescent light glowing above her head on the wall. An IV drip was connected to the back of her left hand and an oxygen line led to her nose. Nearby, a monitor beeped with regular intervals and made a faint typing sound as a continuous paper feed flowed out of the bottom and fell along the floor. It was all so surreal; Doris thought momentarily she was having a nightmare.

Doris tried to swallow but the back of her throat felt clenched like a fist. She batted away a tear and moved next to the bed. She put her hand gently on Avis' leg and then took her right hand in her own. She pulled a chair over and sat with her cheek resting on their blended hands. "Mother," she whispered softly, "I'm so sorry I wasn't there." She wanted to cry in earnest but realized this might upset Avis so she held back. She took several tissues from the box on Avis' nightstand and cleaned herself up. "Now, mother, you're going to be fine. They won't let me stay here long, but I'll be right outside in the waiting room, okay?" She patted Avis' hand, but there was no response. Avis looked small and helpless and almost as pale as her pillowcase. Doris was still rubbing her hand when Nurse Cindy came back to retrieve her.

"I'm sorry, but you'll have to wait in the lounge. We have bedding, and the chairs recline if you want to spend the night." Cindy face was soft and fleshy, with bright green eyes and a sweet smile. Doris was grateful for her face and her kindness.

"Yes, I'd like to do that." Doris stood and kissed Avis' hand, gently placing it back on the white blanket. "If I can come back in or if anything happens, you will let me know, won't you?"

"Yes, of course," Nurse Cindy nodded. Doris had never been ill enough to stay in the hospital, but she remembered sitting with her father for days on end. Some nurses were kind, but many of them were rude and abrupt, probably overworked and exhausted, but still. *Cindy has the right job*, Doris thought, *she is completely convincing and understanding like a nurse ought to be. Too bad they can't all take lessons from Nurse Cindy.*

She asked the nurse for the nearest payphone, and the nurses looked at her oddly. *No, I don't have a cellphone*, she thought to herself. "There's one just past the elevators," one of them said and pointed politely. Doris wasn't looking forward to it, but she figured she needed to call Ted. She didn't know if he should come in or not, but he definitely needed to know their mother was in the hospital. It was nearly eleven o'clock in Kerryville, which meant it would be almost ten in Baton Rouge. Tammy, Ted's wife, answered the phone. She was a pleasant woman, a year or so older than Ted, whose main concern was raising her two kids. Doris sometimes envied what she perceived as the simplicity of knowing where your priorities are at all times, which she assumed was how mothers felt. "Tammy," Doris spoke in muted tones, "This is Doris." Tammy usually greeted Doris with a loud hello and lots of chitchat, but she seemed to sense Doris' mood.

"Hi, Doris, how are you?"

"Well, I'm okay, Tammy, but Mom's in the hospital and I need to speak with Ted. Is he there?"

"Oh, goodness, uh, yes, hold on," Tammy put the phone down, and Doris heard scuffling and muffled voices which sounded like "Avis" and "Doris" and "hospital." Doris didn't hear any kids' voices; she figured they were in bed by now on a school night.

"Doris?" Ted's worried voice came through the line.

"Hi, Ted. I'm sorry to be calling you so late and with such bad news, but Mother is not well. She's had a serious stroke and is unconscious. She's in intensive care now, and I thought you'd want to know."

"Well, of course, Doris," Ted seemed insulted for some reason. *Whatever*, Doris thought. She didn't communicate well with her younger brother—the one who did everything right. "Is she going to be all right?"

"I just got here, Ted, I don't know much. I'll talk to the doctor when I can find her, but I wanted to go ahead and call." The line was quiet for a long minute. "She looks bad, Ted," Doris couldn't keep the sobs from her throat, "all white and helpless. I wish I could tell you more."

Ted's attitude softened. "It's okay, Doris, I'm glad you called." Another long moment of silence landed between them. "Do you think we should come up right now?"

"I don't know. Why don't you wait until I talk to the doctor? If there's no immediate danger you could at least wait until the weekend. I promise I'll call tomorrow and let you know—should I call you at work?"

"Just call my cell." Ted's cell phone, made him immediately available wherever he was. Doris resisted the new technology; she only learned how to use the Internet because it's the only way most students want to communicate and, admittedly it came in handy for research. But a phone you carry with you all the time? Sounded like a nuisance before, but now, she realized sadly she could have received her mother's call right away if she were carrying one. She resolved to get one as soon as possible, as soon as this crisis was over.

After Ted and Doris made calling arrangements and hung up, Doris walked to the desk to ask Nurse Cindy if she could speak to Avis' doctor. "I'm sorry, but she made her rounds right before you arrived. She is here, though, and will be back around in a few hours, but unless there's an emergency, she has other duties in the hospital. Should we wake you up when she comes back?"

Doris nodded and said, "Please." It was the only word she could produce. Cindy nodded and patted her hand. Doris turned from the desk and for the first time realized she was soaking wet and freezing cold. She made a visit to the bathroom where she could wash her face and use the hand dryer to air out her shell and pants. The lightweight material responded quickly to the heat and in fifteen minutes, Doris emerged with mostly dry clothing and only slightly damp hair pulled back into a low ponytail. She entered the waiting room and looked around for a chair. She was surprised to see Martin, lying in one of the recliners already asleep with a stack of papers in his left hand and a red pen in his right. She had completely forgotten about Martin, the man who might possibly have saved her mother's life. Doris smiled at the sight of him. *At least he's here*, she thought; all else was forgotten. Doris took the recliner next to him and tried to focus on the CNN news report an elderly gentleman across the room was watching.

When the nurse entered with her arms full of blankets and pillows, the bustle woke Martin. He tucked the papers into his briefcase and helped the nurse distribute the bedding to the elderly gentleman and a young married couple in the other corner. Doris fixed up makeshift beds for Martin and herself, then asked the nurse if the lights could be dimmed. "Yes, we usually do that," the young nurse, Gloria, said in a friendly but somewhat clipped manner. "We turn the TV off at eleven, also. You let us know if we can do anything else to make your wait more comfortable." She was all business—neat and efficient, but she impressed Doris as being cold and unconcerned. Nurse Gloria went through all the motions and did a good job, but Doris doubted if she ever worried about a family or even remembered a patient's name. She wasn't Nurse Cindy, that's for sure.

Martin settled into the chair and looked over at Doris. He took her hand and asked about Avis. "You were right, it was a stroke," Doris said. "She's still unconscious, so we have to wait."

Martin looked down and furrowed his brow. "I'm sorry I couldn't get hold of you, Doris. And it took me so long to tell you..."

Doris cut him off. "Please. Don't worry about any of that now." He patted her hand and told her goodnight. "You don't have to stay here, Martin. I mean, I know you have classes tomorrow and there's nothing you can do."

"Nonsense," was all he said, pulling the handle to recline the chair completely and closing his eyes. Doris looked at him for a long moment and then followed his lead. But she knew there wouldn't be much sleep tonight. All she could hope for was some quiet rest.

Try as she might, however, Doris could not settle down. She got up as quietly as possible and stopped at the desk around midnight to see if the doctor had come by. Nurse Cindy was gone, off at eleven Doris figured. Nurse Sarah was there with Gloria and they both assured her the doctor would be back around one o'clock and there were no changes in Avis' condition. Doris thanked them and rambled around the hospital.

She strolled down to the cafeteria and got a pint of milk from the vending machine. She thought it might help her relax, but it was so cold all she accomplished was becoming wide-awake. She walked around the lobby, which was virtually deserted. A soft tapping on a computer keyboard came from the receptionist's desk, and occasionally she would pass another family member who couldn't sleep roaming the halls. Doris returned to the Intensive Care waiting area, pulled the play script out of her purse, and retreated to the only unoccupied corner of the room and turned on a nearby lamp to read.

The next thing she knew, Nurse Gloria was gently nudging her hand. She awoke slowly, confused about where she was and who was waking her. Then it dawned on her—she was in the hospital and this was Gloria, and the doctor must be here.

"Ms. Peechum," Gloria whispered, "Doctor Newsome will speak with you about your mother now. Come with me." Gloria helped Doris out of the recliner, which she needed for some reason. Doris put the script in her purse and smoothed her hair back as she walked at the brisk pace of Nurse Gloria toward a small room near the nurses' station with a sofa and two matching armchairs. The doctor was looking over a file with her glasses perched on the top of her head when Doris came in and took a seat on the sofa across from her.

The doctor looked up and stood slightly to reach a hand to Doris. They shook hands and greeted each other cordially, and then the serious expression returned to the doctor's face. Doris sat silently, her fingers pulling at the zipper on her purse. "Ms. or I believe it's Dr. Peechum, isn't it?" Doris nodded slightly and tried to smile. She realized she was holding her breath but couldn't seem to stop doing it. "I'm Elise Newsome. I'm in the same practice as your mother's doctor, Ruby Stapleton. I'm the one on call tonight." She paused and looked at her hands then back to Doris. "Your mother endured a pretty serious stroke from what we can tell. We don't know how much damage there is right now or even if she will come out of the coma. Comas are still mysterious. Some stroke patients go into a coma like this and then come out as good as they were before the stroke—the body sometimes uses a coma to heal itself. But with your mother's age and general physical condition, I don't think we should pin our hopes on that kind of outcome. Her vital signs seem good now, but there could be brain damage or, more likely, some paralysis. There is brain function, but we can't know the extent of any damage until she comes out of the coma, and I can't tell you if it will be today or three weeks from now."

Doris started to breathe again. "What can we do for her?" she asked.

"Wait," the doctor said, "wait and keep her comfortable is all we can do at this point. Spend time with her, talk to her. There's some evidence to suggest coma patients are partially aware of their surroundings—it might help her to hear a familiar voice. When she awakens, she will probably need some intense therapy to recover." There was a long silence between them in which Doris wondered if she should ask the obvious question. Dr. Newsome seemed to be waiting to see if Doris was ready to hear the answer. Finally, the doctor sighed and said, "There is also the possibility she will not come out of the coma. Many stroke patients succumb to a coma before they pass on."

Doris nodded, and a tear began to trickle down her cheek. She cleared her throat.

"What I need to know from you is what we should do if we detect a serious condition. I mean, if she goes into cardiac arrest or kidney failure, do you know if she has a living will?"

"No, I don't think so. She never mentioned anything to me," Doris said. "I should talk this over with my brother."

"Fine. Remember, unless we have a 'do not resuscitate' order from the family, we will do everything in our power to keep her alive, even if it means she will be connected to machines for the rest of her life."

Doris put her hand over her mouth. "I know she wouldn't want that. I am sure of it. I've heard her say it before. Can you tell me with any certainty she wouldn't fully recover if you did try to save her?"

"Sadly," the doctor said, "I can't tell you anything with certainty now. I do need your signature on some papers to give us permission to run some tests." Doris looked around the room trying to remember if her mother ever talked about a will. "We should know more by tomorrow." Doris was strangely silent. "Are you all right? Can we get you anything?"

Doris signed the forms. "I'd like to sit with my mother and read to her. Please?"

"Certainly. I'll arrange it."

2

The day before.

Doris Peechum sat at her kitchen table, with a 1950s green Formica top and chrome edging, as she did every morning. She sipped her coffee and looked over the early newspaper. "Nothing but bad news," she muttered to herself as she folded the paper neatly and laid it on the kitchen counter. She rinsed her empty coffee cup, tucked it into the dishwasher, and gathered her robe tightly around her middle. Felix, her skinny, shorthaired black and white cat, nosed into her calf and rubbed the length of his lithe body around her legs. "Morning, sugar," she said, bending slightly to stroke his fur, affectionately running her hand down his back and along his tail.

"Reow," answered Felix before running back to his breakfast dish.

Doris took a moment to step onto her screened-in back porch to check her flowers and deposit the newspaper in the recycling tub. Colorful pansies in modest clay pots she planted over the weekend lined the southern ledge of the porch railing, catching a light breeze that made them bob in and out of sunlight, illuminating and darkening their bright colors like a flashing sign. She pinched off a few dying blossoms and looked over her tiny backyard, a square of grass shielded from the neighbors by a tall cedar fence, coming to life in the early morning light. She noticed the oleanders and azaleas needed some cutting back before autumn sets in so they would produce glorious pink and white blooms in the spring. Doris let out a deep sigh, wishing she could go right out there and start cutting. "Back to the grindstone," she told a robin sitting in a nearby tree. The bird took flight, and she walked to her room to dress for work.

Doris progressed through her morning bathroom routine with meticulous attention to detail and order. She had performed this same ritual since her high school days and saw no reason to vary it. She flossed and brushed her teeth, scrubbed and moisturized her face, and then pulled her robe off to get dressed. Usually she rushed to her closet, but today, she paused in front of the full-length mirror to assess the effects of aging on her figure. She was proud to see she had not gained any appreciable amount of weight, but the sagging of breasts and tummy was undeniable. "I really need to start walking in the evenings," she scolded her reflection. She turned sideways and decided she liked this view much better, but a closer look at her face showed tiny lines etched near her mouth, eyes and forehead, and the hair around her face was beginning to gray--presenting a stark contrast against the rich auburn. Doris never considered herself pretty; the nose is too pointy, the skin too pasty, and the lips too thin. But she took pride in her plainness and used her intellect and wit to engage others. She used to worry about the freckles on her face, but now, the freckles were the least of her concerns. Dr. Doris Peechum would soon turn fifty, and she was beginning to show her age. She sighed sadly to herself and headed to the bedroom closet.

As she was nearly dressed, Felix started rubbing the sides of his face lovingly against her bedroom slippers. "What is it about these slippers that fascinates you so much, you crazy cat!" She was running late, but she paused for a moment to pick him up and scratch under his chin. She laid him gently on the bed and kissed his head then hurried, into the bathroom to dab on a light coat of foundation, blush and lipstick and then brushed her hair neatly away from her face.

Here we are, halfway through September, and I still haven't put my fall and winter clothes into the closet, she thought to herself. It was going to be a warm day in Kerryville, so she picked out a lightweight top with a pair of tan slacks. "I'll do it this weekend," she vowed, meaning she would put her summer clothes into the plastic tubs she kept under her bed and pack her cold-weather clothes into her drawers and closets. With the finishing touches of a brown leather belt, matching pumps, and a conservative amount of solid gold jewelry, Doris was ready for the day. She picked up her briefcase and headed for Kerryville College, a small private liberal arts school, where she serves as the one and only Associate Professor of Art History.

Entering her office in the morning was Doris' favorite part of her job. She loved turning the key to her door and opening it to her beautifully decorated and highly personalized space. She hadn't done much with her home--she had barely taken the time to paint and hang curtains when she moved in last year--but her office was different. This is where she lived the best part of her life. Six years ago, when the college granted her tenure, she was promoted to Associate Professor of Art History in her hometown of Kerryville, Tennessee. She had spent the following weekend moving into her new office. For the first time in over twenty years of teaching, she had an office with a window.

She painted the walls a pale, soft sage green, and used some of her savings to buy authentic teak furniture--a desk, two shelves and a filing cabinet. She spread a dark green and blue Oriental rug across the painted plank flooring and bought a flower box for her window, which she regularly kept full of potted annuals and greenery. The walls were adorned with authentic etchings by a former school chum, who died tragically before thirty, and the curtain was a dark green velvet valance hung at the top of the oversized window, allowing natural light to flood the room. Luckily, a large evergreen tree stood outside the window, which shielded her from the harsh sunlight of the afternoon and created a peaceful scene, almost completely blocking the view of the golden arches recently built beside the campus. Her final touch was to set up an elaborate system of incandescent lamps, which could be turned on with one switch located on the floor to create a warm, welcoming atmosphere. The only time her large overhead fluorescent light was turned on was at night when the cleaning crew came through or over breaks when she would leave it on for her plants.

Doris put her briefcase down on the desk, slid into her large swivel leather chair and began pulling out the papers she had finished grading the night before. She took out the folders for her first class and absentmindedly clicked on her computer. Her bird clock chimed up a whippoorwill call to let her know it was 9:00 AM and almost time for Art 150--Art Appreciation. The clock was set ten minutes ahead so she knew there was enough time to gather up her materials and get to class on time. She looked over her notes, tucked them, her grade book, and text under her arm, picked up her glasses, and headed down the hall to teach Art Appreciation to eager freshmen in their first semester of college blended with world-weary seniors who waited until the last minute to take their Fine Arts elective.

Lecturing was a special joy for Dr. Doris Peechum. She completed a minor in drama in her undergraduate schooling and had often felt called to the stage. Most of her students could never imagine the intellectual and seemingly conservative Dr. P under the spotlight clipping off an Oscar Wilde witticism or yanking up her petticoats to show a well-turned calf as Jenny Diver. But in her salad days, "Dorie," as her friends called her, knew her way around the stage quite well, having spent most of her evenings and weekends either on it or behind it. Now there was no time for doing theatre. Of course, she usually bought season tickets to the local community theatre and attended all the Kerryville College Players productions on campus, but since she moved back home, she had not pursued any parts even though she secretly longed to.

In her lectures, however, she brought art history to life. She channeled all her dramatic zeal into lively stories about Gaugin and Van Gogh's short cohabitation or an impassioned speech defending the great female artists of the twentieth century. For the most part, her students liked and admired her. She practically lived in her office with an open-door policy, usually available for a chat or advice, and she gave excellent tidbits of wisdom when asked but didn't invade the privacy or dignity of her students.

Some students didn't get it--how could anyone be so crazy about a bunch of old dead farts? But those pupils didn't bother Doris. They presented her with a challenge, and she loved to be challenged. "Honey, you think that hot guy on your favorite soap has it? Look at this painting! If you ran into Gaugin on a beach, you'd take your blouse off, too!" is all she would say to them, and there would be a muffled tittering from the back of the room. "Well, you would," she'd say and then give a devilish grin before getting back to the subject at hand.

Doris finished her lecture on sculpture and handed back the quizzes. "I was disappointed with these grades," she scowled and gave them a shake of her head. "You do yourselves a great disservice in not developing better study habits. You would also do better if you would put your phones away and pay better attention in class. If you have your topic proposals for your oral reports, I'll take them up as you leave today. If not, they are due Wednesday to give me time to look them over during the break." A clatter of backpack zippers and shifting desks ensued as students opened their phones and started dialing or texting before they even got to her desk with their proposals. She just sighed, collected the papers, and erased the whiteboard. As they rushed out of class, Doris pulled her glasses to her chest and left them hanging there by a little necklace especially made to hold them, picked up her books, and filed out behind the students.

On the way to her office, she stuck her head into Martin C. Winborn's doorway. "Are we still on for lunch today?" He looked up and for a moment studied her face, as if trying to place who she was.

"Oh, Doris, yes. I'm sorry, I was deep in thought."

"Well, don't let me keep you. I'll see you around twelve."

"Right." He turned and buried his head back into the book that had so completely engrossed him before her interruption. She lingered for a moment to study him, a nice figure of a man, with white hair, a bushy mustache, and no sense of style in his clothing. Martin C. Winborn taught American history and his office, as she surveyed it, was barren and stark: white walls, old painted wood floors, no window dressing and mixed-matched furniture he probably bought at different garage sales or found in the college warehouse. Stacked on top of every available space were piles and piles of papers, books, reports, files, and magazines. Doris smiled to herself and headed toward her sanctuary.

While unlocking her door, she was accosted by the shrill pitch of Lenny Fernum's voice. "Doris, Doris, wait up!" Doris opened her office door and stepped on the light switch; a warm glow of golden light flooded the room, commingling with the muted sunlight from the window and spilling into the fluorescent blue of the hall lights.

"Come on in Lenny, I need to put my things down." She set the books and papers neatly down in the center of her desk, turned the "student chair" around for Lenny and took a seat. "What has you in such a tizzy, Miss Lenny?" Lenny Fernum held the Assistant Professorship in Theatre Arts in the Humanities Division of Kerryville College. Humanities housed three departments: fine arts, social sciences, and languages and literature. Theatre, art, dance, and music comprised the fine arts department, so Lenny's office was just down the hall from Doris'.

"Doris, I'm pretty sure I've chosen the fall play and I need a humongous favor from you." Lenny, a tall statuesque woman, maybe early thirties, with long dark straight hair, brown eyes, and a peaches and cream complexion, smiled her most ingratiating smile and sank into the chair. She wore no makeup and struck Doris as the kind of woman people in the fifties might have called handsome, like Joan Crawford or Rosalind Russell.

"I know you did a lot of theatre in college and by all reports you were excellent." She looked above Doris' head at a small robin sitting on a branch of the pine tree and then around the room at the etchings. "God, you have divine taste! You must adore being in this office."

"Yes, I'm quite happy with it, Lenny, but it doesn't mean I'm going to design the sets for you. I haven't done that since, well, I don't know how many years."

"Sets?" Lenny's face screwed into a picture of surprise. "What makes you think I'd want you to do the set?" Before Doris could answer, a good-looking young man with jet-black hair, about twenty years of age, poked his head into the open doorway.

"Oh, I'm sorry, I didn't know someone was here."

"It's okay, Jayson. Ms. Fernum popped in for a minute. Do you two know each other?"

"Yes, ma'am, I was in the play Lenny directed last spring—you remember, *Bus Stop*? I played Bo."

"Oh yes, of course, you were very good. I knew when I first saw you in class I have seen you before, but I couldn't place it." Doris nodded at them both; she considered it bad form to allow undergraduates to call a teacher by her first name. *But Lenny, well, she's still young and probably thought she needed to be the students' friend.* Doris tried it at first too, but it had proved to be too hard to be their friend and their teacher when she had to give them poor grades. *They expect favors when they feel close to you, better to keep a professional distance.*

"Thank you, Dr. Peechum. I'll wait in the hall."

"Thanks, Jayson, we won't be long."

"You are coming to auditions tomorrow night, aren't you?" Lenny screeched as Jayson Jeffries backed into the hall.

"Of course, Lenny!"

Lenny looked toward the empty doorway. There was a long pause; Lenny heaved a deep breath in and out, and then turned suddenly to focus on Doris. "Adorable boy," she whispered almost to herself, "too bad I only have one more semester with him." Doris could only imagine what was going through Lenny's head. "So, the favor," Lenny's mind apparently came back to the office. "I want you to audition." Doris opened her mouth to protest, but Lenny jumped in before she could utter a sound. "I know what you're going to say. I don't have time, I don't do theatre any more, I haven't done it in years, yada, yada, yada." Doris sighed and leaned back into her chair, casting a doubtful eye toward Lenny.

"We're doing *Who's Afraid of Virginia Woolf?*, and I don't have anyone else who could do Martha and I remember you talking about it once in the cafeteria—how you've always wanted to play that role." Doris was thinking it was a good thing Lenny didn't try to teach English using run-on sentences like that one. She rambled on, "I got Bill Richards to agree to read for George, but I don't have a good Martha. Please, please say you'll come."

Doris perked up some at the name of the play, one she wanted to do but had previously been too young for. But not now—she was the perfect age now. The play by Edward Albee is a searing depiction of a seriously dysfunctional marriage and is considered one of the best American plays ever written. Martha is one of the greatest contemporary roles for mature women, and Doris was attracted to her boldness and sheer outrageousness, something she herself could never manage in real life. Martha and her husband, George, live near a small college where he teaches and her father is president. Nick, a new professor at the college, and his wife, Honey, are invited over for drinks after a college party. Too much liquor flows, and the couples intertwine in seduction, confessions, and lots of decadent behavior. A few years back she would have loved to play Honey, a reserved and timid character more like her own public personae, but then, well, life happened and she went into teaching and there was little time to worry about acting. But here was a great opportunity being laid out at her feet and try as she might to stay focused, Doris' mind wandered around the Kerryville Theatre stage imagining herself in the role as Lenny droned on. "You don't actually need to audition, all you have to do is come and you have the part. I need to read the Nicks and Honeys with you and Bill. I have to put the group together. You understand, don't you?"

"When is the show?" Doris felt herself being pulled in like grains of sand at the mercy of the ocean's undertow.

"Second weekend in November. Please?" Lenny held her breath, hugging a script to her chest. "Here's the script," she said as she thrust the little yellow book toward Doris. There was a long pause.

"Doris?"

"Let me look over my calendar and think about it. I'll let you know tomorrow." Lenny was elated and virtually sailed out of Doris' office and into the hall. There was nothing to think about and nothing to look at; Doris knew right away she was going to do it. It was too good of an offer and probably her one and only chance to play Martha. She knew Bill Richards; he was a popular local actor at the community theatre who once did some soap opera role on television and a small part in a movie. *Too bad he was already happily married,* she mused to herself. It was settled. She picked up the script—that sacred moment in theatre when an actor makes a commitment to the play. Highlighting the script was Doris' favorite part. It was like slipping an engagement ring on her left hand. Well, she actually hadn't done that, but she imagined it must feel something like taking on a character in a play. She sighed and momentarily came back to reality long enough to notice the figure of young Jayson shifting from side to side in the hallway outside her door.

"Oh, my goodness, Jayson, please come in and sit down. I'm sorry, I forgot all about you waiting out there."

Eyeing the script, he looked up at Doris. "So, you auditioning, too?" Doris looked in his face, amazingly beautiful with Paul Newman blue eyes and a chiseled jaw line, as open and untouched as a new snowfall. "I didn't know you did theatre, Dr. Peechum."

"Well, I used to," she smiled and shook her head. "Now, what can I help you with?"

Jayson needed to make up the test he missed because of some illness or death in the family like those Doris heard from probably a thousand students. Her tests probably killed off more grandmothers than cancer and heart disease combined. She wasn't listening, though, because it didn't really matter. She would allow him to do the test, like she usually did, and she had a play to think about.

3

Doris arrived in the cafeteria a little before noon so she could pick out good seats for Martin and herself. She scanned the dining room, heading toward the large round table near the back windows usually considered the faculty dining area. She put her sweater on one chair and her purse in the other and headed toward the food line. She knew Martin would be late; he usually was. She had her Art History I: Greek to Renaissance class at one so she went ahead and got her lunch. *And besides,* she thought, *I don't want him to think I live and breathe with his every movement* (even though she secretly feared she was a bit too focused on him.) She did well to resist casually passing by his office to remind him again about their standing lunch date. *He'll be here; a man's stomach will usually remind him about food.* She picked the spinach salad with vinaigrette dressing, iced tea, and a small cookie.

As she headed back toward the table, she saw it was filling up with her colleagues who were chatting happily about the weather finally clearing and looking forward to a short work week due to the homecoming break, which meant no classes Friday. Doris smiled at her friends as she took her seat, nonchalantly moving her purse to the seat beside her as if she needed a place to put it, not saving a seat for anyone. She knew, however, this would be the last seat at the table to be taken, so she could hold it for Martin for a while longer without anyone knowing she was holding it. Truth be told, however, most of her colleagues were well-aware of her friendship with Dr. Winborn, although there was campus-wide speculation concerning its exact nature. They appeared at most college functions together, but rarely touched, and certainly not in any kind of romantic way. Were they or were they not sleeping together? No one knew, because no one even entertained the idea of asking either of them, and surely, they never volunteered any information.

Doris munched and sipped, with visions of Martha and George

floating around in her head, waiting for the moment she could share her good news with Martin. He came in the door, finally, and headed for the food line. When he emerged with his tray, a student snagged him into an impromptu conference. Doris' face dropped as he sat at the table with the young man, deep in conversation and concern for whatever plight the student was suffering. *Probably another dead grandmother*, Doris thought bitterly to herself. She managed to carry on a somewhat strained, yet normal conversation with her co-workers, and as the table filled up she offered a chemistry professor the seat beside her. She kept a casual eye toward Martin, who was completely oblivious to her and totally absorbed in the student's story. She finished her salad, made her excuses at the table about having to get back and get ready for class, and left the cafeteria. She walked with her head high across campus, smiling and nodding at students and faculty, but when Doris finally made it to her office, she closed the door behind her, left the lights off and sank into her chair. *Why doesn't he care for my feelings the way I care for his?* She and Martin had been going out together for over a year. He was polite and thoughtful but totally clueless about romance. Doris loved his intellect, his wry sense of humor, but she yearned for something more physical. Yes, they kissed some, but that's as far as it went. When not on campus, they would hold hands walking through a museum or share a box of popcorn at a movie, but when Doris tried to get closer, Martin pulled away.

Angry with herself, she pulled a tissue from its box, dabbed at her eyes and nose, then turned on the lights and picked up the script. It was almost unbearable not to be able to start highlighting her lines, but she knew it was too early to do this, the show wasn't even cast yet, and besides, she didn't have the time to spare.

By one, she finished looking over her papers and made it to her Art History class on schedule. *Thank goodness I don't have to lecture today*, she thought. It was the final day for their oral reports on Greek and Roman architecture, so all she needed to do was sit in the back of the classroom and get lost in grading their presentations. Did they cite their research sources, did they stay within the time boundaries, and did they use good eye contact?

Driving home, Doris ran a few errands. She picked up her dry cleaning, took a paycheck deposit to the bank, and swung by the grocers for some basic supplies. As she drove home a small sprinkle of rain dotted her windshield. "Oh, shoot!" she muttered as she pulled up to her small, but pristine home in the historical district of Kerryville. Old houses are so nice with all the ornate woodworking, creative room designs, and intricate rooflines, but old houses don't have garages. Right now, Doris was wondering if latticework and stained glass windows were worth the price in bad weather. She tugged the large bag of groceries into one arm, hooked the dry cleaning over one finger, hoisted her briefcase under the other arm and held her purse and keys in the same hand. She managed to wriggle out of the car as the rain began to get heavier and huge droplets splattered her glasses and the carrot stalks protruding from the top of her bag. "Oh, dear!" Doris trotted quickly on the brick sidewalk to her front steps, struggling to get the door unlocked without dropping her cargo. The phone began to ring as she turned the key. "Yes, yes, Martin, I'm coming! You finally remembered lunch?" Soaking wet, she set everything carefully on the rug inside the door and ran to the kitchen phone on the wall since it was the closest.

"Hello!" She answered triumphantly.

"Doris? Is that you?"

Not Martin. Sigh. "Yes, Mother, it's me. Who else would it be-- Felix?" Doris' body slumped against the counter. She grabbed a dishtowel and started to dab her face, hair, blouse, and shoes.

"There's no need to be flip, Doris Ann, I just wanted to make sure I had the right number. You didn't sound like yourself."

"I'm sorry. I was running to the phone so I am out of breath. And I got in the door and I am wringing wet—can I call you right back"

"Oh, sure, oh sure. What do you mean, you're wringing wet?"

"It's pouring down rain, Mother, haven't you looked outside lately?"

"Well, no," her mother said as if she were trying to remember what she *had* been doing. "Actually, I've been in the downstairs bedroom going through some things. I told you you'd be sorry when you bought that old house. A house without a garage, well, it's so inconvenient."

"Right, Mother, you did tell me that, and I am so very sorry for buying this beautiful old house."

"Well, you're in a mood, aren't you?"

"It has not been the best day, Mother." Doris said, biting her tongue, trying not to say what she was thinking. She paused and took a deep breath. "I'm awfully sorry, Mother, what were you calling about?"

"Well, you said you couldn't talk right now, so call me back later."

"It's too late, Mother, we've already been talking."

"Right," her mother said. "Okay, well, I simply wanted to double check what time you're coming by to pick me up tonight."

Oh goodness, Doris thought, *in all the excitement about the play and my frustration about Martin, I completely forgot about my standing Monday night date with Mother.* "Let's see . . ." she looked at her damp arm, pulling a sleeve up over her watch. "It's nearly five now, I guess I'll try to get there in about an hour so we can catch the 7:45 show. Okay?"

"Oh, sure, oh sure, that's fine. I'll see you then, Doris."

Doris pushed her thumb into the phone to disconnect the call and dropped her hand to her side. She stood there for a few moments, breathing evenly, seemingly in deep thought, but if you'd ask her about what she couldn't have told you. When the phone rang again she nearly threw it across the room. When she caught her breath, her mood perked up temporarily. Maybe this was Martin, after all. "Yes?" She said in her most professional phone voice.

"Doris? This is Lenny. I am so sorry to bother you at home."

Not Martin. Again. "Don't be silly, Lenny, what is it?"

"Well, I couldn't wait until tomorrow to know if you have made a decision about the play. I may have to cancel it if you can't do it, and I don't want to get a bunch of people down there for auditions if there's no hope for a production. If you're not ready, I understand, I know it's . . ."

"I'll do it."

". . . a big commitment and it will take a lot of your time, but you would be perfect with Bill. Wait. Did you say something?"

Doris laughed, "Yes, Lenny, I looked at my calendar, and luckily my conference isn't until after the play dates. I'm scared to death, but I would love to get back on the stage one more time."

"Oh, God, Doris, I wish you knew what this means to me! I won't forget this. Can you be there a little early tomorrow so I can talk to you and Bill before the others come?"

"Will 6:15 be okay?"

"Perfect. I'll see you then. And Doris? Thanks, thanks, thanks again!"

This time Doris hung up the phone with a definite movement suggesting, "I hope Martin does call so I can *not* answer the phone." She stomped back to the foyer making plans to get a caller ID device for her phone and picked up the groceries. She neatly arranged the vegetables in the refrigerator, the cans in the cabinets, and the boxes in the pantry. She pulled a chilled bottle of white zinfandel from the back corner of the fridge--a place she hoped her mother wouldn't look--and poured it into a small wine glass. Then she hurried back to the foyer to get her briefcase and purse which she set in the living room. Next, she headed to the bedroom to get out of her damp clothing. "Felix! There you are, you bum!" The cat was curled up so tightly at the foot of her bed it was hard to tell where the head was. He looked up at her with sleepy eyes and turned on his back, inviting a tummy-rub. "Oh, you silly, silly boy." Doris' hand rubbed the soft fur gently back and forth and Felix turned his head this way and then that way. He flipped over and butted his nose into her face so she would kiss him and then burrowed his head under her hand to show her how to pet him. "Oh, Felix, I love you so much!" She stroked him from the top of his head to the tip of his tail, his body arching under her hand. She scratched the top of his butt and he lifted it higher and higher until he reached back and snapped at her hand. "Okay. Enough is enough. I get it. I need to take a bath anyway."

Before long, Doris was soaking in a tub of hot water and scented bubble bath, sipping on her wine. She lay there for a good long time, enjoying the feel of the heat, the swirl of the water on her body and the glow of the wine in her throat. But she couldn't stop herself; she started feeling sorry for herself again. *Why can't Martin pay more attention to me?* Felix was nearby when Doris was sad. He sat calmly on the toilet lid, a quiet presence. She looked over at him and reached a wet hand over and scratched his head. When the water hit his nose, he shook his head and left the bathroom. "Sorry!" she said to his backside.

Doris and her mother's regular outing usually included an early dinner and then some kind of entertainment. Sometimes they took in the college play or an orchestra concert, and sometimes it was a movie or an evening of shopping. They had already discussed the movie they wanted to see at the local cinema, so Doris put the finishing touches on her make-up, tidied up the house and headed for the door. September in the mountains of eastern Tennessee could be tricky. Sometimes it was hot as summer and other times it could feel like impending frost. It seemed this year would be a more traditional autumn, with blustering winds and sudden rains which pushed the temperatures down to the low fifties. She grabbed an umbrella from the hall tree in the foyer and opened the door. The rain abated, and the air started turning cooler. Doris was usually hot-natured, but now, for some reason, she noticed it more often. Tonight, however, the rain left a slight chill in the air, and Doris knew it would get colder after the sun went down so she grabbed her favorite blue sweater from the foyer closet. The days were getting shorter, so as she slipped into her car it was nearly twilight.

As she drove up to her mother's front door she tapped the horn. She had tried many times going to the door, and her mother would admonish her for wasting time. So, she tooted again and finally saw the porch light flip on, which was the sign her mother was getting ready to leave. Doris waited patiently in her blue Karmann Ghia, her dream car. Doris' father, an avid classic car enthusiast, purchased the 1972 Volkswagen after she earned tenure as a congratulations gift to his only daughter. It gave her a fair amount of trouble, but she refused to listen when her mother advised her to buy a more sensible car.

Avis Peechum came out of her door backward and tugged on the doorknob to make sure the door locked. She turned her face to the sky and then to the sidewalk assessing the probability of getting her feet wet. She waved a hand to Doris as if to say she would come out the side door, and as she turned to go back into the house she nearly bumped her nose, forgetting she locked the door. She dug in her purse for a good minute; Doris rolled her eyes and heaved a sigh, turning off the engine. Avis finally found her keys, unlocked the door, and toddled back inside. She emerged again from the side of the house, walking gingerly on the edge of the driveway that provided a small pathway above the standing water in the center, which had sunk in a few inches over time.

As she got in the car, Avis said, "You know, when it's wet like this, you might as well pull up into the driveway. I can't walk on that old sidewalk after a rain, there's too much water."

"I tried that once, Mother, and you fussed at me. You said there wasn't enough room for you to get into the car with the bushes where they are."

"Oh. Well, you're probably right. I don't remember," Avis fixed her coat around her knees and twisted herself around to get comfortable. "This car, Doris, it's so hard to get in and out of. And would a little heat kill you?" Doris didn't say a word; she started the car and switched the heat to its highest setting. "Now, that feels good. Where are we going to eat tonight?"

"Don't you remember, Mother, you said you wanted to try the new Italian place close to the mall. But if you want to go somewhere else that's fine."

"No, no, that's good, sure, sure. That's good. I don't remember us talking about it. Are you certain I said that?"

"Yes, I think so." Doris hated heat blowing in her face because she felt suffocated, but she stayed quiet to please her mother.

"Well, okay. Getting old, I guess." Avis tried a small and unconvincing laugh. Doris knew her mother had been forgetful on a more regular basis lately, but she didn't think it was a problem. She could tell by her mother's silent gaze out the car window it was worrying her, though.

"Well, aren't we all?" Doris said and Avis turned to look at her with a puzzled expression. "Getting older," she explained, "Aren't we all getting older?" Her mother gave a half smile and nodded slightly. Doris tried to look upbeat, but she knew her mother's moods better than anyone else. It was time to leave her alone with her thoughts.

On Monday evenings, most restaurants were practically empty in Kerryville, which Doris knew Avis liked. They could get their choice of seats, and it didn't take long to get waited on or served. The hostess showed them to a nice table for four in the rear of the dining room beside a window facing the garden. As they looked over the menu the garden began to disappear into the twilight, but then was suddenly illuminated by a series of well-situated tiny halogen spotlights which captured the color and shape of the trees and flowers in a beautiful display. "My, that's lovely, isn't it, Mother?" Doris was trying to draw Avis from the pit of her dark thoughts.

Avis looked up over her glasses absentmindedly, "Huh?" she said. She saw Doris looking at the window and turned her head to see and then back to Doris. "Sure, sure, dear, it's nice. Do you know what you want to order? I can't make up my mind in these fancy places—it all looks good to me. You order for me."

"Oh no you don't! I did that once before and lived to regret it." Doris scoffed. "You order your meal and I'll order mine, okay?" *Sometimes,* Doris thought, *Mother can be such a pain in the neck.*

Avis looked at Doris with a scowl, as if she might have been thinking the same about her daughter. "All right. Let's see . . . umm, I'll take the spaghetti and meatballs, a small house salad with French dressing, and umm, the New York Cheesecake."

The server appeared to take their drink orders. Avis ordered iced tea, but Doris wanted her favorite, Dr. Pepper. She couldn't believe her mother would come to an expensive Italian restaurant and order spaghetti like a child. *Where is her sense of adventure*, she thought. Finally, Doris decided on a nice house salad with balsamic vinaigrette dressing and a penne dish with shrimp and artichokes in a lemon cream sauce. No dessert tonight, she wanted to lose her tummy pouch.

Her mother was quiet while they waited for their food. She glanced around the room and occasionally out the window at the garden. "Your father would have hated this place, you know." Avis finally said.

"Well, of course, Mother," Doris teased, glad to see her mother come alive again, "there are no hamburgers or steak and potatoes on the menu." They both gave a soft chuckle. Over the years, Doris and her mother were not close. Doris was a daddy's girl all the way; her mother was so critical and opinionated about her every move so Doris never felt comfortable in confiding or sharing her life with Avis. Since she moved back home, however, she had matured enough to deflect her mother's criticisms, and since they seemed to have little effect on Doris, Avis had toned them down considerably. Now with her father gone for nearly two years, Doris and her mother started enjoying each other's company more. Brought together by their common bond of grief over Ed Peechum's passing, they began to truly get to know each other as women, as people, and even as friends. "So," Doris offered, "You said you were going through some things?"

Avis was just now beginning to be able to enter their old bedroom to go through her husband's belongings. She finally distributed the clothing to Goodwill and the church mission drive but could not yet throw out medicine, jewelry, papers and so forth. "Yes, your dad's effects," she looked down at the table and then out the window, "I have some items for you—jewelry, mostly, and his war medals. You can come over this weekend and take anything you want. It will all be yours soon anyway."

"Soon? What are you talking about, Mother?"

"Well, you know, I mean I'm getting close to eighty and that's pretty old. Your dad was eighty-one when he died, and so, when I'm gone, it will all be yours anyway. Teddy won't want anything we have. Well, you can sell the house and then split the money, but he doesn't care about all those souvenirs. You're the only one who ever cared about those kinds of mementos."

"You scared me, Mother. Don't ever do it again." Doris put her hand gently on her mother's.

"I'm sorry, Puddin', I've been thinking about it. I didn't mean for it to sound so serious. Everyone needs to think about a will and what we give to those we leave behind." Avis put her other hand over Doris' and smiled. "I want everything taken care of for you and Teddy when I go. I've already put both of your names on my biggest assets, the house and bank accounts. You and Teddy won't have to worry about inheriting them; you will already own them. A lawyer friend of mine suggested it, and it makes good sense. It helps you avoid the trouble of the will going into probate and you and Teddy won't have to pay inheritance taxes. Wait a minute, you remember Ethan, right?" Doris just smiled and nodded. "I asked him to draw up the papers, and he sent a copy to Teddy for signing. I told him I would just give them to you. All you have to do is sign these." She pulled a set of papers from her purse and slid them across the table to Doris. "Teddy said he couldn't do it since he would benefit from it."

"Sure, whatever you want is fine with me. I think you ought to leave it all to Ted's kids, they'll be going to college soon. But it's your money. When did you meet with Ethan without me taking you there?"

"Oh, well, I thought it might be awkward for you, so I asked Fran to take me. It was several weeks ago, but I don't want to wait any longer to get this finished." Doris stared at her mother, who seemed determined to get this done right away. Fran was her mother's long-time friend and mother of Doris' childhood friend, Tootsie.

She briefly flipped through the papers, but didn't feel the need to read them. If Ethan had prepared them, she trusted everything was in order. Avis handed her a blue pen, and Doris signed and initialed several places.

"Thank you, Puddin'," said Avis and she folded the papers and tucked them into an addressed envelope. "Would you mind dropping them off tomorrow to Ethan?"

"Of course, Mother, I'll do it on the way home after I take you home. But we have many years to think about his," Doris said as the server brought the food with a pitcher of tea and a fresh glass of Dr. Pepper. Doris and Avis moved their hands from the table to accommodate the food, but her mother winked at Doris, which was her way of saying thank you. Doris smiled and nodded.

"I feel so much better now," Avis said and took a deep breath.

"That's all that matters to me, Mother."

"So," Avis began her salad, "what do you want to do next week on your birthday?"

Doris looked down at the lettuce and poured the dressing carefully in a spiraling circle. She knew she was about to light the match of her mother's disapproval, but it needed to be done at some point, and this was as good a time as any. "Well, I'm not sure right now, Mother. I've agreed to do a play at school and we may need to have rehearsals then."

"A play! What do you mean you agreed to do a play? You don't have time for a play—you hardly have time to breathe now!" Doris closed her eyes and took a deep breath.

"First, it's a play I have always wanted to do. Second," her mother started shaking her head and opened her mouth to interrupt so Doris raised her volume slightly, "second, I haven't done any theatre in a long time and I do miss it. Third," Avis pursed her lips tightly to remain silent, "I am an adult and can choose to pass my leisure time in any way I see fit. And finally, if you love me as you say you do, you will support my efforts to get out and have some fun before I'm too old to do it." Avis looked stunned for a moment and Doris regretted saying this last part. "I mean, why not, Mother? I don't have any kids; I'm not dating anyone seriously right now—I want to have a social life. Is that a crime?"

"What about Martin? I thought you two were getting along."

"We are, Mother, but well, I can't put my life on hold for him. He hasn't asked me to marry him, you know."

Avis must have sensed the hurt in Doris' voice. She put a hand on her daughter's and spoke softly, "He needs a little more time to get used to the idea. I can tell he's crazy about you. The way he looks at you when you're together."

Doris looked at her with skepticism. "Really?"

"Absolutely!" Avis furrowed her eyebrows and released a sigh. "You know what, Doris? You're right. You should go out and have fun. It's…Sorry."

Doris was so shocked she almost choked on her tomato wedge, but she smiled at her mother and chewed vigorously. "Thanks, Mother" was all she could manage. They continued to eat and chat about the play and for the first time, Doris felt she and her mother turned a corner. Avis was sincerely trying, and Doris was grateful.

After dinner, Avis said she felt too tired for a movie, and Doris agreed because she had a lot of work to do. She lied about having a pile of papers to grade when she knew all along she wanted to get home and read the play over and over. So, Doris was relieved she would be home early and have plenty of time to study at her leisure.

Against Avis' protests Doris insisted on helping her mother into the house when it was dark. "Next time we'll take my car, ok?" her mother asked as she struggled to pull herself around to get out.

"Of course, no problem. I'm sorry the car is uncomfortable for you. I wish you'd said something sooner."

"It's usually not a big deal, honey, but my arthritis has been acting up some."

"I love you, Mother," Doris said quietly and kissed her mother's cheek.

"I love you, too, Puddin'," Avis said as she gave a little wave.

Doris backed her car into the street and sat there for a few minutes looking at the house where she grew up. Her mother displayed an obvious trail of her movements through the house, turning on a light, and then turning it off when she turned on another. Doris hoped no one ever watched this house, they would know exactly where Avis was at any moment.

The house, Doris realized, was much like her own. It was an old house with white sideboard and decorative woodworking around the front porch railing. The boxwoods she and her father planted around the edge of the front yard were now a dense row of hedging, with an opening for the sidewalk path to come to the street. The sidewalk, however, was more grass than brick these days, but that only made it look more rustic. And, naturally, there was no garage. Doris thought about her mother and what she would do when she died. How would she feel? Would she stay in Kerryville? She didn't know the answer to these questions because she couldn't imagine a life without her mother. *I don't have time to think about all this*, Doris told herself, *I have an audition to get ready for*. She wiped a tear from her cheek and moved the car quietly down the road toward her own little white house.

4

Tuesday started out like any other school day. Doris drank her coffee, read the paper, conversed with Felix, and checked the pansies on the back porch. By the time she got to school, the campus was bustling with activity. Tuesdays were busy days and parking was a nightmare for everyone except the tenured professors who were lucky enough to have reserved spaces next to their office buildings. Doris pulled her little car into the space marked "Dr. Peechum: Art." She gathered her raincoat and briefcase before locking the door. "See ya' later, Carmen," she said and patted the hood of her car. Doris believed if you were good to machines, they'd be good to you.

Doris' first class was a ten o'clock senior honors Art 450 class about careers in art, created especially for art majors planning to become teachers, museum curators, restorers, and even architects. She adored it, teaching a small group of serious-minded learners, intent on her every word, capable of asking thought-provoking questions and offering insightful studies on the evolution of art throughout the centuries. They sat around an old oak table in a remote area of the Humanities Building, which used to be the president's conference room, laughing and sipping out of paper coffee cups. They never used their phones except to take a picture of an assignment written on the white board. This was the kind of class college teachers live for. It was what made teaching sections of general education classes, like Art Appreciation, bearable. It offered the intellectual challenge Doris knew college professors expect to engage in on a regular basis once they begin teaching.

The truth is, until they are tenured, and even then, professors are expected to do almost everything except engage in intellectual debate. There are committees, advising, and teaching core curriculum classes to scores of confused, arrogant, and usually apathetic undergraduates. And, of course, miscellaneous duties like sponsoring campus organizations, attending and supporting campus concerts, ballgames, and social gatherings take up the rest of their time. Then there are those endless faculty meetings where no one is expected to disagree with anything the dean proposes, if they know what's good for them, and Doris did. She held strong opinions about almost everything, but she learned not to be too vocal about them. As a tenured professor, she felt a bit safer. *They can only fire me now for egregious offenses*, she mused, *but of course, there will still be promotions to consider.* Doris spoke her mind politely when it was important, but kept her mouth shut the rest of the time. She knew tenure and promotion are not awarded to those who swim against the tide, and she hoped to go for full professorship soon.

It's all repetitive and boring, Doris thought to herself as she walked down the hall and up the steps. She tried to be more optimistic. Opportunities to do plays, exhibit her art, or be in the campus choir or orchestra were also extra benefits of teaching college. Although she didn't teach drawing or painting, she excelled at both. The other art teacher, Thelma Black, who gave instruction in everything from watercolor to lithograph, often invited her to show in the little college gallery, and she had occasionally accepted. Since she didn't sing, the choir was out, but the play--the play was something to look forward to. She had read the play twice after arriving home and then read Martha's lines aloud looking for the right intonation and expression. But she tried not to think too much about the audition—she needed to work now, she could daydream later. For the first day in a long time, Martin didn't even enter her mind.

Try as she might, however, Doris couldn't keep images of auditions out of her mind; even her favorite class felt tedious to her today. The lines echoed through her head. She felt so excited; she forgot how much she enjoyed working in the theatre. In her undergraduate days at Agnes Scott College in Atlanta, she practically lived in the theatre and the art studio. She designed costumes and posters, painted breathtaking stage backdrops, and carried her own weight in any role. After college, she spent a few years of living as a starving artist in New Orleans. She clearly had an eye for design and better-than-average talent, particularly with watercolor, but she also recognized that she was not gifted as a great artist. Luckily, she discovered art history and fell in love. When she entered graduate school, she was so busy pursuing a degree aimed at preparing her to be a museum docent, there was little and then no time for theatre. While at Tulane she did a few community theatre pieces in the summers when her load was lighter and her sanity level ran low, but that was many years ago. She wondered if she possessed what it would take to do a role this challenging after so much time. "What do you think about it, Dr. Peechum?"

She looked up at the wonderfully curious face of Valerie Ray, an outstanding pupil, who would be graduating in the spring. Doris suddenly realized she had completely zoned out of the entire conversation, and the last comment she remembered was something about the difficult job of restoring Italian frescos. She had no idea how long she had been lost in her thoughts or how the topic may have changed. "Valerie," she said with complete calm, "you know I don't like to give you my opinions about these discussions. What you think and how you defend it is much more important." Valerie's eyebrows arched, she looked down at the table, took a breath, and nodded. "So, what do *you* think?"

Valerie studied a spot on the table for a long minute. "Well, I don't think it's right."

Doris, with no idea what Valerie was referring to, nodded in a thoughtful way and said, "Okay. Tell us why."

Valerie began to explain her point of view and other members of the class chimed in with comments, and soon got Doris back on track. She was so grateful for not being found-out she let them go early. "Remember, I need to see your final paper proposals Thursday," she reminded them as they gathered books, papers, and backpacks, and swept out of the room like one great gust of wind scooping up a pile of fall leaves and dispersing them in all directions. Doris stayed behind to erase the board and gather her papers. As she entered the hall she collided with Jayson Jeffries, and their books scattered all over the hall. "Oh my, I'm so clumsy! Excuse me, Jayson."

"No, I'm sure it was my fault, Dr. P. I'll get it for you." Doris was thinking how polite he seemed outside of class. Perhaps she misjudged him. In class, Jayson did a lot of sleeping, he missed regularly, and he turned in barely passing assignments and tests. "There you are," he said, handing her a pile of papers. "See ya' tonight!" He flashed a bright smile with clean white teeth and then was gone before Doris could utter a thank you.

"Yes, see you tonight," she said, but he was nowhere in sight. She passed by Martin's office on her way back to her own, but this time she did not stop to say hello or remind him of lunch. *If he wants to have lunch with me*, she thought, *he's going to have to come over and invite me and then take me off-campus.* She saw him hunched over his computer keyboard with her peripheral vision as she passed by, but he didn't see her. *Just as well*, she thought, *I have enough going on right now.*

Doris had packed a small lunch so she could stay in her office and look over the play some more. It also gave her a good excuse for not having to accidentally run into Martin in the cafeteria and listen to another one of his lame excuses. She closed and locked her door, turned off her lamps, and read by the natural sunlight streaming in through the huge office window. She read and nibbled awhile and then worked on a midterm exam on her computer. She finished the unit on photography in her afternoon Art 250, Introduction to the Visual Arts, class then returned to her office to prepare a quiz for Thursday. As she finished copying the quizzes, she looked at the clock and suddenly realized it was almost time for the afternoon faculty meeting.

Doris shut down the computer, stacked the quizzes neatly on her desk, tucked the play into her purse, and headed across campus to Hillman Hall, the oldest building on campus. It had a huge Colonial style edifice with red brick and concrete inlay. Large white columns flanked the front entrance, and Doris hustled up the seemingly endless series of steps and then up two flights of stairs inside to arrive five minutes late for the meeting. She stifled her heavy breathing and stood for a moment waiting for them to finish their prayer. Lenny's head popped up, spotted Doris, and tilted her head discreetly for Doris to take the seat beside her. But Doris didn't want to walk across the room so she mouthed a polite thank you but no and Lenny nodded, understanding. At the end of the prayer, Doris slipped silently into the back row near the door. Martin was deep in conversation with another history professor and didn't notice Doris' entrance.

The faculty meetings were usually the same. Motion, discussion, vote. Dean Rogers resented anyone who brought up a question or presented a challenge to any motion from one of his favorites. Anyone who challenged a motion during a meeting received a black mark in a little scorebook Doris was sure Dean Rogers kept on everyone. Too many black marks, and you were out.

It happened four years ago to one of Doris' good friends, Ann Kinsey, the theatre professor whom Lenny replaced. Ann was too honest for her own good, and she believed the hype that the college was a family. It was too late when she realized it was a dysfunctional family. Doris was in much the same position until Ann was denied tenure the same year the college granted it to her. It woke her up; it jarred the whole campus, and it almost destroyed Ann, who eventually gave up teaching altogether and became a chef. The last time Doris spoke with Ann she looked much happier. She was working four days a week and making twice the money she made teaching, but she admitted she was still taking her anti-depressants.

Doris often fantasized about doing another line of work, but she couldn't imagine herself as anything but a college professor. She had decided during her first year of college that it was what she wanted to do with her life. Through all the politics and tiresome undergraduates, she still felt at home in the classroom and being in the academic lifestyle. There were certainly times when she questioned her career choice, but it usually came back to the fact she simply wasn't suited to anything else. She frowned for a moment wondering what she would do if she was ever forced to give it up.

Someone marched to the front, made a motion, there was a second, a token discussion, and then everyone voted. Ann's fate taught them no one is indispensable, so Doris tried to keep her opinions and objections to herself. After she was granted tenure, she spoke up a little more, if the issue warranted it. She even brought up opposing viewpoints for discussion and refused to vote for programs or policies she found disagreeable. She figured if she defended her views diplomatically and kept doing a good job with the students, there wouldn't be too much fall-out. *Appreciating diversity is what college is all about, right?*

There was no direct evidence, but Doris felt certain the reason she had not been asked to chair the Fine Arts Department three years ago was due to her assertiveness. Dan Turner, who had chaired the department for over ten years and hired Doris, finally retired at the age of 68, leaving the position open. Doris did all the right things to stay academically vital. She remained active in her field, published in academic journals, presented at conferences, earned tenure, demonstrated her willingness to be a team player, and possessed more seniority than anyone else in the program except for Howard Archer and Sylvia Granger, who had each expressed a desire to stay in the classroom and not work in administration. Yet, instead of asking Doris, the dean brought candidates in from outside and finally offered the position to a musicologist who had only worked at KC for a few years, Phyllis Hathaway. Doris liked her; she was an effective department head, but Doris was clearly first in line for the position, so there was a little tension between them. She had to admit, however, she wasn't even sure she wanted to be an administrator. Still, it would have been nice to be asked. *It would have been nice.*

Doris' mind drifted back to the play. She doodled on her pad, drawing pictures of Martha and George, Nick and Honey, and writing the play title over and over. When the meeting was adjourned, Lenny rushed over to Doris. "Are you ready?" she nearly vibrated with excitement. Doris felt it too, but she was way too reserved to let it show.

"Yes, I'll be there. 6:15—right?"

"I'll be there even earlier if you want to come before then. But I know Bill is coming then. I can't wait to work with the two of you—thank you so much, again!"

Before Doris could speak, Lenny hurried through the door and down the hall. She watched Lenny's long ponytail bouncing back and forth in rhythm with her gait. Lenny was so open and outspoken, like most theatre people. Doris hoped she wouldn't suffer Ann's consequences.

"Doris," a familiar voice echoed behind her, "Doris, wait up." She paused and turned to see Martin huffing toward her, a clump of papers turned in several directions tucked under his arm. She moved to the side of the hall to let other faculty members pass while she waited for Martin. She saw him at the meeting, in his usual seat near the front. He somehow managed to make faculty meetings early, but not once had he shown up for a date or appointment with her on time. "Doris, I've been trying to call you—have you not been answering?"

"No, Martin, why on earth would I do that? I think I've forgotten to check my voice mail in a day or so—did you leave a message?"

"Oh, Doris, you know I hate those contraptions." He looked down to arrange the papers in danger of falling to the floor and then shoved a lock of white hair back from his forehead. "Well, no matter. I wanted to apologize for missing you in the cafeteria yesterday. I got waylaid by a student and lost track of time. By the time I looked up, you were gone."

"Oh, goodness, Martin, it's okay. I was in such a hurry yesterday with so many papers piled up for grading I forgot about it myself. I ate a quick salad and got back to the grindstone. But thanks for being concerned."

"Well, you know, I thought you might be upset with me. Especially when you weren't at lunch today and I didn't see you at the beginning of the meeting, which is unusual for you."

"Nonsense. After my one o'clock class, I went back in my office to make out a quiz and almost forgot to come at all. I'm going to go home early today, make a big cup of coffee and tackle all those papers. I'll see you later." Doris flashed a noncommittal smile and turned to go.

"Doris," Martin sounded almost desperate. She stopped and turned, thinking how men are all the same. *You show them you are interested, they feign apathy, but the minute you become independent and don't need them—there they are at your feet.*

"I'm sorry, Martin, I thought we were finished. What is it?" Doris amazed herself at times like this. She often thought how lucky it is for the people in her life that she is usually so honest. Doris knew she was a good liar; she had been since childhood. She figured it was all that acting experience, or possibly she was good at acting because she was a good liar, she wasn't sure.

"Oh, well, it's nothing important. I was wondering if I would see you at lunch tomorrow."

"Wednesday," she pretended to go through a mental date book, "I should be there. I'll look for you around noon, okay?" Once again, she twirled around, leaving him in her dust.

He stood there for a moment watching her walk down the corridor. A paper fell from his arm, and when he bent over to retrieve it the whole stack scattered around the hall, along with his glasses from the top of his head and a red pen from his jacket pocket. "Damn," he muttered as he got on his knees to gather his students' essays on the events leading up to the Vietnam War. Doris caught a glimpse of him as she turned to take the stairs but kept her stride, pretending she hadn't.

5

When Doris got home, Felix was waiting for her at the door. This was a bit odd because he was usually lounging on his "blankie" at the foot of her bed or his special window hammock Doris gave him last Christmas. It hooked onto the windowsill allowing him to watch the world go by the front window between catnaps. He didn't seem hurt or alarmed, so she figured it was one of those weird animal behaviors. Who could tell what goes through a cat's mind?

She kicked off her shoes the minute she hit her bedroom and did her pre-audition ritual. This included a long, hot bath with special herbal salts, washing her hair, shaving her legs, and doing a facial and a manicure. It was basically the same ritual she did every weekend, but she used it for special occasions because it made her feel more confident.

With cream on her face and a towel over her wet hair, she donned her favorite chenille robe and headed toward the kitchen. "Something healthy," she said to herself. Felix rubbed around her ankles, back and forth, meowing. "Oh, yes, can't forget the cat!" She bent over to scratch his head and picked up his bowls. "A little fresh water, a little bit of kibbles, and there you are." She placed the food and water on his tray. Felix smelled it then continued caressing her ankles. Doris picked him up in baby fashion and rocked him in her arms. "What is wrong with you today, sugar?" She nuzzled his nose and kissed his head. He struggled to be free so she gently placed him on the floor, and he ran into the living room. "Whatever!" she said with a little giggle.

Doris ate a light supper and tried to relax with a little television, but all she could find in the late afternoon were talk shows and syndicated sit-coms. By and large, she found talk shows boring, overly sentimental, and at times, preachy. Old sit-coms were, well, old sit-coms. She released a heavy sigh, shut off the TV, turned on her favorite Laura Nyro CD at top volume and then washed her dishes. Once the kitchen was in place, she headed to her bedroom to finish getting ready. She picked out a simple, but attractive, pair of tan slacks, a light green shell and a matching, lightweight sweater. She pulled her usual pageboy auburn hair into a sleek ponytail at the nape of her neck with a satin ribbon to match her shell. A few finishing touches of gold jewelry, cologne, and her favorite pumps, and she was ready to go. It was nearly six o'clock, which gave her enough time to get to the college theatre. It took about ten minutes to get anywhere in Kerryville.

She picked up her script and her purse noticing the light on her answering machine was blinking. *Martin must have gotten up the nerve to leave a message*, she mused to herself. *Let him stew in his own juices for once,* she thought and headed toward the door. Felix ran to the door and stared up at her in such a serious fashion that Doris stopped to look at him. "What?" she said with a puzzled expression. "What do you want?" She thought for a moment—the litter box was clean, food and water bowls were full, and his blankie was in its place—what could it be? She squatted down to pet him. "I sure wish you could talk." She stood up to leave and Felix stepped aside. He jumped into the window to watch her get into her car and pull out of the driveway. As she changed gears, she could still see him sitting in the window and meowing. "He's going to the vet tomorrow," she vowed, and drove away.

When she arrived at the college's broken down theatre, she looked around in dismay. The old wooden seats were in a sad state of disrepair, the ceiling and walls were streaked with water stains and the black curtain showed signs of wear, with several rips and stains. When she came for performances, she didn't notice much about the condition of the theatre, but here it was with no special lighting or adornment, and it looked rather pathetic. Lenny was absorbed in the script and some papers in a single chair on stage beneath the work lights. The door made a small noise when it closed and she looked up. "Doris! Hi! Come on up." She got up and disappeared for a moment into the wings then returned with two folding chairs. "Bill should be here any minute. Come on up and sit down."

Doris made her way up the rickety makeshift steps leading to the stage. "Am I early?" she looked at her watch; she came in right at 6:15, as promised.

"No, not at all. I've been here awhile, looking over the scenes I want to read and, well, you know!"

Doris nodded and their attention was drawn to the back of the theatre as the door shut and Bill strode toward the stage. *He is even better looking up close*, Doris thought. A healthy, active man in his early fifties, Bill Richards was the kind of man who looked good without trying. His salt and pepper hair was neatly styled and his beard and mustache trimmed, but he never looked like he took much time with his appearance. He wore a blue sweatshirt with big white letters, "North Carolina," on the front and a nice pair of jeans that flattered his tight behind and long legs. He greeted both women and took a seat near Doris, offering his hand. "I hear we're married, darling," he said, and Doris tried not to blush.

"Pleased to meet you," she said and shook his hand.

Lenny explained to them what she wanted to do with the readings and gave them the scene pages. They both agreed it would be a good idea to go into the greenroom and read over the scenes with each other before the others arrived. Some other mature actors might come; Lenny felt the need to have understudies as they had come in handy more than once. So, it promised to be a long night. "I would like to have callbacks tomorrow night, if that's okay with you two. I'd like to post the cast by next Monday when everyone returns from the long weekend. You can keep the scripts you have." Bill and Doris nodded and headed into the greenroom to rehearse. Lenny spent her time setting up a mock living room and getting scripts and information sheets ready for the onslaught of eager young thespians.

The tacky greenroom had one wall of windows, which wouldn't open, and with no ventilation, the room got stale. Layers of old theatre curtains were piled in one corner near a leaky window and the odor of mildew permeated the room. In another corner stood an old electronic organ that didn't work and next to it was an old Hotpoint refrigerator used to store food props and party drinks. The furniture looked like rejects from a garage sale at a doctor's office. Black vinyl benches, faded brocade armchairs and an olive-green sofa, circa 1968, offered the seating choices and a few banana crates were scattered around for tables. Bill and Doris looked around the room and then at each other and smiled. "Your choice," he said and raised his eyebrows.

Doris took a seat in one of the armchairs and Bill sat across from her on a black vinyl bench which puffed loudly as he sat on it. They both giggled a little and shook their heads. "I don't remember this place being so disgusting when I was here," Bill said as he looked around the room. "Of course, that was some years ago."

"I didn't know you attended Kerryville," Doris said stupidly. "I guess I should have, but well, I guess you don't know where I went to school either, do you?" She was flustered, and her face began to feel hot. Doris couldn't remember the last time she felt like this, and she couldn't figure it out. *He was cute, but geez*, she thought, *he's married and I'm not interested.* "Sorry, I am so nervous about these auditions. It's been so long since I've done any acting."

"I understand, but I'm sure you'll be great." Bill sounded convinced so Doris rolled her shoulders and tried to loosen up a bit.

"So, let's talk about the play," Doris started. "Tell me what you think about Martha and George."

Bill looked up from the script, pushed his sleeves up and rubbed his beard. "Huh? Oh, I think they're a couple of great roles."

"Yes, certainly," Doris' cool air of authority was returning to her. "I mean, what do you think of their relationship, their personalities, you know?"

He looked down at his tennis shoes and picked at something Doris could not see off a shoelace. "Well, I read the part and let all that stuff take care of itself."

Doris was silent for a moment; *a technical actor*, she thought to herself. There are two kinds of actors in the theatre. One is called the technical actor who begins with the outside attributes of the character— voice, clothing, walk, and nervous gestures—and then allows those to reveal the inner character. The other kind of actor, which most American actor training spawned was called the method actor, after the famous acting teacher, Stanislavsky's, "method" for training actors. These actors try to understand the internal life of the character first—the psychology, motivation, and past experiences, which make her behave as she does in the play--and then translate that understanding into gesture and movement. They also use their own life experiences to bring appropriate emotion to a scene. Two actors could work in totally different directions and still arrive at the same goal; Doris knew this to be true. The problem would be the rehearsal process. She began to worry about her character development and how she could get him to cooperate in discussion sessions since she subscribed to the method approach. She looked at Bill, and when their eyes met there was an instant "actor understanding." They both knew the best they could hope for was not getting in each other's way.

"Okay," said Doris, trying to remain optimistic, "Shall we read through some of these scenes then for familiarity?" Bill agreed it was a good idea, so they did. He sat on his side of the room with Doris on hers, and they read the scenes. *Bill is excellent*, she thought, *a natural*. He picked up on little nuances in each scene and was already exploring George's physicality. *Maybe this will be good*, she pondered, *I might learn something new*. Doris wasn't worried about Bill as much as she feared not living up to Lenny's expectations and making a complete fool out of herself in front of her colleagues.

By 6:45, the house started filling up with acting hopefuls. Bill and Doris emerged from the back room and took two seats in the front. Lenny distributed the papers, blue for males, yellow for females, and they busily filled out their contact information and previous acting experience. Jayson Jeffries sat in the third row with his girlfriend, Kayla Washington, by his side. A petite blonde with a large chest, Kayla was gripping Jayson's hand and looking around the room with a scowl on her face. A larger girl sat next to her whom Doris didn't remember seeing before. Doris saw a few familiar students she recognized from classes over the past few years, but Jayson was the only one in a class with her now. She prayed he would not get cast, but she knew he was one of Lenny's favorites, and it was his senior year.

Lenny started out by reading the actors she was certain she would not cast, or at least this is what occurred to Doris. There was one mature woman from the community who gave a nice reading for Martha, and Doris figured she would end up being her understudy. There were no Georges, however, so Bill would need to take care of himself. The rest were college students vying for the other two parts. Lenny read a string of Nick and Honey scenes, weeding out the truly awful from the pretty good. She then announced a ten-minute break so she could smoke a cigarette and hurried out the side door.

Doris looked at Bill who smiled and headed toward the lobby where the restrooms were. She figured this was a good idea and headed in the same direction. She wondered why Lenny even wanted them here tonight, but it became more apparent after the break when Lenny stopped doing the charity readings and got down to business. She called Doris and Bill to the stage to read George and Martha and no one else read those parts the rest of the evening. Lenny was looking for the right combination of Nick and Honey to play against them.

Doris thought she was reading quite well. Her practice was to give as much as possible in an audition, but she knew she would not come alive as the character until the actual rehearsals began. She took on a role slowly, like a moth transforming into a butterfly. Her experience with actors who read well at auditions taught her they were probably doing as much as they would ever do with the role—they rarely moved beyond that first flash of brilliance. Bill impressed her as this type of actor. He read much better than she did, and he may be wondering if she has what it takes to play such a demanding role. But he had not seen her in rehearsal or performance. She would come through; it would take time.

Even her mediocre reading, however, seemed to impress Jayson sufficiently. The look on his face during their scenes together showed how surprised he was. Could this fiery, dominating vixen be the same gentle woman who conducted class so eloquently and with such unruffled style? Doris took some delight in shocking the young man, but she still hoped he would not get cast. Actors get close when they work together. Although getting close to a young man was fine with Doris, especially one this attractive, having to do it with a current student might compromise her reputation if she showed him any leniency in class. She could also foresee problems that might arise if Jayson couldn't separate the Doris he saw in rehearsals from the Dr. Peechum he saw in class. She wondered as she watched the readings if she should speak to Lenny about it.

Doris thought Jayson read wonderfully though. He looked older than his twenty-one years and could pull off a believable Nick. His girlfriend, however, read in the first go-around and was truly terrible. The large girl with dark hair didn't read at all. Probably a friend of Kayla's offering her moral support. Another young man named Moses read well, also, so Doris figured he or Jayson would land Nick and the other would be the understudy. She decided, however, it was not ethical of her to ask Lenny not to cast Jayson. It was his senior year, and he gave a lot of his time and effort to the college theatre. She needed to let the chips fall as they may and perhaps have a chat with Jayson if problems arose.

The girls were plentiful, but there was one real standout for Honey, a senior named Teri Hopper. Doris remembered having Teri as a freshman in her Art Appreciation course, one of the most delightful students Doris could remember. Highly disciplined, infinitely curious, and appropriately respectful, Teri made straight A's in all her courses. She was in pre-med, hoping to become a pediatrician, but she possessed real talent for the arts. Teri did two plays Doris could remember while at Kerryville, and each time, she lit up the stage with her petite figure and beautiful face. Doris hoped she would get Honey, and there were probably five other good women for the part from whom Lenny could choose for the understudy.

The evening ended on a high note with Lenny announcing she would post a callback list by noon tomorrow and hoped everyone could make it. She thanked everyone profusely for their interest and hoped they would volunteer for tech assignments if they didn't get a role. Many of the students were in Lenny's production class, but she always tried to recruit new cadets. Doris nodded to Jayson, and Kayla eyed her suspiciously. Bill said goodnight when they hit the cool evening air, and Doris walked, as if on a cloud, to Carmen, who sat waiting patiently under an old elm tree. She cranked up the stereo and even the heater then headed toward home.

As she approached her house, she noticed a car parked in her driveway. "Who could be here at this hour of night," she murmured to herself, looking at the clock in her dashboard. When she got closer, she recognized Martin's old maroon Volvo and the shape of his head. She pulled up behind him and got out of the car. When she got to his window, she saw he was sleeping. "What in the world?" she asked the car. She tapped the window lightly and Martin roused. It took him a moment to realize where he was, and when he looked over to see Doris it startled him. He rolled down the glass.

"Doris, I've been trying to call you. Could I come in for a moment?"

"Why, of course, Martin." She stood aside to let him get out and then escorted him to the door. In the pale glow of her porch light, Martin showed his age, and the worried expression on his face scared Doris. She saw Felix on his window hammock fast asleep. Somehow, he had managed to get one of her slippers into the hammock and was dozing with his nose partially embedded in the furry toe. *Strange*, she thought to herself, but she didn't say anything. She showed Martin in and asked if he wanted something to drink, but he politely declined. He sat on the loveseat and Doris took the sofa to his left. Between them on the table, her answering machine flashed seven times, indicating seven messages. She absentmindedly thought about checking them after Martin left, figuring they would all be from him anyway. "So, Martin, what is it? You look terrible."

Martin cleared his throat. "Well, after the faculty meeting, I drove home and there was a message on my answering machine from your mother. She was looking for you and thought I might know where you were. I called her back, but there was no answer, so I figured she went out, you know."

"Yes, she goes for a walk almost every evening around five."

"Yes, well I guess that was it. Anyway, I tried to call you a few times but got no answer. I figured you were at school or perhaps you and your mother might be together." Doris looked at him impatiently. "I'm sorry. To get to the point, I tried to call your mother again around seven or so and it sounded like she picked up the phone, but then she didn't answer. The phone stayed off the hook, and I got concerned. I didn't remember her having a cat or anything, so I couldn't figure out who would pick up the phone but not say anything."

"That is odd," Doris looked worriedly at the answering machine and its flashing red light. "Go on."

"Well, I drove over to her house and looked in the window. She was on the floor, Doris, so I tried to get in the house, but couldn't find a way in. So, I broke one of the windows in the back door and called an ambulance. She's in the hospital, Doris. They think she suffered a stroke."

"Oh my God, Martin, why didn't you say that right away!" She got up angrily and virtually flew out the door and to her car. Martin struggled to catch up, locking the door and rushing to his car.

"I'll meet you there," he waved vainly to her car as it sped down the road. Felix sat in the window and watched Martin's car pull away, then jumped down and headed to his dish for a snack.

6

When the sunlight streamed through a small opening in the drapes it hit Doris in the face and made her wince. She woke up in a sudden panic, trying to remember where she was. Her purse fell to the floor with a clatter, but Avis lay perfectly still, not responding to any sound. Doris took a deep breath and rubbed her eyes; the constant beep of Avis' heart monitor kept a steady rhythm. In the daylight, Avis looked even paler and so small in her hospital bed. Doris looked at her watch and realized she should probably go to the lobby to release Martin from his vigil and ask him to make the arrangements for her to miss her classes. She took Avis' hand gently in her own and looked at her mother's peaceful face. "I wish we hadn't wasted so much time," she said quietly. Avis lay quiet and still, a steady flow of breath raised and lowered her chest slightly. Doris entered the bathroom to splash water on her face and then left to find Martin.

The hall was brightly lit and a flurry of activity ushered in the new day. The nurses had not yet disturbed the visitors, leaving them asleep in their armchairs. Unlike Avis' room, the waiting room windows did not face the east, so the light seeping in from under the blinds was muted and dim. The older gentleman in the corner lay with his head back and mouth open, but oddly he did not make a sound. Doris spent a moment thinking he might be dead, but then he wiggled a foot and sniffed. The couple was gone, leaving Martin as the only other camper. He was turned on his side, a small drop of saliva dripped from his mouth onto the pillow.

She sat next to him and gently shook his shoulder. Martin hadn't miss her during the night. He seemed to have no notion she was roaming around or that she moved all her belongings into Avis' room around two in the morning. They discussed Avis' condition, and Martin agreed to take care of everything at school. Fortunately, none of his classes overlapped with hers, so he promised to meet her classes. She gave him the key to her office and asked him to pick up proposals in her first class and show a video in the art history class. A sudden thought pierced Doris' brain—Lenny! She almost opened her mouth to ask Martin to talk to Lenny about auditions, but realized it would take too long to explain everything to him. She decided to thank him for staying the night, and he assured her he would return as soon as possible in the afternoon. She helped Martin collect his things and get on the elevator then she walked to the pay phone to call Lenny and leave a message on her voice mail. Next, she called her brother to let him know she wouldn't know much until the tests were complete. He didn't answer his cell so she called Tammy and gave her the message.

Doris realized she was hungry. She told the nurses she was going downstairs to get something to eat and would be right back. They assured her they would call her if anything changed with Avis. "What's your cell number?" the nurse asked politely.

"Oh, I don't have one." The young nurse looked at her as if she was speaking a foreign language. "Should I just stay here in case?"

An older nurse nearby said, "No ma'am, we can page you if there's an emergency." She scanned a paper on her clipboard. "Peechum, right?"

Doris returned a half-hour later with her muffin and coffee; nurses were in Avis' room changing her bedding. A nurse with Ruth on her nametag came to the door and asked Doris to wait in the lounge. "The doctor will be here shortly, and we will be running several tests on your mother. It would be best if you would wait in the visitor area." Doris looked at Avis and nodded.

"If anything happens, you will come get me, won't you?" Doris was pleasant but firm. "If my mother is going to die, I want to be with her—no one should die without someone there who loves them."

"I understand," Ruth said and put her hand on Doris' shoulder to escort her from the room. Doris took a long look at Avis and reluctantly headed toward the hall.

The waiting room emanated an entirely different tone. The blinds were opened, and the room was flooded with warm sunlight mixed with overhead fluorescents. The television was off, but a hum of muffled conversations filled the room. Doris looked around for a seat and found nearly every chair was taken. There was a large group of people surrounding a plump woman of about thirty who was sobbing and talking almost incessantly. The low murmur of voices seemed to pacify her, and Doris could hear bits and pieces of their conversation. Bike, helmet, speeding, Frankie—Doris tried to make sense out of it. Apparently, the woman's son, Frankie, had been hit by a car while riding his bike without a helmet, and the prognosis was grim. Around the room, smaller groups of anxious family members huddled together looking for subjects to talk about and waiting for the five minutes they would be allowed to visit their loved ones. Doris took a seat in the only open corner and unwrapped her breakfast.

Doris finished her muffin and held her coffee between two fidgety hands. She looked around the room and then stood to study the parking lot from the seventh-floor window. She closed her eyes, thinking about her mother when a hand touched her arm gently. She turned to see Lenny's concerned face.

"Lenny, what are you doing here?"

"I am so sorry about your mother, Doris. I don't have a class until this afternoon and I wanted to stop by and see if you needed anything."

Doris smiled and shook her head. "Did you get my message?" Lenny nodded. "I'm sorry to do this to you. I don't know what to tell you about the play."

Lenny sighed, "Doris, don't be silly. We'll take it one day at a time. I'll finish auditions tonight with Bill there and then post the cast tomorrow morning. I will give you an understudy; if you are able to do the play you can take some nights off when you need it. If you can't do it, we will all miss you terribly but we'll understand. I'll come by or call and see how everything is going over the weekend. Please don't worry about the play— your mother is all that matters." Lenny put her arm around Doris' shoulders and squeezed slightly. Doris did not like being touched without warning so Lenny's affection startled her at first, but then she gave in to having a friendly hug. "Now, what can I get for you?"

"I'm fine right now, Lenny, but thanks," Doris moved to sit, and Lenny took the seat beside her. "They are running some tests today so we should know something soon. I'll need to make some kind of arrangements, but right now I don't know what."

"Well, you call me and let me know. I'll be in town all through the weekend and can come here or take care of your house, or whatever you need." Doris was silent. She didn't realize what a good friend Lenny really was. After all, they only spoke at plays and over lunch, never socializing together. When this was over, she might invite Lenny to see a movie or something. "Okay?"

"I will," Doris said, "thanks." Lenny smiled and said goodbye. She tiptoed into the hall and looked both ways, trying to remember the direction of the elevators. She disappeared to the left and Doris was once again alone in the waiting room. She sipped her coffee, now cold, and surveyed the room. During Lenny's visit, most of the people left, leaving only the plump woman and a man who was most likely her husband, one young couple, and the older gentleman from the night before, who returned to sit vigil. Doris couldn't stomach the coffee and got up to dispose of the cup in the trash. While she was up it made sense to her to ask about her mother at the desk. Nurse Ruth told her Avis was downstairs in radiology, and they would let her know as soon as they knew anything.

Doris sighed and wondered what she should do. The waiting was driving her nearly crazy. She hadn't realized until now how much she depended upon her mother for company. Doris was a rather solitary person who took pleasure in quiet evenings at home along with a good book or an old movie with Felix perched on her legs. She occasionally went to lunch with a colleague or attended campus events with Martin or a group from the department, but she hadn't cultivated any close girlfriends. Growing up here, she had enjoyed some good friends in high school, but only one of them came back here after college to settle down. Gina Michaels, nicknamed Tootsie because of an admitted addiction to Tootsie Roll candies when she was in elementary school, was married with three children so Doris didn't see much of her. They lived in totally different worlds. When Doris wanted to go somewhere or do something on the spur of the moment, she called Avis.

Standing in the hall of Kerry County Memorial Hospital's Intensive Care Unit, Doris considered for the first time what it would really mean to lose her mother. It was hard on Doris when her father died, but even though she was his favorite, they shared little interaction in their daily lives. When he died, she missed the memory of her father and the comfort of having him near, but she didn't miss doing things with him. Avis was the one who accompanied her shopping, eating out, going to a movie or a play. She suddenly realized that her mother was her best friend. This thought overwhelmed Doris so much she barely made it into the bathroom before the tears escaped and streamed down her cheeks. She was crying so hard she couldn't breathe, and all she could think about was what she would do if she never got the chance to tell her mother how much she meant to her.

Doris took some time in the bathroom cleaning up her face and then ambled back to the waiting room. She slowed her pace as she passed the nurses' station in case they wanted to tell her anything, but no one spoke to her. The television was on when Doris sat down. The older gentleman was watching a game show with the sound so low there was no way he could hear it, but Doris was grateful. She took the script from her purse and started reading. The plump woman was alone, and she sat quietly with her purse clutched in her hands. She sniffed occasionally and took a tissue from the table beside her to wipe her eyes. Doris made a point of not making eye contact with the woman—she seemed like the type who would strike up a conversation anywhere at any time with anyone. As sympathetic as Doris was to the woman's situation, she was not in the mood for chitchat or swapping family tragedies. And after all, she was focused on her own situation here. The warm sun streamed in through the window; it felt good to Doris, like a cozy blanket.

When Nurse Ruth touched Doris' knee the script fell to the floor, and Doris realized she had nodded off again. She rubbed her face and looked around. Her watch read nearly noon. How could that be? Ruth was sitting in a chair across from Doris and gave her a moment to recover her composure. "Dr. Peechum? The doctor would like to speak to you about your mother's tests."

Doris wanted to ask for the information right now, but she had visited hospitals enough to know the nurses won't tell you anything. Doris didn't speak; she nodded, gathered her belongings and followed Nurse Ruth to the little room she was in the night before. She took a seat on the sofa and looked around as she waited for the doctor to arrive. Someone had carefully decorated the room with a simple but elegant wallpaper design and color coordinated furnishings. Doris wondered how one picked out wallpaper for a room where most people would be talking about dying relatives, broken friends, and living wills. Still, she thought they did a good job. The room was nice but understated. The Monet prints were tasteful without being ostentatious, and there was no pretense of reading material or entertainment. Studying the decor helped Doris stay sane as she waited for Dr. Newsome's entrance and as she was about to run out of things to think about, the door opened and the doctor came in and took a seat.

"Hello, Dr. Peechum," Dr. Newsome said as she took Doris' hand, "I hope I can answer some of your questions now."

"Good, please call me Doris" Doris tried to smile, but she was so nervous her face wouldn't cooperate. "What can you tell me?"

The doctor put the folder aside and laced her fingers together at her belt, resting both elbows on the arms of her chair. She sighed and looked down and then at Doris' face. "Well, I'm afraid the news we have is not good." Doris felt an immediate grip in her chest and she gritted her teeth. Dr. Newsome explained that Avis' tests showed she suffered a massive stroke, and it would be unlikely for Avis to ever come out of the coma. "Right now, she's breathing on her own, but that could change without warning. She might linger for months in this state, or she might go into cardiac arrest or kidney failure at any time. We don't know what to expect, but we do know the damage to the brain is significant, and if she does come out of the coma, there definitely will be paralysis and probably brain damage."

"I see." Doris held so tightly to her purse her nails made little dents in the leather. "What do we do now?"

"The only choice we have is to wait and see how she does. If her vital signs improve and she continues to breathe on her own, we will need to move her to a constant care facility . . ."

"You mean a nursing home?" Doris' voice sounded strained and thin. "She would hate that. Aren't there any other choices?"

"Well," the doctor paused, thinking deeply, "if she is stable enough there is a possibility she could go home with you, or another family member, and be cared for by a home-care nurse." Doris' face brightened. "But let me warn you, she would need constant monitoring and a lot of special care."

"But a nurse could do it for me, right?"

The doctor looked at Doris. "Yes," she said, "it's very expensive, but yes, it's possible. Sometimes this kind of care can go on for quite a long time though. Her Medicare will pay for a skilled nursing facility for a certain about of time, and as she is, I don't think she is aware of her surroundings at all. Whatever you're thinking, I'd still recommend you get her on a waiting list for a skilled facility, though, because if you decide to put her in one, it can take a while to get a place in the better ones. I can give you a list of some good facilities right here in Kerryville." Doris sat, so heavy in thought she didn't realize the doctor was waiting for her to respond. "Is there anything else I can do for you now?"

Doris came to and looked at the doctor for a long moment before she spoke. "I'm almost afraid to ask this, but we don't know how long she was unconscious before my friend, Martin, found her. Do you think her condition would be better if we'd found her sooner?"

"I can't say for sure, but strokes happen pretty suddenly. Unless you feel definite symptoms before, which is unusual, and even if you do, they are easy to confuse with so many other problems. But if you do feel something before and get to a doctor immediately there is a better chance of surviving a stroke. However, after the stroke has happened, there isn't much we can do to help. I would advise you to focus on the fact she is here now and that you are ready to do everything you can to help her."

"I'll try." Doris' throat felt constricted and her nose was burning.

"I do need to know what kind of measures you want us to take if her condition changes for the worse. If she goes into cardiac arrest, we need to know if you want us to do everything in our power to revive her or do you want a DNR order."

"DNR?"

"Do not resuscitate."

"Oh yes, you mentioned that before. Does that mean you would let her die?"

The doctor paused and smiled, sympathetic to Doris' agony. "No. We would try normal methods for resuscitation, such as oxygen feed, a defibrillator, and even CPR. But her life would not be sustained by machines such as a ventilator. Unless you specify you want no life-sustaining efforts at all. In that case, we would let her go."

"I'll talk to my brother and let you know."

Dr. Newsome touched Doris' hand and smiled in a reassuring way and then took her leave. Doris sat, blankly staring at the Monet print and rearranging her house in her head. "I don't have room," she muttered to herself, "I'll have to move into her house." She sat planning how she could shift furniture around to suit a hospital bed, still staring absentmindedly at Monet's water lilies. Nurse Ruth opened the door to ask if she was all right, and Doris realized she needed to get up and call Ted.

She called his mobile number first, hoping to catch him directly and bypass Tammy, the fewer people to explain this to right now, the better. Ted answered on the third ring. "Ted? It's Doris. I have news about

Mother."

"It's about time, Doris—Jesus, why don't you have a cell phone?"

"Didn't Tammy tell you I called?"

"Yes, but that's not the point!"

"You could have called me here at the hospital," she said, not prepared for an attack.

"Oh, really, and just how would I do that, Doris?"

"I don't know. Call the hospital and ask for ICU?"

"And then the nurses would just let you stand there using their phone to talk to me? This is the twenty-first century; you need to catch up with the rest of the world!"

She was quiet for a moment. Yes, she was here and knew what was going on, and he wasn't and didn't. "Do you want to know what the doctor said?" she asked simply.

7

Ted was obviously uncomfortable with making any decisions about Avis' care, but he finally agreed with Doris that she would not want to live hooked up to machines. Ted said he would arrange to take the next two days off work so he would be flying in later in the evening. Doris told him where her door key was hidden, but he suggested taking a taxi directly to the hospital.

"But what will you do with your luggage?" Doris asked. "Why don't you taxi over to my house and get settled in and then come to the hospital. We'll take it from there. You remember where the key is?"

"Yes. That makes sense I guess," Ted agreed, "but you will call me on my cell if there's any change."

"Of course." Doris assured him and sent her regards to Tammy and the kids.

"And, I'm sorry, Doris."

Doris hung up the phone and approached the nurses' station to tell them what she and Ted decided. If anything happened with Avis, they did not want extraordinary methods used to keep her alive. Nurse Ruth made a note and said she would notify the doctor immediately. "We will have to ask you to sign some papers. If you'll wait in the lounge, we'll come get you when we have them ready."

"Thanks, but I'll be in my mother's room." Doris was tired and suddenly hungry. She looked at her watch and realized it was early afternoon and all she'd eaten was a muffin. "On second thought, I'm going downstairs for a moment to get some food, and then I'll be in my mother's room." The nurse nodded but focused on her computer screen.

Late in the afternoon, Nurse Ruth came into Avis' room to find Doris watching television and commenting to Avis. Doris looked over at the nurse and nodded. "Mother, I'll be right back." She squeezed Avis' hand lightly and followed the nurse to the little conference room.

"Dr. Newsome will be with you shortly. Can I get you something to drink?"

Doris knew Nurse Ruth was trying to be kind in a difficult situation, so she resisted the urge to hold her by the hair and say something like, "I'M SIGNING MY MOTHER'S DEATH CERTIFICATE, WHAT KIND OF DRINK DO YOU THINK WOULD MAKE THIS EASIER!?" She shook her head silently and turned away. Doris knew it was normal to cry in these circumstances, but she still didn't want the nurse to see the tear that trickled down her left cheek. Nurse Ruth took the hint and tiptoed out of the room.

Moments later, there was a faint knock at the door, and Dr. Newsome came in and took a seat. "Doris, we have the paperwork ready for you to sign as Mrs. Peechum's next of kin. I assume you have discussed this with your brother. Do you have any questions?"

"I don't think so," Doris said, wiping her eyes. "I understand you will try normal procedures to save her, but will not attach her to breathing machines or continue CPR if there are no brainwaves." Doris was amazed at how detached she sounded; it all seemed unreal. She guessed it was impossible for anyone to wrap her brain around the reality of death. A part of her seemed to be floating in some parallel universe where she would call her mother as soon as she got home and tell her all about this, and the other part was holding onto a pen and looking down at the paper she was supposed to sign. Doris felt herself floating between the two, trying to comprehend which was real.

"That's basically correct," Dr. Newsome was saying. Doris was watching her mouth but it was as if the voice track was slightly delayed, like what happens sometimes on television. The mouth moves ahead of the voice. She noticed Dr. Newsome's brown eyes were kind and full of concern.

Doris felt as if her head was in a fog; visions of Avis in a new Easter hat, baking a cake in the kitchen, and holding her first grandchild kept flooding through her memories. The doctor was speaking in soothing tones, like a Brahms symphony, but Doris couldn't hear the words at all anymore. She placed the document on the little table near the sofa, signed her name, and pushed the pen and papers toward the doctor. She leaned back on the sofa and put her hand over her mouth. "If it helps at all, I believe you are making the right choice for your mother," the doctor said and reached a hand out to Doris' knee. Doris nodded and put her face in both hands. "If you have any questions or need to talk, please let me know." Dr. Newsome left the room and Doris could hear muted voices in the hall. She didn't care what they were saying; she needed time to breathe. Doris stayed in the little room for what seemed like a long time, but no one bothered her.

When she finally emerged, Doris took a detour to the bathroom to wash her face. The icy cold water felt good--like the punishment she felt she deserved for deserting her mother when she needed her most. She walked past the nurses' station and took the elevator to the third-floor chapel. The little chapel was made mostly of a fine polished wood. Walnut, she guessed. Ed Peechum was an avid woodworker, and Doris learned more than she realized as she hung around her father's workshop. The smell of the wood brought back memories of sawdust, birdhouse kits, and her wood-burning days. There was an altar beneath a stained-glass window lighted from behind. The window featured a dove with multicolored glass surrounding it. There was no cross, crucifix, or other denominational symbols. However, there were banks of candles to the right and left of the small altar.

It had been a long time since Doris had darkened the door of a church. She stood in the aisle for a minute remembering her first communion and the dress Avis made for the occasion. She genuflected from habit and took a seat in a pew near the front. Doris wasn't sure what to do; she didn't pray anymore and didn't think God would be interested in anything she wanted to say. But it felt good to sit there. It felt familiar, strangely comforting, and a little awkward at the same time. As she sat thinking, the plump woman from the waiting room came in and headed straight for the candles. She knelt, lit a candle, and tucked a ten-dollar bill into the little jar nearby. Doris thought she was saying the rosary, but then she realized the woman was sobbing. Her son must be holding on by the same thread Avis was clinging to. *Why do we hold on when all hope seems lost*, she wondered?

Doris wished she could believe lighting a candle would help Avis. She envied people with strong religious beliefs. It would make everything so much easier to believe someone else could take care of her life, there is a grand plan, and all we need to do is accept it. But Doris didn't believe in candles or statues or even crosses. She did believe in God, or at least she thought she did, but she didn't think anyone could define God with statues or faces. *Those things are what we use to make God accessible, more like us*, she reasoned. *How could a Jewish Jesus have blonde hair and blue eyes? Oh well*, she reminded herself, *this is neither the time nor the place to dwell on theology*. However, it felt good for a moment to think about something other than Avis and her own sense of guilt.

Doris stood, genuflected and then rolled her eyes. *I'm like Pavlov's dog*, she thought, kneeling in front of the altar is a conditioned response for Catholics. You walk by an altar, you genuflect. By this time, the other woman was gone, leaving a brightly burning candle in her wake. Doris turned, looked at the altar, and headed to the bank of candles. She knelt, lit a candle, and pulled a five-dollar bill from her wallet. She tucked it in the jar, paused a moment, and then got up to leave.

Before she left the chapel, she turned to see Avis' candle burning strongly, its flame tipping above the rim of the glass. She picked a votive with a picture of an angel, surrounded by rays of light and clouds on the outside. Doris thought Avis would like this one; her mother remained deeply religious all her life and was fond of angels. *And besides*, she thought, *it can't hurt*.

Around six o'clock Nurse Cindy came in to find Doris sound asleep in the chair beside her mother, her hand holding Avis'. She woke Doris gently and told her there was a visitor in the waiting room. "We need to change your mother's IV anyway, so we'll do it while you see your friend."

Doris patted Avis' hand then left to find Martin in the waiting room. He met with her classes, took up the Art 150 proposals, and had looked over her syllabi to give them and the Art History class their assignments. He told her not to worry about school; he took care of everything. "Some of your students were concerned about you. A young man named Jayson asked about you after class. He was worried about you not being able to do the play. What play is that, Doris?"

"I wanted to tell you about it at lunch on Monday, but remember, we missed each other? Lenny has asked me to play Martha in *Who's Afraid of Virginia Woolf?*, and I agreed. That's where I was last night when . . ." tears threatened to escape again, so Doris sniffed and threw her head back.

"Well, it certainly would be exciting. I'm happy for you. That's a demanding role. Do you think you'll be able to do it?" He paused momentarily, and realized she might take offense at his comment. "I don't mean will you be able to handle such a demanding role, I'm sure you can.

I haven't seen you act, of course, but you've told me how active you were in college. I meant will you have time now, because of your mother, I mean." Martin's face showed distress and the white lock of hair fell over his left eye.

Doris smiled and gently pushed it aside. "I don't know, Martin, I'm taking this one minute at a time." Doris sat back in the chair beside him and closed her eyes. She knew she wanted to continue in the play, if possible, for her own sanity. The few moments she spent thinking about the play were the only times she felt calm and relaxed. It was good for her to have something to look forward to amid all this sadness, but at the same time, she felt more guilt for trying to go on with her life when her mother was apparently at the end of hers.

"Doris, I know you are exhausted. I'm going to insist you go home and eat and rest while I sit here with Avis." Doris opened her mouth to object, but Martin forged ahead. "No arguments. You are in the same clothes you came in here with. You need a few hours alone—if for no other reason than to be of better use to Avis. Now go." Doris was silent; she knew he was right. She started to speak, but Martin read her thoughts. "Yes, I will call you the second anything changes."

"But will they let you stay?"

"I'll think of something, go."

They both stood and Martin gave her a slight kiss on the cheek and watched her get into the elevator. He looked around and then headed for Avis' room. He sat in the chair Doris had moved over, opened his briefcase, and yanked out a group of papers to grade.

Doris pulled into her driveway and saw Felix in the window meowing and rubbing against the glass first one way and then the other. She rushed to the door and inside to take him into her arms. His wet nose butted up against her chin, and he licked her jaw and neck affectionately. Felix was warm and living and felt so good to her; she carried him over her shoulder like a baby around the house as she walked around straightening up and putting things in order. As she fluffed the pillows on the sofa, she noticed the flashing light on her answering machine. Thinking these were old messages from Martin she pushed the button and sat down long enough to make sure. Felix scampered toward his food bowl in the kitchen and began making noises to remind her it was nearly suppertime. "Yes, Felix, I know," she smiled. The answering machine rewound and beeped and then she heard the voice of her mother.

"Doris? This is your mother, Doris, if you're home please answer." There was a silence while Avis waited. "Well, I guess you're not home. I haven't been feeling too well today and I wondered if you'd be able to drive me to the doctor tomorrow." There was another pause. "Well, that's all, really. I'll call back later." The machine beeped again, and then Martin's voice came on.

"Doris, this is Martin. I, uh, well, I wanted to talk to you. I thought we might have lunch tomorrow. Let me know." Doris stared at the machine and leaned back on the sofa. The machine beeped again.

"Doris, this is your mother again. I wanted to let you know I'm going to bed early—I'm still feeling lousy. So, don't call after nine. Call me when you get up tomorrow. Bye now." Doris was thinking if she knew her mother wasn't feeling well, would she have gone over to see her? *Would she have been there when she had the stroke? Would it have made any difference?* The machine beeped again.

"Doris, this is Martin again. Your mother called me looking for you. She seemed kind of worried. I'm going over to see her—hope that's okay. I'll talk with you later." The machine beeped again, but Doris was already sobbing. "Doris, this is Martin. I, uh, went to your mother's house and uh, she was passed out on the floor. I took her to the emergency room and got her checked in. They said it looks like a stroke. So anyway, I'm calling from the hospital and since you're not home, I may drive by later and see if you want a ride over here. Uh, yes, well, I'll see you later then. Sorry." The machine beeped three times, signaling that all messages had played. It clicked and rewound and clicked again and then was silent. Felix jumped up on the sofa next to Doris and reached out a paw and gently rested it on her knee.

"That's what you were trying to tell me yesterday, wasn't it? But I was too busy to listen—too into myself to pay attention." She picked him up and stroked his soft fur, her eyes swollen and burning and a pile of tissues wadded into small balls in front of her. She sat there rubbing his head, trying to clear her mind when she drifted off to sleep with Felix on her chest.

Felix's hunger finally got the best of him, and he jumped down to check for leftover morsels in his bowl. The movement stirred Doris, and she awoke to a darkening living room, the sun all but gone. She looked around and realized where she was and sat there for a moment listening to her breath. Felix meowed, and she got up to feed him. She set up a weekend food feeder that allowed a continuous flow of food, which she used when she needed to go out of town for a few days. She also fixed up a continuous water bowl, too, knowing full well Felix's favorite watering hole was the hall toilet. Doris fixed a light supper, watched the news and tried for some sense of normalcy. Afterwards, she took a long, hot bath, washed her hair and packed a small travel bag so she could stay at the hospital if needed.

She checked her machine—no calls while she was in the bath. She pushed the button on the machine to save the old messages; it might be the only way she could ever hear her mother's voice again. She entered the guestroom and made sure there were clean sheets and towels for Ted. Doris wrote him a short note with the hospital phone number and an invitation for him to eat whatever he could find and pinned it to a pillow. She realized it was time to go back, so she did her make-up and hair, picked up her bag, kissed Felix, and took off.

When she arrived in Avis' room with her briefcase and an overnight bag, Martin was still grading papers with his glasses on top of his head, pushing back the wild lock of hair, and a red pen dashing off curious notes of corrections. He didn't see her at first, and she enjoyed a few moments of watching him work on the papers. He occasionally commented to himself and then to Avis about the sad state of his students' grammatical incompetence and then shook his head. Doris made a small movement drawing his attention to the doorway. He stood, slipped the papers into his briefcase, and moved toward the door. Doris raised her eyebrows in a question, but Martin shook his head. "No change," was all he said. She thanked him and told him to go home and get some rest. "Oh, yes, just in case they say something, I told them I was your husband so they'd let me stay--I hope you don't mind."

"Of course not, Martin, I appreciate you staying with her for me."

"I can take your classes again tomorrow," Martin said.

"That would be so wonderful, thank you," Doris said and started writing down her class schedule and assignments. "Pick up final paper proposals from my seminar class and just give the quiz to my art history class."

She explained where to find the quizzes and gave him a quick kiss. He promised to return tomorrow and then picked up his briefcase and left.

Doris put some of her belongings into a small cabinet near the window and then resumed her vigil at her mother's side, calmly looking over final proposals from her first class. She knew that some people wouldn't understand how she could carry on her work when her mother was so ill, but Doris always needed something to keep her busy, even in the worst of times. It kept her grounded. She read and commented on them until she fell asleep.

8

Ted arrived at the hospital around midnight, and knocked on the door of Avis' room to get Doris' attention. He hardly looked at Avis, which Doris found a little disturbing, but she chalked it up to fatigue and worry. She gathered up her papers and showed him to the waiting area, and they found a quiet corner to talk. Most of the family members had fallen asleep so they didn't want to disturb anyone. Doris explained the situation to him, offered her keys, and urged him to go back to her house to rest. "Take my car. You've been up since early this morning. I know you're tired from the trip. Get a good night's rest and come back in the morning." He made a small protest but finally relented. When he gave her a hug, Doris tried to reciprocate, but her arms didn't want to work. The gesture shocked her; they were not a physically affectionate family. She wondered what kind of private hell her brother was going through--*do we ever truly understand the experiences of others?* Before she could respond, he turned to walk away. They didn't even say goodbye.

Doris sat for a few minutes in the waiting area, looking around at the oversized recliners, muted wall colors, nondescript but tasteful art, and incandescent lighting, all carefully designed to create a soothing ambiance for grieving families. She pondered for a long minute how they taught this in interior design school. What would the course be called and what kind of exam must one take? She stood up, abandoning the thought, and returned to her mother's room.

When the nurse came in to take Avis' vital signs the next morning, her movements woke Doris who had nested herself in the recliner, clutching a pillow in her arms. "Good morning, Dr. Peechum," the nurse said. Doris wasn't wearing her glasses and couldn't read the nametag, but she knew this was someone she hadn't met yet. "Dr. Newsome will be by to see you soon."

"Is there news, about my mother?"

"I don't know. She makes her rounds here early, so she should be here soon. Is there anything I can get you in the meantime?"

Doris asked for tomato juice and the nurse took off. It was fifty minutes before she returned with the juice, by which time Doris had dozed off again; she sat up in the chair and took Avis' hand. "I saw Dr. Newsome down the hall, so she should be in here soon."

"Thank you," Doris muttered and opened the juice. She pulled a bottle of vitamins from her purse, swallowed one, then walked into the bathroom to comb her hair and try to look presentable. When she came out of the bathroom, Ted was standing in Avis' room just staring at his mother.

When the doctor arrived, Doris introduced her to Ted, and they walked down the hall to the little Monet room. "Dr. Peechum, sorry, Doris, and Mr. Peechum, your mother's vitals have stabilized." Doris sighed in relief and gave the doctor a smile. "I wish this could be better news, but all it means is her heartbeat and breathing are not labored or erratic."

"Isn't it good she's still breathing on her own?" Ted asked.

"Well, it can be, but with your mother's condition it means she is not in any immediate danger. We will monitor her the rest of the day, and if her status stays as they are now, we will move her to a regular room either tonight or tomorrow morning."

"What exactly does that mean?" Doris read the concerned look in the doctor's face; *there's something she's not telling me.* "Please, be honest with us."

"Well, I don't think your mother is suffering. I wish we knew more about strokes, but we don't. We can monitor brainwaves and vital signs, but no one in a coma can tell us what's going on, and no one has remembered anything from a comatose state--so it's all pretty much guesswork. Which I know is not what you, or any other concerned family member, wants to hear."

"Okay," Doris couldn't think of anything else to say.

"What this means for you, is your mother could remain in this state for a long time to come, or could have another stroke or other failure at any time. I'm so sorry, but I want you to be prepared."

"Couldn't she recover?" Doris asked, noticing Ted had leaned back in his chair and was staring into the middle distance.

"Well, no, I don't see that happening. We think she suffered a major stroke, one which caused a great deal of brain damage. Not in the areas that control involuntary functions like breathing and heartbeat, but in other parts vital to cognition."

"Are you sure--absolutely sure?"

"Well, when we're talking about the brain, there are no absolutes. But our tests show she will most likely never recover full function and may not come out of the coma. But if you'd like to get a second opinion I would certainly understand. However, I must tell you if she levels out in the next few days, in other words, her condition becomes stable, we will need to move her to a continuing care facility--a nursing home."

"I thought you said I could take her home."

"Well, it is possible, but she would have to have almost round-the-clock nursing care, and it is prohibitively expensive. Given that Medicare doesn't cover it, or certainly not enough of it. You and your brother should start looking for a place immediately. Because of Mrs. Peechum's condition, we can probably get her placed if there's any room at all, so we need to know your preference of facilities."

"Okay," Doris said again, feeling ignorant and inadequate.

"Here are some brochures, but I am not trying to push any of these places on you. I suggest the two of you take some time and visit them. Let me know your first few choices as soon as you can."

Doris took the brochures and looked at Ted. The doctor put her hand gently on Doris' shoulder. "Again, I'm so sorry." And then she left.

"I'm going downstairs for coffee," Ted said suddenly. "You want anything?" Doris just looked at him and shook her head.

There is a technique in filmmaking, which Doris understood fully at that moment for the first time. The person of the audience's focus stays in one place while the camera moves farther and farther away--emphasizing how completely small and alone this character is feeling. This was the only way Doris could understand what she was feeling right then. Shock? Anger? Sadness? Yes, definitely, all of that. But more than anything, she felt alone, like a piece of driftwood floating on an ocean wave with no direction or anchor. She had Ted, Martin, friends; she knew this. But for some reason, none of them could have reached her, none of them seemed likely to be of any use in helping her find her footing.

And why, she asked herself. Why did she feel this overwhelming feeling of impending doom? She sauntered down the hall and returned to

Avis' room. She looked at her mother and knew immediately. It was because her mother was lost to her. Yes, she was breathing, but she knew instantly her mother would never be the vibrant person she was on Monday, and probably not able to communicate, to acknowledge triumph or defeat, or share in any way in her daughter's life. *What is it Emily Dickenson said? "Hold dear to your parents for it is a scary and confusing world without them."* For the first time, Doris felt the full import of this quote, but felt oddly comforted that someone else obviously felt the kind of terror that enveloped her now.

She pulled a chair over and sat beside her mother, taking her hand. "What is going on in your mind, Mother? Do you feel any pain? Do you even know I'm here?" She rested her head gently on Avis' hand. And she cried.

For a long, long time.

9

Doris did arrange for Avis' tests to be reviewed by another doctor, but the results and prognosis were the same. There were no classes Friday because of homecoming so Doris and Ted decided to check out local nursing homes, and Martin sat with Avis. They walked into the first one and were shocked to see patients in wheelchairs all over the halls and lounge, some sitting fast asleep with their heads uncomfortably buried in their chests or heads thrown back, mouths open, and snoring. Some were moaning, one woman was asking anyone who walked past, "Can you take me home?" An old man, rail thin with bent feet, whose face lit up when they entered, said, "Jenny? Jenny, is that you?" Doris looked at Ted, then went over and took the man's hand.

"No, I'm sorry, it's not Jenny." The man's face fell into a mask of sadness and broke Doris' heart. He rolled himself away, and Doris wiped a tear off her cheek. She knew it would not be pleasant but didn't imagine it would be this painful. The staff walked quickly by, paying no attention to anyone, on their ways to whatever was so important. A couple of women, possibly nurses, were chatting at the desk, laughing occasionally. Ted started to approach them, but Doris took his arm and ushered him out the door. "There is no way I'm putting our mother in a place like this!" She rushed to the car, and Ted didn't speak.

By Friday afternoon, Avis' condition remained the same, and the doctors decided she was stable enough to be moved. She was transferred from the ICU into a regular hospital room with close monitoring. Martin and Ted spent most of the evening moving Doris' necessities over to Avis' house. She rearranged things to her liking in the big bedroom downstairs, connecting her stereo, VCR, and television. Martin found a reason to leave the room when she started to unpack her lingerie. Finally, they brought Felix in so he could sniff the entire contents of the house, which any cat must do before settling into a new, however temporary, home.

On Saturday, Ted and Martin helped Doris rearrange Avis' house to make her huge dining room into a makeshift hospital room, with a bed, a TV, and comfortable chairs for her visitors. They all decided this room was the best choice since the master bedroom was nearby with a large bathroom between it and the dining room area. Doris could sleep in this downstairs bedroom and be able to hear Avis' monitor. Also, it would be more convenient with everything on one floor. Together they lovingly wrapped all of Avis' beautiful china, crystal, and silverware and stored it in an empty closet in a bedroom upstairs. Ted also secured the help of a few neighbors to move Avis' furniture into a large room in the rear of the house she used as a sewing nook and miscellaneous storage room.

Ted spent a few moments visiting Avis off and on, but it was clearly making him uncomfortable to see her in this condition. Doris suggested he go home to take care of his family, and he was obviously relieved—having been given permission to leave without guilt. He took off early Sunday afternoon, and Doris promised to call if anything changed. He offered to take care of their mother's bank accounts and pay the bills since Doris was the one giving up her time to care for their mother. That seemed reasonable to Doris. She didn't want to leave her mother's care in anyone else's hands anyway, and Ted couldn't stand the idea of changing her urine bag or giving his mother a bath. When he left, they were both satisfied with the arrangement.

On her rounds Sunday afternoon, Dr. Newsome asked Doris if she had found a place she liked for Avis. Doris tried to keep her emotions in check and simply told the doctor she was planning to bring her home. "I'll have my nurse give you some brochures on home healthcare," Dr. Newsome said as Doris stared at her mother. "You will need to move her soon, hopefully by Tuesday." Doris nodded. The doctor paused and waited, to see if Doris had any questions, but she said nothing. She took Avis' hand in hers and looked up as the doctor was leaving the room. Martin and Doris sat with Avis, grading papers and sipping coffee, with very little conversation.

Doris held her classes on Monday, returning the Art 150 proposals and discussing Medieval painting in the art history class. She didn't keep her office hours, rushing home in the afternoon to interview candidates to be her mother's private nurses. She found a company she liked so she hired a retired registered nurse to come in while she was at work to take care of medical needs such as her IV, catheter, and medications, and a licensed practical nurse for the evenings. She could change linens, bathe Avis, and monitor her while Doris had rehearsals. She and Lenny worked together to make out a reasonable schedule so Doris could be with her mother as much as possible. Lenny told her not to come on Monday and Tuesday evenings since she could work with the other three actors on character analysis and with the technical crew. Doris arranged for the two nurses to come over in the afternoon to see the house and meet each other. By the time they left, she was feeling more confident and less like warm Jell-O.

Tuesday morning, Doris returned paper proposals to her Art 450 Senior Seminar in Art. It seemed so long since she had seen their curious faces, and it felt good to be back--in the safe cocoon of academia. At one, she met the Visual Arts class long enough to return their quizzes give them their assignment, which was to find a copy of the movie, *Citizen Kane*, and be ready to discuss it. Afterwards, she drove to Avis' house, making it before the ambulance arrived. Doris took charge, showing them where to put everything; Avis lay still and quiet, no expression, no movement. They rolled her bed into the once stylish dining room that was now rearranged into an antiseptic care facility. The hospital bed, monitors, IV drip, and tables with instruments and trays looked oddly out of place in the periwinkle blue room with expensively framed Georgia O'Keefe prints and dark blue velvet curtains that framed the large bay window. Doris left Avis' miniature garden of herbs and flowers she kept in the windowsill and the chandelier, which once suspended gracefully over the nineteenth century cherry dining table. It needed to be raised to accommodate people walking under it, but Doris refused to remove it.

She insisted the bed be turned toward the bay window, so Avis could see her window garden and the sunlight when she woke up (which Doris still believed could happen.) Although this arrangement made everything a bit harder in terms of wiring and plugging in, the staff complied without complaint. Once everything was set up, the transfer team gave her a few last-minute tips for Avis' care and left her a booklet for easy reference in case of an emergency. Martin saw them to the door while Doris tugged and tucked at Avis' blanket. She stopped for a moment and then quickly ran up the steps and into her old bedroom. Martin stood at the base of the steps waiting, listening to the opening and closing of doors and then the tap of Doris' shoes on the wood floor as she returned. Her arms held a beautifully crocheted afghan of many colors Avis' mother made many years ago. It was Avis' favorite possession. Doris carried it respectfully to Avis' bed, draped it over her legs gently and then patted her hand.

"There, Mother, your favorite cover." Martin came up behind her and gently placed his hands upon Doris' shoulders. She turned to embrace him and found herself in tears. Martin patted her back softly and murmured everything would be okay.

Doris and Martin spent the next few days juggling school and Avis' care and familiarizing the day and night nurses with Avis' house. It was hard for Doris to drive off and leave her mother come Wednesday morning, even though she knew Avis was in the capable hands of Harriet. She was an experienced, retired geriatric nurse who now worked solely in home healthcare. She was nearly sixty, came highly recommended, and was pleasant to work with. Still, in most ways, Harriet was a stranger, but Doris told herself to have faith.

She finished off her breakfast, dressed, greeted Harriet, kissed her mother's forehead, and patted Felix. It felt good to rev up the Karmann Ghia, but as she pulled away from the little white house her mind was full of worries and fears, but she knew it was the best thing to do. She needed some time for herself, and she knew her mother would want her to get on with her life.

Sunlight streamed through the pine branches outside her office window. She took her little can down the hall to the bathroom to fill up with water for her pansies, dieffenbachia, and some vine she liked but didn't know the name of. "Drink up, sweeties," she almost sang to them as she treated them to a badly needed drink. She sat at her computer, leaned back in her armchair, and for the first time in over a week, took an unlabored breath. *Goodness, it is good to be back home*, she thought. *This is who I am, who I want to be.* Since she was tenured, Doris felt secure in the knowledge she would stay at Kerryville until she retired. Without a husband and children, her job was the only part of her life that made her feel secure. She complained sometimes, but she loved being a professor and having a place in the little college community she could be proud of.

"Morning!" a cheery voice disturbed her reverie, but she didn't mind when she saw it was Martin.

"Oh, Martin, I can't believe how good it feels to be back at work full time!"

"I understand," he said and gave her a wink. "I'll come by around twelve to escort you to lunch, if that's okay."

Doris was amused. So much could change in such a short amount of time. "Well, my class ends at ten and then I'll be in the library doing some research on my conference paper until eleven thirty so I'll meet you at the cafeteria afterwards--okay?"

"Righto!" Martin said and was gone.

Doris shook her head and gathered up her materials for her Art Appreciation class. Jayson sneaked into class five minutes late, interrupting Doris' lecture on the evolution of architecture. He looked red-eyed and bushy haired, as if he had just awakened. Doris wondered why he scheduled a nine o'clock class if he couldn't get up for it. He looked at her sheepishly and grinned, but she gave him no special recognition. Their assignment for Friday was to finalize their proposals and conduct research on famous 20th century architects. One petite girl, who looked too young to be in college, stopped by Doris' desk on her way out. A boy, apparently with her, lingered just outside the door.

"Dr. P, I have to miss class next Monday, and I was wondering if we're doing anything important that day." She pushed her thin blonde hair off her face and twisted her body from side to side.

This was not the first time Doris had been asked this question, but it always infuriated her. She took a breath, trying to keep her temper in check. "Yes, Abby, I know you may find this hard to believe, but I consider everything we do in class important. So, what do you mean by important?"

The girl pulled her head back, darting her eyes around the floor. "Well, I guess something graded, like a test. Or something that will be on a test, you know?"

"Do you have your syllabus?" Doris asked her as politely as possible.

"Yeah, somewhere."

"Why don't you pull it out and let me show you how to tell what we're doing each day in class."

"No, that's okay. I think it's in my room." The girl started backing toward the door. "I can figure it out."

"Wait, here, I have a copy," Doris said, smiling. She showed Abby how to read the syllabus and where to find her class policies about absences.

"Ok, thanks." The girl sighed and left the room. Doris just scratched her head and picked up her books and notes.

"What did she say," the boy asked.

"Nothing important," the girl responded, took his hand, and pulled him down the hall.

Doris found her sense of humor and just smiled as she followed them down the hall.

She and Martin shared a pleasant, albeit short, lunch, and then she hurried back to the Humanities building for her afternoon Art History class. The students wanted to know how her mother was, if they could do anything to help, and how she was holding up. *By the time they become juniors and seniors*, Doris mused, *they really become adults.* That awkward self-absorption she found so tiresome in the freshmen and sophomores dissipates into a pleasant level of maturity around age twenty or twenty-one. She didn't think college had as much to do with it as her colleagues seemed to believe; she noticed it happened to most people whether they were in college or not. *But college doesn't seem to hurt anyone*, she reasoned. She wondered for a moment who in their wisdom had set the legal drinking age at twenty-one.

Once she assured them things were as good as could be expected and she was trying to get back into a routine, the students brought up questions concerning their reading assignment. They spent the rest of class discussing pageant wagons and mansions used for Medieval stage settings. Doris often took intellectual discourse for granted, but as she made her way back to her office she realized she needed it more than food--certainly more than she needed sex. She didn't understand the big deal over sex anyway. *Great for men, but for women, the intimacy is far more enjoyable. Martin is good at cuddling; perhaps*, she thought, *life with Martin would be stimulating enough.*

Lenny dropped by during her late afternoon office hours to see how Doris was holding up. "Hey, Doris, how's your mom?"

Mom, Doris thought, *I never in my life called my mother "Mom;"* Avis wouldn't allow it. "She's the same, Lenny. I'm sorry I haven't been in touch with you about the play. My life is so topsy-turvy right now. But I am hoping to make it to my first rehearsal tonight."

"Doris, I told you not to worry about it," Lenny said as she took the extra chair in Doris' office. "I thought you might want to know who got cast as Nick and Honey." Doris nodded, encouraging Lenny to continue.

"Jayson Jeffries and Teri Hopper." Doris furrowed her eyebrows at the mention of Jayson's name. She was worried again about being in the play with a current student, but Lenny must have interpreted her scowl as disapproval. "They are both good actors and easy to work with. I think you'll like them once you get to know them."

"Oh, Lenny, I know Teri—she's a former student. And I'm sorry I didn't tell you this sooner, but I know Jayson, he's in one of my classes this semester. I am a little worried about playing Martha against him because of that. Martha and Nick get pretty physical, you know."

"Oh, god, Doris, I didn't even know that. Oh, shit, I can't un-cast Jayson at this point—I wish you'd told me."

"I started to, Lenny, but I didn't want to knock Jayson out of such a great role when he is clearly so deserving and talented." She patted Lenny's hand gently. "I'll talk it over with Phyllis and see what she thinks. If she gives me the go-ahead, then at least we're covered, right?"

Lenny looked visibly relieved. "Good, you let me know what she says and what you decide to do. I hope you can be with us, but I will understand if you can't."

"I want to be with you, too, Lenny. I have so much on my plate right now; I need to give it some serious thought. I will still come by tonight, though. I know how important the first read-through is." Lenny smiled, sighed, and nodded before she slipped out the door and down the hall.

Having done hardly anything but work and watch after her mother for the past week, Doris wanted to run a collection of errands in the afternoon. She already told Martin she wouldn't see him again until the next day at lunch. She drove by her house first to check on things in general and water her flowers. It was obvious from the closely shorn grass and neatly edged landscaping that Martin had come over recently to mow and trim the yard. Hopefully, this would be the last time before winter set in. Doris tried hard not to get too involved in her house; she missed it terribly. It was better if she stayed detached, not thinking too much about anything. She took the sheets and towels Ted used and put them in the laundry room, made up the bed and tidied the hall bathroom, so she could stay in her house longer. Afterwards, she gave one final look, sighed, and locked the front door.

Doris swung by the dry cleaners and dropped off a few outfits, picked up a new battery for her watch at the jewelers, then sat looking over class notes while a bevy of young grease-smeared men hovered over Carmen giving her an oil change and check over. Finally, she stopped by the grocers to pick up some staples like bread, milk, and chocolate ice cream before going back to relieve Harriet before six.

"No cha-unge," Harriet said in a thick accent Doris thought sounded Appalachian. She picked up her sweater and purse, patted Avis' hand, which Doris found touching, and headed for the door. "That ca-ut," Harriet turned to look at Felix at the foot of Avis' bed, "wuz reel good comp'ny. He luvs yore mothur. I hope yew 'preciate him." Before Doris could respond, Harriet closed the door and was heading down the steps to her little Honda.

Doris picked up Felix, stroked his soft fur and scratched under his chin. "I think I appreciate you, don't I?" Felix purred. She kicked off her shoes and carried the cat around the room while she tidied up—gathering parts of the newspaper, folding blankets, and so on. She chatted happily to Avis about her day as if Avis was sitting at the kitchen table having coffee. Felix hopped down from Doris' embrace and curled up at Avis' feet. "Good boy," Doris said, and sauntered into the kitchen to fix a light dinner.

After her bath, she watched the early news with Avis and admitted the evening nurse, Sandy, who appeared and behaved quite differently than Harriet. Harriet was soft and round, with a sincere smile and seemed comfortable with a moderate amount of messiness. Sandy's hair was blonde and cropped short and close to her head, she wore small wire-framed glasses, and had a too-thin, even boney body bearing a white nurse's pantsuit. She was amiable to Doris, but headed immediately toward Avis to check her IV and catheter. "Harriet takes care of her baths in the morning," Doris offered. Sandy nodded and made a small noise, which sounded somewhat like okay. "She also changes the linens every day."

"That's wonderful, Dr. Peechum," Sandy said in a mild reassuring tone she must have developed in her work with geriatric patients. Doris found it a little condescending, but didn't say anything. "I still have to check everything. I want to make sure your mother gets the best care. You understand, I'm sure." She removed the catheter bag and replaced it with a fresh one and disappeared into the bathroom before Doris could speak. Doris wasn't sure if she liked Sandy. She heard flushing and the sink running and then Sandy reappeared with a towel, drying her hands.

"Well, okay, then," Doris muttered, feeling like a visitor in the house she grew up in. "I guess I'll be off. I'm not sure what time I'll be home, but I know it will be by ten."

"Yes," Sandy said as she straightened Avis' sheets and put Felix on the floor so the blanket could be smoothed out. "You mentioned that when we first met."

"By the way, Sandy, unless Felix is getting in the way of your medical care of my mother, do not disturb him again." Doris finally had enough.

"Well, I wanted to smooth the blanket. And animals can be unsanitary."

"Perhaps, but they are also a great comfort. If you are uncomfortable with Felix being on my mother's bed, you might want to re-think this position."

Sandy looked demure now, not so arrogant. "Whatever you wish will be satisfactory to me. I didn't mean any offense."

"Fine. I didn't either," Doris said. "My mother adores that cat and vice versa. You understand, I'm sure." Sandy gave Doris a surprised look, but said nothing. Doris picked up a lightweight sweater, gave Felix a pat and her mother a kiss, and exited through the side door. She stood to unlock her car door, watching Sandy through the big dining room window. She resumed her straightening up ritual so Doris got in the car and drove to the Kerryville College Playhouse.

10

There is nothing quite as exciting for an actor as the first rehearsal. One finally gets a chance to see who got cast in all the parts and hear them read their roles in the first read-through. Lenny had thoughtfully postponed the read-through two days to allow Doris to come. She had spent the first two nights of the week getting them started on the set building and instructing some of the new students in how to operate equipment.

If she thought she could have made a living at it, Doris might have pursued an advanced degree in theatre; she loved it so much. She arrived a tad early, as usual, but she wasn't the first one there. The rehearsal room was a large rectangular room with one wall of windows and an odd assortment of tables, chairs and wooden boxes butted up against the far wall in a completely random arrangement. At the director's table, Lenny was hunched over her promptbook in deep conversation with Jayson, who maintained a surprisingly intense gaze on Lenny, nodding occasionally. The door had a delayed action and when it closed, Jayson and Lenny looked up abruptly, as if a gun had gone off in the hall.

"Oh, Doris, come on in," Lenny was up and all smiles, ushering Doris toward the table while Jayson fetched a chair for her. "Jayson and I were talking about the set while we were waiting. Did you know Jayson is the designer for this one?"

Doris raised her eyebrows and looked at Jayson who was trying not to beam. She noticed for the first time how muscular his arms were. "Well, no, I certainly did not! It's wonderful you let undergraduates take such a major role in the productions, Lenny."

"They can't learn it from a book, you know. And well, it's his major project for the stagecraft class--the course where they study costuming, lighting, set design, and so forth.   And . . ." Lenny leaned over and whispered in Doris' ear, "it gives me an excuse not to have to work too closely with Tom, if you know what I mean."

Doris didn't, but she nodded politely and said, "Tom?"

"The technical director for the theatre," Lenny said in a whisper and then rolled her eyes. Doris nodded again. Loud once more, Lenny said, "Jayson has several creative ideas."

"God, Lenny, that's enough," Jayson gave Lenny a playful shove. Doris thought he might be a little embarrassed. "Dr. Peechum knows me-- I'm in her art class."

"Oh, yes, I forgot!" Lenny was so cheerful, Doris observed, about everything. How does one manage to pull that off? "Well, that's good."

Doris looked over at Jayson, "Well, if I had known you could design sets, you could have done a set design for your oral report in my class."

"Oh, I didn't even think about that. Is it too late?" Jayson looked at her hopefully.

Doris stared at his hopeful face, mentally trying to justify letting him do it. Sometimes it was hard for her to be completely objective. Teachers are, after all, only human. "Well, the final proposals are due Friday," she paused and dug in her purse for her little pocket calendar. "Let's see, I have an appointment after our class tomorrow. Oh, I have you down to make up the test at 2:30 after my afternoon class. Why don't we discuss it after that?"

"That would be perfect, thank you, Dr. P!"

Lenny for once was not sure what to say so she stepped outside to have a cigarette. As Doris lingered in her thoughts the door swung open, and Bill entered chatting with Teri. As seven o'clock neared, the crew members and understudies floated in, hands full of bottled water, junk food, and sporting backpacks that made them look like an onslaught of tortoises approaching the ocean on the Galapagos Islands.

Lenny came back in right before seven and asked everyone to move the boxes and chairs into a circle for the reading. She instructed the two couples to sit together, with Nick and Martha beside each other. There weren't enough seats so several of the college kids sprawled out on the floor, one's head on another's stomach, one's feet resting on someone's knee. *Ah*, Doris thought, *to be young, carefree and so trusting.* She didn't realize she was staring and smiling until one of the girls looked up and smiled back.

Doris nodded and nervously riffled through her script. She hadn't even taken the time to highlight her lines yet or start on her character analysis. Avis' condition had consumed her so totally for the past two weeks she almost forgot she had another life. She loved her mother dearly, but she admitted it felt good to be out of the house.

After Lenny handed out copies of the rehearsal schedule she discussed technical assignments and encouraged everyone to come for the all-day Saturday set building sessions. She handed out scripts to the cast, understudies, and crew leaders, and then talked a little about the play, the characters, and her ideas for the production. The more Doris got to know Lenny, the more she liked her. She was a thoughtful, talented young woman. Lenny then asked everyone to introduce themselves to the group, what part they were playing or tech job they oversaw, and anything else which might help the group get to know them better.

Doris cringed, wondering what to say. She wanted to be a pal, a mature actress here to have fun being in a play with a bunch of kids. But she was painfully aware she was not just an actress here--she was also a professor. The title carried a lot of privilege on campus, but privilege carries responsibilities. She didn't want any special treatment at rehearsals. Doris wanted to be one of the gang but wondered if the students would allow her to do that. She told everyone her name and what she did at K. C., she explained about her mother's condition in case she missed rehearsal, and then told them she about her cat, Felix. Everybody smiled, and she heard a few "awwws" before Bill recited his acting resume, which Doris perceived as being in poor taste.

Lenny asked her stage manager, Stacey DeBenedetto, to read the stage directions in the script, and the read-through began. It took a moment to place her, but now she remembered Stacey as the girl sitting next to Kayla at the auditions. She seemed like a serious student, possibly Latina, a little overweight with an unfortunate complexion. She read with little to no inflection and basically no facial expression; Doris understood immediately why she was not an actor.

It was so exciting for Doris to listen to the actors read their parts. She could already envision them on stage in make-up and costume. She hoped she would do a good job so she might get an opportunity like this again. And, of course, she didn't want to let Lenny and the rest of the group down. After the second act, Lenny announced a ten-minute break, stressing ten, not twenty, minutes. Doris smiled at the others and watched them disperse into various groups. Some of the college students dashed across the street to the campus grill for a cup of coffee, others stepped outside with Lenny for a smoke, including Bill, and Doris decided to stretch her legs and visit the restroom.

When she came back to the rehearsal room, almost exactly ten minutes after leaving, only Jayson was back in his seat. "No one ever sticks to the ten minutes," he joked, "not even Lenny." He picked up a can of Dr. Pepper, took a gulp, and offered her one of his potato chips.

"No thanks, but your drink looks good," Doris said, "Do you think I have time to get one?"

"Are you kidding?" Jayson gave her a look. "It only takes exact change; do you have it?" Doris pawed in her purse and found her billfold, but before she could get it open Jayson was up and at the door. "What do you want?"

"I'm sure I have it, Jayson . . ."

He interrupted her, "Don't worry, I'll get this one. I'm sure I will have occasion to bum change from you!"

"Well, okay, uh, diet something--anything."

"You got it!" he said and disappeared down the hall.

Doris wondered if Jayson would expect special favors in class now. Some students were clearly mature enough to maintain a close friendship with a teacher and still defer to her authority in the classroom. Many students, however, thought if you allowed them into your inner circle they were somehow immune to the consequences of shoddy schoolwork or juvenile behavior. It could be a most uncomfortable position for a professor, so most of them kept students at arms' length until the relationship was tested or until they graduated. *Children aren't taught anything about decorum these days*, Doris thought. The death of civility was becoming a growing concern for Doris. She guessed she was getting old.

She only hoped Jayson's politeness was offered without a fee. No one received special treatment from Dr. Peechum in class--no one. She took pride in her efforts towards fairness and hoped the young people would profit from it. Many didn't realize any benefit, however, until they were out of college and on their own. Then they would write Dr. P letters thanking her for her tough standards and challenging courses. But now, while they are in the class, many of them think "Dr. P" rhymes with "B," which stands for "bitch."

The others filtered back into the room, chatting happily and sipping on drinks or munching on chips. Jayson joined in the reverie and set Doris' drink on the table near her. "There you go. Sorry, it's all there was," he said.

"Oh, thank you, Jayson. Actually, I like this kind." He unknowingly got her favorite, Diet Dr. Pepper.

"Good!" he smiled and took his seat. Doris noticed for the first time how charming his smile was with perfect teeth. *He is such a nice-looking boy*, she thought; Jayson had jet-black hair, an even tan, and obviously worked out regularly. Doris' attentions came back to the room when Lenny got back to business by asking Doris to pick up the first line in Act 3.

The reading went well and there was a dead silence as Bill and Doris read George and Martha's impassioned lines at the end. "Oooh, that gave me chills," said one girl who sat near Jayson wearing overalls, a black long-sleeved leotard, and three silver hoops on her left ear and one in her left eyebrow. Doris smiled at her, wondering if she was a dancer. She had a short pixie haircut with black roots and platinum blonde hair with pink tips. Doris realized she had been staring and quickly averted her eyes.

Lenny drew everyone's attention to the schedule for the coming week. Most of it would be character work, and Doris noticed she was supposed to work with Bill the following night and then Jayson the following Monday. No rehearsal Friday night, she noticed with pleasure, and started making mental plans for a date with Martin. The students impressed her when everyone disposed of their drinks and chip bags and tidied up the room before leaving. Doris sauntered slowly out to her car, noticing the moon was full and casting a beautiful glow on the campus buildings. The quaint streetlights of K.C. were burning brightly and a light mist seemed to envelop the campus, giving the lamps a fuzzy, almost halo appearance. *Like Vincent Van Gogh lights*, she thought.

Footsteps came up behind her, and she realized it was Jayson and the girl who spoke at the end of the play who managed props. "Man, is that your Karmann Ghia?" the girl with the pink tipped hair asked Doris. "What a sweet ride!"

"Yes, it's mine." Doris was desperately trying to remember the girl's name.

"It's so sick--I'm crazy about these cars!" she was peeking in the windows and admiring Carmen's rear-end. Jayson strolled to the front.

"Is the trunk in front?'" he asked.

"Yes, you dope!" the girl responded, "All Volkswagens did in the seventies. I don't know if they still do that--I only like the old ones. I want a red Beetle someday—not the new ones, the old model--that's my dream car!"

"Well," started Doris, "they're pretty reasonable, especially on gas, but the Karmann Ghias need a lot of repairs. I think the Beetles are better, though. Some night when we get out early, I'll take you for a drive around campus, if you like."

"Oh, wow, that would be awesome!" the girl nearly screamed.

"Come on, Winnie," Jayson was already across the street on the sidewalk, "if you want me to walk you to the dorm, you need to move your butt! I have a test to study for tomorrow--right, Dr. P?" He looked at Doris and winked.

Winnie, yes, thought Doris. "Right!" she said and waved, trying to remember if Jayson's make-up test was scheduled during her Thursday break. The girl reluctantly dragged herself away from the car and joined Jayson. They both waved as Doris got in and revved up the engine. As she drove away, Doris looked back in her rearview mirror at Winnie, who was still standing at the edge of the street pointing at the car and talking to Jayson, who was nowhere in sight.

11

Doris pulled into her mother's driveway and sat for a few minutes looking at the house. She probably couldn't have told anyone what she was thinking, but she knew she needed a moment to catch her breath. When she entered the side door, she was greeted by Sandy's thin voice reading a section of the Bible Doris didn't recognize. Avis was lying still and quiet, Felix was curled up at the foot of the bed, and Sandy sat in an old rocking chair she had dragged in from the living room. She peered up at Doris over her little half-sized reading glasses and smiled. "Everything was fine with your mother, Dr. Peechum," she said as she tucked her Bible into her bag and poked her arm into her sweater. "Since the day nurse bathed her, I rotated her some to prevent bed sores and checked on all her medicines, drips and bags." Sandy gave Avis' hand an affectionate squeeze and bid Doris a goodnight. The night nurse had settled down some and was acting more personable, Doris noticed. She kept the outside lights switched on until Sandy drove out of sight.

Doris headed to the kitchen to make a cup of decaffeinated raspberry zinger tea, tidy up, and do the dishes. Felix jumped up on the counter, and Doris scolded him to get down. She puttered around the house, talking to her mother and getting the house ready for bedtime. She laid out her school items, a crisp pantsuit, and set her mother's fancy coffeemaker to go off at seven. As she came out of the bathroom to curl up in bed with some classwork, the phone rang.

Martin wanted to see how rehearsal went. They talked in hushed tones, like teenagers on the phone after bedtime. Martin could talk intelligently about so many different subjects; they discussed a Bergman movie they saw recently at the art cinema, Doris' seminar class, and finally something about American paintings during the Civil War. Before they knew it, an hour passed, and Doris mentioned she had some reading to do before bed. Martin let her go, setting up a date for lunch the next day.

"Goodnight, darling," he said. Doris held her breath. "I'll swing by to get you for lunch tomorrow," he prompted.

"After my first class, I have something to do. I don't have my calendar in front of me, so, of course, I can't remember. Why don't you just meet me there at noon?"

"Whatever you want, Doris. I'll see you there."

"Yes, you will," Doris said, "Goodnight, Marty."

She sat wondering what he thought of the new nickname she gave him. She wondered if Marty really fit him--no, definitely not, she decided. Oh well, they could discuss it tomorrow. Doris checked on her mother one last time and then switched off the light and thought about Martin, how well suited they were for each other. He allowed her to be whomever she wanted to be, and he was the only man she knew who could sit through Bergman's *Cries and Whispers* and appreciate it. They would sit together for long periods on the sofa without speaking, each absorbed in preparing materials for their classes. *If he were more demonstrative with his affections*, she thought, *everything would be perfect*.

Thursday morning her seminar class discussed careers in commercial art, and she returned to her office to find a student waiting for her. *Oh yes*, she remembered, *Rosemary wanted to discuss her grades*.

Thursday, in the cafeteria, she met Martin at the faculty table. Her colleagues greeted her and inquired about her mother. *What a nice little family this is*, Doris thought to herself. It felt so good to be included in the group, even though Doris was, for the most part, somewhat of a loner. She knew instinctively this was where she belonged and doubted she would ever leave.

Her afternoon class, Introduction to Visual Arts, moved into the unit on film, which was usually everyone's favorite. As they discussed *Citizen Kane*, some of them thought it was overly dramatic and many couldn't understand why Orson Welles would do a movie in black and white when all the other movies of the same period were done in the newly perfected Technicolor. "Well, why do you think he would choose black and white over color?" Doris asked a young man in the back who wore torn jeans and had shaggy black hair.

"I dunno," he said, "I was hoping you would tell me." The other students giggled and Doris put a hand on her hip and shook her head.

"Sorry, Steven, that's not how it works. Your assignment for next Tuesday is do some research on the movie and come up with an answer to your own question--why did Welles use black and white for the movie." An audible groan swept across the room. "At least two sources, one of which may not be from the Internet." A louder groan and lots of muttering followed this declaration. "Well, I can see you aren't happy with the research assignment."

"Man, Dr. P, where do you find things if you can't go to the Internet?" one girl in the back of the room whined.

"We have this cool building on campus," Doris said. "It has all kinds of books and magazines and newspapers--it's called a library. In the olden days, that's where we could go to find information on almost any topic. Check it out, you might like it."

"Not much chance of that," the girl said with a sneer. "I walked in there once for an English paper and couldn't find anything. It's rows and rows of junk on shelves. Are we supposed to go walking down the aisles reading the titles of every book until we find the one we need?"

Doris stared at the girl in complete amazement. "Did you not have a library in your high school?" she asked.

"Yeah, but it was the same thing. Confusing! We never used it for anything."

Some of the students were nodding in agreement; others were suppressing smiles and rolling their eyes. Doris didn't know if this student was serious or not. "No one ever taught you how to use the library?"

"No." The girl crossed her arms and looked out the window.

"Okay," Doris said. "Next Tuesday we will have class in the library. Meet me in the front lobby. For Tuesday, instead of doing the research, watch the movie again and come up with one major question you would like to know the answer to. Bring your question to the library and we will see if you can find the materials necessary to answer it. Okay?"

Doris thought this would make them all happy, but instead, they all gave out heavy sighs and looked up at the ceiling, one boy smacked his hand on his desk. The girl with all the questions, whose name Doris could not recall, slammed her books together and walked out without a word or any acknowledgment to Doris. Sometimes, she couldn't understand students. They don't seem to like anything remotely to do with academics. *Why in the world do they come to college?* She stood in the front of her classroom and wondered suddenly if this was where she really wanted to spend the rest of her working life.

She decided to go by the library to talk to the librarian about holding class there and, also, to do some research for her conference paper in November. Maybe it would help get her mind off the class. When she arrived back at her office around four, she ran into Jayson leaving a note on her door; "Hi, Jayson, what can I do for you?" She tried to maintain a pleasant tone even though she was still feeling residual resentment from her Visual Arts class.

"Well, I came by at 2:30 to take the test, but somehow missed you. I was trying to catch you after class to set up another time."

"Oh, goodness, Jayson, I am so sorry. Please forgive me. With everything that's happened in the past week, I can't seem to keep my head on straight."

"No problem, Dr. P, it gave me more time to study." He smiled his winning smile, which was just lopsided enough to be adorable, and she realized he was being extremely polite; he probably sat here for a long time thinking she would return any moment. It was rude of her to stand him up, and she felt genuinely regretful. She forgot to look at her planner and took for granted there was nothing special scheduled. "I'm sorry I was late for class yesterday morning, Dr. Peechum," he said pathetically. I was up later than I thought I'd be, studying for an English test and fell asleep without setting my alarm. I wanted to say something at rehearsal last night, but I figured you wanted to keep rehearsals separate from class work."

She was impressed with his insight. "Yes, that's probably a good thing for us to do," she smiled. "You know, Jayson, you might want to buy one of those alarms that stay set after you turn off the buzzer."

"They make something like that?" He looked genuinely perplexed by the magnitude of modern technology. "Cool. I'll look for one of those."

"Do you feel ready to take the test now?" He looked down at his hands and then up at her and nodded. "Okay, if you can leave your book-bag in here, I can sit you next door in the empty adjunct office. let me know if you have any questions." Doris was ushering him to a desk near the door. Jayson, sluggish and moving slowly, dug into his bag for two pencils and then took a seat where Doris was waiting for him. "Good luck," she said and stepped back into her office to prepare for her Friday classes.

Jayson finished the test in twenty minutes, too quickly, Doris thought, to have put much thought into it. He handed her the test and shoved his hair back off his face. He smiled, picked up his book-bag, and turned for the door. "Again, I apologize, Dr. P. Do I work with you tonight?'

"Uh, I think you are working with Teri this week, and I work with Bill. I think we do some work on Monday." Doris tried to sound casual about the schedule knowing full well she had memorized every detail. That she could remember. It distressed her a little that she hadn't memorized her work week as well, something she usually does on Sunday evenings.

"Oh good. I'm looking forward to it. By the way, did you make a decision about letting me use my set design for my oral report?"

Doris looked up. "Well, you can't do the set design for one class and then turn in the same work for my class. I don't mind you using the set design, however, as a springboard into a research project. Perhaps you might find out who designed the original set for Broadway and do a study on him--or her. It would help you in your future theatre studies and would probably provide enough material for a satisfactory oral report. Do some preliminary searching and let me know in class tomorrow if you want to do that."

"Thanks, Dr. P, I appreciate it." He started to back out into the hall but then came back suddenly, his hand on the doorframe. "You know, I'm not always such a screw-up. I'm really disciplined about my acting."

Doris turned, taken aback by his unexpected declaration. "I'm sure you are, Jayson. I don't consider you a 'screw-up', as you put it. I do, however, think you need to realize your grades would benefit from applying the same discipline to all your courses, not just your theatre work."

"Yes, Ma'am," he said, nodding his head slightly. "See ya' tomorrow." He disappeared into the hall. Doris took a deep breath and looked over his test. He, of course, barely passed.

Character work with Bill on Thursday night went smoothly. Doris was developing a growing respect for Lenny as a director. She understood the value of script and character analysis, but didn't give in to the kind of maudlin, emotionally indulgent work Doris was forced to do with other directors. In graduate school at Tulane, Doris took the summer off from classes to earn some money and ended up in a small community production of *Romeo & Juliet* outside of New Orleans. She played Lady Montague and was asked to act out the grieving loss of Tybalt and Romeo with graphic expression. It wasn't completely a waste of time; it was certainly a cathartic exercise for all her pent-up frustration over school, but she didn't think it did much for her acting. Doris favored script analysis with judicious use of improvisation and emotional recall.

Lenny had to pull nearly every answer from Bill, who took to this kind of rehearsal in the same way most cats take to a good bath. However, it seemed she touched a nerve with him when they were discussing George's suppressed rage. Doris thought she saw a tear in his eye, but he put an end to it quickly by making a joke, which only he laughed at.

Doris needed to do some class prep, so she was grateful for a short rehearsal. She was home and in her favorite chair by nine-thirty, with her hot tea and a stack of books on the table beside her. Sandy tidied up and bid goodnight to Avis.

The presence of her comatose mother in the house with her was almost surreal to Doris. It felt weird to walk around the bed, back and forth to the kitchen, without talking to Avis. And yet, when she did talk to Avis, she felt a pang of guilt like a twisting knife in her stomach, and tears welled up in her eyes. *I could cry about this all the time*, she thought, *if I would let myself, but life has to go on.* She had to go to school, and she needed to go to rehearsal and out with Martin. Having the play to focus on and Martin to enjoy was keeping her from losing her mind, and she was thankful to have both.

While lost in her thoughts, the phone rang suddenly and made her drop the book in her lap. The telephone in Avis' house was set to an unusually loud ring, which Doris decided right then to re-set. "Yes?"

It was Martin, again, to say goodnight. It was so nice to have someone who would listen to her complaints. She talked about rehearsal, her thoughts about her mother, and the classwork undone. Martin chuckled at the last part, telling her about his stack of papers to grade but didn't have rehearsals to blame. They made plans for a date on Friday night, but she warned him she wouldn't be at lunch because she needed to finish her work, so he could come by the house around six.

Doris laid out her clothes, checked on Avis, and then tucked herself into her parents' old four-poster bed. Memories flooded back of weekend mornings when she and Teddy would burrow under the covers between their parents and snuggle. She remembered days when she was sick and home from school; her mother would let her stay downstairs in their bed during the day. Avis found a teaching substitute so she could stay at home. She served Doris homemade soups and pastries, and on every tray, there was a small toy or trinket to cheer her up. And then the nights she had nightmares and couldn't go back to sleep, Doris remembered crawling under the covers between her parents while they were asleep. *This bed*, she thought, *was my safe place*. Tears threatened so she opened her book and tried to read. It was no use, she decided. It would be best to turn off the light and try to get some sleep.

12

Friday morning, Doris took up the oral report proposals in her first class. Jayson turned in a paper with a new proposal about William Ritman's original set design for the play in 1962. In the afternoon, Doris let Harriet go early and sat at her mother's bedside reading the play aloud to Avis. Martin knocked on the door then popped in with a beautiful bouquet of flowers. Doris looked up and smiled at him, "Oh, Martin, how sweet. I wish Mother could see all these beautiful flowers everyone has sent her. Her church, the college, friends, family--even Phyllis, if you can believe that! It's beginning to look like a garden in here!" She took the flowers and looked for a pitcher to put them in, finally resorting to a tall glass from the kitchen.

"Doris, I have already sent a bouquet to your mother. These are for you. Don't you remember what day it is?" Martin wore an impish expression on his face Doris couldn't remember ever seeing before.

"Uh, Friday?" Doris was thinking he'd lost his grip on reality.

"Yes, Friday, September what?"

"Oh, my goodness, I completely forgot!"

"Happy birthday, Doris," Martin awkwardly put his arms around her and gave her a peck on the cheek. "I have a nice evening planned for us, so I wanted to come by and let you know I will pick you up around six."

"What about Mother," Doris looked up and asked.

"Already took care of that. You get ready, the night nurse will be here before six!"

"Ok, great," Doris said slowly, "I'll see you then."

"Righto!" Martin said and with a bounce in his step as he turned toward the door. "I'll see you at six. Ta-ta, Avis!" He waved to them both and nearly floated out the front door.

Doris was so stunned she stood holding the flowers and looking toward the doorway for a good minute. "Martin has something planned for tonight, Mother. I can't imagine what it could be. Dinner and a movie, I guess." She puttered around the room, pinching dead flowers off Avis' bouquets, straightening up the clutter on the chairs and tables. Avis lay quiet and still, as she had for the past week. Doris watched as a gentle breeze outside danced with the autumn leaves. She sat back down, picked up her script, and resumed her reading. She couldn't concentrate, however, because she couldn't get her mind off Martin.

Finally, she gave up and switched on the television. "Look, Mother, your favorite soap is on." Doris hadn't watched *Days of Our Lives* since she was home from college for summer vacation. She was surprised she still recognized a few of the actors. She sat watching the TV, holding Avis' hand, and daydreaming about Martin.

When the soap ended, she kissed her mother on the cheek, set the TV on another channel for Avis, and began to get ready for her date. Felix jumped up to Avis' bed and curled around her feet. "Good boy," Doris said, scratching his chin. She was bathed and dressed by 5:45 in a smart pantsuit with her hair tied at the nape of her neck with a leather clasp. She was slipping on her shoes when the doorbell rang and Sandy, the night nurse arrived. When she opened the door for her, Doris saw Martin's old maroon Volvo puttering up the driveway.

She greeted Sandy, then squeezed Avis' hand and patted her leg, promising to be home early. She grabbed her sweater off the back of her chair and met Martin on the porch, took his extended arm, and allowed him to escort her out the door and to his car. "So, where are we going?" Doris asked as Martin opened her door and helped her in.

"You'll see," he said with an impish grin as he secured her door, pushed the wild flap of hair off his face, and practically skipped around the car to get in. Doris thought he was acting like a teenager—a very strange teenager. But she smiled because he was making her feel like one, too.

They drove into the Old Town Square of Kerryville, a recently updated area with beautifully restored Victorian houses converted into boutiques, cafes, art galleries, and antique shops. The whole place was re-landscaped with flora typical of this part of Tennessee and edged with handmade bricks taken from old houses in the area, which were too far gone to repair. Doris liked antiquing and shopping here. It was so historic and modern at the same time. The people were friendly, and the ambiance was pleasant and calming. The little green market played classical music, served hot coffee, and specialized in homemade baked goods that melted in your mouth.

Martin pulled his car into the back lot of a little white, ornate building called Le Petit Café, one of Doris' favorites for lunch, and came around to help her out. "I didn't know they served dinner," she commented as they entered the romantic little bistro. The entranceway was adorned with an arched lattice covered with vines of greenery, flowers, and tiny white lights. The interior was small but decorated beautifully with elegant wallpaper and drapery, and soft candlelight gave the place a warm glow. The hostess showed them to a reserved table near a window overlooking the quiet little street and handed them each a huge menu. She rattled off the specials for the evening, took their drink orders, and disappeared.

Martin's eyes were alive and excited as he stared at Doris. Being a Friday evening they were surprised to find the place nearly deserted. One other couple sat at a table across the room, and as Doris and Martin waited for their drinks a young woman came in and took a seat by herself near the entrance. A female server brought goblets of water, introduced herself as Candice, spoke with what seemed to be an authentic French accent, and asked for their orders. Doris agreed Martin could order for her, so he asked for an expensive grilled salmon dish served with a lavish amount of side orders. Doris said she couldn't eat all that, but Felix would appreciate the leftover salmon. Martin chuckled nervously and studied the street outside the window. Outside the restaurant little white lights twinkled in a row of holly bushes almost ready to produce little red berries, and the old-fashioned streetlights were beginning to pop on in random order down the tree-lined street.

"So?" Doris asked and Martin jumped, moving his hand to push back the stray wisp of hair and, simultaneously, knocking over his wineglass.

"Oh, good grief!" he exclaimed and started dabbing at the burgundy mess with his petal pink damask linen napkin. The server, who was headed toward another table, made a quick left turn and pulled her hand towel from her over her arm and caught the spill before it trickled onto the floor. Doris moved her purse and offered her napkin as well. "I'm sorry, oh dear!" Poor Martin's worried eyes darted back and forth from Doris to the mess to the server. "I'm so sorry."

"Il n'est pas un problème, Monsieur, zese sings happan all zee time," the server said with a professional cool which Doris found admirable and was impressed with her French. Doris was no expert, but she studied French in college, did a semester in Paris during college, and spent a year there after finishing her MFA. "Ici, let me geet zee whole sing, hol' zee glass, s'il vous plaît, Madame?"

"Merci, Candice," Doris said. She picked up her glass and a few condiments and sat them on the windowsill nearby. Martin watched the server mutely as she wrapped up the tablecloth, camouflaging the spill, and nearly sprinted to the kitchen.

Martin looked sheepishly around the room and noticed the other diners gave him a furtive glance and then quickly averted their eyes toward their tables. He looked over at Doris, who smiled and asked how much grading he needed to do. He seemed grateful for the diversion and chattered on about this paper and that project while Candice replaced the tablecloth, their napkins and Martin's wine. She sat the condiments and other accouterments back on the table and exited without a word. Doris hoped Martin would reward her efforts with a generous tip.

Martin asked Doris about the play, if she was satisfied with her mother's nurses, and about anything else he could think to ask. They chatted happily through the salad, the salmon entrée, and when the server brought dessert, Doris gave Martin a look of condemnation. "Martin, I couldn't eat another bite. I already have Felix's next two dinners in my doggy bag."

"Just nibble at it, then, while I have my dessert," Martin pleaded. Doris put her regular sweetener and cream in her coffee and then picked up her fork to taste the chocolate fudge cake. "See?" Martin interjected, "Isn't it delicious?"

"That was never in question, Martin," Doris said and laughed.

"Doris," Martin started and then hesitated. "Doris," he said in a way that made Doris put her fork down.

"Martin? What is it?" Doris was becoming concerned. *Is this a farewell dinner,* she wondered? *Is this how Martin breaks up with a woman?* Now, while she was taking care of her mother and trying to do a play and teach school, she already realized there would be very little time for Martin. Maybe he was realizing the same.

"Doris, I've been thinking a lot about us." Doris gritted her teeth and waited in patient silence. She laced her fingers together and placed her hands in front of her, resting barely on the edge of the table. "We've been seeing each other for over a year, and I enjoy your company so much." He leaned forward with his elbows on the table and took one hand to push back his hair and the other to take Doris' left hand. She used her right hand to push the dessert aside so her sleeve wouldn't be smudged. "We've gotten so much closer in the past few weeks; I was hoping we might take our relationship to another level." Doris looked at him, eyebrows raised and mouth slightly open. "I was wondering, well," Martin dug in the inside pocket of his corduroy jacket and finally pulled out a little box. He sat it in front of Doris, who by this time felt all the blood rush out of her head and into her feet. "I was wondering if you would do me the honor of becoming my wife." Doris stared in silent shock, her mouth still open. "Would you consider marrying me, Doris?"

The next thing Doris saw was the dangling end of the lace tablecloth near her head, Candice on one side of her with a damp towel, and Martin on the other side holding her hand and fanning her face with his napkin. "Doris? Doris? Are you all right?" Doris shook her head and blinked her eyes open. Somehow, she was on the floor, but she couldn't figure out how she got there.

"What happened?" she asked Martin. Regaining her composure, she tugged at her pants, so grateful she wasn't wearing a skirt, and stroked her hair into place. She sat up to see all the diners and servers looking in her direction with concern on their faces. "Oh dear, how embarrassing. Help me up, Martin. I'm fine," she turned to everyone in the restaurant to assure them they could go on with their meals and try and forget the crazy lady near the window. "Thanks for your concern, but I'm fine."

Martin helped her into her seat, and she looked at him and around the room, satisfied everyone had stopped staring and were resuming conversations over their meals in hushed tones. "God, Martin, what in the world did I do?"

"Well, I asked you to marry me and your eyes rolled back into your head and then you fell over." Martin looked wounded, which Doris couldn't understand, but right now, all she truly cared about was her lost dignity.

"Could we please go somewhere else?"

"Certainly," Martin seemed ready to leave, also.

"I'll be in the restroom repairing myself." Doris made a quick exit from the table, and Martin put the ring box back in his jacket and waved for the server.

In the car, they were quiet. Martin was afraid to say anything, and Doris was deep in thought, almost unaware of his presence. Finally, Martin broke the silence. "I planned for us to go somewhere after dinner, but if you're not up to it, I will understand."

Doris, back to normal enough now to recognize the hurt in Martin's voice, put her hand gently on his knee. "No, let's go somewhere quiet where we can talk, okay?"

Martin nodded and drove the Volvo. Doris stared out the passenger window until Martin pulled the car into the parking lot of a small bar on the other end of town, far from the campus. The blue neon read "Benny's Jazz Club." "We can get a good glass of wine here, the music is nice, and it's dark and private," Martin said, helping Doris out.

"You know a lot about the nightlife in Kerryville, Martin, you'll have to tell me how you got so experienced!" She was teasing, trying to lighten the mood. But Martin was still tense, worried, wounded, and didn't get it.

"It was a favorite of Sarah's. I'm sorry to bring her name up, but it's the only way I know to explain."

Doris stopped him and turned him to face her. "I don't want you to ever be afraid to talk about Sarah. She was your wife, an important part of your life. I wish I could have known her; she sounds like a wonderful woman." Martin nodded and smiled, and they walked on.

The place was busy but didn't feel crowded. A pianist in the far corner was playing soft jazz, and there were exquisite art reproductions on the dark plaster walls. They were shown to a small round table in the rear corner, and Martin ordered two glasses of Valpolicela. "It's no wonder Sarah liked this place so much--what a treasure!"

A male server dressed in black dress pants, white collared shirt, and a bow tie, brought a bottle of wine and two glasses to the table. He removed the cork and let Martin sniff it. Once approved, the server poured a small bit of wine in a glass and handed it to Martin, who swirled then smelled it, held it up to the light, and tasted it. "Excellent!" Martin said, and the server poured two glasses and left the bottle on the table. "We better let this breathe a little before we drink."

"A wine connoisseur too?" Doris leaned back, looking at Martin with a new appreciation.

"Sarah again. We used to go to wine tastings with some friends from the college. I picked up a few pointers."

"I'd say more than a few." Then an awkward silence fell between them.

"Martin," Doris started, taking his hand in hers. "Thank you so much for everything you did for me tonight. It's been a long time since a man took so much trouble on my behalf. I'm so sorry I passed out. I can't explain it; I haven't done that in a long time."

"You don't have to apologize, Doris," he looked down at his knees, taking his hand back to pick up a wineglass. He expertly poured the wine and handed the glass to Doris. "I'm the one who should apologize. Here you are with your mother ill and all kinds of stress and I spring it on you out of nowhere . . .."

"Nonsense, Martin. It was such a lovely gesture; I think we need to talk about it though." Martin nodded, resigned to the rejection he was sure he would soon receive. "I am so flattered and thrilled you think enough of me to ask me to marry you, Martin. You know I hold you in high regard and am so grateful for everything you do for me. But . . ."

"You don't love me." Martin said.

"Well, the truth is, I don't know if I love you. We have been seeing each other for over a year, but it has always been on more of a "good friends" level, I wasn't sure if we were dating or simply keeping company. You've never told me you love me, you haven't taken me home to meet any of your family, you've never even kissed me beyond a peck on the cheek. I don't think we're close enough to decide about marriage yet. Do you understand?"

"I'm so bad when it comes to romance. In my day, you courted a girl for a good amount of time before you kissed her, and then after some more time, you asked her to marry you if she was a 'good' girl. I was only interested in Sarah, and it all came so easily with her. We dated for a while and then got married. We were so young. I'm not sure how it happened, so I'm not sure how to do it again."

"Well, you know, Martin, the concept of good and bad girls, based on their appetite for sex, is pretty outdated."

"Oh, I know. It was such a pre-historic notion anyway, but you know what I mean. I was a teenager in the early '70s, and girls were either considered good or bad, depending upon whether they 'put-out.' I know it was the time for "free love" but not in Fall River, Kansas. I'm so bad at courting I didn't want a girl to put-out anyway, so I guess the girls thought of me as a gentleman. The truth is I wasn't comfortable with them."

"Well, Martin, dating has changed a little. I don't go out much either, so I'm certainly no expert here, but I think we should become more physically comfortable with each other before we think about marriage. Even though I went through my adolescence during the early 80s, I would never have gone to bed with someone on the first date like some of my friends. But being single all my life, I have had a few experiences that taught me a lot about what I do and do not want in a sexual partner."

Martin visibly blushed. "You talk about this so openly. It's refreshing, but hard for me. I'm sorry."

Doris smiled and touched his cheek. "Martin, I find your shyness so sweet, but if we are going to be husband and wife, we need to be able to talk about everything openly. If you can't do that with me now, it just confirms that we're not close enough . . . yet."

"So, you're not completely ruling it out?" Martin asked hopefully.

"Of course not, not at all," she swiftly reassured him. "I think we need to start having dates instead of chance meetings and convenient excursions. I don't even know when your birthday is or what the C in your name stands for. I could never marry a man I haven't been more, well, more intimate with."

Martin blushed, but he was smiling. "I'm so clumsy with romance. I guess I'm old-fashioned, but I still think folks should leave that stuff for marriage. But I know everything is different today. I don't know if I can change, but I can try." He took a sip of his wine and scooted closer to her. For the first time since she'd known him, Doris became acutely aware of the eleven years separating their ages. She was finally starting to understand his odd ways, it wasn't fear of commitment he felt, it was plain fear. He was outgoing and friendly at school, but painfully shy with the opposite sex.

"You hang onto the ring, Martin, and ask me another time, okay?"

"Okay," he said and kissed her gently, albeit quickly, on the lips. "Cecil. It's Cecil. I don't ever tell anyone because I hate it so much. It reminds me of Cecil the Seasick Sea Serpent. Do you remember him?"

Doris was laughing now. "Sorry!"

"A puppet on a kids' TV show in the fifties. The children at school made fun of me. When the teacher called me down, she'd say my whole

name. At recess the kids were terrible. Making Cecil's dopey voice."
Martin started laughing too. "I guess it's time to get over it, huh?"

Doris had tears from laughing so hard. They both knew this topic was
not funny enough to laugh so hard about, but Doris had cried so hard in the
last week she needed the release of a good laugh, her soul needed it. She
collapsed under his arm and rested her head on his neck, sniffing and
sighing, and trying to calm down. Martin squeezed her shoulders like a
child might hug a favorite teddy bear.

"Do you want to go somewhere else?" he asked her hair as he took a
deep whiff.

"Well, that's another problem, Martin," Doris sat up and leaned her
elbows on the table, and Martin steeled himself. "As much as I'd like to
stay out for a while, I feel like I ought to get back home. With trying to
take care of Mother, doing the play, and teaching school, there won't be
much time for dating until the semester break." She turned to face him,
placing a hand gently on his knee. "I want you to know I won't be putting
you off, I simply won't have much time."

"I understand," Martin said, taking her hand in his. "I can do some of
those things with you. Let's go to the house now, and I'll stay there awhile.
We can watch a movie on TV."

"I have a better idea," Doris said, as she finished her wine and stood
up.

They headed back to Avis' house, but this time, Doris sat near the
middle of the long car seat and Martin looked over at her and smiled
occasionally. They pulled into her driveway. Felix was asleep in his
window hammock and awoke only when he heard the key in the lock. After
Sandy drove away, Doris headed toward the kitchen.

"Have a seat, Martin, I'll fix us a glass of wine. Sorry, all I have is
white. I don't know anything about wine, I just drink the ones I like."

"That sounds good," he said and bent over to pet Felix. Felix adored
Martin who had a great affection for animals but knew himself to be too
absentminded to care for one properly. Martin contented himself with
bestowing affection on his friends' pets, buying them Christmas presents,
and bringing them special treats when he visited. "Sorry, old boy, no treats
tonight." Felix seemed to understand Martin and decided to jump down
and take a snack in the kitchen. Martin tucked his hands in his pockets and
walked around Avis' living room, which was adjacent to the dining room

where Avis lay in clear sight through the wide archway flanked by built-in bookshelves. He studied the watercolors on the wall; there was one of a calico cat sitting in a window and one of a house, this house, he realized. When Doris came in with two wineglasses, he politely waited for her to take a seat before sitting beside her on the loveseat.

"Are those yours?" he asked Doris.

"Oh, heavens, yes. From college."

"They're really good, Doris."

"Well, thank you, but I learned pretty quickly how hard it is to make any money as an artist. The cat was my favorite pet as a child--Cally."

"She was beautiful. And you really captured the spirit of this house, not just the architecture."

She leaned toward him, and he put his arm around her shoulder. They sat together till midnight, reading *Who's Afraid of Virginia Woolf?* aloud to Avis, who listened without comment.

13

On Saturday, Doris and Martin graded papers, played Scrabble, and watched an old Doris Day movie on television. They both got used to having Harriet work around them, taking care of Avis and reading her book. Sandy would have to come to check on Avis, but Doris could let her leave early. After she left, Doris prepared a magnificent dinner of chicken and pasta for the two of them, and afterwards, they settled in front of the fireplace. Even though it wasn't cool enough for a fire, Doris turned on the gas anyway and opened a window to even the temperature some. Martin laughed at her and wrapped his arms around her shoulders when she joined him on the couch. He kissed her on the mouth, tentatively, and she did everything she could to encourage him. But he pulled away and buried his face in her shoulder. Doris wondered for a moment if he could be gay.

Doris realized she was going to have to take the initiative, even though she felt a definite weirdness with her mother in the next room. "Let's go sit in the bedroom," she whispered in his ear. He didn't argue.

She took him by the hand and led him to the old four-poster and sat down beside him. She nuzzled his neck and playfully licked at his ear, occasionally sucking on his earlobe. His hands rubbed her back, edging toward her sides and nearing her chest. Her fingers were running through his hair when she realized this scene felt eerily familiar. She hadn't been this close with Martin, she thought as her mouth moved down to his neck and under his collar. Ethan! It was Ethan Anderson, she remembered. She and her high school boyfriend necked like this many, many times in this same house, albeit on the sofa.

"Oh, dear lord," she said as Martin's hands found their way to her breasts. Martin, thinking Doris was in the throes of ecstasy continued his clumsy fondling, but Doris was stifling a giggle. It had been a long time since Martin touched a woman's breasts, so he wasn't sure what kind of reaction to expect, but he felt certain giggling was not the usual response.

Finally, she couldn't hold it in any longer, and a long trill of laughter rolled out, and then she gasped for breath, looking at Martin desperately.

"Am I tickling you?" Martin pulled his hands away and froze in suspense. Doris realized what a terrible mistake she was making. This could shut Martin down for a long time, when he was venturing forward. She recognized a lucky break when she saw one.

"Yes, I'm so sorry, I'm terribly ticklish--especially when I'm nervous." Martin's face seemed to relax. "I was enjoying it, Martin, you have such gentle hands." Doris took his hands to her lips and kissed them sweetly and rubbed her cheek against them. She leaned over and kissed Martin on the lips, and they fell into a warm embrace.

When Martin said goodnight, he kissed Doris and gave her a hug. Felix rubbed around his ankles until Martin rubbed his head and picked him up. "Should I come by and get you for church?" Martin asked Doris.

"Church?"

"I never asked you which church you go to, but I thought perhaps we could go together tomorrow."

Doris' mouth was open, but no sound was coming out. "Where do you go," she finally asked.

"St. Bartholomew's. Episcopal. You?"

"My mother goes to Our Lady of Mercy--Catholic. I used to go there, of course." Martin looked at her expectantly. "Martin, I want to be honest with you. I don't go to church anymore. I'm not even sure I believe in God anymore."

"Really?"

"Really."

"Well then."

"Yes, well then." She paused, Martin was scratching Felix's chin and nuzzling his nose into his soft fur with the wild flap of hair hanging over his eyes. "Does that mean it's over?"

"Oh, for heaven's sake, Doris, of course not! I'm Episcopalian! Haven't you heard--we're very liberal."

"Ok, that's good. I guess."

"So, does it mean you don't want to come?"

"No. Not necessarily. Yes, you can pick me up. What time?"

They made plans for church and kissed goodnight. She stood at the screen door waving as he backed the Volvo out of Avis' driveway and pulled away, blowing his horn till he was out of sight. Doris hoped the neighbors weren't in bed yet, but she was smiling as she watched the taillights fade into the darkness. She took Felix and put him at the foot of Avis' bed, where he decided to sleep each evening and got ready for bed. She walked over to Avis' bed and stroked her arm. She pulled the rocker closer to the bed and laid her cheek gently on Avis' hand. "Oh, mother," she said, "I wish I could talk to you."

She made one last check on Avis' machinery and was heading for her room when she distinctly heard her mother's voice. "Doris?" Avis' eyes were closed and she lay perfectly still.

Doris rushed to her side. "Mother? Mother?"

Avis blinked a few times and slowly and looked around the room. "Are we having company, Doris?"

"No, Mother, this is all for you." Doris was so excited she wanted to jump and scream, but she knew she must be calm and quiet for Avis' sake.

"Tell your father I need some things from the store."

Doris hesitated. "Uh, well, I can go, Mother. What do you need?"

Avis gave Doris a look of disgust. "Tell me how you're going to go when you can't even drive!"

"Mother, do you know where you are?"

Avis looked around the room until she spotted the chandelier above her head. She looked at Doris' anxious face. "Isn't this the dining room?"

"Yes, Mother, oh yes, it is your dining room!" Doris squeezed her hand. Instead of pleasure on Avis' face, however, she saw a look of sadness.

"Ed is gone, isn't he?"

"Yes," Doris wasn't sure what to say. "He's been gone for a few years."

"And I'm sick aren't I. Really sick."

"Well, you have been."

"Do you remember where your father kept his gun, Doris?"

"Yes, Mother, I do, but what does that have to do with . . . "

"I want you to go get the gun and shoot me. Right now. I don't want to live like this, and I'm too old to live anymore anyway."

"Mother, you can't be serious." Doris' eyes were filling up with tears despite her best efforts to stay in control. "You're scared right now, but that's okay. I'll be right here with you. I'll do anything to help you."

"You don't understand, Doris," Avis looked so determined and so sensible it scared Doris. "I don't have much time and I sure as hell don't want to live the rest of it lying out like a buffet in my own dining room."

"Well, now that you're better, you can stay in your room. You can watch television and I'll read to you. It will be fine, Mother, you have to let me help you with all this."

"Bury me in my new silk dress, Doris. I know it's a little fancy, but shoot, who cares? Do you know which one I mean?"

"Mother, I wish you'd stop talking about death and dresses. You're going to be fine now; I can see that."

"Doris!" Avis said with such urgency Doris was alarmed. "Do you know which one I mean--the new blue dress with the little jacket?"

"Yes, Mother, I know the dress, the one you wore for Easter Mass." Doris said, almost angry, scolding an unruly child. Then she softened, pulling Avis' hand to her cheek. "I'll even take you to Mass, Mother, if you'll stay with me." Doris' eyes filled with tears, but she didn't even notice. She kissed her mother's hand and laid her head against Avis' hip.

"Doris, you've been a blessing to me, do you know that? I love you so much--don't ever forget that. Tell Ted I love him, too."

"Oh Mother," Doris leaned over and kissed her mother on the cheek and hugged her shoulders. "I love you, too. And I've missed you so much. You stay right here; I'm going to call your doctor."

Doris ran to the phone and called the hospital, but Dr. Newsome wasn't available. "Please page her to call me immediately. It's about my mother, Mrs. Peechum." She hung up and walked back to her mother, who was sleeping again. "Mother?" Doris didn't know if she should try to keep her awake or let her rest. "Mother?' she whispered softly. Avis lay still with no recognition or movement.

By the time the doctor called it was after four o'clock and Doris was asleep in the rocker. She told the doctor what happened. "Yes, well, strokes are still pretty mysterious to us. Some patients have episodes like this and then descend back into the coma. Some come out of it for good and some don't come out at all. If she saw you and spoke to you, well, that's quite remarkable, but not completely out of the ordinary. If she is sleeping again, let's let her rest for the night. I will try to stop by tomorrow morning on my way in to see if she is sleeping or back in the coma."

"Can't you come now?" Doris knew she was asking a lot, but this was her mother's life, after all.

"I don't think there's much I could do now can't be done in a few hours, Dr. Peechum. If you're really worried, you could call for an ambulance. However, it might disturb your mother's rest. Why don't you try to get some rest, and I'll see you before I go home--about six thirty, okay? And Dr. Peechum, call me immediately if she wakes up again. Here's my cell number."

Doris was disappointed but knew the doctor was probably right. Since she was in her pajamas already, she took a blanket and pillow off her bed, reset her alarm clock for six, and curled up on the rocker to sleep. For the first time in a while, Felix jumped up in her lap and fell asleep in her arms.

Doris' alarm rang in the bedroom at six o'clock, and it startled Felix into jumping on the floor and under the sofa in the living room. Doris was groggy from having too little sleep, but she managed to make it to the clock so she could throw it across the room. The alarm stopped abruptly, followed by a little whimper of metal falling on the hardwood floor. Doris hated the old-fashioned alarm clock with its loud ticking and little gold bells on top, which woke her with the exigency of a three-alarm fire drill. How she longed for her own bed and her own radio alarm clock. She decided that would be an errand today--bring her clock radio to her mother's house.

She passed Avis' bed, checking briefly to see if she was still asleep then sauntered into the kitchen to grab a muffin and a glass of milk from the fridge. She munched on the muffin while she turned on the coffeemaker switch and prepared her cup with artificial sweeteners. While the coffee perked, she changed into a casual pair of slacks, brushed her teeth and combed her hair. Her straight, thick auburn hair was dangling almost to her shoulders and she made a mental note to get a trim this week.

It was almost time for the doctor to arrive, even though Doris guessed she would be late. Harriet wasn't due to arrive until eight thirty. She decided to check on her mother and then try to look over schoolwork for Monday. She looked over at Avis, who was lying still and quiet as usual. A fleeting thought ran through Doris' mind that perhaps she dreamed her mother had spoken. She noticed Avis' arm with her IV was swollen significantly, and this concerned her. She also noticed something was different. She couldn't put her finger on exactly what it was, but she studied her mother closely for several minutes without moving. Suddenly, Avis seemed to be struggling to breathe. She'd take a deep gulp of air, then lie perfectly still, then another deep, painful sounding gulp of air.

Doris felt herself beginning to panic. *Thank goodness the doctor was on her way*, Doris thought, looking around the room as if there might be something nearby to help her mother. She put her hand on Avis' arm and was shocked to notice her mother's skin was cool to the touch. She felt for a pulse, but couldn't find any movement at all. Just as she was getting ready to scream and rush to the phone, the doorbell rang and she ran to the door.

Dr. Newsome took one look at Doris' face and rushed to Avis' bedside. She pulled her stethoscope from her bag and put it to Avis' neck and chest. Doris stood nervously near her, gently rubbing Avis' feet. Felix was perched at Avis' hip, but Dr. Newsome didn't seem bothered by his presence. The doctor pulled up Avis' eyelids and then checked her arm. She removed the stethoscope from her ears and let it lay around her neck like a cowboy tie. She turned off the IV drip and turned to face Doris. "I'm so sorry, Dr. Peechum, I don't have good news. I'm afraid she's dying." Dr. Newsome put a hand gently on Doris', but Doris didn't notice. She was looking at her mother's face. "The swelling is a result of her system slowing down--the body isn't absorbing the fluid at a normal rate and it's collecting in the injection site. I'm so sorry." Dr. Newsome walked slowly to her bag and pulled out some papers. Doris stood staring at her mother.

"What about the breathing—what is happening?"

"It's what's called agonal breathing. It's not unusual."

"How can that be?" Doris asked, "She was alert and talking to me last night."

"Well, I have heard of it happening before--a moment of clarity before death--as if the mind knows what's going to happen and forces the patient awake to finish important business. It's rare, but not unheard of. Her body is in the process of shutting down. She still has a faint and periodic pulse, but she is unconscious and probably has been for several hours." Doris was too stunned to say anything else. "I'll uh, step into the kitchen and let you have some time with her. Call me if you need anything." Dr. Newsome patted Doris' hand and left the room.

Doris lay her head down on the bed next to Avis and sobbed. Felix nestled next to Avis' hip and stretched out a paw to touch Doris' hand. Doris, however, was too distraught to take comfort. She slid into the rocker and held Avis' hand on her cheek. She couldn't talk or even open her eyes; she felt as if she had been holding her breath for hours, sinking to the bottom of a swimming pool. When her weeping finally subsided, Doris rubbed her eyes and grabbed the box of tissues from the table near Avis' bed. The gasps began getting farther apart and finally slowed, with long periods between them. Doris blew her nose and then rested her head on the bed, holding her mother's cold hand next to her cheek.

Some time passed--Doris could not have guessed how much--and Dr. Newsome returned to the room. Without disturbing Doris or Felix, she put her stethoscope on Avis' neck and listened patiently. Avis made a loud guttural rumbling sound, which Doris guessed was a death rattle. She had heard of them before, but never witnessed one. It was the saddest sound Doris ever heard. Dr. Newsome took a deep breath and then sighed. "She's gone. I'm sorry, Doris." She folded her stethoscope and tucked it into her black bag. "Would you like for me to call a funeral home? Since I witnessed her . . . well, since I was here, I can sign a certificate and release the bod . . . uh, let the funeral home take her today. Unless you want an autopsy done."

"God, no," Doris finally caught her breath and was finally able to speak. "She has endured enough torture. I'll call the Kerry County Funeral Home. She has an acquaintance from her church who works there. But thank you, anyway."

"Is there anyone I can call for you? Family? Friends?"

"You're so kind, but I think I need to make those calls myself." Doris dreaded placing the calls, but she knew it must be done. She began making a mental list of everyone who needed to be contacted in order of importance and necessity. She had gone through this once before when her father died. She helped her mother make funeral arrangements, call relatives, write an obituary for the paper, and orchestrate the funeral. It helped her tremendously to feel needed and like she was helping. It felt too hopeless to have nothing to do.

"Will you be okay, or would you like for me to stay with you?" Dr. Newsome brought her back from her thoughts. She was filling out the death certificate.

"Oh. No, I'll be fine. Thank you for everything."

"I wish we could have saved her," she handed the paper to Doris.

"Give this to the funeral staff when they arrive. I'll keep a copy for the hospital, and you will need to send a copy to your insurance companies and retain this original for other legal proceedings. The funeral home will probably give you a folder explaining all the procedures you have to go through when a loved one passes." She paused, but Doris sat quietly, staring at Avis. "God bless you." The doctor patted Doris' shoulder, picked up her bag, and let herself out the front door. Doris was left with her mother and Felix and some calls to make.

14

Doris sat beside her mother with Felix in her lap until the funeral home staff arrived. They respectfully covered Avis' face and then wheeled her out the side door and into a waiting hearse. Doris stood, mute, watching them as they deftly managed the hospital bed without disturbing the body. It was all very precise, very practiced, and very impersonal. Felix ran to a window to watch them drive away, but Doris closed the door behind them and then returned to the dining room and looked around.

It was almost eight. She first placed calls to Harriet and Sandy. Harriet was about to leave her house to come over and expressed sincere regret and sympathy. Sandy's machine picked up, curt and efficient, it asked Doris to leave a message at the tone. The next call she made was to Martin who moaned with genuine upset. He would be over in a few minutes. She took a deep breath and dialed Ted's home number. Baton Rouge was an hour earlier than Kerryville, and she could tell she woke Tammy. Doris wanted to tell Ted directly, but it seemed silly to not tell her sister-in-law. Tammy assured Doris they would be there as soon as possible. Doris told her to plan on staying at her house like Ted had before. She would have to stay at Avis' until after the funeral anyway, to greet visitors, and start the sad task of packing up the belongings. *And besides*, Doris thought, *the teenagers won't be underfoot.*

Doris took a breath and decided to take a break from calling once she contacted the most important people. She picked up all the remaining hospital paraphernalia and packed it into a big box from the basement. She put it in Avis' sewing room out of sight and proceeded to straighten up the living room and kitchen to receive guests. She made a mental note to get Martin to help her move the dining room set back in and to lower the chandelier.

Martin arrived with a cardboard tray holding two coffees, pound cake, and a bag of muffins. They sat together on the sofa eating breakfast, not talking. She asked Martin to move as much of the dining room furniture as he could, then she searched Avis' closet for the silk Easter dress and the matching hat. Avis was raised Catholic; women wore hats to church. It was one reason Doris hated church--she looked horrible in hats. It didn't matter to Avis that the rules changed, and it was too late for Doris to care. She started to pick out a pair of shoes but stopped herself, realizing the shoes would not show in the coffin. The coffin, she thought. It was impossible to picture her mother's face in a casket. She took a deep breath and focused on stopping her tears from creeping down her cheeks. She wiped her face, put the clothing in a shopping bag, and laid them near her purse.

She and Martin spent the rest of the morning working on the house, and after lunch she called Father Kasper about the funeral arrangements. Tuesday morning was decided on, and the priest assured Doris he would take care of all the arrangements on the church end. She called Avis' sister in Knoxville. Aunt Clara was the only surviving member of the Daugherty family. She was upset, but not surprised. Clara was five years younger than Avis and said she would come up the next day. Doris, of course, invited her to stay in Avis' home, and she accepted. Doris secretly hoped Aunt Clara would reject the offer but knew she wouldn't.

A call she dreaded but needed to make was to Phyllis, her department head, who assured her it would be all right to take Monday and Tuesday off and asked if she could do anything to help. Doris wasn't sure the time was right, but Phyllis was hard to catch. *Better ask her now,* Doris thought, *while I have her on the phone.* "Phyllis, do you remember I asked you about doing the play? Well, I need to discuss something with you once I get back to school."

"That will be fine, Doris," Phyllis said in a thoughtful tone, "we can meet Friday. Set something up with Vivian."

"Thanks, Phyllis, I appreciate it."

"Let me know if I can help with anything else." Doris knew this was what Phyllis was supposed to say, but she would not be doing too much for her in this difficult time. She and Phyllis worked together as colleagues but not friends. The fine arts faculty tried to remain friendly with each other, but they were all so overworked there wasn't much time for socializing. Doris and Phyllis saw each other at college social functions, fine arts performances, and activities, but they rarely saw each other off-campus.

Lenny was out, so Doris left a message. Finally, Doris called Avis' best friend and Tootsie's mother, Fran Michaels. Avis met Fran while they were both teaching at Our Lady of Mercy, a private high school for girls. Fran taught mathematics, and Avis taught history. Doris and Tootsie became friends almost as immediately as their mothers had, feeling like sisters. Fran and Avis shared babysitters and then, of course, put Doris and Tootsie in the same classes once they got to high school. Hearing Fran's voice brought a rush of memories back to Doris, along with genuine regret she hadn't worked harder to stay in touch with Tootsie. Mrs. Michaels, as Doris called her, was deeply moved and offered to call Avis' friends in town, including her bridge group and close friends at the church. Doris was grateful for not having to make those calls. Fran also said Gina, because she wouldn't call her daughter Tootsie, always asked about Doris and was hoping to plan a lunch sometime soon. Doris missed Tootsie, too, she told Mrs. Michaels, and agreed they needed to catch up.

Doris made sure the downstairs bedroom was suitable for Aunt Clara and moved her essentials to her old bedroom upstairs. In the early afternoon, she put groceries for Ted's family in her own refrigerator and took care of a few other errands. She arrived at the funeral home around four to make the final arrangements for a casket and burial. The funeral director, Ernest Watson, was tall, with extremely pale skin and white hair. As they all did, in Doris' experience, he wore a black suit with a subdued tie. His handshake was firm but his hands soft and fleshy, like a priest's. Mr. Watson expressed sadness at the loss of Avis Peechum and remarked that the church bazaar would miss her marvelous pies.

Doris was surprised to find that Avis made all the arrangements for her funeral in advance. She selected a pale blue casket, specified an open casket if she "looked good," as she put it, a funeral Mass at Our Lady of Mercy, and burial in the Evergreen Hills cemetery beside her husband. Since she paid for the entire package in advance, Mr. Watson assured Doris everything would be taken care of in accordance with her mother's wishes. He gave Doris a copy of the contract and asked if she had any other questions. Doris sat with her mouth slightly open and her brows furrowed toward her nose. "When did she do all this--she never mentioned it to me."

"Shortly after your father passed, Doris," Mr. Watson's voice was smooth, like a late-night FM radio DJ. "She said she didn't want you to have to worry about all these details. Now, if it's all right with you, we can do a family viewing tomorrow afternoon, an hour before the public wake.

Then we can oversee another public viewing one hour before the funeral Mass at the church the following day. I will work this out with Father Kasper so you won't have to worry about anything, Doris. After the service, we'll then take the body to the cemetery and oversee the service there and the internment."

Doris thanked him, and he told her not to worry about anything. The family could come by any time after five tomorrow. Doris cringed at the thought but thanked him again and left. After her father's funeral, she had decided on cremation for herself and now she was certain. Doris didn't want anything to do with funeral homes after this.

Driving home, she looked forward to a peaceful evening with Martin to rest and try to wrap her brain around the reality of her mother's death. Indian summer was making her sweat, so as soon as she got into the house, she kicked off her shoes, turned up the air conditioner, and as she started to make a cheese sandwich, the doorbell rang.

In true southern tradition, the doorbell continued to ring for most of the afternoon and then well into the evening. Avis' friends from church, the neighborhood, and her bridge club came in and out of the house with casseroles, vegetables, soups, and every imaginable form of dessert. She and Martin moved Avis' dining room set back where it belonged as a necessity--she needed somewhere to put all the food. Finally, they worked out a system where Martin would greet people at the door and show them to a seat while Doris took care of serving the food and washing the dishes. "I know people mean well," she whispered at one point to Martin, "but this is more work than I feel like doing right now--I'm exhausted!" Martin gave her a sweet kiss on the cheek, which seemed to be the magic she needed at that moment.

Doris tried to stay in the kitchen as much as possible, entering the living room briefly to pick up dirty plates and cups, and say a respectful hello to Avis' admirers. "Your mother was the salt of the earth, Doris, I hope you know that," Mrs. Eckles from the church remarked as she gnawed on a chicken leg.

"Thank you, Mrs. Eckles, I know she thought highly of you, as well" Doris lied. Avis hated the way Vera Eckles took every opportunity to remind her that Doris never darkened the door of the church whereas her daughter, Irene, was there every weekend.

"How is Irene?" Mrs. Eckles jabbered on about her daughter this and her daughter that while Doris feigned as much interest as possible. The charade was almost more than she could bear. Irene and her mother wouldn't forgive Avis for giving Irene an F in American history, even though she never turned in an assignment and failed all her tests. The doorbell rang giving Doris a welcome excuse to leave Mrs. Eckles alone with her chicken leg.

Fran Michaels came around eight and, as a true friend, pitched in to help Doris with the food and cleaning up. "Here, Doris, you sit down awhile and I'll wrap up some of this food for the fridge." Doris was grateful for the help, but realized she was happier in the kitchen with the dirty dishes than in the living room trying to keep up a brave face and engage in banal chitchat. All she could think about was Avis, lying all-alone in the cold funeral home--waiting to go into the ground forever.

"Thanks, Mrs. Michaels, but I don't mind doing it--keeps me busy, you know," Doris stopped a tear from leaking out.

Fran Michaels touched her arm gently, and said, "I understand, dear, but let me help, at least."

"Thank you. How is Tootsie these days?"

"She's well. Still trying to work part-time; she and Sam are taking care of Hayley's kids, you know."

"No, I didn't." Doris didn't think it polite to ask for details.

"Hayley made some mistakes, as we all do, and ended up broke with two little ones."

"That must be so hard on everyone."

"Yes," Mrs. Michaels admitted, "but Tootsie is enjoying it too."

"Well, that's good, at least," Doris struggled to find something positive to say.

Doris put dishes into the rarely used dishwasher in Avis' kitchen while Fran put aluminum foil over casseroles, scraped some of the food into small plastic bowls, and managed to stack everything neatly into the refrigerator. Martin played host, escorting visitors in and out in a timely fashion. By nine, the pace slowed considerably and the last guest was in the process of saying her good-byes to Doris and Martin at the door. Fran wiped down the dining room table, the kitchen counters, and the sink. She then started fluffing sofa pillows and picking stray bits of food from the floor.

"She was a fine lady, Doris, and I know she thought the world of you," Ms. Harvey was saying as she picked up her purse and headed toward the door. "I wish you could have heard her brag at church about her daughter the professor." Ms. Harvey was Doris' tenth grade English teacher when she was just out of college and barely seven years older than her pupils. She was the only divorced woman Doris had ever known until she attended college. Doris Harvey, a pretty woman even today, suffered quite a scandal in this small hotbed of Catholicism, but she held her head high and carried on. As far as Doris knew, she never remarried.

"Thank you for coming, Ms. Harvey. It's so good to see you again," Doris ushered her onto the front porch while Martin joined Fran in the clean-up.

"I wish it was under better circumstances," Ms. Harvey said, patting Doris' hand. Doris nodded and watched her former teacher drive away. She went inside, turned off the porch light, hoping it would discourage any additional visitors. She looked around the house in amazement. Everything was perfectly tidy, and Fran was putting away Avis' apron and picking up her purse to leave.

"Now, Doris, funerals are hard on the family--you call me anytime you need help, okay?" Fran draped a white sweater around her thin shoulders.

"You have been so wonderful, Mrs. Michaels," Doris was saying as she followed Fran out, "No wonder my mother thought so highly of you."

"Why don't you call me Fran, Doris? And remember, you and Teddy were her pride and joy--she talked about you all the time and how proud she was of you both. I'll tell Tootsie to give you a call."

"Please do, it would be great to see her. And thanks again, Mrs. Mich . . . uh, Fran," Doris said. Fran gave her a motherly hug and walked away quickly, fighting the tears in her eyes.

"Well," said Doris as she turned to face Martin.

"Well," he said. "Well," Martin said again, stretching and reaching for his jacket and flipping back the unruly wisp of hair. "I guess I better head out. I know you are exhausted and tomorrow will probably be harder than today."

Doris bit her lip, watching him prepare to go out the door. Suddenly his unmanageable wisp of hair was looking awfully good to her. She dreaded the thought of sleeping alone in this house where death had been. "Martin," she said hesitantly. Martin stopped and looked at her, eyebrows raised, mouth ajar. "I wish you'd stay."

Martin, thinking Doris needed some comforting, put his coat down and came over to hug her. "Sure, honey, I can stay for a while--as long as you want me to."

Doris buried her face in his jacket and breathed in his scent. She couldn't quite place it--perhaps a combination of English Leather cologne and coffee. She wrapped her arms around his waist, inside his jacket and moved her forehead to his chin. Afraid to look at him, she whispered, "Could you stay all night? You don't have class till tomorrow afternoon. I don't want to be alone right now."

Martin didn't show any sign of response; his breathing was measured and even and his arms around her shoulders didn't move. "Of course," he whispered in her ear, kissing it gently and smelling her hair.

Doris moved her head up and caught his lips in the kind of kiss she had given up hope of ever feeling again. They stood in the archway between the dining and living rooms for a long time, kissing and hugging. Doris led him upstairs to her old room; her parents' room was out of the question. Aunt Clara would be sleeping in there and Ted's room was converted into her father's study many years ago and remained untouched since his death. But there should be plenty of time. She wasn't expecting Aunt Clara until late morning or afternoon. Leading Martin up the steps to her room reminded her of her first time, leading bashful, intelligent Ethan up the steps. But this memory didn't make her laugh; it made her smile.

They lay on the bed, still kissing and caressing, as jackets and belts and shirts were removed in a slow and methodical way. Doris pushed back the lock of hair covering Martin's face so she could kiss him while she unzipped his pants and her slacks. There isn't any way to be romantic taking off pants, so they both shucked their clothes off until they were finally down to their underwear. Martin wore a pair of blue boxers with little maroon diamonds and a tank style t-shirt, like her father used to wear. A disturbing memory ran briefly through Doris' mind, but it soon dissipated into panic when she tried to remember the last time she shaved her legs. Having not planned this event at all, Doris was wearing her favorite white bra and high briefs made of cotton. She felt awkward and plain, until she looked at Martin who was assessing her fifty-year-old figure with an admiring stare. He heaved a deep breath and looked her into the eyes. "You're beautiful, Doris," he said and took her in his arms to show her how much he appreciated her.

Doris could tell Martin was somewhat inexperienced with women, but she found it rather endearing. It made her feel even more special--not another conquest. Martin was married once before but was widowed many years ago. His only child, a son named Cedrick, graduated from a prestigious university and began his own college teaching career in Ithaca, New York. After his wife's death, Martin poured his enthusiasm and passion into teaching, research, and guiding undergraduates toward an appreciation for history. In the past ten years, he became one of America's leading experts on World War I, having presented numerous papers and guest lectures on the subject across the country.

Doris found two features attractive in men: a sense of humor and intelligence. She didn't focus on looks, age, income, or any of the other traits usually associated with sexual attractiveness. Martin wasn't much in the humor department, but his brains attracted her when they first met at a party offered by the college president to welcome new faculty.

Now that they were in bed together, Doris was trying to imagine what her life might be like as his wife. She wouldn't change her name--why do it when she didn't want children? And she hated the title Mrs.; she felt a woman should not have to change her title because she did or did not have a man in her life. Ms. or Dr. would do fine, thank you very much. Martin kissed a nipple and Doris remembered what she was supposed to be doing. She tried to stay focused on Martin and his hands on her body. It felt good to have someone make love to her again. And even though Doris didn't realize it at the time, it felt good to have something other than her mother's funeral to think about.

Martin came to a hasty crescendo and lay on Doris, exhausted and sated. She, on the other hand, was left wanting more. But this was their first time, she told herself, it would get better once they became more comfortable together. He rolled him off her, and she snuggled up under his arm, laying her head on the sporadic gray hairs dotting his chest. Martin rubbed her shoulder gently and then fell into a deep sleep almost immediately. Doris lay still, listening to his heavy breathing, for a long time. Finally, she got up to go to the bathroom to brush her teeth and wash her face. She put on her nightgown and then came back to bed. Martin had rolled to his side, facing away from her. Doris slipped under the covers and cuddled next to him in spoon fashion and tried to sleep.

It was no use. Memories of Avis flooded her thoughts. She turned to her back and stared up at the light fixture she had picked out with her mother and the curtains Avis made. It was going to break her heart to sell this house, but she knew she couldn't keep it. To move into it would only move her backward instead of forward, and the idea of renting it to someone who wouldn't appreciate and nurture it was unthinkable. She would have to sell it and let it go--never to come back. She and Ted had a lot of work ahead of them.

At some point, early in the morning, Doris fell asleep from sheer exhaustion. Martin snored lightly beside her without moving, and Felix finally came in to curl up at her feet. She dreamed of Martin and her first boyfriend, Ethan.

The morning sun of early autumn crept in between the blinds and past the curtains right onto Doris' face. She winced and turned over toward the dark side of the room. At first it startled her to see Martin, still on his side, snoring peacefully, but then she smiled. It felt nice to wake up with someone besides Felix. She rubbed his back then moved her hands to his stomach so she could embrace him. Martin slept soundly without movement. Doris buried her face in the area between his shoulder blades and focused on trying to go back to sleep. Felix moved to her pillow and sat next to her head, purring in her ear.

15

She must have dozed off for a while because she jumped to attention when the doorbell rang suddenly and repeatedly. "Martin, Martin," she was shaking him vigorously; Felix scampered down the steps. "Martin, wake up! Someone's at the door!"

Martin roused slowly, rubbing his face, "Good morning, sweetness," he said, but Doris was up, frantically snapping and zipping her clothing and stroking her hair.

"What's the matter, Doris?"

"I don't know who it is, but I definitely don't want the neighborhood to know about my sex life, thank you very much!" She threw his clothes on the bed. "Please get up quietly, get dressed and stay in here until I get rid of whoever it is." She rushed out the door, closing it securely behind her, before Martin could say another word.

Doris took a moment at the top of the steps to be sure her hair was smooth and all the buttons and zippers were closed. She walked down the steps at a leisurely pace, as if she was tidying up the house; she had no idea what time it was. The figure at the door was unmistakable, even though Doris could only make out the silhouette through the leaded glass. She took a deep breath and opened the door.

Clara Daugherty's face and body reminded Doris of a bulldog. One eyebrow seemed to be permanently up and the other down, and a scowl turned her mouth down on both sides. Her arms were crossed under her ample bosom, resting on her belly, and her luggage sat beside her feet, which were adorned in the latest style of comfortable shoes. "What took you so long?" Aunt Clara bellowed as she shoved past Doris into the living room. Doris struggled to get both suitcases in the door and set them down at the bottom of the stairs. "My, that was a hot ride, even though the weather is quite pleasant," Aunt Clara took her sweater and purse and laid them on a chair. "You won't mind if I visit the potty, would you?" Doris' mouth was still open, but so far, she hadn't found a chance to speak. She nodded, and Aunt Clara explored until she found the bathroom. Doris looked worriedly up the steps; Felix disappeared as soon as Aunt Clara spoke.

Doris considered what to do about Martin. Should she go upstairs and rush him out the door? If he left now, the neighbors would be buzzing, but if he stayed, how could she explain him to Aunt Clara? The neighbors were probably buzzing already since Martin's Volvo was still parked in her driveway. Perhaps she should let him come down and admit he stayed here to support her but had slept upstairs while she slept downstairs? God, she felt like she was seventeen again. Why did she care so much what people thought? *No one can tell my parents now*, she thought sadly. She chose to let him stay and decide later how to handle the fallout.

"Whew, that feels better! I feel all refreshed now." Aunt Clara almost shouted as she emerged from the bathroom, looking exactly the same as when she went in.

"Aunt Clara, how did you get here? I told you to call me when you got to the bus station."

"Oh, well, I didn't want to wait around in that nasty place. I took a cab over here." She was looking around the house, up and down the walls, walking in and then out of the kitchen. "Avis made a few changes since the last time I was here. She always had the weirdest taste!" She was looking at the O'Keefe prints in the dining room.

"Well, everybody's different, Aunt Clara." Doris finally got her voice to work. "Can I get you something to eat or drink?"

"If you offered me a cup of coffee, I wouldn't turn you down!" Aunt Clara said and then laughed as if this was a terribly funny joke. Doris looked at her awkwardly.

"No problem, I was going to make a pot anyway. It will take a few minutes, so why don't you have a seat and rest."

"Well, Doris, I'd like to get settled. Where am I sleeping?"

"I was going to put you in the master bedroom, Aunt Clara. I slept in there last night, but I've already changed the sheets for you." Doris picked up the suitcases and carried them into the bedroom.

"Nonsense, I can sleep in your old room, Doris."

Doris stood at the bottom of the steps. "There's someone in there, Aunt Clara." Aunt Clara turned slowly midway up the steps, and her other eyebrow shot up to meet the first one. "There was a late night of company here, and my dear friend stayed with me to help clean up and then take care of visitors today. I'll introduce you two later, but right now I think he's still asleep."

Both of Aunt Clara's eyebrows sank toward her nose. "He?" she said, making it two syllables. "You mean there's a man up there?" Clara looked up the stairs toward Doris' room with her mouth open.

"Yes, Aunt Clara, Martin is a man. He has been a great help to me while Mother was sick--taking care of her yard and my house. Mother adored him. I think you will, too." Aunt Clara's mouth was still open, but now she was staring at Doris. "I'll put your suitcases in here, so you can fix up the room however you like." She lugged the two suitcases into the room and came back to the living room. "I'll check on the coffee. Would you like a muffin?"

"No thank you." Aunt Clara said formally. She pursed her mouth and ambled down each step in a deliberate manner, brushing past Doris as she entered the bedroom.

Doris rolled her eyes and strolled into the kitchen. She prepared a nice arrangement of muffins, fruit, and coffee on a tray and sat it on the dining room table. She retrieved silverware, napkins, plates and cup, then knocked lightly on the master bedroom door. "Aunt Clara, your coffee is ready." Then she climbed halfway up the steps and yelled, "Martin, there's coffee and muffins if you're ready for breakfast." Martin emerged slowly from the room and stood at the top of the stairs. His eyebrows went up, to ask Doris if it was all right to come down, and Doris nodded and headed back to the dining room.

Martin crept down the stairs, getting to the bottom at the same moment Aunt Clara opened her door. "Well, you must be Martin," she said, looking at him up and down with her arms crossed and her head tilted to one side.

"Yes ma'am," Martin said politely, "And you must be Aunt Clara. What a pleasure it is to meet you. Doris has told me so many wonderful things about you." There was a small crack in Aunt Clara's glare. Martin gestured for her to go in front of him and when they got to the dining room, he pulled out the chair for her. Doris suppressed a smile.

"Well, I see you two have met," Doris said brightly. "Anyone want milk or juice?"

The phone rang; it was Ted who had arrived at the airport in nearby Chattanooga. He told Doris they would be taking a rental car into town and would come by the house first. Doris urged him to go to her house and get settled, and they would come by and get them before going to the funeral home. As much as she loved them, Doris couldn't stand the thought of having the kids around today. Ted insisted, however, on coming by his mother's house first, and Doris realized it was futile to argue.

By the time they arrived, Doris had cleaned up the kitchen, helped Aunt Clara get settled, ordered flowers for her mother's casket, and was reading a book. Martin decided to leave to teach his classes and take care of a few appointments at school and then be ready to take everyone to the family viewing at five. Aunt Clara was exhausted from her trip and decided to take a nap. Tammy and Doris greeted each other with a hug, and Ted gave his sister a quick peck on the cheek. Ted's children, now 16 and 13, gave their aunt a warm hug and agreed to a snack of milk and muffins.

"Where's Aunt Clara," Ted asked, taking a seat on the sofa. "I thought she'd be in here redecorating the house." His humor was dry, sometimes even hard to catch, but Doris smiled and nodded.

"She's napping. She got here this morning around seven. Why she insisted on leaving Knoxville in the middle of the night is beyond me-- she's afraid the bus will break down, or there will be some horrible storm, and she might be late." Doris took the rocking chair and pulled it back to its normal place in the living room. No one spoke for a full minute. Doris sighed and looked at her brother. "I hope you can stay for a few days, Ted, so we can get everything settled about Mother's estate."

"Yes, I was planning on it. As executor of her estate, I would have to do it anyway."

"She made you executor?" Doris asked in surprise. "Why didn't she ask me--I mean I live here and could easily take care of it?"

"I don't know, Doris, I asked her the same question. She said she wanted me to do it. I guess it's because I'm a lawyer." Ted sounded exasperated with his mother, and Doris took offense at his tone and at his being chosen executor of the will. When it all boils down to basics, she thought, Ted was still her mother's favorite.

"Well, all right," Doris said, trying not to show her disappointment, "let me know if I can be of any help."

Before Ted could respond, Aunt Clara came through the bedroom door pushing her hair into a tight gray twist at the back of her head. "Well, Teddy, I didn't know you all were here. Where are those adorable babies?" She rushed over to give Ted a big hug and then, by default, hugged Tammy. The kids looked at her with suspicion. They hadn't seen Aunt Clara since Doris' father's funeral, five years before, and they clearly did not recognize her. Eddie, the sixteen-year-old, stared in mute silence, and thirteen-year-old Betsy gave her little more than a passing glance, intent on her muffin. It was apparent to everyone she was expecting them to drop their muffins and run to greet her--like they would have surely done with Avis. Tammy intervened, making an excuse ". . . you know teenagers!"

She whispered to Aunt Clara, in a conspiratorial way, they needed a little more time. Doris could see the disappointment on her aunt's face, but she pushed up her mouth and nodded. "Well, then," she said as she took over one side of the sofa, "tell me how life is in Baton Rouge--hot, I guess." She laughed too loudly, and Tammy nodded and smiled at Ted. The kids finished their snacks and pulled out their phones. *My mother would've killed me if I acted that way—no one makes young people follow social graces anymore,* Doris thought.

Around lunchtime, Doris and Aunt Clara started laying out the remaining food from the night before and prepared fresh lemonade and tea. Everyone nibbled on the food without much conversation, and while Doris cleaned up, Aunt Clara took her bath. Ted took his family over to Doris' house to get unpacked. Doris felt relieved to have a few minutes alone, even if it was just to clean up the kitchen. She decided to leave the food out since people might drop by or the family might want to snack.

She heard a soft tapping at the front door and opened it for Martin who greeted her with a warm hug and kiss. He finished everything up at school and wanted to come back over and help. Doris offered him a late lunch, which he gratefully accepted, but then cleaned up after himself. It was good, Doris decided, to be with a man who has lived alone and is used to taking care of himself--he didn't expect her to be a maid like Avis had been to her father and Tammy was to Ted. That was a good thing since Doris Peechum decided a long time ago not to become a servant to any man. She wanted a real partnership, not a domestic job.

They prepared two cups of coffee and went outside to sit on the front porch rockers. The weather was beautiful, a cool seventy degrees. After a mostly blustery September, the days had warmed in its last few days. "Are all the men in your family named Edward?" Martin smiled and asked.

"My grandfather, Edward Howard Peechum was the first, and they called him Edward. My father was the junior and everyone called him Ed. Ted is Edward Howard Peechum the third, and Eddie is a fourth. It's good they picked a name with so many nicknames, I guess."

"Yes, and by the time Eddie has his son, he can start all over with calling him Edward." Martin was trying to lighten up Doris' day, and she appreciated it. However, she knew nothing was going to make these next two days much easier. The best she could hope for was to get through them with her sanity intact. He took her hand, and they sat holding hands, sipping coffee, and rocking gently back and forth.

Aunt Clara came out to join them and took a seat on the swing, fanning herself with a magazine. She was wearing a simple housedress and the front of her hair was in rollers. With no make-up, she didn't look so severe, and Doris mentioned how pretty she looked. Martin offered to go inside and get her some coffee, but she declined. "I'm still hot from my bath," she remarked, but smiled at him.

As the day wore on, Martin's considerable charm was beginning to soften Aunt Clara's resolve to disapprove. When he headed home to dress for the family viewing, she even made a comment to Doris about what a nice young man he was. Doris agreed and giggled at the image of Martin as a young man.

Ted called and told Doris they were planning to meet everyone at the funeral home. The kids were taking baths, and Tammy wanted to lie down awhile. Doris assured him it would be fine, but she didn't mention how relieved she was. She loved them all, but right now the only company she really wanted to keep was Martin's.

Doris told Aunt Clara to make herself at home while she took her own bath and got ready to leave. Felix was sitting in his window hammock, watching all the activity but not wanting to get involved. He seemed to Doris to be depressed--missing Avis. But perhaps it was Doris' imagination.

16

Everyone was dressed and ready to go to the funeral home by five o'clock. Martin held the door of his car open for Aunt Clara and then for Doris, who sat in the back. This was the part of the whole ordeal Doris dreaded the most--seeing her mother laid out in her silk Easter dress in the blue casket. It was hard for her to grasp that this would be the last time she would ever see her mother's face. She told herself Avis was gone, but the reality had not yet touched her. She looked at Felix sitting in his window hammock watching them in the car. Suddenly she opened the car door and ran up the steps into the house. Martin looked at Aunt Clara who shrugged her shoulders. He got out of the car and looked toward the house. "Doris," he yelled, "Are you all right?"

A few minutes later, Doris emerged from the house holding a small canvas pet carrier with Felix inside. Martin looked at her in surprise and then concern. "This is a family viewing, isn't it?" Martin nodded. "Well then, Felix should be there." Doris said. "He loved her and she loved him."

Doris slid into the backseat with Felix beside her in his carrier. Aunt Clara shook her head. "They are not going to let you bring that cat into the funeral home, you know."

"Yes, they will," Doris said and left it there. No one spoke anything further on the ride to the Kerry County Funeral Home.

Mr. Watson and one of his young protégés met them at the rear door of the funeral home. They looked at Doris' cargo and opened their mouths slightly. "Dr. Peechum," Mr. Watson said, "Would you like for me to keep your cat in my office?"

"No thank you, Mr. Watson, my mother would want him near her." Doris didn't wait for a response. She pulled her sweater together in the front and walked through the door. "Oh," she said, turning, "My brother and his family should be here any moment. Please show them in when they arrive."

"Yes ma'am," the younger man said, going to the car door to help Aunt Clara out.

Doris noticed the sky looked decidedly dark and foreboding. "Oh dear," moaned Aunt Clara, "I hope it doesn't rain tonight." But Doris was hoping it would. Fewer people would come out in the rain, fewer people to deal with.

Ted drove up in the little compact rental car with his wife and children in tow. They all looked a bit cramped, especially Eddie who looked as if he'd grown two feet since Doris saw them at Christmas, but, somehow, they managed to emerge unwrinkled. Ted had a nice-looking family, and Doris smiled thinking how proud Avis was. She wondered how much Ted and Tammy told the kids about Avis' death. They were teenagers now, and she doubted they remembered much about their grandfather's funeral. She wondered how you tell children anything important. Suddenly she was regretful, and then relieved at the same time, that she had elected not to have any.

They entered the somber room with dark paneling and blue-gray carpeting. Some loathsome organ music was playing softly in the background, and an array of flowers encircled the altar and the open casket. Oak pews with velvet blue cushions lined the small chapel and beside the entryway stood a little lighted table with the guest book.

Clara stood by the coffin first, sobbing into a lacey handkerchief. Ted and Doris looked at each other. Doris stepped into the foyer to request the organ music be turned off. She suggested a nice quiet classical CD, but if not, no music would be better than the sappy organ music. "But, Dr. Peechum, I think your mother would like to have music playing. This tape contains many of the same hymns she sang in church."

"Mr. Watson, she sang them because she was in church, and I am sure she liked the hymns. But my mother hated organ music--said it sounded like a chorus of sick cats. Now, I would appreciate it if you would abide by my wishes and defer to my expertise concerning my mother since you saw her once a week at Mass, and I lived with her or near her for most of my life."

"Yes, ma'am, of course," Mr. Watson said, smiling in a condescending manner. He turned to speak to his assistant who rushed out of the room. "Please let me know if I can be of any further service." Mr. Watson nodded to Doris and disappeared into his office. Doris was nonplussed by his aggravation. If you couldn't fight for what you want, what is the point? Regardless of who Mr. Watson imagined himself to be, to Doris he was an employee, the services of whom were prepaid at great expense by her trusting mother. He wasn't going to push her around. *You don't teach college for twenty-five years and not learn how to stand up for yourself,* she thought.

When she returned to the chapel, there was no music playing, and Ted was looking down at his mother in the coffin. Martin put out an arm for Doris to return to. Tammy and the kids were still waiting, and Aunt Clara took a seat in the front pew. Betsy squatted down next to Felix's carrier, and he was rubbing his side back and forth against her hand. When Ted sat down in a pew across the aisle from Aunt Clara, she looked at him with a hurt expression. Tammy looked at Doris before taking the kids to the casket. They looked at Avis' face with furrowed brows and open mouths. Soon they turned away and went to sit with Ted.

Doris nudged Martin to go next, and he moved next to Avis' body and looked at her sadly for several minutes. Without saying a word, he took a seat on Aunt Clara's pew, leaving a space for Doris.

Doris realized this was the moment she had dreaded since the funeral director took her mother's body out of the house. She drew a deep breath and walked slowly toward the casket. A large spray of irises, Avis' favorites, stretched across the body of the casket. The spiraling ribbon said in gold glitter "Mother." Doris found it easier to focus on the flowers than on her mother's face. She pulled Felix up next to the altar and took him out to see Avis. He looked at Avis and tipped his nose down toward her hands to smell. Then he climbed back into Doris' arms with his head nuzzling against her ear. She stood cradling Felix like a child, rocking him slowly from side to side, while she looked at her mother's peaceful face. She tucked her lips between her teeth to keep from crying. Finally, she returned Felix to his carrier, then returned to Avis. She kissed her fingertips and gently placed them on Avis' hand. "Goodbye, Mother," she whispered.

Ted looked at Doris like she was crazy. Doris took a seat between Martin and Aunt Clara and handed Felix to Martin who sat him on his knees. She then reached over to squeeze Aunt Clara's hands and received a teary-eyed look of gratitude in return.

They all sat without speaking for a long time. Eddie and Betsy played on their phones, and Ted seemed to be checking email on his. Tammy kept an eye on the kids, and Doris thought she was a good mother, even if she let her teenagers play on their phones too much. Doris knew, however, she could never be selfless enough to be a good mother. Suddenly she found herself envying Tammy, Avis, and even Tootsie. Perhaps she made the wrong choice after all. *Who will be there to make sure there's no organ music playing at my funeral,* she wondered. Doris made a mental note to consider cremation arrangements and payment plans as soon as possible. She scowled, remembering she hadn't prepared a will or living will. *I must do that at once*, she thought.

The guests began to arrive, and there was a steady stream of mourners from six until almost nine o'clock. Doris was touched to see the whole cast and crew of the play enter with Lenny. She apparently canceled or suspended rehearsal so they could attend the wake. They each came over and expressed their sorrow for Doris. Lenny assured her all was well with the play, and they were ready for her whenever she could return. Doris felt like it had been a year since her first rehearsal. It was hard to imagine how she could ever get back into it, but she didn't mention it to Lenny. This was neither the time nor the place. She thanked them all for coming and promised she would see them soon.

She was pleased to see Phyllis and many of her colleagues from school. A long line of Avis' church friends paraded in and out, expressing their regrets to Ted and Doris, not knowing who Aunt Clara and Martin were. Doris couldn't introduce any of them because she didn't know many of them. A few of them were schooled enough to offer their names, and Doris was relieved to reciprocate. Avis' neighbors were more familiar, and of course, Fran Michaels came in with a group of Avis' oldest friends whom Doris had known for years. The ladies who visited the night before with casseroles of food showed up about the same time.

Ms. Harvey entered alone, and Doris heard an immediate chorus of whispered comments. She visited the coffin briefly then came to speak with Doris. As she stepped away, Doris looked up in surprise to see Harriet signing the guest book. "I know I niver got to know yore mother, Dr. Peechum, but I felt close to her in those last few days. I'll keep yew in my prayers." Doris thanked her and wiped a tear away.

Tootsie came in later than her mother and without her husband and Hayley's kids. *People don't bring children to wakes like they used to*, Doris thought. Doris started going to funerals with Avis when she was about four, maybe younger. It was as common for her as attending a wedding, a reunion, or any other big social event. Tootsie hadn't changed much since high school except gaining about forty pounds or so. She still bore the sweetest smile and curliest hair Doris had ever seen. When she spotted Doris, she came over and gave her a big hug. Doris, not much for hugging, tried to respond, but it was awkward in a seated position.

Tootsie pulled back, holding onto Doris' hand. "I was so sorry to hear about your mother's illness and passing," she said. "Mrs. Peechum was so nice to me when I spent the night with you and so much fun. She made the best caramel popcorn balls in town."

Finally, a genuine remembrance, Doris thought. "Thank you, Tootsie," Doris said, squeezing her old friend's hand. "We need to get together for lunch sometime soon. I'm so sorry we've lost touch with each other."

"Oh, well, me too. But we're both so busy and in such different places. Me volunteering to cut out paper pumpkins and ghosts at preschool and you lecturing on art history at the college." Tootsie giggled and gave Doris her great smile. "I want to catch up with you, though. Please call me when everything settles down and you have time to go out. We'll do a movie and pizza like the old days, okay?"

"Sounds wonderful," Doris said and meant it. She introduced Tootsie to Martin, Aunt Clara, and Felix. Tootsie bent down to talk to Felix face to face. Doris could tell right away she was a cat person. She held out the back of her hand for Felix to sniff and then rubbed the net side of the carrier to pet him. She then said she needed to get home and relieve Sam, who was taking care of the grandkids. *Grandchildren!* Doris thought; she hadn't thought of Hayley's kids as Tootsie's grandchildren. The word didn't describe the vibrant, young woman who stood in front of her. But then, Tootsie got married right after high school and started her family right away. *Yes,* she realized, *we are that old.*

"God knows if the house will be standing when I get back!" She patted Doris' shoulder then spoke with her mother before leaving. Doris watched her thinking it was probably best she came without the grandchildren.

By nine, the crowd thinned down and most of the visitors were putting on their sweaters or jackets to leave. As they left the funeral home, Doris noticed it had rained, bringing in a cool wind whipping her hair around her face. Ted took his family to Doris' house, and Martin took the women home to Avis'. He said he would come by after breakfast on Tuesday to take them to the funeral service. He helped Aunt Clara up the steps and into the living room then gave Doris a brief kiss and hug. She stood in the doorway watching him drive away before turning off the porch light and going into the house.

Aunt Clara disappeared into the downstairs bathroom. Doris told her goodnight and to let her know if she needed anything and then headed up the steps to her old room. Martin had made up the bed as nicely as it was before and left no visible traces anyone enjoyed a forbidden night of romance in the room. Doris did her bedtime ritual and then tucked herself under the sheets. She turned to Martin's pillow and sniffed in the faint scent of English Leather, coffee, and sex. She wrapped her arms around the pillow and fell asleep instantly. Felix curled up next to her feet.

The funeral was well attended by almost everyone belonging to Our Lady of Mercy and Avis' few friends who were not Catholic. It was a confusing mix of standing and kneeling for the Protestants, but in the end the service proved profoundly moving for Doris. It surprised and touched her to see Ethan Anderson and his mother near the rear. She spoke to him briefly after the service, introduced him to Martin, and invited him and his mother to come back to Avis' house with the rest of her close friends so they could catch up. But first the cars lined up behind the hearse containing the coffin to process to the cemetery for the graveside service. Doris dreaded this part most because it was so final. After today, her mother would be gone for the rest of her life, and she was going to have to figure out how to handle it.

A handful of devoted friends gathered with the family to say a final and somber goodbye to Avis Peechum. Doris lost control and sobbed openly at the sight of Avis' blue casket resting on top of the immense hole in the ground. Martin put his arm around her and kissed her hair as Father Kasper uttered the truth everyone comes to in the end: "Dust to dust, ashes to ashes . . . "

Doris was still weeping softly as Martin led her away from the grave and toward his old Volvo. Aunt Clara elected to ride with Ted and Tammy, squeezing herself into the tiny backseat of the rental car like cotton candy stuffed into someone's pocket between Eddie and Betsy who didn't seem happy with the arrangement.

Like most Southern funerals, the services were followed by a potluck lunch and gathering at the home of the deceased. Fran Michaels, Tootsie, and a few of Avis' bridge club friends acted as hostesses and served the food, keeping dirty plates picked up and glasses full of tea and lemonade. The crowd spread onto the porch swing and rockers and into the backyard. Eddie stared at his phone while Betsy played around Avis' garden with a small child, and Tootsie's husband, Sam, was holding a toddler. Doris assumed these were Tootsie's grandchildren. Doris and Martin greeted the guests and thanked them for coming and for their concern for Avis. Countless people remarked on Avis being their favorite high school teacher or laughed about how well she played bridge. Doris' hands were rubbed and squeezed so much she could hardly feel her fingers. Mrs. Eckles and Irene carried plates piled high with every available food while most visitors nibbled on a ham biscuit or a slice of butterscotch pie. It turned out to be a hot day, so only a few people drank the coffee Fran set up beautifully with Avis' china and lace napkins.

Doris and Ethan enjoyed a nice conversation about their families and current jobs. Ethan was a lawyer, like Ted, so when her brother joined the conversation it became boring for Doris. When Ted moved on, Doris and Ethan entertained Martin with some funny anecdotes from their high school days. Ethan attended public high school, but stayed in touch with Doris through church. The girls at Ethan's school were filled with jealousy when he brought her to the prom, and Doris was one of the few girls in her class who had a date for every party. Consequently, neither of them enjoyed much popularity in their own schools, but it only made their special bond stronger. Doris gave Ethan a hug; this was the first time she had seen him since they broke up over twenty-five years ago, and he still smelled the same, British Sterling. She looked in Ethan's eyes and remembered all the times he comforted her, made her laugh, and feel special. She suddenly realized she missed him, maybe they could become friends again. She guessed he had finally forgiven her for breaking his heart all those years ago, but they both knew there was no going back. One of life's greatest tragedies, Doris thought, is the bittersweet loss of something dear and intangible, which can't be replaced.

Doris stood for several minutes watching Ethan interacting with Fran and Tootsie and tried to imagine what her life would have been like had she married him. He never officially asked her even though they discussed types of houses and names for children. Ethan turned and smiled at Doris as if he knew what she was thinking. She smiled back and raised a glass of lemonade, toasting him, and wondering why he never married after their break-up. But then, of course, she hadn't either.

Doris was exhausted when the house cleared out. Martin helped Fran, Aunt Clara, and the other ladies clean up the kitchen and put away the china and silverware. Tootsie took the children home for naps. "You should have plenty to eat on for a few days, Doris," Fran said. "There's still enough food to feed an army--despite what Bertha and Irene Eckles ate!" She laughed, and it released the tension in the air. Doris and Martin joined in, and soon they were all caught up in the frenzy of a giggle fit. Doris' eyes watered and her glasses fogged up, she laughed so hard. It felt damn good.

After the guests left, Martin, Doris, and Aunt Clara sipped Fran's delicious coffee with flavored cream on the front porch. They were all worn out so Martin and Aunt Clara fell asleep. Doris rocked gently with her eyes closed, listening to their heavy breathing. Ted and Tammy soon joined them on the porch with glasses of lemonade while the kids watched a rented movie. They all wanted to sit together until it was time for Ted's family to go to the airport. The kids had school the next day, so they were flying home with Tammy. Ted promised to stay a few days to help Doris settle Avis' estate, put her house on the market, and make arrangements for her belongings.

Doris did not wish to spend another night at Avis' house, but she knew she would have to stay once more so she could take care of Aunt Clara and get her to the bus station the next morning. So, when Ted took his family to the airport, Doris, Martin, and Aunt Clara ate a late supper from the food in the fridge.

Doris tried to concentrate on some television shows with Aunt Clara, but she couldn't keep her mind off all the things she needed to take care of the rest of the week. She turned to Aunt Clara to wish her goodnight and realized she had nodded off. *She looks almost peaceful*, Doris thought, *while she's sleeping*. Doris flicked the television off, and Aunt Clara came to life.

"You know, Doris, I'm going to miss my big sister. Avis and I fought like cats--no offense, Felix." Felix heard his name and looked up from his slumber on the arm of the sofa. "But I loved her. She was good to me, and now I'm all alone in the world." She leaned her head back on the sofa and closed her eyes. Doris wondered if she was crying.

"You're not completely alone, Aunt Clara," Doris said and laid her hand on top of Aunt Clara's, who took her hand, gave it a slight squeeze, and then said she needed to pack and go to bed if she wanted to catch the bus the next morning. Doris figured this would be the extent of Aunt Clara's sentimentality—an emotion she rarely, if ever, allowed herself.

Doris kissed her aunt goodnight and watched her carry her robe into the bathroom. She looked at Felix then climbed the stairs to her room. He jumped down from the sofa and ran ahead of her. She bathed, looked over some papers for school, made a list of things she needed to do during the week, and floated into sleep with her light on and a pen in her hand. When she awoke, Avis was sitting on the edge of her bed. It startled Doris at first, but then it seemed natural. Doris was waking up in her old room, in her old bed, and here was her mother in her housecoat, gently nudging Doris' shoulder telling her it was time for school.

"I know, Mother," Doris said into her pillow, rolling over to turn her back to Avis.

"Doris, it's time to get up. Now, you get dressed, and I'll have breakfast on the table when you get down there." Avis walked to the door and turned around. "Doris Ann!" she said in a stern voice, "Don't make me have to come back in here." When she left, Doris jerked up in her bed and looked at the door. It seemed undisturbed from the night before. Felix looked up at her, still curled neatly at her feet. She flopped back onto her pillow and looked out the window, tears running down her cheek. Felix stretched, first the front then the back, then walked up to Doris' pillow and curled up next to the back of her head. She turned over to face him and hugged his body next to hers so tightly he began to squirm.

17

Doris managed to go to school the rest of the week but drove back and forth from Avis' house to hers to school, trying to move her belongings back home and get Avis' house ready to abandon. It all began on Wednesday morning when she drove Aunt Clara to the bus terminal, held her classes, and scrambled to make up missed material. In the afternoon, she moved Felix and her most important things back into her house. She delivered the leftover food to a soup kitchen, took piles of clothes, linens, and knickknacks to Goodwill, and recycled away an enormous amount of old newspapers, magazines, and the like.

She and Ted emptied the contents of their father's safe, and Doris agreed to take care of insurance bills and credit card debts from Avis' account since her mother never removed Doris' name from her checking account. Doris used the account in college to pay for tuition and rent. It kept Avis from having to send checks through the mail, which she hated doing, and made the money easily accessible to Doris for things she needed but couldn't afford. Her parents did the same with Ted, but once he got married, his name was removed. Doris smiled when she looked at the checks. *According to my mother you don't grow up until you get married.* Of course, now Ted's name was back on the account, but Doris still felt she should pay the bills.

Since Avis took such good care of her finances there were no large outstanding bills or debts, and thanks to Avis' foresight, they both owned the house now. Neither one of them wanted to keep it, so they agreed it would have to be sold. Ted suggested they turn it over to a real estate agent and let them hold an estate sale to sell the contents, then sell the house and property. Doris agreed it was a good idea--it saved them the trouble of packing everything up and hauling it off to a charity or trying to sell it in a garage sale. This way, they could use the money they made to pay the real estate agent and then split the rest. Doris volunteered to donate her part toward college funds for Eddie and Betsy, but Ted refused.

Martin helped as much as he could in the days that followed, but it was a hard time for Doris. She tried to balance teaching, going to rehearsals, and packing up the items she and Ted wanted to keep--which wasn't much. Doris kept the china, silverware, and the dining room suit with the Oriental rug. It was the one area of her new home Doris had completely neglected to outfit. At present, her dining room had her mother's old card table with three folding chairs. No one could explain satisfactorily what happened to the fourth.

She took the photo albums, a few of her father's old war medals and some memorabilia Avis had already packed up for her, and finally some mementos from her own room. As Avis had predicted, Ted didn't want anything, but Tammy requested the master bedroom suit--a huge antique bed with matching dresser and chest. She needed something nice for their guest room, which up until now contained a futon and lots of boxes. Ted arranged with a shipping company to come by while he was there to pack it up and send it to his home in Louisiana. Doris hired the same company to move the large furniture she had selected to her house--for convenience and to be sure her belongings were handled carefully.

It felt so good to be back in her own home. Even with Ted there, it was good to be in her own kitchen and her own bed. Martin spent Wednesday night hooking up her VCR, TV, and stereo while Doris was at rehearsal. He and Ted found a football game and decided to watch it until Doris returned home.

Doris was apprehensive about doing character work with Jayson. As Martha, Doris would have to do some heavy flirting and panting around him, and it made them both a little nervous. It wouldn't be the first time Doris had done this on stage, but it would be the first time with a student-- and worse yet, a current student. *This probably wasn't such a great idea*, she thought to herself as she parked Carmen in front of the Humanities building.

Doris was a little early so she strolled along the sidewalk of the small campus, enjoying the new color in the trees and the brisk breeze that tussled the leaves. It was twilight, the last gasp of daylight, and as she gazed at the rose-colored sky, Doris could hardly believe all that happened in the past few weeks. She felt a rumble in her stomach, like life changing forever, and she wrapped her sweater tightly over her chest against a sudden chill.

When she arrived at the rehearsal room, Jayson and Lenny were going over set ideas again. They both looked up and Doris smiled weakly.

"Doris," Lenny began, "if you're not up to a rehearsal tonight, it would be fine. You've been through a pretty rough time."

Doris smiled again at Lenny's thoughtfulness. "No, Lenny, thanks, but it helps me to keep busy. Otherwise, I sit and dwell on things. I know we were supposed to do this on Monday, so I appreciate your rearranging the schedule for me." Jayson got up to pull a chair over for her, and she nodded at him. "Thank you, Jayson."

"It's no problem, Doris, I had to work George with Nick and Honey with Nick as well, so we did those rehearsals on Monday and Tuesday. Okay folks, let's get into it." Lenny handed them some papers to fill out which Doris was already familiar with because she completed similar forms with Bill. Jayson and Doris were encouraged to discuss their answers so the information about their relationship would be mutually understood by them both. The first question was: "What was your first impression of this character?" Doris was supposed to answer as if she was Martha and Jayson was Nick, and Jayson was to do the same.

They both agreed there was an immediate attraction on Martha's part at the party earlier in the evening. It may be the reason she invited them back to the house. Nick's motives, however, were completely political, they thought. He's a new professor on campus; Martha's father is the president--not hard to figure out.

Lenny led them through a series of questions such as these, and they read parts of the script focused on the burgeoning relationship between the two characters. It was exciting and exhilarating work for Doris, and she was impressed with Jayson's professionalism. In rehearsal, he was a different person than she encountered in class--slinking in late, falling asleep, barely passing. Here, he was always early, alert and curious, and truly insightful for one so young. She decided this might not be so hard after all. Jayson was being a grown-up and making it easy for her.

After they read some of the scenes and discussed the characters, Lenny asked them to face each other in their chairs. She then asked them to take turns touching each other and trying to communicate something by body language--nothing verbal. They both looked up at the ceiling and then back in each other's eyes. No one did anything for several minutes and Lenny said, "What's happening?"

Jayson broke the tension and smiled. "Nothing, Lenny," he said, "You didn't tell us who should go first." He had apparently played this game before and knew the rules. Doris sat motionless hoping someone would take charge because she didn't want to.

"Well," said Lenny, "It's interesting you said that, Jayson. I was figuring Martha, being who she is, wouldn't wait for anyone to tell her to go first when it comes to touching a handsome young man."

Doris blushed and covered her cheeks with her hands. "Oh, gosh, I didn't even think of that."

"It's okay, Dr. P, Lenny does this kind of thing all the time. I have done this exercise many times with her, and she always tells us who should start. You want to know my guess, she forgot and was trying to put it on someone else." He looked at Lenny and grinned knowingly. Doris saw it was more than a student calling Lenny by her first name--they were friends. And they felt like colleagues, not teacher-student. She envied them.

Lenny heaved a sigh and rolled her eyes as she pulled her cigarettes out of her purse. "Okay, okay, smart ass, you got me. Let's take a break. I need a smoke, and you both need some air. Why don't you take a walk together and get acquainted a little--as friends? It can help a lot when you're trying to do this kind of intense work together." Doris and Jayson looked at each other and nodded. "I'm going up to my office to do some work, so you guys come on up when you get back. Go to Foster's and get some coffee--bring me some."

"I know, Lenny," Jayson said as he stood up, "black, one sugar."

Lenny nodded and left them alone. Jayson looked at Doris, expecting her to get up and go with him. She sat quietly, studying the two of them and wondering if there was an affair going on. "What?" Jayson asked.

"Nothing, nothing," Doris came out of her reverie and slung her purse over her shoulder. She started toward Jayson and then on second thought headed back to get her sweater. The evenings were getting cooler in the small Tennessee town of Kerryville, especially after the sunset. Soon the time would revert to Eastern Standard, and Doris would hate it.

She and Jayson strolled over to Foster's, the campus grill and coffee shop, and found it buzzing with activity. Students were sipping from huge plastic cups and burrowing through tomes on philosophy, Civil War history, and European literature. A few groups were talking and laughing, going back and forth to the jukebox, while one or two sat with their backs on a wall, sound asleep. Doris didn't know if this was an ordinary night or an unusually busy one. Jason pulled out a chair for her and said, "Good, it's not as crowded as usual," Jayson said. "What can I get you?"

"Oh no, you don't," Doris scolded him, "I owe you one. So how do you take your coffee?"

"To tell you the truth, I hate coffee, but some hot zinger tea with honey would be awesome." Doris raised her eyebrows, smiled, and turned to the order window. When she returned, she saw Kayla, Jayson's girlfriend who came to auditions, sitting next to him. She was preoccupied with rubbing Jayson's arm and didn't notice Doris at first. Doris decided it would be best to take another table, so she sat a few feet away and proceeded to put sweetener and cream in her coffee. A few students came by and nodded to her or called her by name. She turned to say hello to one of them and was surprised to find Jayson standing beside her with Kayla attached to his arm.

"So, Dr. P," he said, "you ready to get back to the grindstone?" Before Doris could answer or say hello to Kayla, Jayson turned to kiss her on the cheek. "Sorry, baby, Lenny's waiting on us."

"She won't mind if I sit in," Kayla was whining; it was so unattractive. Judging by the expression on Jayson's face, Doris surmised this must be a familiar argument between them.

"Kayla, you know Lenny has closed rehearsals. I've told you before. I asked her several times if you could come, and she said it was a blanket policy--nothing personal." He tickled at her chin and then stroked her cheek gently. "I'll probably be late getting in, so I'll see you in English tomorrow--okay?"

For Kayla, it was clearly not okay. She puffed out her feathers, gave Doris a disdainful look, and sauntered back to her friends' table. Doris recognized a girl from the play, Stacey, the stage manager? *Shouldn't she be at rehearsal*, Doris was thinking. Doris and Jayson walked out in a hurried, business-like manner, as if they had been sent to get coffee in the middle of an extremely important session. From the corner of her eye, Doris could see Kayla and Stacey watching them, huddled together. It made her feel awkward, like she was doing something wrong when she knew good and well she wasn't. She suddenly realized in their haste to escape they completely forgot to get coffee for Lenny. *Too late now*, Doris thought. She didn't want to go back to endure more of Kayla's scrutinizing. The lights from Foster's, along with Kayla's disapproval, faded into the misty darkness of the campus.

"She's always driving me crazy about this," Jayson said. "She's a real sweet girl, but she's pretty immature--clingy, you know?" Doris nodded, remembering she was once a lot more like Kayla than she would ever admit.

"Well, she's young, Jayson, she wants to be with you."

"I know, but geeze! She's so childish."

"Wasn't that Stacey the stage manager with her? Shouldn't she be at rehearsal?"

"Well, I guess in some theatres she would be," Jayson said, looking both ways to cross the street, "but Lenny likes these character sessions to be private, to help the actors feel more comfortable."

"Oh," Doris said, not sure what he meant. "So, where do we go to have this talk?" she said as they climbed the steps of the Humanities building.

"Is it too cold for you out here?" he asked. "You can have my jacket; I never get cold."

Doris laughed, "I was going to say the same thing--I usually freeze everyone to death!" They dusted off the marble steps and sat close enough to talk, but far enough away to see each other. The only light fell on their backs from the bright lights in the foyer of the building, but it was filtered through a double set of steel and glass doors. The streetlights along the sidewalk were only bright enough to light their immediate surroundings so Doris and Jayson looked at each other in silhouette. One side of Jayson's face lit, the other dark, like the Beatles on their first album cover, Doris thought.

Doris handed Jayson his tea, and even though it had cooled down significantly, he poured the honey in and stirred it with his finger. Doris sipped her coffee and tried to think of something to ask him--or tell him.

"So," Jayson started, "I'm so sorry about your mom. My mom and I are pretty tight, and I can't imagine what it would be like to lose her. You know, go home and her not be there."

"Thanks," was all Doris could muster. They were quiet again. Then Doris took a deep breath. "I guess I'm not ready to talk about it yet--I don't think it has actually sunk in."

Again, a pregnant silence fell between them. They sipped and looked up at the thin sliver of the moon. "Have you ever wanted to go up there?"

Jayson suddenly asked her. Doris looked at him as if he was crazy. "Be an astronaut? I was totally into it when I was a kid, but I outgrew it."

"I'm sure your mother is grateful." Doris smiled, reflecting on the fact she was old enough to be his mother.

"Well, ummm, actor--astronaut. She might prefer me sailing to the moon than trying to make it in this business."

"Does she support you in your acting?' Doris finally loosened up a little, and it was becoming a pleasure to chat with Jayson instead of an assignment. They talked about their acting experiences--the one thing they had in common--and some funny accidents that happened to them on stage. Time, it seemed to Doris, decided to stand still. No one was walking around on campus, and only a few cars passed by. Clouds skated past the moon as the two of them sat on the cold steps. Doris was feeling relaxed and comfortable, something which had eluded her in the past few weeks. They heard a door open behind them and turned to see Lenny approaching.

"There you are," she said, squatting between them. "How'd it go?"

They smiled at each other and then at Lenny. "Cool," Jayson said. "Oh, my god! I just remembered you wanted some coffee!"

Lenny laughed. "No worries, Jayson. Without the caffeine, I might actually get to sleep early tonight." She looked at Doris and smiled; an awkward silence ensued. "Well, I think we've done enough tonight. I'll be working with the two of you again; we have plenty of time. Thanks for a great rehearsal--I'll see you both tomorrow." Lenny stood up and strode to her car like a champion racehorse with a wreath of flowers on its neck, boots clacking on the sidewalk.

"Well," Doris said, "I guess it's later than we realized." She pulled up the arm of her sweater to reveal her watch--it was nearly ten thirty. "Oh, dear, I'll never get up tomorrow."

"You should buy one of those alarm clocks that stays set even after you turn them off." Jayson said and winked. He stood and offered his hand to her. Doris smiled.

"Touché," she said, taking his hand and rising. "I'll see you tomorrow."

"Good night, Dr. P." Jayson practically jumped down the steps and bounded out of sight toward the dorms. Doris revved up Carmen's engine and drove towards home.

She was feeling much better. Her spirits were lifted by the chance to work on a play again, and she was regaining some of her confidence about being able to pull off such a demanding role. She drove up to her driveway and noticed Martin's car was still parked in front of the house. Felix was in his hammock sound asleep, waiting for her. She unlocked the door on the dark porch and entered to find the television blasting some football game's final moments. "Anybody home?' she asked playfully. Felix jumped down and ran into the living room. Ted and Martin were asleep in their respective chairs, a bowl of popcorn and two beers sitting on the coffee table. Doris wondered for a moment if she really wanted to live with a man.

Felix jumped in Martin's lap, jolting him awake. He pushed back his unruly lock of hair and looked around to get his bearings. He saw Ted and then Doris and started to chuckle. "Well," he said, "the game was good at first, but I guess it got a little boring."

Doris clicked the set off, and Ted wiped his hands over his face and stretched his legs out. "Hey, Sis, how was rehearsal?"

Doris shook her head and picked up the popcorn and beer cans. "It was good, we . . ."

"Dear god, look at the time," Martin interrupted, pushing his feet into his loafers and stroking at his hair. "I think I got everything hooked up right. Ted helped with the stereo. I don't have one of those, so it was good to have an expert on hand."

"Hardly an expert," Ted said as he got up to shake Martin's hand. "I'm going to hit the sack. See you later, Martin." Ted disappeared into the bathroom, and they could hear bath water running. When Doris was in high school, Ted would linger around her boyfriend and sometimes hide behind the sofa while she was necking with Ethan in the living room. But tonight, Ted was giving Doris a little time to be alone with her boyfriend. *I think Teddy has finally grown up,* she mused to herself.

"Well, I'll see you tomorrow at school, Doris," Martin put his arms around her waist and gave her a kiss. She put her head down on his shoulder and pulled him closer.

"I have so much work to catch up on, I don't know if I will even see you," she told the side of his neck. "Maybe you can come over for supper with Ted and me. Why don't you two catch a movie or something? I hate to walk out and leave a guest here alone--even if he is my brother."

"Okay, I'll come by around five and we'll see what Ted wants to do."

They kissed again, and she walked out on the porch with him. He drove off in his Volvo and Doris sat on the edge of the porch looking up at the sky. Felix stood behind the screen door, watching her curiously. It was a cool fall evening and getting colder as she sat there, but she couldn't seem to pull herself away. The night air, the clear sky, her beckoning future presented irresistible forces for her contemplation.

18

Doris arrived home from school Thursday to find Ted weeding her flower garden. She invited him in for lemonade, and they sat chatting awhile. He did a few repairs in Avis' house and helped a shipping company pack up Avis' dining room table set for Doris and the master bedroom set for Tammy. It felt odd to Doris, talking to Ted like a regular person, not a brother. She noticed he was quite charming, in a lawyer kind of way, and possessed a better sense of humor than she remembered. When he left to take his bath, she picked up Felix and took her lemonade to the back porch. The air was getting nippy, even in the afternoon, but Doris liked fresh air. She stood surveying her yard, making mental notes of all the work she needed to do some weekend, and stroking Felix's soft fur. Martin arrived around five, and since Doris wasn't hungry and needed to get some laundry done before rehearsal, Martin and Ted decided to go out for dinner and then catch a movie at the mall. Doris told them she wasn't sure when she'd arrive home, but she would see them sometime later. It felt good to have her house all to herself, even if it was only a couple of hours. Ted had set up the dining room furniture, and it looked beautiful. She washed clothes, ate a light snack, played with Felix, and then got ready for rehearsal.

The evening rehearsal was for the whole cast so Winnie and Stacie observed. Lenny asked the actors to sit in a circle and read the whole play. This time, however, she gave them a small sponge ball and told them to throw it at the person they were directing the line to. "It may not be the one you think you're talking to," Lenny said, "look for times when you are talking to one person but actually directing the line to someone else. Also, look for times you are directing the line to the obvious person, but look at the mood you are in when you do it. There may also be times when you are saying the line for your own benefit. In that case, throw the ball to yourself." Everyone looked at each other, a few eyebrows went up, but no one spoke. Bill, above all this Doris supposed, rolled his eyes. *How rude,*

she thought, *like my students. Does no one have any manners anymore?*
"Okay, here's the ball--someone has to start."

Lenny laid the ball on the floor in the middle of their circle. Doris faced Bill with Jayson to her right, facing Teri. Doris picked it up and started. She threw the ball up in the air and then caught it. Bill grabbed it away from her, and then she took it from him. Once they all warmed up to the exercise it became easier to determine what the lines were about and who was talking to whom. It got intense near the end of Act 2, so Lenny called a break. The smokers headed outside for a cigarette, Winnie ran to the bathroom, leaving Doris and Jayson alone, again.

"Wanna coke?" Jayson asked Doris.

"Yes, but I'll walk with you. I think I need some air as badly as they need nicotine." Jayson laughed and waited for her at the doorway.

"So, what do you think of Lenny as a director?" Jayson seemed sincerely curious, not making small talk.

"I like her a lot. She certainly gets to the heart of things. It's like she cares, but she doesn't push or dictate." Doris was trying to sort it out more for herself than for Jayson. "Yes, I do like her," she concluded.

They made it to the drink machine and stood looking over their choices. "There's never anything left at the end of the day--the guy comes every morning to refill it." Jayson put in his money and punched his choice for a bottle of water. While Doris did the same, he picked up the topic of Lenny again. "I like her, too. Did you know the woman who was here before her--did you ever work with her?"

"Well, working in the same building we got to know each other pretty well. Ann was a great person, but I never worked on a play with her." They took their water outside and sat on the side steps of the building. It was dark and cold, but the sky was clear with bright stars and an iridescent moon. "My, what a beautiful evening."

Jayson sipped his water and looked around. "I guess so," he said, "you know I never pay much attention to the weather. I've seen you walking on campus, though, stopping to study a group of flowers or pull a red leaf from a maple tree. You must be really in tune with nature." Doris was a little taken aback by his confession of watching her on campus. He must have sensed something in her face because he quickly added, "Not that I'm stalking you or anything!" They both laughed, but Doris started wondering. "It's . . . I sit out here a lot or under a tree. I can't study in the dorm, it's too noisy, and there aren't many quiet places. I come here to sit on the steps or sometimes I like to sit on that bench over there," he was pointing toward the library. "I look up sometimes and see you, like I do everyone else. You're the only one who stops to look at the world around you, though, so I guess that's why I noticed it. Everyone else has their noses buried in their phones."

"Ugh, cell phones," Doris said, "the bane of a teacher's existence!"

"I know I didn't have one as a kid, but now, I can't imagine life without having one."

"It was different, for sure, Jayson. Maybe better in some ways. I still don't have one."

"No, really?" Jayson was incredulous. "How do you stay in touch with people?"

Doris had to laugh. "Well, I do have a regular phone—a 'land-line' they call it now." Her mood darkened briefly at the thought of her mother trying to reach her. "Recently, though, I have had some experiences that make me think it would be a good thing to get one." Jayson, sensitive to her mood, didn't pry.

They sat silently for a moment. "It's okay, Jayson. And you're right--I do enjoy nature, especially the change of seasons," Doris leaned back, resting her head on the hard stone wall. "Sometimes I take a long walk at lunch, winding around the campus, looking at the bright colors in the trees right now. I guess it has something to do with being a visual artist."

"I hope you don't mind my saying this, Dr. P, but I think you're a great theatre artist too." Doris was almost blushing. "I couldn't believe you at auditions--you blew me away."

"Jayson, I think you are exaggerating some," Doris smiled, flattered by his attention.

"That's one thing I never do, Dr. P. I don't tell anyone they're good unless I really think so. If I'm not impressed, I try not to say anything." He looked so earnest and sincere, she believed him.

"You know, Jayson, it's important we maintain some formality in class together, but at rehearsals, why don't you call me Dorie. It may sound strange, but we're going to have to work so closely together it's too weird to be Dr. P here."

Jayson studied his water bottle. "Okay, I'll try." Doris got up to stretch, and Jayson followed her into the Humanities building and down the hall to room 106.

They finished the read-through and then discussed some of their choices. Both Teri and Jayson were still calling Doris "Dr. P." After Lenny reminded them about the rehearsal schedule for the rest of the week, Doris made a general announcement she'd rather be called by her old nickname in rehearsal. "Like in *Finding Nemo*?" Winnie asked. Doris looked at her blankly.

"It's a Disney movie," Jayson whispered.

"Yes, I guess so!" Doris said smiling and making a mental note to do some research.

Everyone agreed to the nickname, and Jayson looked more at ease, since Doris included Teri and Winnie. Lenny smiled at Doris knowingly; Doris wondered what was on her mind.

After everyone gathered up jackets and scripts, they headed for the door; Lenny touched Doris' arm and nodded for her to stay. "Doris, uh sorry, Dorie, have you ever smoked?"

"No," Doris said hesitantly. Jayson looked back as he got to the door, but realizing it was a private conversation, he closed the door gently and raised an open palm to them. They smiled and nodded, but Lenny pulled Doris back into the conversation.

"Well, you know, Martha does, and," she paused, "I don't know how you feel about it, but there are some lines about her cigarettes I don't think we should cut. I'm a big fan of saying all the lines the playwright wrote."

Doris was stunned at first, why hadn't this occurred to her? She read the play so many times and somehow failed to realize that if Martha smoked, *she* would have to smoke. "I don't want to have to smoke, but if you think it's necessary, I can try," she finally said.

"Let me look over the script carefully, Doris. There is a part where she asks George to light her cigarette, but he refuses. I expected Nick to light it, but I guess we could have her put it down or throw it at George. I'll let you know about it later. However, you still need to look like a smoker."

"How do I do that?" Doris was beginning to think the understudy should take over.

"Well, a smoker handles a cigarette as if it is a part of her body—like an eleventh finger. She can put on make-up, drive, play cards, do anything with a cigarette in her hand, without dropping it or burning herself. You need to get a cheap pack of cigarettes and start carrying one around all the time. Pretend it's lighted and do everything except teach class with it in your hand—cook, grade papers, set your watch, brush your hair— everything. Okay?"

"Sure, I think I can do that."

"Some of the time, I would suggest you light it, because you also need to learn how smokers handle the smoke itself—keeping it out of your face, not burning your sofa or your book. Here are a few to get you started." Lenny hit the pack on her hand and out came three cigarettes. She pulled them out and handed them to Doris.

"Okay." Doris felt a deep churning in her stomach.

"One other thing, I wanted to ask you why you changed the 'goddamns' to 'damn.'"

Doris squirmed a little. "Uh, well, I figured this being a church-related school, we'd soften the language some."

"Do you have a religious objection to the language?" Lenny was trying to be sensitive to Doris' feelings, she guessed, but it only made her more uncomfortable.

"No, I guess not." Doris looked around at the others, who found reasons to stare at their scripts. "If you want me to say goddamn, then goddamn it, I guess I will!" She laughed, and it lightened the tension considerably.

Lenny smiled. "Thank goodness! I didn't want to put you on the spot, but the language is so important in defining these characters. She thanked Doris for being so cooperative, and they walked down the hall and then to their cars mostly in silence. Doris rode home with the windows down in Carmen. The air was cold but thrilling. She felt as if all her senses had been asleep for years and were now beginning to wake up and notice the world. It seemed an odd paradox to her; she felt so sad because of her mother's death, and yet, was beginning to feel alive for the first time in decades. It didn't concern her for the time being. She decided to let herself cry when she needed to and laugh when she wanted to.

Doris stopped at the first corner gas station she passed to fill up with gas, and while there she purchased her first pack of cigarettes. She looked around to make sure no one saw her, as if she was still in high school and could incur the wrath of her father. There was something sinister about it, but instead of scaring Doris, she felt somehow liberated. It was a strange sensation for her, pleasant but a little uncomfortable. She asked the clerk for the mildest cigarettes available. On the way home, she pulled the pack of cigarettes from her purse and tugged at the cellophane awkwardly.

"Some heat wouldn't kill you, Doris," she heard her mother say. It seemed so real, she turned to her right, expecting Avis to be sitting there in her little white sweater and green polyester pantsuit. But she wasn't there. The pack of cigarettes fell under her legs and there was no way to get them until she came to a stop. She decided to let them stay there until she got home.

Doris popped a CD of Beethoven's fifth symphony into the stereo and turned the music to top volume with the wind whipping her hair around. A few years ago, she finally gave up her old cassette player because she couldn't find the tapes anywhere. A car audio specialist installed a CD player so neatly into the old spot it looked like it had come with the car. She made a sudden turn and drove down a little dirt road, which followed a winding river for several miles before rejoining the main road. It was a drive she and Ethan took many times in their youth. The cold air swirled around her head and feet, the music assaulted her eardrums and the stillness of a country road, as she drove much faster than normal; Carmen didn't complain. Doris patted the dashboard with affection and looked in her rearview mirror to see billows of dirt left in her wake, reflecting the glow of her taillights. It felt like religion.

When Doris pulled up to her house, the lights inside were extinguished, and there was no sign of life. She tucked the cigarettes into her purse and headed for a good night's sleep. She turned off the porch light, locked the door, and looked around the house. Felix was sacked out on his blanket at the foot of her bed, one of her slippers under his chin, and through Ted's cracked door she could see the outline of him asleep in bed. She tiptoed back to the kitchen for a glass of milk and found a note from Martin. He and Ted enjoyed their movie, and he would catch her at lunch the next day.

Doris held the note to her chest and thought how nice it felt to have a man leave a note for her and yet, it still felt a little awkward. Doris wondered if perhaps she had become so accustomed to living alone that adjusting her lifestyle to suit someone else might not be possible. "You're stuck in your ways," her mother would say. Well, surely it was possible, but was it desirable? She sipped her milk slowly, staring into the middle distance of her thoughts about her past, her present, and her uncertain future.

Felix wrapped himself around her legs, bringing her back to the present. She bent down to pick him up and rocked him gently on her shoulder while he nuzzled into her hair. Doris finished her milk and took Felix back to bed like a child, stroking his fur and humming to him softly. He stretched his front paws into her face and then rolled himself into a tiny ball. She curled up next to him, lying across the width of her bed, and fell asleep in her clothes.

Friday's classes were uneventful, and afterwards, Doris met Ted back at the house to finish up some last-minute arrangements about Avis' estate. He had planned to have dinner with a few of his high school chums, which suited her just fine. She drove off to rehearsal which was mostly about working on lines and subtext, what the character is *really* saying with a line, for Act 1. When she arrived home, Ted was in bed, and Martin had left a message on her machine, asking her about plans for Saturday. She called Martin, waking him up, to tell him she would be taking Ted to the airport, and would call him afterwards. "Sorry for waking you up, Martin," she whispered.

"I'd rather wake up to your voice than sleep through any night, Doris. She smiled to herself and bade him goodnight.

The next morning, she drove Ted to the airport, which was an unexpectedly emotional goodbye for them both. On the way home, she stopped for groceries. By evening, Doris was exhausted. She had been going full-steam all week and hadn't realized how drained she was. She called Martin to let him know she needed some time alone--there were papers to grade, lines to learn, television to watch, and peace and quiet to find. He understood but made her promise they'd have a date the next day.

Finally, she thought, *some time to myself.* Doris did some serious housecleaning, fixed herself a nice dinner, and spent some time on class preparation. When her eyes started burning she settled into her favorite chair with Felix to watch some television—all with a cigarette between her fingers. The house was cold, the way she liked it, and she could stay up late or go to bed early--whatever she wanted. She wondered if the reason she had remained single for so long was because she wanted to be single. She imagined it was because she hadn't found the right man or was too busy with work to socialize. She scratched Felix's head and wondered if she was ready to get married. When she woke up two hours later the television was still on, and Felix had jumped down from her lap and headed toward the kitchen. "Oh, dear," she said to herself and shuffled off to bed.

Doris started the next day in the same way she had started her days for the past several years. She ate a light breakfast, stepped into the shower, and cooled off with a cup of coffee while reading the paper on her back porch. She tried lighting the cigarette and gulped in a puff of smoke, which made her cough so long and so hard she was sure she wouldn't be able to talk. Finally, she settled down, took several sips of coffee and kept waving the smoke away from her face. She picked up Felix and stroked his fur, but he did not like the smoke and quickly jumped down. She snubbed the cigarette in a little saucer and went in the kitchen to refill her cup. She looked at her cat and then around the kitchen and suddenly felt tired of the wallpaper and the color of her dishtowels. "I'm in a rut," she whispered to Felix, who hurried to his dish to get a drink of water.

On her back porch, her pansies bobbed up and down with the breeze, and she looked at their happy faces and tried to remember when she first started planting flowers on her porch. When did she start thinking about how her yard looked or whether a late frost would kill the oleanders? When did she become so domestic? She took another cup of coffee to the porch and shielded herself from the cool air with the big chenille bathrobe she inherited from her grandmother. In college, she could barely imagine herself married, much less such a "homebody." She lit another cigarette and struggled to keep the smoke away from her face.

She thought about Tootsie and Tammy, happy in their domestic lives, surrounded by adoring children and devoted husbands. The thought of having children brought a momentary sadness to her mood. She once thought she was pregnant when she was in college, but it turned out to be a false alarm. The incident scared her so badly she stopped dating Ethan and had rarely dated since then. *Should I have married Ethan*, she wondered. *How would my life be different?* She couldn't answer and knew that dwelling on what might have been was a horrendous waste of time.

When she looked down at the cigarette there was an ash nearly an inch long. "Oh crud!" She tapped it lightly and the ashes caught an unseen breeze and swept about the porch and onto her robe. Furiously dusting them off her arms, Doris turned to enter the house. "How do smokers put up with this nonsense?" she muttered to herself, snubbing the cigarette into the saucer.

She assessed herself in her bathroom mirror. The hair was good and she particularly liked her eyes. But the small breasts were still a disappointment, as were the freckles. All in all, however, she was not bad looking for a fifty-year-old spinster. *Possibly it's time to get new glasses,* she thought. *And some new clothes wouldn't hurt either.*

She went to her stereo and shoved past a stack of CD's to the albums lined up behind them. She flipped slowly, looking for the right one. It was an album she probably hadn't listened to in twenty years, but she still knew all the songs by heart. Cat Stevens' voice rang clear and strong, and Doris headed to the kitchen to wash her coffee cup and heat up a muffin.

For the first time in a long time she finished reading the entire newspaper in one sitting. The cigarette was beginning to feel better, but she wondered if she would ever be able to manage a lighted one. Around noon, she got dressed, kissed Felix on the forehead, and headed to the mall. Sunday, all the optical shops were closed. *Better get my eyes checked anyway*, she thought, and made a mental note to set up an appointment. She browsed through some of the big department stores and looked through the racks, pilfering through stacks of Laura Ashley sweaters and holding up pairs of slacks. She was amazed nothing seemed to appeal to her. They were beautiful ensembles, quality clothing, but when she studied them closely Doris thought they suddenly looked too old for her. Had she turned fifty in her thirties?

On her way to find something to drink, she passed a store that sold cell phones. She stared at the logo for a long minute then decided to enter. The sales clerk, Natalie according to her nametag, nearly accosted her and, being polite, Doris said she was just looking around. Natalie shoved her brown hair off her face and curled it behind her ears, then pushed her glasses up her nose. *She looks too young to have a job like this*, Doris thought. "Well, we have some nice smart phones--they do just about everything, you know."

"Do you have any dumb phones?"

Natalie laughed, but Doris' face remained somber. "Oh, you're not kidding, are you? Well, no, uh, we only sell the latest models."

"Do you know where I might be able to find one that is just a phone?"

"I don't think they make those anymore, well, maybe those disposable things."

"Disposable telephones?"

"Yes, you can buy a phone that you just use till it runs out of time then toss it. I really don't know much about those."

"All I want is a phone that I can carry with me for emergencies. I don't want to play games or twit or do Facespace."

Natalie suppressed a giggle. "You mean tweet and Facebook."

"Whatever. You get the basic idea, right?"

"Ok, I could sell you a stripped-down model with a low monthly fee. But there would be a two-year contract," Natalie paused, tucked her lips between her front teeth, and looked around the store. She moved toward one corner and picked up a display model, and Doris followed. "If you've never had a cell phone before, you might want to start out with a pre-paid phone from a store like Kmart. That's what my grandmother did." *Her grandmother*, Doris thought, *how old does this kid think I am?* "She used one of those for about six months, and it helped her figure out what kind of phone she wanted. Please, just don't tell anyone I told you that." She looked nervously around the room again. "If you decide to go with a more permanent phone, one that offers you more features, including service and repair, I hope you'll keep me in mind."

Doris tried to smile, thanked her for the advice, and made a hasty exit.

She strolled down the nearly empty halls of Kerryville Mall, looking in the windows of stores she seldom entered. One store, apparently aimed at a younger market, caught her attention. Did she dare even try anything on? Why not, she said to herself, no one I know will see me. She picked out a cute little leather skirt with a black turtleneck, a pair of white wool slacks, and a black lace teddy.

The salesgirl smiled at her slyly--was she laughing at her or admiring her spunk? *Who the heck cares,* Doris thought, and smiled back. The teddy looked great, a shocking contrast against her alabaster skin. She giggled when she thought about Martin and what he might think of it. The white pants were too small, but she was surprised she liked the skirt and sweater. It reminded her of an outfit she wore to class at Agnes Scott. Could she wear this to teach in? It was so much shorter than the skirts she usually wore. If not to teach in, then where could she wear it? She was never able to answer any of these questions, but she bought the lingerie, skirt, and sweater, anyway. She glanced at her watch. It was nearly suppertime, so she packed her treasures into Carmen's trunk and headed home.

Once home, she opened her packages and grimaced as she studied the leather skirt. "Maybe not," she said, deciding to take it back. But for the other items, she smiled as she removed tags and put them away. As she emerged from her bedroom, Martin suddenly appeared at her door. He entered without knocking or asking permission. "Doris, are you all right? I've tried to call you all day."

"Oh, Martin, I'm sorry. I woke up with a headache and turned the phone off so I could go back to sleep. I'm feeling much better now." It concerned her that she felt the necessity to lie to Martin. *Why did I say that,* she wondered, *he would understand I needed some time alone.*

"Oh, I'm sorry you weren't feeling well, and I barged in like this."

"It's ok, Martin, I'm so sorry I worried you. I am so thoughtless sometimes."

"Have you eaten?"

"No, shall I cook you something?"

"Don't be silly, I'll take you out."

"As long as it's not Le Petit I'm game!" Doris grabbed her sweater from the hall coat tree, and Martin helped her on with it and out the door.

Martin pulled into the parking lot of a nice little seafood place Doris had frequented many times. Once they sat down and ordered, Doris pulled a pack of cigarettes out of her purse.

Martin stopped in mid-sentence and stared at her. "Doris, have you started smoking?"

"Goodness, no," she laughed. "I'm sorry I forgot to tell you—Lenny asked me to handle them as much as possible so I could look like a real smoker in the play."

"Do you have to smoke in the play?" Martin was trying to sound neutral, but Doris could see the strain on his face. The wild flop of hair fell over his eye, and he didn't even notice it.

She touched his arm gently, "I don't know, I hope not. Lenny is going to try to have me handle them some but not actually smoke them."

"Oh," Martin sounded relieved, suddenly noticing the hair and pushing it back. "I, well, you know it's what killed Sarah. Lung cancer."

"Oh, Martin, no, I didn't know." Doris felt horribly insensitive and quickly tucked the cigarettes back into her purse. "I knew she died of cancer several years before I came here, but I didn't realize it was from smoking."

"It's okay, I, well, I wouldn't want you to develop the habit. It's terribly hard to quit, you know, Sarah tried a million times."

"I promise to keep that in mind, Martin. I'm only doing this for the play."

"Okay."

"Look, here comes our wine." Doris was talking to him like a child who didn't get to go to the carnival.

His mood lightened. "I think you'll like this one, Doris."

Doris smiled, grateful Martin was so flexible. The wine was great; the food was divine. Martin may not be a passionate man, but he was certainly sophisticated, brilliant, and generous. Maybe this was enough.

19

Monday night's rehearsal was another all-cast read-through. It was Lenny's last chance to do script work. She told them they would start blocking on Tuesday, which means organizing the physical movements of the actors. "And," she said with a grin, "I was able to find a good copy of the film version of the play. I'm going to watch it Friday night so everyone's welcome to come—bring a friend, bring some food and I'll supply the soft drinks."

Everyone looked around at each other. There was nothing on the rehearsal schedule for Friday so Teri said she already had plans. "My wife's out of town so I'll be there," Bill offered.

"Me, too," Jayson said. "Lenny has the sickest parties. You have to go, Dr. P, uh, Dorie, if you can."

"Sickest? Is that a good thing?" she asked, looking around with her eyebrows scrunched.

"Yes, Dorie," Winnie laughed, "sick is good."

Doris felt all eyes on her. Rehearsing with students was one thing, but going to a party with them was another. She wasn't sure what to do. She knew it would be great to see the film with the other actors and she was curious about Lenny's home. "I'll have to check on something," she said, "but it sounds like fun." Everyone seemed content with her answer.

Lenny gave them each an assignment for the read-through. She told Bill to over-emphasize the word "Martha" every time he said it. Jayson and Doris were supposed to do the same with "I" and Teri had to emphasize any reference to another person. Doris wasn't clear about why Lenny wanted them to do this, but as they read the play in this unnatural way, it helped her see how self-absorbed Martha is and how focused George is on her. *Interesting exercise*, she thought, *it wouldn't be a bad idea to do in real life.*

During the break, Jayson and Doris met at the drink machine again.

"Do you think you can go to the party?" he asked Doris, who was trying to pull a bottle of water from the mouth of the machine.

"Darn, the bottle is stuck!" She was pretending to be preoccupied with her beverage. Jayson stepped in and put his hand on the theft-proof flap, lifting it so Doris could pull the water free. "Thanks," she smiled at him.

"This machine does that all the time." Jayson stood with his hands in his pockets while Doris opened the water and took a gulp. "Plus, it's hard to do with a stupid cigarette in your hand, isn't it?" Doris smiled and nodded, and then headed back down the hall. Jayson turned slowly to walk with her. "So, do you think you'll be able to come Friday night?"

"I don't know. Are you bringing Kayla? I'm only asking because I'm trying to decide if I should ask Martin."

"Martin? Oh, Dr. Winborn? I didn't know you two were hooking up." Jayson was smiling, being friendly Doris realized, but in her opinion too invasive. Of course, she realized, she was the one who mentioned his name.

"I'm not even sure I know what hooking up means, but we're good friends, and we planned to do something that night. So, I'll check with him."

"I never invite Kayla to cast parties. I tell her it's restricted to people working on the show."

"Don't you want her there? Isn't she your girlfriend?"

"Well, I'm not sure how long that will be the case, anyway. She is so damn jealous. If I joke with Winnie or Teri, she's all over my case."

"I knew someone like that once, so I know what you mean. Do you think you should be dishonest with her, though? I'm sorry, Jayson, that's none of my business."

"No worries, Dr. P., I don't mind. And no, I don't think it's good to be dishonest, but she makes it real hard to be honest." Jayson shuffled his feet and looked away. "I guess it's time to break up. It's . . .well, we've been together for so long, I don't want to hurt her."

They stopped outside Room 106. Jayson leaned against the wall and Doris stood in front of him, sipping her water. "Well, Jayson, you have to do what's right for you. If you don't love her, then it's unfair to lead her on. It may hurt at first, but letting her go on to someone else may be best for her." He was looking down at his feet, nodding and sighing. "Of course, if you do love her, you can work it out so you can be honest with her."

"You're right, Dorie. I need to do some thinking about it." Doris looked at him, her face full of concern and, she was surprised to discover, genuine caring.

They noticed Lenny and the group returning to the circle and picking up their scripts. "We better go back in," Doris said. "Are you all right?" Jayson smiled and nodded. She patted his shoulder—like a pal, a sister, maybe a mother, no, an aunt? It felt unfamiliar to Doris at first, but it felt right.

Fortunately, the first blocking rehearsal was for Doris and Bill the next evening. Doris kept thinking about Jayson and his perfect white teeth, his sweet smile, his musky aroma. Not English Leather or British Sterling--something new with a fresh bouquet, but very masculine. *Focus, focus* she scolded herself. An actor cannot afford to be preoccupied at rehearsal. One former director told Doris to pack up whatever was on her mind, put it in a little suitcase, and leave it by the door. He assured her it would be there when she left—and it always was. It was good therapy for Doris in general. Letting things go for a few hours usually served to give her a clearer perspective which led to fewer impulsive actions. She started packing her bag as she locked Carmen's doors and headed toward the rehearsal studio.

People who have never done theatre probably have no idea how long it takes to block a few pages of script, Doris thought.

Lenny clapped her hands and ask them to get ready. They discussed the floorplan while Stacey, the stage manager, arranged some chairs and old tables to represent George and Martha's living room. Winnie brought in some "shadow props," items to be used as props during rehearsals until the real ones could be found.

Doris and Bill tried several patterns, moving around during the opening scene. Lenny explained to them how important these first few minutes are in establishing the characters and their relationship. Doris chose to wear a skirt and heels since Martha has been to a party before her first entrance, and she felt it would get her used to working in them. Bill wore his traditional rehearsal blue jeans and sweatshirt, but he did carry a pipe around and chewed on it through most of the scene. Lenny explained they would be working on the script slowly, doing what they could handle at one time. She liked building the production organically this way throughout rehearsals.

Lenny shaped the scene and set the blocking while the stage manager, Stacey, recorded it in the promptbook. After they ran it a few times Doris knew her lines. The next rehearsal would add Nick and Honey to the mix.

Wednesday morning, Doris slept later than normal. Evening rehearsals were beginning to take their toll on her routines. She caught a glimpse of her clock and realized she was running late--very late. She started to rush around, skipping steps in her ritual to get out of the house on time. Then she looked at Felix relaxing on his hammock, bathing his ear with his right paw. *Why am I hurrying to a class no one wants to take?* She stopped in the middle of her kitchen for a long minute.

Doris picked up the phone from the wall and punched in the number of the department secretary, Vivian. She suddenly hung up, realizing she needed to have a cigarette in her hand. She rushed to her purse, grabbed one, and then punched in the whole number again.

"Department of Fine Arts," Vivian's voice sounded like the low growl of a rabid dog.

"Yes, hello, Vivian, this is Dr. Peechum. I need a favor."

"Yes, Dr. Peechum, what can I do for you?" Vivian's tone picked up some, but the growl was still there.

"I am not feeling well this morning, I think it's a migraine, but I need to cancel my morning classes."

"Well, I'm sorry to hear it, Dr. Peechum. I'll put a sign on the classroom door."

"Great, Vivian. Add a note stating we still have the midterm on Friday--they can email me with questions. I'll let you know by noon if I need to cancel my afternoon class. If you don't hear from me, don't worry about it."

"Sure thing. Hope you get to feeling better."

Doris hesitated for a moment; she never once played hooky, not in her entire life. Maybe it was time. She swallowed an overwhelming wave of guilt, and her breath caught in her chest. *I have taken off several classes already this semester*, she thought, and *I'll have to cancel one day for the conference.*

"Dr. Peechum? Are you all right?" Vivian broke her concentration, and she blurted out she would come in later if she possibly could and then hung up.

Doris turned around, wondering what she would do with her free morning. A "lagniappe" morning, as they would say in Louisiana. The word lagniappe means a little extra--an unexpected find. This was her lagniappe time.

She looked around her house. First, she called her optometrist to see if she could get an appointment, and by some stroke of luck she had an opening at 10:30. *Now what?* Glasses! She visited several optical shops looking for a smart new pair of frames she could order when she got her prescription. She finally picked out a pair of modern, small and square-shaped glasses to replace the large gold metal pair she had worn for the past five years. The rims were blue plastic, flecked with silver. Doris would normally never buy colorful glasses; she usually bought something sensible, such as metal, brown, or gray. But something unfamiliar seized her as she studied her reflection. The blue set off her green eyes nicely, and she suddenly didn't care if they matched everything she wore. She asked them to hold the frames until the doctor called in the prescription. Although she was hoping to pick them up in the afternoon, they told her she'd have to return in two days to get them. *What a shame,* she thought, *suddenly I can't stand the thought of wearing these old glasses for one more minute.* For the sake of innocent pedestrians, however, she made the sacrifice.

The eye doctor, Margery Brown, asked her if she was having any problems. Doris explained that she was having some trouble reading up close, which had never been a problem for her before. "Well, yes, Doris, as we get older the eyes actually change shape. Even though you're still nearsighted, you may discover you can now see distances better without your glasses than you did before and the close-up reading you're used to doing without glasses is getting harder."

Doris scrunched her nose and eyebrows in a worried frown. Dr. Brown patted her hand gently. "Don't worry, Doris, it's natural for someone your age."

Someone my age, Doris repeated in her mind.

". . . and easy to fix. Doris, I think you will probably be happier with bifocals."

"Bifocals?" The color drained from her face and she felt a little weak. "The thick glasses that have lines across them, like my mother wore?"

"Things have come a long way since your mother started wearing her bifocals. They call them "progressive" lenses. The distance vision is still in the top half of the lens and the reading portion is at the bottom, but there's no line. People don't even know you're wearing anything but regular glasses. See? I'm wearing them now."

Doris had to admit she couldn't tell, but bifocals? *Holy Moses, does everyone fall apart when they hit fifty?*

"You might have to give yourself a little time to adjust to them, but once you get used to them, you'll wonder how you ever survived without them—like a cell phone!" Dr. Brown gave her best "atta-girl" smile. Doris' face remained frozen in a resigned expression.

"Can you fax the prescription to the eyeglass place?"

"Of course, we do it all the time." The doctor sat still for a moment. "I'm glad to say your eyes are extremely healthy, and unless you have a problem, you don't need to come back for two or three years."

Doris nodded and the doctor left. The nurse came back in and handed her a paper. "You take this to check-out and you're all done. Do you have sunglasses with you? Your eyes are dilated so you can pick up a pair of disposable ones at the check-out if you need them." Doris nodded, took the paper, and followed the signs to the check-out.

She felt guilty already for taking the morning off, but at least she had gone to the doctor and not flittered the morning away. She looked at her watch and realized she had plenty of time to make it to her Art History class, especially since all she had to do was give them their midterm exam. She stopped by a fast food restaurant and gobbled down a burrito on her way to school.

After class, she started home but then decided to buy groceries for the seven-layer dip she intended to take to Lenny's party. She went to a large discount store, and as she was checking out she noticed a rack of prepaid cell phones. *Why not*, she thought, so she picked up two of them and tossed them on the counter.

At rehearsal, Lenny wanted to block Nick and Honey's entrance up to where the women leave the room. "After we block that part, we'll go back and run it with what we did last night. Seeing where we've been will help us understand where we have to go." Everyone nodded, so she suggested they start at the beginning of the scene and walk and talk through a couple of pages. Once they got started they all began to feel the rhythm of the writing. Doris marveled at Albee's mastery of natural dialogue.

Lenny stopped them before they got to the part where Martha and Honey leave the room. "Great work," Lenny told them. "Let's run it now starting at the top of the play. I'll work with Nick and George tomorrow, so ladies that will give you a bonus night off." Teri and Doris smiled at each other. Handling scripts and props and trying to remember blocking made the run clumsy, but Lenny seemed content so no one argued.

Once they hit the cool night air, everyone walked briskly to their cars waving goodnights to each other. Doris had parked in the direction Jayson had to walk toward the dorms. *On purpose, she wondered? No, I drove around the circle twice looking for a place*, she told herself. As they walked toward Doris' car, she mused about Martha's next costume. "So, while the men are chatting, Martha is upstairs 'changing.' I can imagine what kind of costume I will get stuck wearing!"

"Umm, well, Ms. Tandberg is a good costumer, so I'm sure it'll be right for the character." Doris smiled and nodded. "You may hate it, but Martha will rock it!" Jayson flashed those magnificent blue eyes, and Doris laughed.

"Rocket? Like a spaceship?"

"No," he couldn't help but laugh. "Rock, like rock 'n roll. It's an expression; it means she will . . . wear it with style."

"Oh," she said, feeling ignorant, "Well, I guess I got myself into this, didn't I? Somehow, I didn't consider all these things when I came to auditions. I feel like I'm too old for this."

Jayson looked genuinely stunned. "You *are* kidding, aren't you?" Doris stared at him. "Everyone knows you're the coolest teacher on campus."

This came as such a surprise to Doris she was sure Jayson was pulling her leg. "Right, Jayson, I wasn't born yesterday, either." As soon as she said it she was sorry, Jayson looked offended, perhaps, hurt at her sarcasm. "I mean, you're kind to even suggest it, but somehow, I have a hard time believing anyone your age would find me anything but dull."

"I don't think you're dull at all, Dorie." Jayson opened the door and started to head out. His tone was so serious Doris couldn't think of anything to say. "I think you're cool. See ya' Friday, then." Before she could comprehend his words, he was gone—sprinting across the street into the campus mist.

20

Classes on Thursday went well. Doris had arranged to meet Martin at Foster's for lunch. After they placed their orders and found a table, Doris pulled the phones out of her bag. "I bought these the other day for us. I haven't even taken them out of the package, but I think it's high time we start using them."

Martin looked skeptically at the phones. "Oh, Doris, I can't think of anything worse than having a cell phone!"

"Well, I can think of lots of worse things, but I think I know what you mean. I never wanted one either, but now I find that I want to try one. Did you know you can buy disposable phones?"

"No, but I'm not at all surprised. There isn't much in today's world that's not disposable."

"We're going to give them a try."

"Oh. Well, okay. Maybe you're right. I'll make the effort."

As they munched on salad greens and croutons, Doris and Martin tried to figure out the new phones. Doris had picked out the simplest model she could find—a flip open phone with just calling and texting capabilities. They read the instructions and thought they understood what to do. "So, we just need to charge them overnight and we're good to go, right?" Doris said optimistically. Martin gave her an uncertain look.

"Martin, I know I had to cancel on you for tomorrow night. I just found out last night that Teri and I don't have to be there tonight." She saw hope on his face. "But I really need some down time to get work and grading done. I hope you understand. We'll spend time together over the weekend, ok?" He nodded and kept eating.

Friday morning, Doris was surprised to see Jayson in class early. He was chatting with a neighboring classmate when she walked in, as she typically did, exactly five minutes before the beginning of class. She liked to have some time to arrange the room to her liking, get her notes in order, and have a moment of quiet before starting. It rarely happened, however, because she was usually accosted by students looking for answers to questions that should be handled during office hours. *It's this "on demand" society we have today,* Doris ruminated, *everybody has to have everything right now—whenever they want it—whether it inconveniences someone else or not.*

Jayson looked up, smiled, and raised his palm slightly to acknowledge her. She nodded and erased the board and scooted the lectern back to its proper place. It didn't matter where the lectern was because she would be sitting at her desk while they took their midterm exam. Still, Doris liked things in their proper places.

Jayson finished his exam in a reasonable amount of time, turned it in, and left. Near the end of the hour, Doris had two students remaining who seemed to be completely clueless about the whole exam. Pages fluttered back and forth, fists rapped on desks, and nearly inaudible sighs occasionally escaped from the boy. At five minutes past the end of class, Doris stood to signal time was up. "I'm sorry, but we have to clear the classroom for others waiting in the hall," she said as sympathetically as possible. The girl rolled her eyes. "Do either of you think more time would help you?" They looked at her blankly, as if lost in some enormous eddy of swirling water. The boy finally spoke up, "I guess not, Dr. P. Thanks anyway." He gathered up his papers and headed toward the front. The girl gave up also and turned in her paper on the way out. She didn't speak.

"Oh, dear," Doris kept saying to herself as she graded the exams during her office hours. "Don't they know they have to study for an exam--learning doesn't happen by osmosis?" After all these years of grading exams, she still marveled over the ones who waste their time in college. Some students, admittedly, try hard and study all the time to pull a C. She respected those students. But the ones who were capable of better grades but did just enough to get by infuriated Doris. "I could shake Rosemary Connors," she mumbled. "I know she can do much better than this."

"Talking to yourself again, Doris?"

Doris jumped and put her hand to her heart. Martin's head was peeking through the small opening in her office door with the unruly strand of hair hanging over his nose. "Martin! You gave me a start. Is it eleven thirty already?"

"Do you have time for lunch today?" he asked, wiping his hair back and catching a book that threatened to fall from the stack he was carrying.

"Oh, gosh, well, yes," Doris stammered in confusion. "I want to have lunch with you since I had to cancel on you tonight." Martin's shoulder pushed the door open farther for her. "Come on," she said, grabbing her sweater.

After lunch, Doris held her afternoon Art History class, giving back a stack of graded midterms. These were mostly students majoring or minoring in art, so the exams were quite good, and she commended them. After class, she tidied up her office, gathered materials she would need at home over the weekend, and took off to run errands. She needed to pick up her new glasses, take clothes to the dry cleaners, and drive by the cemetery to check on Avis' grave marker.

It was Doris' first visit to the cemetery since the funeral, and she felt uneasy. The office was located near her parents' graves, so she parked in front of the small building. The attendant told her the marker had been engraved with the date and was back in place. Doris thanked her and walked the fifty yards or so to check it out. Although her mother's name had been on the marker for several years, this was the first time she really noticed it. When she came here before with Avis to put flowers on her father's grave, Doris usually focused on his side. Now they were both there, lying side by side as they did every night for over fifty years of marriage. Doris stood staring at the graves, unable to move or speak. Another car pulled up and stopped nearby, and she heard distant conversations that brought her out of her stupor. She took a deep breath and started walking back to her car. The other car pulled away, and she began to sob. She couldn't tell you how long she sat in her car and cried, but when she finally drove away, she felt completely spent.

She stopped to pick up her new glasses. On her drive home, she kept looking at herself in the rearview mirror to decide if she liked her new look. She had to move her head up and down, trying to find the sweet spot to see close and then distant. She decided she liked the look, but now her hair needed something. Before she could decide exactly what it was, she pulled into her driveway.

She busily prepared the dip for the party or rehearsal or whatever it was. She had purchased some tortilla chips and a few liters of her favorite soft drink, as well. Felix rubbed around her ankles, nudging his head into her sock feet. "You already stole my slippers; you want my socks too?" She laughed and picked him up. She cradled him in her arms like a baby, gently rubbing his chin and rocking him slowly around the kitchen. The glasses infuriated her, as she tried to adjust which part of the lens to look through.

"How's mama's baby?" Doris made baby talk in a high-pitched voice Felix responded to with a slow blink. When Doris returned the favor, he climbed onto her shoulder and nuzzled his nose into her hair. "I haven't been at home much, huh, baby!"

She carried the cat into her bedroom and placed him gingerly on his blankie, next to her slipper, and then started running a hot bath. She lay in the bathtub for a good while, relaxing and coming to terms with lying to Martin. He was so disappointed, but she couldn't tell him the whole truth. Doris told him Lenny called an extra rehearsal to watch the video together and discuss the characters. She didn't mention the "rehearsal" was at Lenny's house or she was taking party food. She wasn't sure why she didn't want Martin there, but she knew she didn't. Perhaps she wanted this to herself, or he might do too much talking, or it would be too much like a date and not enough about the play. Whatever it was, she still felt guilty. Even though she promised to make it up to him by cooking a special dinner the next evening and treating him to a rented movie at home.

After her bath, Doris pulled out a cigarette to practice holding it. She dressed in a casual pair of khaki slacks; she didn't own a pair of jeans. She kissed Felix's sleepy head, gathered up her food basket, and a lightweight jacket, breaking the cigarette. "Oh shoot!" she mumbled and scraped the tobacco into her hand. New glasses, new phone, new cigarettes—maybe it was too much all at once. She decided to wait until she got in the car to try another one. The television meteorologist predicted temperatures in the thirties so she thought she might feel a slight chill. She put on her jacket, picked up her basket and purse, and took off. She managed to lock the door and pack everything into Carmen's passenger seat. As Doris walked around the car a raindrop hit her new glasses. First one, then another, then it turned into a fine drizzle. "Oh, shoot!" she moaned as she folded herself into the driver's seat. "Maybe it won't last long," she said hopefully. She turned the key in Carmen's ignition, but nothing happened. "What the . . ." Doris tried again, but the car was dead as four o'clock. "Great!" she said angrily, "Now what?"

She stewed for a moment trying to decide what to do. The sky turned suddenly darker and Doris noticed the dome light barely glowing. "Did I leave it on? When would I have done that?" She prowled through her memories of the day and remembered she turned it on at the cemetery so she could read the receipt for the marker engraving. Then she got out of the car, visited the graves and drove home in bright sunshine. "Stupid!" she scolded herself. "Well, nothing else to do."

Doris pulled herself out of the little car, blinking in the rain, which was getting harder and colder, feeling like little pins falling from the sky. Mumbling to herself about her own stupidity, she gathered up her food basket and purse and scurried back into the house. She took her script from her purse and looked at the folded list of rehearsals and cast phone numbers Lenny gave them. Wiping rain from her face with a dishtowel, she punched Lenny's number into the dimly lit keypad and waited through four rings. Lenny finally answered, laughing.

"Lenny, this is Doris."

"Doris, hi, where are you?"

"Well, I'm still at home. I was all ready to come and my car won't start. I think the battery's dead. I'm sorry I won't be able to make it."

"Oh, don't be silly, Doris! You're not far away. One of us will come get you, wait there!"

"No, Lenny, I don't want to put anyone to any troub--" Doris stopped short, realizing Lenny had already hung up. She put the phone back in its cradle and caught a glimpse of herself in the hall mirror. "Oh, dear, I better do something about this!"

She rushed to change into dry clothes, another pair of khakis with her new sweater. She repaired her make-up and blow-dried her hair. This time she pulled her long raincoat with the hood from the closet and grabbed a good umbrella. She patted Felix's head, which he didn't even acknowledge, and then gathered up her purse, script, and food and stood waiting on the porch. By now the sky was a darkening twilight, and the rain slacked into a steady downpour, which convinced Doris to go back inside and change into boots; she hated wet feet. When she emerged again, Jayson was bounding up her front steps. "Hey, Dorie! My car is a mess, but it will get us there—you ready?"

"Hi Jayson. How'd you know where I live?"

"Lenny had your address from the audition form. It's a beautiful house."

"Thank you. Lenny hung up before I could give her directions so I wasn't sure anyone would find me!"

"Lenny always has the bases covered!"

"I really appreciate this, Jayson."

"No trouble at all."

Doris nodded, and Jayson grabbed the food basket. He tucked it neatly into the back seat between a pair of sneakers and a large textbook.

Jayson was wearing a high school letter jacket, which made him look much younger than his twenty-one years. Rain dotted his face and the wool on his coat. His skin seemed flawless and smooth, and she noticed, for the first time, he had one dimple on his left cheek. Doris experienced one of those moments when you study someone for a moment, but it feels like an eternity. She wasn't sure why, but she knew she would remember this moment, the cool damp air of early October, and the way Jayson looked in the fading sunlight, for as long as she lived. It was like capturing the perfect picture of someone in her mind exactly the way they are in that moment, and she knew she would recall that perfect image many times in the future.

Jayson's car was an old Honda Civic, red with black interior. Fast food cups and bags littered the tiny back seat and schoolbooks were strewn along the back window and protruded from an open book bag that sat on the floor behind the driver's seat. She noticed his Art Appreciation textbook lay on top of an old army blanket. The car smelled like Jayson's cologne—musky but floral. She decided she liked Jayson's cologne better than Martin's and made a mental note to get some for Martin for Christmas.

"Let me know if I freeze you out—Rhonda does have a heater; I don't usually turn it on."

"Rhonda?"

"Rhonda the Honda!" Jayson said, laughing. "I always name my cars."

"Me too," said Doris.

He flashed his winning smile, dimple and all. "No, wait, you like it cold, too, right?"

"Right," Doris nodded, "not wet though—I hate being wet."

"Oh. Well." Jayson shrugged. "Nothing I can do about the rain." This made Doris laugh a little and relax. She wondered if it was against school policy to be riding in a student's car. Jayson turned on the engine, put

Rhonda in reverse, and then stopped suddenly to stare at Doris. She looked back, frightened slightly by the attention. Finally, he burst out, "New glasses! That's what it is!"

"Oh, yes," Doris smiled with relief. "I thought for a moment there was spinach on my teeth or something."

"Sorry! I noticed something different as soon as I saw you, but couldn't put my finger on it. I like them—very fashionable!" Doris blushed a little; she felt a little embarrassed, like a schoolgirl, when people gave her compliments on her looks.

"Thanks," she finally managed to say. "I was so tired of the other ones. I'm having a little trouble getting used to them, so if I bump into anything just steer me away!" They both gave a half-hearted laugh. She had no intention whatsoever of telling him she was now wearing bifocals. Jayson backed the car into the street and headed toward Lenny's house. Doris pulled out a cigarette to hold in the car.

"It's a bitch, isn't it," Jayson said. The term bitch startled Doris a little and she turned to stare at him. She didn't know what he was talking about. "The cigarettes, you know, they're hard to get used to."

"Oh, yes, I hate them." Doris relaxed again. "I can't imagine why anyone wants to pick up a habit this annoying, smelly, and dirty!"

"Lenny made me do the exercise when I played Brick in *Cat on a Hot Tin Roof*. The first time I lit up I nearly choked to death."

"That happened to me, too." They both laughed. "I haven't tried it since."

"Lenny taught me how to inhale. You wouldn't think you'd need lessons for smoking, but well, it helped a lot."

"I'll ask her, then." Doris looked down at the cigarette, which was laying on her knee. She would have set herself on fire if it had been lit. She rolled her eyes and looked out the side window. "Is everyone else already at Lenny's?"

"Everyone except Teri, she had other plans already, remember?" Jayson was driving sensibly. Doris wondered if it was for her benefit. "What do you have in the food basket—it was pretty heavy!"

"Oh, I'm sorry, I could have carried it."

"No, Dorie, I'm kidding. I was wondering if you brought enough to feed an army." Doris felt stupid; of course it was a joke. She sat silently for a full minute. "Well? What did you bring?"

"Sorry, I zoned out there. Uh, I made a Tex-Mex bean dip. It's layered with refried beans, tomatoes, cheese, sour cream, guacamole, crushed chips, and black olives. There are some extra chips in there, too, and diet Dr. Pepper."

"Oh, man I dig Dr. Pepper. I take it to every party because no one ever has it."

"Me too! I will drink other soft drinks, but I have a real addiction for D. P." Doris was loosening up. *Even if this is against school policy, who's going to know,* she thought to herself.

"I like Tex-Mex a lot, too, so I will look forward to tasting the dip. Oh, well, here we are already!" Jayson pulled his car into the driveway behind Bill's red Dodge. Lenny's house was more like a bungalow. A low-slung roof dipped over the front entrance, and the sidewalk was flanked by lush Mondo grass. The yard was small but well-maintained, with dormant azalea bushes flanking the entrance and a large river birch tree at one end. Lenny came to the door when they pulled up and stepped out onto her small porch. A medium size dog who looked like a cocker spaniel bounded down the sidewalk and jumped all over Jayson's legs. His arms were full with the basket, though, so Doris bent over to pet him.

"Sorry about Sophocles, she is enthusiastic about guests. Sophie, get down! Come here!" Lenny snapped her fingers, but the dog ignored her.

"She's fine, Lenny, I love animals." Doris said as she struggled to walk on the sidewalk with Sophie at her feet. She suddenly noticed it wasn't raining anymore and Lenny's sidewalk was nearly dry. *How long were we in the car,* she wondered.

Lenny took the food basket and made hungry sounds as she added Doris's dip and chips to the odd assortment of snacks already on her dining room table. There were Oreo cookies, a loaf of homemade bread, a large bowl of potato chips, and little wieners simmering in barbeque sauce in a crock-pot. "You're doing well with the cigarette, Doris. Oh, don't tell me we have another Dr. Pepper freak!" Lenny laughed as she pulled the two-liter bottle out of the basket. "Jayson, I think you have a soul mate!" Jayson laughed and then glanced at Doris. She smiled and nodded.

Lenny introduced Doris to a small woman with dirty blonde hair cut short, one side shaved closed to her head, and several rings in her right ear. "This is my partner, Charley, short for Charlotte. Charley, this is Doris. She teaches art at the college, and she's playing Martha."

Charley looked rough around the edges, in faded jeans, Birkenstock sandals, and a flannel shirt. *Partners? Like in business*, Doris wondered. Charley offered her hand to shake. "Oh yes, Lenny has spoken of you often. I'm so glad to meet you but want to say I was sorry to hear about your mother. I lost my mother a few years ago, so I can relate to what you're going through." She may look a bit rough, but she had a lovely speaking voice and impeccable manners.

"Thanks," Doris said and then became silent, not being able to think of anything else to say.

"Okay, everybody, get some food and something to drink while I cue up the DVD." Lenny turned on the TV and DVD player and popped in the movie. She adjusted the lighting and the volume and then cuddled up on the sofa with Charley. Doris knew immediately Jayson and Lenny were not having an affair as well as what kind of partnership Lenny had been referred to. Doris tried not to stare at them, but she was intrigued. She harbored no ill feelings against homosexuals, but she never had the opportunity to know many. She knew a dear male friend in New Orleans, a fellow graduate student, who helped her study for exams and encouraged her to join him for partying in the French Quarter a few times. Doris, however, never felt liberated enough to go to a gay bar. But she really liked him, and they stayed in touch by mail for many years after school. He died of AIDS right after Doris moved back to Kerryville, and because of her teaching schedule she was unable to attend his funeral. She has regretted it ever since.

Lenny looks so happy, so content with herself. Doris wondered whether she would be so open in front of other faculty, not to mention the students. You never know who will be on your tenure committee or what actually happens in the faculty board meetings. Doris didn't intend to ever reveal Lenny's living situation to anyone, of course, but she doubted if she, herself, would be as trusting.

Doris realized she didn't eat supper and was getting hungry. She took a little bit of everything on a small plate and sat on the floor next to Bill. She leaned up against the sofa, next to Lenny's legs. The dog sat on the sofa behind her, and Winnie and Stacey shared a big Papasan chair. Being so casual with anyone from school felt weird to Doris, but she liked the feeling. *I need to get used to it,* she told herself.

Lenny stopped the movie occasionally to ask a question or probe a discussion. Doris was glad she didn't invite Martin. No one, other than Lenny, had their significant other with them. Charley sat quietly through everything, but she was probably accustomed to this kind of gathering. Martin might think it was his place to answer the questions. This was all complicated enough for Doris right now—it was better to keep everything separate. At least, that's what she told herself. After the movie, everyone gathered up the dishes, and Doris noticed the dip had been a big success. "Not much left there, huh, Dorie?" Jayson nudged her with his elbow.

"Yes, I wonder who ate all this," she glared at him in jest. She knew he visited the table several times to refill on dip and Dr. Pepper. "Hmmm, no D.P. left, either. How could that have happened?" Jayson looked up at the ceiling and started to whistle. Doris laughed. "Lenny, do you mind if I wash out this dish before I go?"

"No, Doris, you may not wash out your dish!" Doris stared at Lenny for a moment with her mouth open. "Oh, god, I'm kidding! Of course you can wash out your dish!"

Charley stood up and picked up a few plates and glasses to carry them to the kitchen. "You'll have to excuse Lenny, Doris, she must have been raised in a bar." Doris laughed. "Here's the soap, scrape the leftovers into the sink—we have a garbage disposal."

"Thanks, Charley." Doris washed out her pan and started drying it with the clean dishtowel Charley laid out for her. "So, what do you do—where do you work?"

"Mostly at nursing homes, I'm a geriatric physician. I'm also on the staff of all the area hospitals, though."

"Oh, my, it must be interesting. There aren't many people who want to go into the field."

"Well, it's sad, you know. I lose most of my patients, because of age. But helping them feel better gives me a lot of satisfaction."

"How wonderful. I doubt if I would have the strength to do it." Doris finished drying the pan and started to gather up her coat and purse.

"Don't forget your basket," Lenny said, coming up behind Charley.

"I'm so glad to have met you, Doris," Charley said and extended her hand again. Doris took it and looked at Lenny.

"Thanks, me too. You have a great house."

"Well, you will have to come back!" Lenny said and ushered Doris to the door where Jayson was waiting. "Jayson, drive carefully. It's late on a weekend night and streets are wet."

"Yes, mother!" Jayson said, hugging Lenny tightly. "Bye, Charley!"

The rain returned but was only a sprinkle. Doris put up her umbrella for herself and Jayson. He held the door for her and then packed her basket into the back seat. "Well, that was fun," Doris said as Jayson got in and started the car.

"Lenny is so awesome. She usually has the cast over several times during rehearsals. And then she also has everyone over for the final cast and crew party. We've become great friends."

"Well, I noticed it the first night of rehearsal. I think it's wonderful you have such a close mentoring relationship with your major professor." Doris was sincere. She thought her student relationships were close, but she never hugged any of them. She gave nice dinner parties for her seniors and helped celebrate special events like engagements or special awards, but she knew now she was missing out on something special. *Of course, it's never too late to start,* she thought.

They were both lost in thought and drove most of the way home in silence. When they pulled into Doris' driveway, the rain became a bit heavier. Jayson offered to help her get the basket into the house. He escorted her under the umbrella and showed her to the door. "Why don't you come in for a warm drink. I have some zinger tea," Doris offered. She could see Jayson was uncertain but willing to try.

"Who is this big guy?" Jayson called from the foyer. Felix jumped down from his hammock in the window to check out the new visitor. "Hey, buddy, how you doin'?" Felix appreciated anyone who would come down for a closer view. He rubbed back and forth against Jayson's hands.

Doris pulled zinger tea and hot chocolate from the cupboard and poured water into the cat teakettle Avis gave her last Christmas. "You mean Felix? He must approve all visitors. Hang your jacket on the hall tree and make yourself comfortable in the living room." Jayson stood up and did as he was told. "I forgot, do you take cream in your tea? Or would you prefer hot chocolate? I'm having that."

"No thanks, hot tea with a little sugar." Jayson put his hands in his pockets and strolled around the room looking at Doris' books on the shelf and her original prints on the walls--the inner sanctum of Dr. Peechum. When she entered with a mug of chocolate and the tea for Jayson, he was staring out the back door onto her screened porch. "Sweet! You must enjoy this when the weather's warm," he said.

"I stay out there as much as possible. And Felix sits on the ledge there and watches the birds in the trees."

"Do you ever let him into the yard?" They stood side by side looking through their reflections to the porch beyond the French doors.

"Well, there's no fence. I'm afraid he would stray away. . ." Doris dropped her gaze toward her cocoa, "I don't think I could stand to lose Felix."

Jayson smiled. "I understand, but . . ." he hesitated and then closed his mouth.

"What?" Doris challenged.

"No, it's not important. He's your cat; you know what you're doing."

"Tell me, Jayson." Doris turned to face him.

Jayson sighed as if he wished he hadn't started this. "Well, I can't imagine not being free. You know, having the chance to run in the yard and chase those birds instead of dreaming about it. That's all."

Doris looked at Felix sadly. "Yes, you might be right. I'll think about it."

"God, I'm sorry! I didn't mean to be such a downer. Can we just sit and talk?"

"Certainly," Doris said. Jayson took the corner of the sofa and Doris sat near him in the chair. "So, had you seen the film before?"

"No, I didn't even know it existed—isn't that awful? But it was great. I liked the guy who did George—what a great voice!"

"Yes, Richard Burton, one of my favorites."

"Are any of them still alive?" Jayson's face was curious and innocent. Doris felt a deep pain somewhere in her middle.

"Sadly, I think only George Segal is still around--the one who played Nick." She sipped her cocoa, playing with the little marshmallows on top with her finger. Felix jumped up on Jayson's lap and nudged his hand for petting. "Well, you definitely met with Felix's approval," Doris said and laughed. Jayson stroked the cat's head and took a final gulp of his tea.

"Well, I guess I better head off, it's getting late." Jayson gently placed Felix beside him on the sofa and stood to stretch. "Thanks for the tea, it hit the spot. I think I'm out in the dorm, and I like to have a cup before bed."

Doris headed to the kitchen. "Here, take the rest of this box, I have another one in the cupboard."

"No, Dr. P," Doris gave him a shocked look, "I mean Dorie. I can stop at the store on the way home."

"Nonsense! It's rainy and late at night, and I want to pay you back in some way for giving me a ride to Lenny's." She paused and they stared at each other. "Please." Doris thrust the box toward Jayson, and he reluctantly took it.

"Okay, if you're sure. Thanks." He headed to the hall tree to get his coat and turned to see Doris picking up Felix and rocking him like a baby. "Will you need some help getting your car up and going tomorrow? I'd be glad to come by and give you a jump."

"I don't think so, but thanks. I'll call you if I do." Jayson walked under the dim porch light, turned to wave, and Doris nodded. He curled the collar of his jacket around his ears and walked briskly to his car. Doris stood in the door, watching him. As he pulled out of the driveway, he flashed his headlights. Doris waved and closed the door. As his taillights disappeared into the foggy dampness of the October night, she flicked off the porch light and headed for bed. She didn't see the other car parked in the shadows of the huge oak across the street. Once Doris had gone inside, the car moved slowly into the moonlight toward the stop sign at the end of Doris' street, then the headlights came on, and the car sped away.

21

Saturday morning came streaming into Doris' window in bright golden tones, lighting up the beige walls and lace curtains of her bedroom. She groaned and turned over, pulling the covers over her face. Felix sat patiently on the pillow next to her head, purring loudly, but otherwise, making no movements or sounds. Outside the sun was shining so brightly the remaining moisture from the rain was evaporating quickly, creating a cushion of warmth between the still air and the slight breeze stirring the trees. Doris caressed Felix's head and then flung the covers aside to get up. She splashed cold water on her face, wrapped herself in her favorite bathrobe, and padded in sock feet to the front porch to get her paper. She checked to make sure the floor was dry and then looked around the neighborhood to make sure no one would see her in her robe. She rushed out the door and as she picked up the paper, she heard a familiar voice. "Hi Doris."

She turned sharply to see Martin rocking in her swing. How had she not seen him? "Oh, god, Martin, go away! I don't want you to see me looking like this!" Martin laughed and started toward her.

"You look beautiful, Doris." She escaped into the house and was running to the bathroom to repair her face. "Doris, stop! You look fine to me."

"Well not to me!" She disappeared behind the door and Martin was forced to take a seat in the living room and wait.

"Would you like some coffee?" he yelled to the door.

"Yes, that would be nice, thank you." Doris' muffled voice answered back. Martin, up and dressed since dawn, patted Felix's head and shuffled to the kitchen to make coffee. He pushed the unruly strand of hair back into place as he passed the hall tree and noticed a book laying on the floor. It was a script for *Who's Afraid of Virginia Woolf?* which he assumed was Doris'. He began to flip through it and noticed the lines highlighted were

Nick's, not Martha's. He screwed his eyebrows toward his nose and tossed it onto the seat of the hall tree. By the time he had fixed the coffee and set the mugs on the counter, Doris emerged from her bedroom dressed, made-up, and composed.

"You always look great to me, honey, but I kind of liked the real Doris better. You looked so cuddly." Doris gave him a look and took the mug of coffee. She took a sip and stood staring at him.

"So, what in the world are you here for this early?" she asked. "I promised you dinner tonight but not breakfast."

"Well, I have missed you, so I thought I'd come over and see if I could convince you to spend the day with me. I want to take you to Sweetwater to visit some antique stores and have lunch at this wonderful little cafe I read about. Then, I hoped we might go to the art cinema and see part of the Hepburn-Tracey festival. And . . ." he paused, Doris cocked her head and smiled, "if you will give me your day, then I will cook dinner for *you* tonight. What d'ya say?" Martin smiled, flipped his hair back, and took a sip of coffee.

Doris sighed. "Well, I suppose I could grade papers and memorize lines tomorrow. I do have to meet the real estate lady at Mother's house at ten, but afterwards, I'm game."

"Terrific! Let's go grab breakfast at the Lazy Bagel, and I'll drive you to your mother's house."

A sudden realization hit Doris. "Wait, I forgot, Carmen won't start. We'll have to see if you can jump her off first. If not, I'll have to make arrangements for the garage to come pick her up."

"What happened to Carmen? How did you get to rehearsal last night?"

"I think I left the dome light on yesterday. One of my students who is in the show came by and picked me up. Do you know Jayson Jeffries?"

"Wasn't he in *Bus Stop*; we saw it last spring? He's playing Nick?"

"Right, he's the one. Yes, he plays Nick."

"Well, that explains why his script is here."

"Really? Where"

"On the hall tree."

Doris had no other option, she needed to tell Martin about Jayson's visit. And why not, she thought, all we did was drink tea and cocoa. "It was cold and rainy when he brought me home so I invited him in for some tea to thank him. He hung his coat on the hall tree; I bet the script fell out of his pocket. Oh dear, he's going to panic when he realizes it. We're supposed to have our lines for Act 1 memorized for Monday."

"Well, call him and we can drop the script by his dorm on our way to breakfast."

"Martin, you are such a doll!" Doris looked at the cast list hanging by her phone in the kitchen and called Jayson's number. By the way he answered she could tell he was not used to getting up at seven o'clock on Saturday mornings. "Jayson, this is Dorie," Martin looked at her strangely but she forged ahead, "Your script fell out of your pocket at my house last night." She was silent, smiling at Martin while she listened to Jayson. "Well, no, it's okay. I'm going to be out all day, so I thought I'd drive by campus and drop it off for you this morning." She fell silent again. Martin took her mug to the sink and washed it out with his and sat both upside down in the drainer. He took the leftover coffee and poured it into a sealed container, put it in the refrigerator, and washed out the coffeemaker. "Well, if you're sure. I don't mind, though." She paused again, watching Martin cleaning up the kitchen. "Okay, I'll put it inside the screen door. come by anytime to get it. Okay . . . yeah, me too . . . okay, bye."

She hung up. "I heard," Martin said, "so let's go eat!" Doris checked Felix's food and water, grabbed her purse and coat, placed the script in the doorway for Jayson, and tried to start Carmen. Martin dug in his trunk looking for the jumper cables. It took a bit of doing to get Martin's Volvo close enough to Carmen for the cables to fit, but they finally got Carmen running, and Doris drove her around the block a couple of times to make sure the battery was fully charged. She parked the car back in her driveway and blew a kiss to Felix who was sitting in his window hammock. She smiled at first and then frowned slightly, thinking of Jayson's comment about being free. She wondered if Felix would be happier outside.

"Doris? You coming?" She turned to see Martin, the errant flop of hair waving in the cool October breeze, sitting in his idling Volvo and waving his arm.

"Sorry!" She tucked the tail of her jacket into the car, checked to make sure the papers necessary for the estate sale were in her purse, and then nodded to Martin as she pulled the seat belt across her chest. "Ready, captain!" she said, saluting him. Martin shook his head and laughed as he slowly pulled out and headed to the college shopping strip for breakfast.

They both knew only the hard-core morning people would be there before nine on a Saturday, so they could have their pick of tables and fresh hot Danish.

When they got to Avis' house it was quarter to ten, and the real estate representative wasn't there. Doris hadn't been to the house since Ted left, and it felt eerily empty and unfamiliar. She let herself into the back door with Martin trailing behind her, watching her carefully for signs she might need him. She looked around at her mother's kitchen table, the pictures in the dining room, and the velvet sofa she and Ethan did their necking and heavy petting on during their high school years. Memories of Avis rocking in front of the television, carrying hot casserole dishes to the table, or fussing around the room with a feather duster came flooding back to Doris. Her feet on the hardwood floors made a subtle knocking noise, and her hands reached out to touch the dark blue curtains she and Avis argued over for nearly two weeks. Everything not nailed down bore price tags hanging down or stuck in some inconspicuous place.

Doris could barely stand it. She turned with tears in her eyes to look for Martin who was watching her from the kitchen doorway. "I'm going out onto the porch to wait," she said simply. Martin nodded and followed behind her. They sat on the porch swing, Doris' head on his shoulder, for nearly twenty minutes waiting for the real estate agent to show.

Finally, a smartly dressed woman of about thirty-five pulled up in her black BMW and parked inside the driveway, behind Martin's Volvo. She had brown hair in a pixie cut, black framed glasses, and pouty little lips the color of watermelon. She came up the sidewalk, dodging the damp grass and a few residual puddles from yesterday's rain. Martin and Doris stood to greet her as she held out her hand to shake theirs.

"Hello, Dr. Peechum, my name is Sheila Grindstaff, we spoke on the phone several times. I'm sorry to be a few minutes late, but I got held up at another meeting. I hope you will forgive me."

"Yes, hello, it's quite all right, Ms. Grindstaff. This is my friend, Martin Winborn." They all made nice chitchat noises about the weather turning colder and how badly they needed the rain. Ms. Grindstaff suggested they go inside to look over the papers and discuss the estate sale. This was the last thing Doris wanted to do, but she realized there was no realistic place for the three of them to meet on the front porch, still damp with humidity.

Ms. Grindstaff spread papers out on the kitchen table and handed Doris a stack to read over. Doris tried to keep her focus on the contract and forget her mother died in the next room a few weeks earlier. Martin was quiet, sitting beside her with his arm on the back of her chair.

"Now, these papers, Dr. Peechum, are the ones you have already looked over with your brother and signed. They give us the right to come into the home, appraise, and price all the items you see here with tags on them. We discarded any broken or unusable items such as the toaster in the kitchen and your mother's underwear, medicine, toiletries, and so on." Doris' face turned pale, and she realized she was holding her breath. "Now this set of papers," Ms. Grindstaff handed Doris a few sheets of legal length NCR pages (no carbon required) that made several copies of the first page and was perforated at the top for easy separation. "The first one is the contract we need for you to look over which gives us permission to sell at any reasonable price the belongings on the estate and hold the money in trust until the house sells." She paused to see if Doris wanted to comment or ask a question, but Doris stared at the papers and tried to remember how to swallow. Ms. Grindstaff continued, "This other set gives us permission to sell the house and property, taking our customary percentage. It also guarantees we will not sell the house for less than your asking price without your permission. However, we do have some liberty to increase the price above the bottom line. Do you have any questions about any of this?" Doris looked at the woman and shook her head. She tried to say no, but no sound came out of her mouth, so she cleared her throat and shook her head again.

"Okay, good. This last set specifies that once the house sells, we take a percentage of the estate sale revenue and then give you a check for the remaining profit for the sale of the house and its contents. By signing here," she pointed to the large X at the bottom of the page, "you agree to this percentage. If at any time we receive an offer below your asking price, we will bring it to you for approval. If you do approve a lower price, it could mean your profit will be lower than ours, or that we may need to use profit from the estate sale to insure our fee. If you don't have any problems with this, then you sign at the bottom and we give you a copy, retain a copy for our files, and send one to our lawyers." She paused, the sound of her voice echoed against the near empty walls. She pulled her sleeve up to check her watch, giving the impression she was on a tight schedule. Still, she looked at them and said, "Why don't I take a final look around to make sure everything is priced and so on while you read the contracts and make sure you want to sign them."

Ms. Grindstaff tiptoed discreetly upstairs to give Doris and Martin more privacy. Martin was reading over one of the contracts while Doris read another. Doris finally found her voice and looked at Martin. "Do you understand all this?"

"They look pretty cut and dry to me," Martin said, folding up his reading glasses and tucking them into the inside pocket of his corduroy blazer. "But if you like, my lawyer friend Pete could look these over. Or you could fax them to Ted in Baton Rouge. I'm sure they can wait a few days if you aren't sure."

"I don't see any reason for that. This company comes highly recommended. Ted made sure of all that before he left." She paused and took a deep breath, trying not to give in to the tears, which threatened to escape. "I want it to be over with, you know? I can't stand being in this house any longer—I don't want to see it empty, or meet the buyers. I want to remember it all the way it used to be—with my mother here and the house warm and inviting--not the department store sale table it looks like now!"

Doris stood up and walked around the room. She paused at the window and noticed the leaves on Avis' favorite tree, a small dogwood near the fence, had deep maroon leaves. She remembered the day her father planted the tree; he planted four of them along the fence. For some reason this one was the only survivor. The man at the nursery said they probably weren't getting enough sunlight, so he gave them boxwoods instead, which Ed Peechum planted at the edge of the yard. Doris sighed, and tears streamed down her face and onto her blouse. Martin's arms wrapped around her from behind, and his face rubbed her ear.

"Why don't you let me take care of it?" She turned and let him hug her, resting her head on his shoulder. "You can sign the papers or wait, whatever you want, but I'll take care of the leg work. You won't have to come here again. I'll make sure all future meetings are in Ms. Grindstaff's office or your home, okay?" Doris nodded into his shoulder and held him tighter.

They heard the click-click of Ms. Grindstaff's heels on the wooden steps and turned back to the table. Martin pulled out his handkerchief and handed it to Doris who took it into the bathroom to blow her nose and clean off her face. When she returned to her seat, Martin was explaining the terms to Ms. Grindstaff, who nodded professionally. The one raised eyebrow, however, told Doris she considered all this an inconvenience.

"Dr. Peechum, I'm sorry, but I have to be at another meeting soon— well, in fact, I'm already late. Could we finish this later this week?"

Doris, unsure of how she felt said, "No, Ms. Grindstaff, we were here on time. We need to finish this today."

"Certainly," Ms. Grindstaff said quietly, as if she was afraid of what Doris might do next. She looked at Martin steadily, but he was watching Doris.

"I don't mean to be rude, Ms. Grindstaff, but coming back to this house is difficult for me. I need to finish this today."

Sheila Grindstaff nodded. "Of course, I didn't mean to sound insensitive."

Doris picked up the pen Ms. Grindstaff had placed near the contracts. She signed her name and handed the copies to the real estate agent to tear apart. Ms. Grindstaff told them the estate sale was planned for the following weekend so she would be in touch after it was over. Doris said she wanted anything left over to be donated to an organization that helps abused women.

"Certainly, Dr. Peechum, we can arrange it." Ms. Grindstaff shook their hands and bid them a good day. She checked her watch again, hurried to her car, and pulled out with a shriek. Doris took a last look around the house, smelled it one more time, and then left the way they came in, locking the door behind her.

Doris sat for nearly a half hour sobbing uncontrollably in Martin's car. He tried to comfort her as well as he could, but she was inconsolable. Martin tried a few intermittent comments, but Doris was in a mood he didn't recognize. Her face was white except for the red around her eyes and nose. She used up all the tissue in her purse and nearly the whole box from Martin's glove compartment.

Doris finally stopped crying, but her breathing seemed permanently affected by her outburst. She tried to speak, but her breath caught in short intakes of air, like a case of multiple hiccoughs. It was impossible for her to continue so she nodded and buried her face into Martin's chest. He put his arm around her shoulder and sat watching leaves float from the old dogwood tree.

The storm subsided, and Doris' breathing slowly returned to normal. Her eyes were swollen and her nose raw, but she didn't seem to care. She pulled herself away from Martin and leaned her head on the car's window. "Get me out of here, Martin, please." Martin looked at her for a long moment then started the car and without a word pulled out of the driveway and onto the street.

"Do you still want to go to Sweetwater today?"

"I'm sorry, Martin, but I think I need some time alone. I have so many papers to finish grading and then lines to work on. Could I call you tomorrow if I get all the work done? We can plan something then?"

It was hard for Martin to mask his disappointment, but he tried. "It's okay, I understand. If you want some company, I need to grade some papers, too. Plus, I could help you with your lines."

Doris looked away at the houses and cars passing by. "Maybe later. I need to take a bath and clean up. I also need some time to think about all this. I'll call you later, okay?" She turned and tried to smile. Martin patted her hand and nodded.

Martin pulled the Volvo into Doris' driveway and started to get out of the car, but she reached over and gave him a kiss goodbye. "I'll be fine, Martin, I need to go inside myself when I get this upset. I want some time, but I will call you soon, I promise." She got out of the car and ran inside her house without looking back.

Doris wondered as she approached her front door if she ever wanted to get married. *How do you ever have time alone*, she wondered. She pulled the screen door open, and Jayson's script hit her toe. She unlocked the front door and replaced the script, thinking Jayson might come while she was in the bath or taking a nap. She heard Martin's car pull away and felt a twang of regret.

Doris walked slowly into the kitchen, poured a glass of wine, put a Laura Nyro album on the stereo, and headed for the bathroom. She drew a hot bubble bath—along with chocolate it was her cure for almost anything, and baths were less fattening. She slipped into the tub and completely under the water, wetting her face and hair and immersing herself in the comforting heat. She pulled herself up and laid her head on the back of the tub. She smelled the new soap—raspberry and vanilla—and spread the smooth lather all over her body. She soaked for a long time in the bath, sipping her drink and listening to Laura's clear soprano voice echo throughout her house. It felt like healing, like release, like her mother's arms around her.

As usual, she let the water out of the tub while she shaved her legs and then stood in the shower to wash her hair and rinse suds off her body. She wrapped herself in her terrycloth bathrobe, twisted her hair into a towel turban, and headed to the kitchen to rinse out her glass. She shifted the towel on her head and wrapped it back into a turban, then headed to the stereo to flip the album over. As it started to play, her doorbell rang. Figuring it was Martin she pulled the door open, "I told you I will call . . ." she stopped short realizing it was Jayson.

"Hi Dorie. I am taking a break from set-work and thought I'd come by to pick up the script and heard the music. I like it—who is it?" Doris stared at him through the screen door. She felt naked in her robe with her hair wet, no makeup, and her feet bare. A cold gust of air blew through the screen and she shivered slightly.

"Uh, her name is Laura Nyro. She was big in the 1960's and early '70's as a songwriter, but I like her own versions of her music." Doris realized she was being rude. "I'm sorry, Jayson, come on in out of the cold."

"Thanks," Jayson stepped in, closing the door behind him. Doris kept her hands tightly on the belt of her robe. "I was wondering if you wanted to go though some of the lines together later?"

"Oh," Doris awkwardly pulled the towel off her hair and pushed her fingers through it. "That's a good idea, Jayson, but I haven't even started to memorize them."

"Oh, it's okay, Lenny doesn't actually expect you to have them memorized for Monday. She doesn't want us having our noses buried in the books, you know. It's hard to move around. She likes for us to be familiar with the lines. She lets us keep our books so we can write down the blocking. Are you coming over today?"

"Oh," was all Doris could muster. "Coming where?" Her hand moved down to the opening in her robe to be sure it was completely closed.

"Set-work. You don't have to be there, but it's usually a lot of fun."

"Well, I have a bunch of papers to grade and then I was going to start on the lines. I'm sorry, but I didn't plan to come today. I'll call you later if I feel ready to work with someone."

Jayson finally realized his art teacher was standing in front of him in her bathrobe with wet hair. "Oh, yeah, well, that's a good idea." He rolled the script in one hand and banged it against the other one. "Oh! I forgot what I wanted to give you." He shoved the script into his right pocket and pulled a box of tea from his left pocket. "Here's a box of tea to replace the one you gave me last night."

"Oh, Jayson, that's so sweet. You didn't have to . . ." She let go of her robe to step forward and take the tea. They both looked down as her leg emerged from the robe. Doris tried to casually take hold of it again, but the belt loosened some and the robe threatened to open completely. She quickly tucked one side under the other and tightened the belt. "Well, I better get to those papers."

Jayson forced his eyes back to hers and tried not to imagine Dr. Peechum under her robe. He backed away toward the door. "Hi Felix," Felix remained asleep in his window hammock since before Doris came home; he did not acknowledge Jayson's greeting. "Well, I'll see you later, Dorie. Thanks again for letting me know about the script—I would have panicked if I started to work on my lines and couldn't find it."

He hurried down the steps and Doris stood at the screen door holding her robe with one hand and waving the tea in the other. "Thanks for the tea!" she yelled. He hopped in his car and drove away. Doris closed the door and stood with her back against the glass window and lacy curtain. She stood with her eyes closed, her arms hugging her middle, breathing deeply. "Oh dear," she sighed.

22

Doris felt a sudden pang of guilt after Jayson's visit, so she immediately called Martin to set up a dinner date with him. She spent the afternoon furiously grading papers and doing class prep for the week. Martin took her back to Le Petit Cafe for a nice seafood dinner then they saw Spencer Tracy and Katherine Hepburn in *Pat and Mike* at the art cinema. Doris' new phone rang loudly during a quiet part in the film, and she received glaring dirty looks from the few people seated around them. "Sorry," she whispered. Martin just shook his head and munched on popcorn—Doris didn't recognize the number so she turned the phone completely off.

When they got back to Doris' house, she was exhausted but managed to serve him coffee and go to bed with him. For once, however, she was grateful for Martin's wham-bam-thank-you-ma'am approach to lovemaking.

He stayed most of the next day after serving her a delicious breakfast in bed and helped her run lines. He read rather well, impressing Doris with his sense of character. For supper, she cooked her "specialty," an original chicken and pasta dish while Martin prepared the salad, dessert, and arranged the table. He left after dinner to stay at home and get ready for school. Doris headed straight to bed and tried not to think. Still, images of Avis' house, Jayson, and Martin haunted her dreams.

In rehearsal Monday night, Lenny said, "Doris, I have given it some thought, and I'm afraid you will need to smoke a couple of times in the play. Have you been practicing?"

Doris knew this was coming; she completely forgot to carry a cigarette around on the weekend. "Yes, but I haven't been actually smoking them. I don't know if I can—the only time I tried I almost choked to death." Bill and Lenny laughed knowingly. "No offense, guys, but I don't know how you two can actually like it."

Lenny's voice softened, but she remained firm. "Well, I completely understand, and I would advise you to keep hating them, but I do want you to start working on it. I can help you if you need me or wait . . . I have a better idea. Jayson learned to smoke for a play so he might understand better how to start from scratch. I've been smoking since I was seventeen!" Doris gave an unconscious expression of disapproval, but Lenny plowed on. "So, believe me, I don't want anyone getting hooked on them. But the character needs it, so let me know what I can do to help you."

"Don't they make some kind of fake cigarette?" Doris tried one last time.

"Yes, they do. And they even light up on the end and emit smoke, but you must blow into them to do that--not suck, the way a smoker does. I just don't think they look real."

"Don't they have rules about smoking in the theatre, though? Won't audience members object?"

"Well, that's a consideration. However, I have received permission for us to use real cigarettes, and I will make an announcement during the curtain speech. You smoke so short a time, I don't think it will be a problem."

Doris sighed, knowing it was no use to argue or protest any further. She nodded and looked over to Bill who was avoiding eye contact. They ran through the first part of Act 1, and Doris surprised herself by knowing a great deal of her lines. Lenny did allow them to carry their scripts (as Jayson predicted), but encouraged them to avoid using them as much as possible. She had a harder time following the chicken scratch notations for blocking in her script and holding a cigarette at the same time.

"Okay, let's take ten, then we'll come back and see if we can run it without books."

Only Lenny and Bill left the room to smoke. Stacey and Winnie had to reset props, and the others studied lines. Lenny gave them permission to call line, which means they can just say "line" if they're lost, and Stacey would read the line to them. Doris made it through the opening scene with Bill but still struggled with the cigarettes. She realized how much the intensive blocking session they'd had on the scene helped her feel secure in the role.

Doris did better than she had expected and found that not having the script in her hand was helpful. Bill, of course, couldn't get past their entrance scene so Lenny, trying to hide her frustration, told him to just use his script.

The following day Doris met Martin for their now-traditional lunch at Foster's, and he chatted almost nonstop about a promising new history undergraduate in his Survey of American History class. She tried to stay interested, but her mind kept wandering back to Saturday morning—Avis' house, Jayson, her robe, Martin's wonderful kisses and lackluster lovemaking. She nodded and raised her eyebrows occasionally to keep Martin talking; she didn't want any responsibility for the conversation right now. Students rushed in and out, as usual, as Doris and Martin calmly sipped tea and nibbled at the salad of the day. *How out of place we look,* she thought, *no other faculty members ever eat here—why do I want to be here?* It was too warm, noisy, and hurried—everything she hated in an eatery. They did have better food than the cafeteria, but she was beginning to miss the camaraderie of lunching with her colleagues. Martin was a dear, but she needed more than his company day in and day out. Doris suddenly wondered if that was bad or healthy. She was trying to decide when someone patted her on the shoulder. It was Lenny.

"You did a great job last night, Dorie, the show is going to rock! Hi, Martin." Martin swallowed his clump of lettuce and nodded to Lenny, the unruly strand of hair fell over his eye. Doris got a sudden urge to ask him to get his hair restyled. "I gotta class I'm late for so I have to run. Don't forget what I said about the smoking, Doris, I'll be glad to help anytime, but I think Jayson is your best bet." The campus bell tower began to ring. "Oh, God! I gotta go! Bye, you two." Before Doris could utter a word, Lenny was out the door. She turned to look at Martin who pushed his hair back while she wasn't looking. He chewed calmly and, it seemed to Doris, tried not to jump to conclusions about what Lenny said.

"So, you *are* going to smoke in the play?" Martin said, trying to sound casual while he took a sip of tea. "How do you feel about it?"

Doris took a deep breath. "Terrible. She told me last night at rehearsal. I tried to talk her out of it, but it was no use. I hate carrying them around, much less having to inhale the smoke. The one time I tried I almost choked to death." She reached out and touched Martin's hand. "I don't think there's much chance of me starting to like them."

Martin's face looked visibly relieved, but he tried to conceal it. The unruly flap of hair fell over his nose, but he let it rest there. "Good," was all he said and took another bite of salad; then a thought occurred to him. "I hate to ask this, but I would appreciate it if you wouldn't smoke around me. I have so many bad memories of Sarah . . ."

Doris didn't speak, but she nodded and patted his hand. She took her other hand and pushed the hair back, making Martin smile as he wiped his mouth. Martin asked her about rehearsals and how they were going, and they conversed for the remainder of their lunch break about the play, the characters, and Lenny's directorial approach.

Doris felt better during the afternoon. What did she have to feel guilty about? Nothing, she told herself. All she did was answer the door; she didn't know Jayson would be standing there. On her way home Doris stopped to pick up some dry cleaning and ran into Tootsie.

"Oh dear, Tootsie! It is so good to see you," Doris said, and meant it.

"Doris, how are you doing? I think about you so often."

"I'm better, thanks. Tootsie, I am so sorry I haven't called. I keep meaning to, but life just keeps getting in the way."

"Well, I haven't called you either, so no worries." They talked awhile about the weather and the price of dry cleaning. The Korean gentleman behind the counter gave them a sneer, so they moved to the street, walking toward their cars with their plastic bags of pressed clothes waving in the wind.

"What are you doing this Friday night?" Tootsie asked suddenly. "It's kind of my night off from the kids. Sam takes them somewhere and I read a book, go out with friends, shopping, whatever!" Doris felt sorry for Tootsie and Sam, taking care of their grandchildren so often and not really having much time alone together.

Doris stammered, thinking. "Gosh, I really don't know right off hand, I'll have to look at my rehearsal schedule."

"Rehearsal schedule? For what?" Tootsie had always supported Doris in her artistic pursuits and sounded excited about the prospect of attending an upcoming performance.

Doris briefly explained the play situation and promised to call Tootsie as soon as she got home. "Ok, here's my cell number," Tootsie was writing on a little scrap of paper, then handed it to Doris.

"Oh! I have one of those too! I just got it so I leave it off most of the time." She gave Tootsie her number and hoped they could see each other soon. *I need some womanly advice about Martin*, she thought as she hugged Tootsie, and they parted ways.

Doris barely made it to rehearsal on time Tuesday night. She tried to run too many errands in the afternoon, leaving her with less time than usual for supper, bath, feeding Felix, and all the other things she thought she needed to accomplish before going out. She rushed down the hall to room 106 and nearly burst in the door only to find Jayson and Stacey talking about the set, Winnie setting up the shadow props, and Lenny smoking a cigarette with Bill on the terrace outside the back door. Jayson and Stacey looked up and smiled then resumed their conference. Doris rolled her eyes and strolled back down the hall to go to the bathroom—a luxury she had denied herself in order to be on time. *Lenny runs rehearsals on "Southern time,"* she thought to herself. When she returned, Lenny and Bill entered, and Jayson sat on the makeshift sofa of three metal chairs pushed together. Teri came in behind her apologizing for her tardiness.

"No problem, Teri," Lenny smiled, "You're right on time, we were just going to get started." They first read and walked through the second part of Act 1, finding their movements in an organic way. They bumped into each other occasionally, so Lenny started orchestrating their movements. "Okay, let's take ten," she yelled to everyone, "and then we'll run the whole thing from the top." Lenny rushed down the hall toward the ladies' room, Bill headed for the terrace to smoke, and Jayson sat down beside Doris, who busily recorded her blocking in the tiny margins of her script.

When she returned from her break, Lenny pulled Jayson and Doris aside. "Jayson, would you mind helping Dorie with her smoking sometime this week?"

Jayson winked at Doris and said, "Sure!" Doris muttered a quiet thank-you and hoped Lenny would move on to something else. "I'll talk to Dorie," Jayson volunteered.

"Sorry," Jayson said. Doris looked up confused. "I mean, I'm sorry you have to smoke in the play. I did it once, and it was a real pain." Doris smiled, a little relieved Jayson was so mature about everything. Then he reminded her of his age. "I had some trouble explaining the cigarettes in my pocket when I went home one weekend!" He laughed, but not too sincerely.

"Well, it goes with all the glamour of working in the theatre, right?" Doris now saw a genuine smile on Jayson's face. "I appreciate your willingness to help me. I will probably be a terrible student because I hate them so much!"

Jayson laid a hand gently on her arm. "No problem, I do, too. So, when do you want to get started?"

"Well, the evenings are full of rehearsals, so how about late afternoons?"

"That's good for me except on Thursdays when I have a biology lab. Should I meet you in your office tomorrow after lunch?"

"No," Doris said quickly, "I don't want to stink up my office, and I'd rather not do it on campus, anyway, I don't want people to see me. Would it be too much to ask you to come over to my house? We could smoke on my screened-in porch." She regretted this the moment after she said it. *This may not be proper*, she thought, *I should have arranged a meeting somewhere else, like a public place.* She did *not* want to be seen on campus, or anywhere else for that matter, smoking cigarettes.

"Course not, what time?"

"Wednesdays I have a class until 2:00, and then I have office hours till 4:00. Well, basically, I'm here till about 4:00 most days. If you would come by to help me around 4:30 tomorrow, then I'll pay you back with supper—okay?" *It'll be fine*, Doris assured herself, *they will be rehearsing. Who could object?* She wondered if she should invite Martin to supper, too.

"Sweet," Jayson said, looking down at his hands, a slight smile cracking his face, "But don't go to any trouble. I don't need to be repaid—this is part of rehearsals."

"Well, I still appreciate it, and besides, we could run lines or something while we eat." *No, better not invite Martin, he might complicate it, make it a social event instead of work.* Jayson had the bluest eyes she could ever remember seeing. She panicked suddenly trying to remember the color of Martin's eyes. *Green? Hazel? Brown?*

"Okay, if you're sure," Jayson said, checking Doris's face for his answer. "Well, I better visit the rest room before we get started." He escaped down the hall, bounding like a gazelle. Doris watched him through the big glass window which comprised half the door to room 106, sighing in amazement at his energy level. She took a moment to pull out her phone and call Tootsie. She got voice mail.

"Tootsie, I'm so sorry, but I do have rehearsal this Friday night. But I promise to call you soon with a possible time to get together." She hung up just as Lenny returned to the room.

"You have a cell phone now, Dorie?"

"Oh dear, I completely forgot to give you the number. I hardly ever have it on though." She tucked it back in her purse and wrote the number down for Lenny. She also handed little pieces of paper with the number on it to Stacey and her cast mates.

Lenny asked them to go through the scene several times. In a particularly quiet moment, someone's phone started ringing loudly. Everyone looked around at each other, startled. "Is anyone going to get that?" Doris asked.

"I think it may be your phone, Dorie," Lenny said. "We have a pretty strict policy at rehearsals that phones are to be turned completely off and stored out of sight."

Doris turned several shades of red as she rushed to her purse to dig the phone out. Sure enough, it was ringing loudly. She opened it up and of course had to talk to whoever had called her. It was Tootsie. "I'm sorry, Tootsie, I'm in rehearsal, I'll call you back soon." A slight pause, and then she turned the phone off and tucked it away. She looked sheepishly around at the others who were just smiling at her. "I'm so, so sorry! I am just not used to carrying one of those things around." Everyone assured her it had happened to them, and Lenny told her not to worry about it.

By the end of the evening, Doris knew most of her lines for this part of the play. She was blessed with an easy memory—lines were never a problem for her. *Thank God,* she thought to herself, *I have enough to worry about right now.*

They all walked out together, chatting about the play, the weather, the football season, and headed toward their cars. Doris noticed a little white car parked near them with the engine on and the lights out. "Damn it, Kayla, get over it!" She heard Jayson say behind her. "Don't look at her, Dorie, if you ignore her maybe she'll go away."

"I assume Kayla did not take the break-up well," Doris muttered under her breath.

"You could say that," Jayson scoffed, "You could say that, but it would be the greatest understatement in the history of Kerryville College."

Doris laughed, but she worried about Kayla and about Jayson. "She's young, Jayson, give her time."

"I know, but if I'm nice to her at all, she takes it as a sign I want to get back together."

"Try being civil—not friendly, but not so mean, either. There's no reason to hurt her any further. I'm sorry. Once again I'm sticking my nose in where it doesn't belong."

"Don't be silly, Dorie. We're friends, it's okay to tell me what you think. See ya tomorrow at 4:30. Come on, Win, I'll walk you to your dorm."

"Right," Doris said, but they were already gone. Doris folded herself into Carmen and noticed that as Jayson and Winnie disappeared into the campus fog, Kayla turned on her headlights and followed them. She wondered what kind of entanglement Jayson would have to contend with when he got to his dorm. Kayla would most likely get there first and be waiting for him at the door. "Oh dear," Doris said as she revved Carmen's engine and pulled out of the parking lot and into the street toward home.

23

Doris was a little ashamed of herself for getting up early to tidy up the house. *My goodness,* she scolded, *he's a kid! Who cares what he thinks about my house. I'll bet his dorm room is a pigsty.* Still, she cleaned and tidied, even changing the litter box two days early. Felix stood nearby and stared at her. On the way to school, she stopped for gas, some cigarettes, and tampons. Her last period had exhausted her supply.

Her Art Appreciation class was especially good. Several students gave their oral presentations.; she allowed them to present on anything having to do with the art world so they usually picked something they were passionate about. A quiet boy named Nathan, who always dressed impeccably, gave an outstanding report on the Louvre museum in France, complete with PowerPoint slides. Jayson's report on the original set for the Broadway production of *Who's Afraid of Virginia Woolf* and the designer, William Ritman, was scheduled for Friday. Lunch with Martin was nice, also. Another Indian summer suddenly swept into Kerryville with temperatures in the upper sixties and bright sunlight. Doris convinced Martin to take their Foster's sandwiches out on campus to a bench near a huge maple tree with a few clusters of vibrant red leaves still clinging to life. Fall invigorated Doris, and she reveled in the cool breeze and air scented lightly with damp leaves and fresh dirt. Martin, she noticed, was rubbing chill bumps on his arms and trying to enjoy his lunch for Doris' sake. She smiled at him, grateful for his sweetness.

When she arrived for her Art History class, Doris was in such a good mood that even the weary arrogance of upper class art majors could not dampen her spirits. She taught class with a vengeance, challenging them to think beyond the small circle of their own interests and experiences. They responded with a collective groan at the idea of turning in their research papers on Friday. "Remember, a minimum of three primary sources." Students mumbled under their breath at the idea of spending the next two days and probably nights in the library doing research. Dismayed by today's students' tendency to consider research some version of surfing the Internet, Doris required them to cite at least three kinds of sources—one of which could *not* be from the Internet. "And by the way," she added. They all stopped momentarily and looked up, "go out and sit in the sun today and enjoy this beautiful day!" She nearly floated out of the classroom and down the hall to her office. The students looked at each other with "what's up with her" looks and hurried on to their next class or the nap waiting for them in the dorm.

She finished her class preparations and grading, quickly checked her email, and then locked up her office and headed home a little early. On the way, she picked up some fresh chicken and vegetables at the green market. She put the seasoned chicken in the oven, placed the broccoli in the steamer, and was boiling water for tea when her doorbell rang. She looked through the peephole at Jayson's eyes as they surveyed the ceiling of her front porch. He came in carrying a liter of Dr. Pepper, which made her laugh. "I have water on for tea, or perhaps we should open the bubbly!" she said, feigning a British accent.

"I'm good either way," Jayson said with a little chuckle, clearly nervous. "I like D.P. with dinner and figured you might, too."

"Thanks, Jayson, you're so thoughtful." Doris tucked the drink into her fridge and prepared tea for them both. "Make yourself comfortable on the porch, I'll join you there in a moment." Jayson stooped to pet Felix, then picked up the cat and carried him to the metal mesh table on the screened-in porch. Felix thoroughly sniffed at the cigarettes, the ashtray, and the lighter laid neatly on the table before jumping into his favorite chair where he slept much of the time. It was the only chair with a cushion; Doris kept it there for Felix.

"Okay," she said, carrying a nice tray of tea and condiments to the table, "I guess we better get started." She sat down next to him at the table and handed him a cup of tea.

Jayson took a sip and smiled. "I dig porches like this. I think I would live on it."

"Well, I do spend a lot of time out here—reading, grading papers, or just sitting with Felix. But today is so especially beautiful, I can't imagine being anywhere else. Besides," she said in a confiding tone, "I definitely don't want to stink up my house with cigarette smoke."

He nodded. "Cool. Okay, Dorie, it's not hard to smoke. The mistake most people make in starting is inhaling deeply directly from the cigarette."

Doris gave him a puzzled look. *Isn't that what smokers do,* she thought, *inhale cigarette smoke?* "Yes, you must inhale the smoke," he said as if he read her mind, "But you take the smoke into your mouth first, then inhale it. It's a two-step process. Let me show you." Jayson tapped the pack a few times against the palm of his hand like an expert.

"Why do smokers hit the cigarettes?" Doris asked, genuinely curious.

"It's to 'pack' the cigarettes—make the tobacco tighter in the paper." Doris gave him a raised eyebrows expression and nodded. "Kinda the way cereal settles toward the bottom of the box. You just want to make sure you pack them toward the filter. The filters are at the top of the pack." Jayson deftly unwrapped the cellophane and foil, hit the pack against his left hand until one cigarette protruded. He pulled it out and lighted it. "Okay, first the inhaling."

"I need to learn the opening ritual you did, too."

"Yes, you're right, but that's the easy part." Jayson showed Doris how to take the smoke into her mouth and then inhale it. She coughed or sneezed almost every time and then washed her mouth with a sip of tea. He made her try it several times before she got the hang of it. Still, she knew she looked awkward.

"I look so stupid doing this," she said. "And I don't want to do it enough to get good at it, but I guess I don't have any choice."

"I understand. But I also know you want to do the best Martha possible, and Martha loves smoking." Doris nodded reluctantly. "Something else is learning how to hold the cigarette. You can fool people pretty well, if you learn to make the cigarette a part of your hand like smokers do."

"I have been trying. I hold one all the time, except when I'm teaching or sleeping. But I still think I look clumsy."

Jayson demonstrated several ways smokers hold their cigarettes and discussed some theories concerning what it revealed about their personalities. "I did a lot of research on this. I never knew there was a whole culture wrapped up in this one little bad habit."

"Yes, I didn't either. It's fascinating." They spent nearly an hour practicing different holds, ash tapping, lighting postures, and inhaling methods, including the French variety in which half of the smoke is taken into the nostrils, which Doris found completely disgusting.

"The chicken should be done, Jayson, let me check on the broccoli, and we can eat out here while we run lines."

"Don't forget to hold a cigarette, Dorie," he said as he handed her a fresh one. She took it and gave him a sarcastic smile. "Can I help with anything?"

"Sure, bring the tea paraphernalia, and you can pour the Dr. Pepper for us."

"It's not the diet type, is that ok?" Jayson asked.

"Ooh, what a luxury! Of course."

Jayson not only brought the tea set inside but also rinsed the cups and put the condiments on the counter. He poured the drinks, added ice, and carried them to the table. "What kind of napkins do you want?" Doris pointed at some napkins and pulled open the silverware drawer for him. She covered the broccoli with melted cheese and placed a breast of chicken on each plate, Jayson set the table and petted Felix while he waited. *Darn,* she thought, *no bread. Oh well, we're better off without it, fewer carbs,* she decided.

When they finished dinner and cleaned up the plates, it was time for them to get ready for rehearsal. He thanked her for dinner, she thanked him for the lesson, then they stood awkwardly looking at each other in the foyer. Felix broke the tension by rubbing around Doris' legs. "Oh-oh, is it suppertime for kitties, too?" She picked him up and scratched his chin while Jayson smiled, looking at Felix's satisfied expression.

"Well, I guess I will see you later, right?"

"Right," Doris said, putting Felix over her shoulder so he could nuzzle in her hair.

"Thanks again," she said as she waved at his car. Doris mechanically put food and water in Felix's bowls, poured some wine, put a cigarette between her fingers, and prepared for rehearsal.

Lenny asked them to run Act 1 twice with the last run-through off-book. Doris was pleased to see great improvement on everyone's parts, and it was beginning to take shape. Lenny was so pleased she let them have Thursday night off. "That is," she added one caveat, "if you promise to have all lines and blocking under your belt for the entire first act, with no coaching, for Friday." Everyone nodded eagerly, not sure they could comply, but willing to face the consequences if they didn't. "Since we won't have rehearsal tomorrow night I'll arrange for Ms. Tandberg to meet with you for costume fittings. Ida wants to double check measurements and have you try on some stock costumes so she can figure out what she needs to find or make." They all looked at each other. *So much for a night off* their faces said.

On her drive home, Doris suddenly realized she was never going to have a free night during the week and should call Tootsie to see if she could arrange to meet her somewhere on Sunday—maybe an afternoon together. At a stop sign on the edge of campus she turned on her cell phone, dug Tootsie's number from her purse, and dialed the number. She felt so modern using a phone in the car, but of course, she realized she was still so far behind the times she had to giggle.

"Of course!" Tootsie squealed. They set up a meeting for late lunch at a little Mexican place near Le Petit called El Hombre. "You want to go to a movie after lunch?"

Doris considered, "Ummm, let's just play it by ear, ok?" She wasn't sure how long her talk with Tootsie would last. After all, that had so many years to catch up on.

Doris spent Thursday after school preparing a lecture for an upcoming class and doing laundry. The rest of the time, she sat with Felix watching television. She had started her period during the night Tuesday, so she felt bloated and uncomfortable. She was surprised, however, it seemed to be ending already. Normally her periods lasted for a full week. She didn't know why but was grateful just the same. *Probably the stress I've been under the past few weeks,* she thought to herself. Since the beginning of September, she had lost her mother, started a play for the first time in years, been proposed to for the first time in her life, and found herself attracted to a student for the first time in her career. Doris surprised herself for even thinking about Jayson—even admitting the attraction to herself. She regretted doing so, however, because now it was real, and she would have to deal with it. She felt terribly immoral, guilt-ridden, pathetic, and titillated all at the same time—a confusing mix of emotions.

Costume fittings were Doris' least favorite aspect of being in a play. She always felt fat and ugly and pitied the poor costumer who had to make her look presentable. Ida was wonderful, though. A plump little woman with gray wiry hair and an infectious smile who chatted nonstop about the play and how much she loved Elizabeth Taylor and how sad it was that she never got that magnificent body back. Doris uttered a few words in Ida's brief pauses, but mostly just stood there and did as she was told. Ida's student assistant, whom she introduced as her godsend Patty, looked familiar, but Doris figured she had seen her at the read-through. She didn't say a word, taking measurements, making notes, or running to the back for clothing items. *A perfect match*, Doris thought, *Ida the extrovert talkative one helped by quiet introvert Patty*. Doris noticed that almost all successful couples she knew had one of each. *Opposites do attract*, she concluded.

The actors and understudies were all there to try on clothes so it was a hectic two hours. Doris realized Ida seemed a bit disorganized; other costumers she had worked with scheduled each actor individually, but this was pretty much a free-for-all. In the end, though, Doris saw the logic in Ida's methods because she had a neatly compiled notebook of everyone's sizes, which stock costumes were assigned to them, and what she would have to find or make.

Friday morning, Doris entered her classroom only to find Jayson busily setting up his audiovisuals for his report. He opened PowerPoint and loaded his presentation on the computer, set his notes on the lectern, and placed a variety of set models on Doris' desk. He was carefully covering them with small pieces of cloth when Doris entered. "My, this looks wonderful, Jayson."

"Thank you, Dorie—Dr. Peechum. I hope it's okay for me to get set up; it would take a lot of class time to get ready."

"Not at all, Jayson, that's what I hoped everyone would do. I can't wait to hear the report." Doris positioned herself in the back of the classroom where she usually sat during student reports. From a distance, she could better judge the effectiveness of the report, plus it gave her a safe distance from the students' so she wouldn't add unnecessarily to their anxiety level. She set up her grade book, the individual evaluation sheets for today's speakers, her stopwatch, and several pencils. "I think it's about time, Jayson, are you ready?"

"Yes ma'am," he said dutifully. He began with a summary of the play then discussed the set design. Doris did a quick survey of the room for attendance purposes then gave Jayson her undivided concentration. She was impressed with his organization of the information, his use of visual aids of his drawings, and the models, which she figured he saved from his Stagecraft class with Tom, the technical director. She listened intently to his explanations about set angles, levels, and seating areas. Doris found herself completely wrapped up in his dissertation, unable to put pencil to paper in any form of constructive assessment of his strong and weak points. *What weak points*, she mused, admiring the smooth bulk of his arms as he held the models up for better visibility and the barely crooked smile that materialized when he made a mistake or mentioned some human-interest tidbit about the original production of the play.

Suddenly she heard her name mentioned and realized he was talking about his set design for the play, explaining the rationale for his choices, and how the design would work for the production. She was wondering how he managed to be born with such jet-black hair and clear blue eyes all at the same time when the class broke into applause. Her hand jerked to stop her watch and record the time, and then she opened her mouth to request his notes and research bibliography. She produced no sound, but lucky for her Jayson was headed her way with a folder in his hands. She took it and smiled.

"How'd I do?" he asked, sincerely wanting her approval. She didn't know if she felt more like his friend or his mother.

"Fine, fine, Jayson. It was very interesting," she commented, trying to shuffle to the papers for the next student. "Now we will hear about the Vietnam films directed by Oliver Stone from Jennifer Messer." Jennifer timidly approached the lectern as Jayson moved his materials to a large windowsill. Her only visual was a movie poster for the movie, *Platoon,* which she had glued to a sturdy board of some kind. Doris recognized the look of inadequacy in her face, knowing the young woman sincerely wished she didn't have to follow Jayson's report. She did well, though, and Doris tried to give her as much positive feedback as possible. Doris knew Jayson had a distinct advantage in selecting a topic from his major and being able to use materials constructed for another class. She would have to balance this into the grading equation, she reminded herself.

The final report covered the sculptures of Rodin and barely finished before the time ran out. Doris collected her materials and pushed them into her briefcase while Jayson stacked his models into a cardboard box, which was originally used to ship a large quantity of toilet paper, probably to his dorm. They looked up at each other occasionally, but didn't speak. When the other students were gone, Jayson asked her how the smoking was going. She smiled and told him she still hated it, but she was getting a lot better. "You'll see an example of my mastery tonight at rehearsal, I guess," she laughed.

"Sweet! Lookin' forward to it," Jayson said, locking up the top of the box by layering one flap over the next. Doris held the door for him and then watched him walk down the hall, hips swinging to maintain his balance, chin resting on the top of the giant box. As he disappeared among the onslaught of bodies rushing to class or lunch, she took a deep breath and headed in the opposite direction to her office.

At noon, she talked Martin into returning to the cafeteria for lunch. The faculty members who regularly ate with them before their Foster's diversion welcomed them back. They made their excuses—change of pace, more student contact, better food, etc.—but most of their colleagues interpreted their absences as a sign the relationship had moved to the next level. The teachers politely accepted their explanations without question, however, and commented on how they were missed. This made Doris feel better than she expected. She felt grounded, back in her element, home to her true self.

She felt she should explain to Martin about her plans on Sunday. "Tootsie and I haven't had a chance to get together for some girl time in so long, I hope you understand."

"Of course, I hope you have fun." Martin said and continued eating. "There's a Feline festival at the cinema this weekend, maybe we can catch some of that on Saturday?"

"That sounds wonderful, Martin, but I'll have to see what's going on at rehearsals. I'd love to see *La Dolce Vita* if possible." He nodded and carried on about something else.

24

Friday's rehearsal promised to be a long one. The goal was to run all of Act 1 twice without scripts, but Doris doubted it would be accomplished. In her opinion, Lenny took too much time to block a few pages at a time, using repetition and character work along with it. *This is a wonderful way for actors to work,* she thought, *but not if it puts us behind and we end up not ready for opening.*

Doris got there early to look over her lines and practice smoking. She guessed Lenny would expect her to start smoking in rehearsals when they started running through long sections. She joined Lenny, Bill, and Stacey on the back steps to smoke and realized it wasn't the act of smoking that could become so attractive; there was a social aspect she hadn't expected. Still, she didn't think it was worth the price of one's health.

Jayson and Winnie spent most of the pre-rehearsal time arranging the set. He brought in the sofa and chair from the greenroom, and Winnie set up a lot more props. Room 106 was sometimes used for acting classes but would now be devoted entirely to play rehearsals until they moved to the stage, which would probably be about two weeks before opening. Kerryville College put their small stage to constant use with recitals, visiting shows, a student film series, and large meetings. Set building sessions were relegated to afternoons and weekends, with most of it crowded into the small shop area behind the back wall of the stage. Doris, not being a student, was not required to attend any set-work sessions, but she realized to be a part of the group she should probably try to go the next morning.

Lenny started rehearsal by explaining she needed to crunch the blocking for Acts 2 and 3. She explained she was used to working with shorter plays and having more time to spend on script exploration along with blocking, and since this play is a three-act, she wanted to move a little faster. Doris nodded silently, glad to hear Lenny was aware of her shortcomings and was willing to admit to them. Otherwise, Doris found Lenny a lot of fun to work with.

"All right," Lenny said, "We'll run through all of Act 1, and I'll try not to stop you. Winnie will have the breakaway bottle for George. First time through, you may call line. And Martha, I mean, Dorie . . . would you please smoke this time through. One in the beginning and then, of course, the one when you--"

"Ask George to light it for me," Doris interrupted, making notations in her script, "Yes, that's fine."

Lenny had to bite her tongue a few times to keep from stopping them, but they went through Act 1 with most of the lines learned, even though Bill was still holding onto his script. Lenny gave a few notes then let them have a break. When they returned, she ordered them to put their scripts down and call "line" any time they needed it. "Otherwise we won't stop unless you skip something or really mangle the line. Stacey will be taking line notes so be careful not to paraphrase Albee's brilliant dialogue. We're not the playwright, it is not our job to re-write the script." Bill looked around and reluctantly put his script down.

Doris was surprised and pleased at how well she and the others did. Even Bill did a decent job. After Lenny gave notes she reviewed the rehearsal schedule for the following week. "Remember, we have another run-through of the first act Monday night with the understudies. After that, we will be moving faster in the blocking." Everyone nodded. "So, who wants to go to The Shipyard?"

The Shipyard? Doris asked herself, though she remained silent. Everyone but Bill and Doris raised their hands. Bill said his wife was back in town, so he wanted to go home and "veg out" with her. Everyone looked at Doris. "I don't even know what it is," she said, looking around.

Jayson spoke up first, "It's a gay bar where we usually go dancing on Friday nights after rehearsal. We never have enough guys and the girls don't want to get hit on all the time, so we go to The Shipyard to dance and let off some steam. It's a lot of fun, you ought to go at least once!"

"There's a gay bar in Kerryville?" Doris was astonished.

Winnie and Stacey giggled. "No," said Lenny, "Charley and I have to drive over to Chattanooga to be able to dance together. But we usually carpool, so it's not too bad. We do have a lot of fun."

Doris tried to avoid looking at Lenny. She didn't care about Lenny being gay, but she wondered about the ethics concerned with a teacher taking undergraduates to a bar—gay or otherwise. *Are they all drinking age?* At the same time, she didn't want to look like a prude, and after all, she needed to observe some intoxicated people as research for Martha. Doris had never been drunk; she drank socially but never got sloppy. "Well, I guess it will be all right," she finally said.

"Sweet!" said Jayson as he bounded up to help Winnie put up the props and clean the room. "Who wants to ride with me?" Doris looked up surprised. Winnie said she and Stacey could go with him.

"Why don't you let me drive," Doris volunteered. "Winnie has been wanting to ride in my car, and Jayson, I could pay you back for teaching me how to smoke. I should warn you guys the backseat is painful, but if it's not too far, you should be fine. Okay?"

Winnie exploded with shrieks of excitement, jumping up and down and hitting Jayson on the head with sofa pillows. Stacey looked at Doris and smiled, "I think she's okay with it, what do you think?" Doris laughed and nodded.

Jayson and Stacey climbed into the back so Winnie could sit in the front. Doris revved up the engine and pulled out with Jayson navigating. Teri decided to ride with Lenny, who wanted to go home first to retrieve Charley. Winnie rubbed her hands over the dashboard and asked questions about the car the entire way to the bar, some of which Doris couldn't answer. Jayson and Stacey pulled snacks from their backpacks and passed them around. Doris took a few bites, but couldn't eat and concentrate on driving a stick shift.

When they arrived, Doris was surprised she needed to purchase a membership to enter. Jayson and the others showed their cards to the doorman, who looked perfectly normal in every respect except he was wearing a pink feather boa around his neck. Doris studied the card as Jayson explained gay bars didn't get hecklers and protestors if they were "private." "Also," he said, "you can show your card on the first night and get enough free drinks to pay you back for the membership."

"It seems like an awful lot of trouble," Doris said, looking at the card. "I mean, aren't gay bars kind of common now?"

"You would think so," he said, "but some people would still come in and throw smoke bombs, or worse!"

"That's terrible. Why can't people just live and let live!" Jayson just smiled and nodded.

The bar was divided into several sections. The large open dance floor was vibrating with loud music and swaying bodies, some scantily clothed, illuminated only briefly by occasional colored lights rotating in a variety of directions. A gathering of tables with chairs surrounded the dance floor, and smoke and vapor permeated the air. Doris' eyes began to water as she stood looking around. On the balcony above, overlooking the dance floor, were pool tables, video games, and another bar. A small room to the left featured more comfortable seating and led to a large outdoor patio lit up with tiny multi-colored lights, like the ones she put on her Christmas tree last year. Doris felt a tug at her arm; it was Jayson asking her what she wanted to drink.

"UH...I GUESS I SHOULDN'T DRINK SINCE I HAVE TO DRIVE EVERYBODY HOME," she yelled.

"IT'S UP TO YOU," Jayson said, "BUT STACEY AND WINNIE ARE TOO YOUNG TO DRINK, AND I'M ONLY DRINKING BEER, SO WE WILL HAVE OTHER DRIVERS."

"WELL, OKAY, I'LL TAKE A RUM AND COKE." Jayson grinned and headed toward the bar. Winnie motioned for Doris to follow her and Stacey as they navigated through the crowd to find a table big enough for everyone. Stacey took a tissue from her tiny purse and wiped the table before sitting down and pulled two more chairs over to accommodate all seven of them. It was another fifteen minutes before Lenny and Charley entered, but they located Winnie right away, so Doris figured this must be their regular seating area. Jayson came carrying everyone's drinks, beers for himself and Lenny, soft drinks for Stacey, Winnie, and Charley, and Doris' cocktail. Everyone claimed a chair and talked about the crowd. Doris sipped her rum and listened. She prayed a strange woman wouldn't ask her to dance.

"TERI DECIDED TO GO HOME—HAS A BIG PAPER DUE MONDAY." Lenny yelled to be heard above the music. Everyone nodded in response.

"I THOUGHT YOU COULDN'T SMOKE IN TENNESSEE IN BARS." Doris yelled to Lenny.

"IT'S A PRIVATE CLUB SO THEY CAN DO WHATEVER THEY WANT." She shrugged and smiled, Doris nodded.

Jayson stood up and asked Doris to dance, but she shrugged,

"MAYBE LATER. I NEED TO GET USED TO THE MUSIC AND LIGHTS!"

"WHAT?" Jayson yelled, cupping his hand to his ear.

"LATER!" Doris yelled.

Jayson nodded and smiled and held his hand out to Winnie who gladly grabbed it and bounced up out of her chair and onto the dance floor. Charley watched Winnie with envy, "IF ONLY I HAD THAT MUCH ENERGY AGAIN!!"

Doris nodded and smiled. "I DON'T THINK I EVER DID!" she yelled. The music assaulted her eardrums, so she pulled small sections of her drink napkin and surreptitiously stuffed them in her ears. *Ah, better,* she thought.

A nice-looking waiter, dressed in tight white shorts with two rows of buttons in the front, a sailor's collar & scarf but no shirt, and a little white hat tipped to one side, arrived to take their orders. Doris ordered another round for her group and asked Lenny and Charley what they wanted. She noticed the waiter wore red Converse high-tops with no socks as he left the table. She looked around and saw Jayson was getting a lot of attention on the dance floor. He and Winnie weren't doing anything unusual, but she noticed in a sea of regular-looking people, Jayson stood out like Michelangelo's David in a lawn statuary lot. They danced through two songs and then headed back to the table for their drinks. Winnie was sweating from every pore, but only Jayson's forehead glistened in the dim lighting.

Doris started her second drink and began to feel a lot more comfortable and relaxed. *I worry too much,* she told herself. A slow song came on so Jayson held out his hand to Doris, and Lenny got up with Charley. Jayson smelled like sweet floral musk, his arms strong and confident. "YOU'RE THE FIRST MAN I'VE EVER DANCED WITH WHO ACTUALLY KNOWS HOW TO LEAD," she yelled near his ear. He smiled and swung her around.

"I GREW UP IN AUGUSTA, GEORGIA, MA'AM," Jayson said, adopting an exaggerated Southern accent, "EVERY TEENAGER LEARNS HOW TO BALLROOM DANCE IN AUGUSTA." He dropped the accent and added, "AT THE TIME, I THOUGHT IT WAS PRETTY LAME, BUT NOW I'M SO GLAD I DID IT. IT HAS HELPED ME MORE THAN ONCE IN THE THEATRE."

"AND ON THE DANCE FLOOR!" Doris added, pressing her ear to his cheek. Jayson rubbed her back in a way Doris thought was a little too familiar, but it felt so divine she didn't stop him. She squeezed his hand, rubbing her thumb on his. A brief thought of Martin crossed her mind; she wondered why he never took her dancing, but then she realized Martin was probably not the dancing type.

"OKAY, HERE COMES A FAST ONE, ARE YOU GAME?" Jayson leaned back to look at Doris. She threw her head back and pulled away from him, spinning under his arm and laughing. As they danced, Doris noticed Lenny and Charley were back in their seats, but Winnie was jumping around Stacey on the floor.

When they got back to the table, Lenny had bought another round of drinks for everyone. Doris finished her second one and held the third one for a long time. Two was her limit. *I'm not going to learn what it feels like to be drunk unless I get drunk,* she thought. She sipped slowly, watching the dancers, studying the light pattern, and smiling as she listened to the others yelling at the table. Jayson stood up again, inviting anyone interested to dance. Everyone was still using their cocktail napkins to wipe the sweat from their necks and foreheads. Lenny shrugged and joined him. They danced like best friends, anticipating each other's moves and rhythm changes. *What a great relationship they have,* Doris thought with envy.

"THEY HAVE A GREAT RELATIONSHIP, DON'T' YOU THINK?" Charley was pointing at Jayson and Lenny, voicing Doris' thoughts so well she wasn't sure if it was she or Charley who made the comment. Doris nodded and smiled.

"LENNY IS SO COOL, I THINK SHE'S GOING LET ME DIRECT THE ALPHA PSI SHOW NEXT YEAR," Stacey finally spoke. "YOU KNOW, LIKE JAYSON WILL IN THE SPRING."

"ALPHA PSI OR PHI?" Doris yelled.

"ALPHA PSI OMEGA--THE THEATRE HONOR SOCIETY."

Doris caught most of it so she looked at Stacey and jiggled her head again. She was beginning to feel like one of those "bobble-heads" you see in the back of people's cars, the body is still, but the head is attached to a spring and bounces up and down with the slightest movement. She hated yelling, though, so she kept her comments to essential pieces of communication.

"I need the bathroom—anyone know where it is?" she asked.

"WHAT?" Charley yelled.

"BATHROOM?"

Charley nodded understanding. "OVER THERE," she pointed to a little room with red walls. Doris finished off her drink and headed toward the women's. When she got there, she was horrified to see there was only one huge bathroom with stalls but nothing to distinguish the men's from the women's.

Oh dear, she thought to herself, but she really needed to go. She looked for the most remote booth near the back and sneaked in quickly. She muttered a quiet prayer of thanks that no one came into the stall beside her. While washing her hands, a tall woman exited a stall and came toward the row of sinks and mirrors. Doris tried to be discreet, but she couldn't help but stare. She thought this must be the most beautiful woman she had ever seen. As she reapplied her lipstick and combed through her hair, Doris noticed the woman was having trouble with an earring, possibly due to her extra-long fingernails.

"Damn it!" she said in deep resonating tones. Doris realized right away this was not an ordinary woman, perhaps not completely a woman yet at all. Doris decided to let her be and make a hasty exit, when the baritone voice stopped her. "God, honey, I would kill for your red hair. Is it natural?"

Doris looked around. Yes, she was the only other person in the room. "Yes," she said hesitantly, "But I have fair skin because of it and lots of annoying freckles."

"Don't kid yourself, honey, those freckles are cute." She then turned back to the mirror and fiddled with her ear. Doris muttered a quiet thank you and left.

Doris had a little trouble steering through the crowd after three drinks; she didn't think she should have any more. Back at the table, there was a fourth round of drinks. Winnie had a beer this time, but Doris didn't think it polite to point out her age. Everyone seemed to be winding down some. Lenny and Charley whispered to each other, Winnie and Stacey went upstairs to play pool, and Jayson sat sipping his beer and looking at the lights. Doris looked at her watch; it was nearly midnight.

"I'M NOT IN A BIG HURRY, JAYSON, BUT WHEN YOU GUYS ARE READY, I SHOULD PROBABLY GET HOME."

"LET'S FINISH THIS LAST DRINK AND THEN HEAD HOME,"

Jayson yelled. They sat quietly, taking occasional sips, watching the dancers, and rocking slightly in their chairs. Doris rested her head in her hand and nearly fell asleep.

She wasn't sure how long she sat there, but she sipped the rum slowly, enjoying the burn as it trailed down her throat. With her eyes closed the room disappeared and images of the past month swirled around inside her head: her mother in the casket, Martin at the movies, Tootsie holding a child, Jayson playing with Felix, fall leaves, Avis' house, Jayson teaching her to smoke, Felix sitting on her pillow, Jayson on her pillow. *Wait!* She bolted upright, widening her eyes and looking around. *Oh god,* she thought, *what is wrong with me?* Winnie and Stacey were standing next to the table and Jayson gently poked her arm.

"ARE YOU READY?"

Lenny and Charley gathered up their purses, took a last swig of their drinks, and joined them on the way out. Doris stood and suddenly the room began to whirl around her. She looked in dumb confusion, not understanding. *Am I at an amusement park,* she thought, *no, I'm at a bar. Oh dear.* She sank into her chair and held onto it so the room would stop spinning.

Her friends were nearly out the door when Jayson turned to ask her if she was okay to drive, but she wasn't there. He told the others to wait by the cars, he'd go back and find her. When he found Doris at the table her head was down on the table and her arms hung limply down at her sides. "Dorie?" he whispered in her ear. He rubbed her back and she came to, turning her head to look at him.

"I THINK I'VE HAD TOO MUCH TO DRINK, JAYSON." She yelled even though it wasn't necessary; the music was slow and at a soft point. Several people around them looked at Doris and grinned, shaking their heads and commenting on the well-dressed drunk.

Jayson put one arm around her shoulders and rubbed her arm with the other hand. "Can you walk?" Doris raised up and pushed her hair back. She nodded. He helped her stand, grabbed her purse, and practically carried her outside to the car. As they left the bar, they heard a spontaneous round of applause.

"IS THAT FOR ME?" Doris looked at Jayson pathetically.

"No," he lied, "Someone did a split on the dance floor."

"OH, GOOD." Doris said, raising her eyebrows. They finally got to her car, and he threw Stacey the keys.

"Dorie isn't feeling too well. Stacey, I know you don't drink, so why don't you drive. Winnie and I will get in the back."

"Uh, Jayson, I've never driven a stick shift before—have you?" Stacey protested.

"Yeah, my dad is a nut for old cars. Okay, get back there with Winnie, I'll drive."

"But Jayson, you've been drinking," Stacey said.

"Yes, but only three beers, and I ate all those snacks on the way over, remember? I'm not drunk at all." Stacey gave him a look. "Stace—you've seen me drunk—do I look drunk to you?"

"Well, no," she admitted. "But I think it's safer for me to drive a stick shift than for you to drive after drinking. Coach me, okay?"

"Why don't you and Winnie ride with Lenny and Charlie, and I'll take Dorie home."

"No, I'll be fine. Put Dorie in the front, then you can crawl in behind me." Jayson helped load Doris into the front passenger seat and then climbed into the tiny backseat where Winnie was already sleeping. He rolled down his window to say goodnight to Lenny, who was concerned about Doris. Jayson assured her and Charley that he would take good care of Doris and make sure she got home safely. Charley didn't consume any alcohol either, so she took the keys from Lenny and climbed into their Chevy.

The chilly air of a fall evening invigorated Doris enough to gesture a goodbye to Lenny, but she was asleep by the time Charley drove off, with Lenny's hand out the open window, waving wildly. Stacey started the engine, after quite a bit of lurching and stalling, she pulled out of the parking lot and drove slowly toward Kerryville. It was nearly two when they pulled up to the girls' dorm. Winnie and Stacey bid Jayson goodnight as he took over the driving to get Doris home. Winnie bent down to the closed window on Doris' side. "Bye, Dorie!" she waved frantically. Doris responded by turning her head away from the window and curling her legs up on the seat. Winnie laughed, blew Jayson a kiss, and joined Stacey in the doorway of the dorm.

Jayson pulled the car into Doris' dark driveway and sat for several minutes planning how best to get her safely into her house. "Dorie?" he said softly, "Dorie, you're home." She made a small whimpering sound and turned her head toward the voice. "Dorie?"

She opened her eyes and said, ever so sweetly, "Hi Jayson," then closed her eyes. Jayson got out of the car and came to Doris' side to let her out. He opened the door, but she did not move.

"Dorie?" he said again, shaking her gently, "Dorie, wake up, you're home." She stirred enough for him to help her out of the car and hobble up the steps to her front door. Jayson fumbled with her keys on the dark porch, trying first one then the other while Felix eyed him curiously from his window hammock. Finally, he found the right one and the lock turned. He hoisted Doris on his hip and shoved the door with his shoulder. Felix jumped down from the window to investigate but kept a safe distance. Jayson kicked the door closed with his foot and carried Doris through the house to her bedroom where he propped her up with her pillows. When he returned, Doris lay on her side, hugging a pillow, with Felix smelling her hair and wearing an unpleasant expression.

"I'm so thirsty," she mumbled.

"Okay, I'll get you something," Jayson went to the kitchen and poured Doris a tall glass of water. "Here you go," he said, sitting her back up and putting the glass in her hand.

Doris took a few tiny sips and started to look around. "How did I get home?"

"I drove you," Jayson said, standing near her but not sure he should sit beside her on the bed.

"Oh," Doris said and took another sip, but as she became more alert, she was seized with a sudden and overwhelming urge to throw up. She pushed Jayson aside and rushed to the toilet in her bathroom. She didn't even have time to close the door. Jayson stood a respectful distance away, but leaned in occasionally to make sure she was all right.

Doris wretched and coughed with a terrible guttural sound, hugging the cool toilet for balance. *Thank god I cleaned the house Wednesday,* she thought to herself. When she was sure she was finished, she flushed the toilet and pulled some tissue paper to her mouth, wiped her lips and nose, then put her face down on the cool tile of the bathroom floor. It felt so solid and cool she did not want to move.

In the meantime, Jayson emptied her water into the sink and put the glass into the dishwasher. "Dorie?" he said as he turned the corner into her bedroom. There was no answer. He peeked into the bathroom where he found Doris sound asleep on the floor with Felix curled up beside her. She looked so peaceful he smiled, but he knew he could not let his art teacher sleep all night on the hard floor.

He lifted her arms around his neck and picked her up. As he carried her to the bed, she nuzzled her nose into the crook of his neck and whispered, "I love you." Jayson had experience with a lot of intoxicated people, so he figured it was an outburst from some alcohol soaked dream. For all Doris knew, she was still on the bathroom floor.

"I love you, too, Dorie," he said, smiling, as he laid her on the bed. He took her shoes and belt off, pulled the covers over her, turned off the light, and searched for extra pillows and blankets for the sofa. Doris pushed one foot from the covers and planted it on the floor to keep the room from spinning.

25

In the morning, sunlight streamed into Doris' bedroom and bounced off the white sheets right into her eyes. She moaned and covered her face; Felix sat patiently beside her head on the pillow. A throbbing pain came from her subconscious into the front of her forehead, and she turned restlessly from side to side to make it stop. It didn't work.

She opened one eye and looked at Felix, who took this as an opportunity for some morning affection. He found her hand sticking out from under the pillow and burrowed his head forcefully under it. Her fingers scratched behind his ears, but her heart wasn't in it. Doris sheltered her open eyes from the light with the other hand and looked around the room. She tried to organize her memory of the night before, but the pounding in her head and over her nose made it virtually impossible to concentrate. She scratched an itch on her leg and realized she was still in her clothes. Beside her on the night table lay her belt, rolled up neatly, and on the floor sat her shoes. She squeezed her eyes closed, trying to focus, then let out a deep sigh, rolled onto her back and looked up at the ceiling. "Oh god, what in the world did I do last night?"

"You tied one on," Jayson said from the doorway. He had been up for an hour, making breakfast and tea and studying his lines.

Doris jumped nearly an inch off the bed, then quickly took the edge of the white eyelet sheet and covered her face in embarrassment. "Go away!"

"You don't want me to do that, Dorie, because I have the perfect hangover remedy. You will feel like new in no time."

"I can't look you in the face, Jayson, go away."

"Don't be silly, Dorie, this was character study. Believe me, Martha will be better for it. Now you need to go into the bathroom and clean up. Take a nice hot bath or shower, wash your face, brush your teeth, and then come into the kitchen. I promise you will feel better." He smiled and turned away, heading back to the kitchen.

Doris flipped the covers off her face and stumbled out of bed then rushed to the door to lock it. She stood for a long moment to re-establish her balance. She breathed deeply, rubbed her face, and headed for the bathroom. She sniffed her clothes; they smelled like a fireplace. She made a face and threw them into the hamper by the tub and started the water. Her nose wrinkled when she took a whiff of the stale smoke in her hair. She looked down at the toilet and a few residual pieces of regurgitated food on the seat. *Oh, my god,* she thought to herself, *please don't tell me I got sick in front of a student. Oh, god I will never be able to look at his face again.*

Doris took the cleaner she kept in the cabinet and scrubbed down the toilet and floor, then caught a glimpse of herself in the mirror. She almost screamed but then realized it might make Jayson dart in, and she most definitely did *not* want that. She cupped a hand over her mouth and then closed her eyes as she stepped into the tub. She sank into the warm water, covering her head and face, her knees sticking out of the bubbles. When she came up she felt reborn. The heat on her skin and sweet aroma of jasmine bath oil felt like redemption, but she knew it wasn't going to last. Sooner or later, she must go into her kitchen and face Jayson.

Doris finished her bath ritual, and although her headache lingered, she was beginning to feel a lot better. She put on a fresh set of clothes, combed out her wet hair, dabbed the slightest bit of make-up on her face, and stepped out to confront her humiliation.

She found Jayson sitting on her sofa reading his script, sipping tea, and watching cartoons. He turned to look at her and smiled. Without a word, he scurried to the kitchen to pull a plate of scrambled eggs and toast from the microwave and a tomato juice concoction from the fridge. He sat the food down on Avis' dining room table Doris had recently acquired, with a linen napkin, and a small cup with three of Doris' pansies from the back porch.

Doris opened her mouth to complain, but Jayson hushed her. "No talking," he instructed, "sit down, sip on your drink, and eat slowly."

She did as she was told, and Jayson pulled up a chair beside her. "I need some ibuprofen," she said pathetically, "my head is killing me."

"No, you don't," Jayson said, "I have a much better cure, and it's all natural."

She didn't argue, she trusted Jayson, so she didn't question his tactics. He sat quietly reading his script while she nibbled on the food. She took a sip of the red beverage and made a face, "What is in this drink?"

"That's a secret," he said, smiling, "but if you drink it all, I'll tell you.

Deal?"

She nodded and sipped. She ate in silence, trying not to look at Jayson. Finally, she asked, "What time is it?"

"Nearly eight thirty," he said, checking his watch. "I need to go pretty soon. I have to be there for set work sessions at nine."

"Oh, yes," Doris said, "I forgot. I really meant to go today."

"You still can if you want," Jayson said eagerly, but then he looked at her face and retracted. "But I know you're not feeling well, so don't worry 'bout it."

"It's not that," she said, "I, well, who saw me last night? I mean, I know who was at the bar, but who saw me . . . what the heck *did* I do?"

Jayson laughed. "You got a little woozy at the bar, that's all, then you fell asleep on the way home. Stacey drove us to the dorms, and I brought you home."

"What about Lenny?"

"Well, I won't lie, Dorie, we all knew you drank a little too much." Doris expression changed from one of depression to horror. "But," he quickly added, "I have seen almost everyone who was there in the same condition. And they have seen me drunk, too, except for Charley. She's a recovering alcoholic, so she doesn't drink anymore. But I have driven Lenny home, and they've done the same for me."

"I don't think I can face them," Doris said, at the edge of tears.

"It means you're part of the group, Dorie. We've all been there, so don't sweat it."

Doris wasn't too sure, but she knew it would be better to face them at a set work session than during a class day on campus. If they were going to ask about her hangover or make jokes about her dancing at the bar, better they do it at set work than in front of Martin. *Martin, oh god,* she thought, *this was the first time he even crossed her mind. How will I explain this to Martin?*

"You are a miracle worker, Jayson, I am feeling better. If you can wait for a few minutes, I'll get some old pants on and take you over there. I don't know if I can do anything to help, but I would like to try." She got up and took her dishes to the sink.

"You *are* kidding, aren't you?" Jayson followed behind with his cup. "We'd be stoked to have you. Don't you remember how hard it is to get people to do tech work? Everyone wants to be a star—nobody wants to do the grunt work."

"Well, I do," she handed him a dishtowel to dry his hands and headed into the bedroom. She donned a pair of old denim overalls she used for garden work, along with a tailored flannel shirt, and her one pair of perfectly white tennis shoes. She pulled her hair back with a band, and took three Advil tablets. *What he doesn't know won't hurt him,* she mused.

"Should I take anything?" she asked. Jayson smiled at her in her overalls and perfectly ironed shirt.

"No, just you. You look great," he said, opening the door for her.

"This old thing?" she said playfully, "Oh, pshaw!"

"Pshaw?" Jayson said as she locked the door. Felix jumped into his window hammock and watched as Doris pulled the car out of the driveway and headed toward Kerryville College without ever noticing the blinking light on her answering machine.

When Doris and Jayson arrived at the theatre, no one seemed surprised to see them come in together, and no one asked about the night before, or even if she was feeling better. Winnie and Stacey said hi, and Lenny came up to tell her how grateful she was for her help. "I know you don't have to be here, Dorie, so it's great you came out to help the students."

"Well, we'll have to see how much help I can be, but I'm willing to try," Doris smiled.

"I know Jayson will be glad to use your art training to do some of the detail painting."

"Point me in the right direction—I aim to please!" Doris gave a salute, which made Lenny laugh out loud as she walked away.

Tom began getting tools and paint out of the storage room, and Jayson asked various students to begin different tasks. Doris recognized a lot of them from auditions and the first read-through. They nodded hello as she passed them and smiled. She walked up to Jayson as he was showing two skinny boys how to brace the doorframe. Once they started working, he turned to her. "Dorie, I could really use your help with painting. The chair rail and window frames are ready, and I would like them painted with this," he reached over for a can of paint and a brush, "and then aged—like an old house that hasn't been kept up. Can you do that?"

Doris took the brush and paint and said, "I will do my best. Where should I work?" Jayson showed her an open area where she could lay the wood down to paint and dry, so she started working while Jayson helped the next crewmember.

Doris laid out all the railing and frames and began stirring the paint. She put newspapers under the areas she would be painting so no drips would get on the floor. As she started her delicate brush strokes, Tom walked by and asked her what she was doing. She explained what Jayson instructed her to do, and Tom made a face and sighed. "I told him not to use that color—it will look all wrong on the flats."

"Do you want me to wait until you speak with Jayson?" Doris didn't want to get in the middle of any artistic disputes. Set designers, she knew, were another kind of artist, and artists had specific opinions about how they wanted things done. The problem presented by Jayson being the designer and Tom being his teacher would complicate it. "I'm sure I can get busy with something else."

"No, I guess not," Tom said, taking off his dirty baseball cap and scratching his head, "He'll have to learn the hard way. You can't tell these kids anything." He put his cap back on his head and walked off. Doris resumed her painting, wondering what the flats looked like.

Around noon, Lenny yelled for everyone to meet in the greenroom for pizza and drinks. Doris wasn't aware Lenny ordered lunch for everyone who came to set work on Saturdays, but she thought it was a wonderful idea. Students swooped into the small room like a hoard of locusts, grabbing sodas and food, and then sat outside on the patio or under trees to eat. Lenny, Jayson, Tom, and Doris took what remained and sat around in the uncomfortable leather benches and chairs to eat. "Oh, Dorie, I wanted to know if you could come to a special rehearsal tomorrow afternoon around two?" Lenny asked with her mouth full of pizza.

"Uh, well, yes, I guess so, if you think you need me. I have some work to do, but I think I can rearrange it."

"Great, I appreciate it so much," Lenny said, taking a swig of her diet cola. "The lady who is understudying Martha cannot come Monday night for the run-through, so I wanted to move it to Sunday. Everyone else said they could come, so we'll meet in 106 to do a run-through for the understudies to watch and take notes, and then we'll let them run it. It helps the actors to watch someone else do their parts; I think you'll find it interesting."

Doris cringed a little. "What time?"

"We plan to start at 2:00."

Doris didn't reveal her inner disappointment, but mentally tried to calculate if she'd have enough time with Tootsie. "Okay, I will be there. I'll finish up the painting I'm doing and then take off so I can get some work done." She noticed that Jayson ate quietly and listened. "Will that be okay, Jayson?"

"Sure," Tom said, Jayson looked over at him but didn't speak. "We're so glad you could come in at all today, right Jayson."

Jayson looked at his pizza and nodded. "It's no problem, Dorie, thanks for doing the painting for me."

"Even though it's the wrong color!" Tom mumbled under his breath as he left the room, tossing his trash into the big can which was holding the door open. Jayson sighed and rolled his eyes, and Lenny patted his hand and smiled.

Doris leaned over and whispered, "Personally, I like the color!" Jayson smiled and looked at Lenny and then back to Doris. "Well, I better get back to work so I can finish up the painting." Doris tossed her trash, dusted her bottom off, and headed back to the chair rails.

Jayson could be heard outside yelling "Okay, everybody, let's get back to work!" About an hour later, Doris finished her job, closed the paint can and set it back on the shelf, and then washed out her brush. She walked up to Jayson and said, "I didn't get the aging done today, but I will come back next Saturday and do it, if it's okay."

Jayson smiled in appreciation, his art teacher asking for his permission to go home. "That's no problem, Dorie, we won't put those details on the set till the end. You were great today—thanks a lot."

"So were you," she said, "You make a good manager, delegating work to others and patiently showing them how to do it." She started to turn, then stopped and said, "by the way, you owe me a drink recipe!" Jayson laughed and nodded as Doris fetched her purse and car keys. "See ya' tomorrow," she said as she headed toward the door before he could respond. From the corner of her eye she spied a figure in the shadows by the door. It was Kayla; her arms were crossed in front of her, and she leaned her shoulder against the brick wall. Doris paused for a moment and smiled at her, but Kayla's gaze held steady on Jayson as he instructed Moses how to brace, or secure, the flats.

Winnie looked up and said, "Bye, Dorie, thanks for coming!"

Doris remembered herself and passed through the door with a little wave to Winnie. She walked to her car with an odd feeling of renewal mixed with anxiety. The medicine started to wear off; the headache still lingered in her temples. But the red and gold leaves stirred around her feet, the sound of the pep band could be heard from the football game at the stadium, and a cool breeze tugged at her shirt. She stopped for a moment to look at the blue sky above her then closed her eyes and breathed in the woodsy fragrance of an eastern Tennessee autumn.

Doris ran a few errands before heading home. She rummaged around the mall looking for show presents for the cast. She found a nice tie clasp with drama masks for Bill, drama mask necklaces for Teri and Lenny, a good pen and pencil set for Stacey and Winnie, and something more personal for Jayson. She smiled as the clerk wrapped it.

By the time she got home, Doris' headache came back in full force. All she wanted was another round of Advil and her bed, but she knew she must get some schoolwork done. Her conference paper lay open on her dresser, reminding her to spend some time in the library to update some of her research. Fortunately, it was an excerpt from her dissertation on a comparison of the painting technique of lesser-known Impressionist female painters. She freshened Felix's bowls and took three pills before spreading her work in front of her on the dining room table. As she was placing a fresh cup of coffee on the table, her doorbell rang. "Who in the . . ." she muttered as she headed toward the foyer.

She opened the door to find Martin standing there with a look of sheer terror on his face. The unruly flap of hair that usually falls in his eyes was held back by a brown velvet fedora she had often seen him wear during the winter. "Doris? Where in the world have you been? Are you all right?"

It took a moment for Doris to answer; she was trying to remember the last time she talked to Martin. "I . . ." she started, opening the door wider to let him enter. He put his jacket and hat on the hall tree while Doris shut the door, still staring at him. "I rehearsed till pretty late last night," again she hesitated. Should she tell him or not? *No, not yet*, she decided. "And I went over to the theatre this morning to help with the set. I think I told you I might do that."

"Yes, well, you might have," Martin said as the tension eased in his face. It seemed enough for him she looked well, dressed in her overalls and tennis shoes. "I called your cell phone and got no answer so I came by the rehearsal room last night to surprise you, and no one was there. So, I drove back here, thinking we might make plans for the weekend, you know." Martin moved naturally into the living room and sat down on the sofa. Doris trailed behind him, finally resting on the chair to his right. "Then you weren't here either. I sat for about twenty minutes, thinking it would take you about that long to get home, if I'd missed you *en route*." Martin rubbed his hands together, Doris thought to herself only a college professor would use the term "*en route*."

"Well, you didn't show, so I drove around town looking for you, but, obviously, I didn't find you." He was avoiding eye contact. Doris knew he was embarrassed to be so worried, especially since he had found her safe and sound. "I finally returned home and called to leave a message. Your light is still blinking. Don't you ever check your messages, Doris?"

Doris moved next to him on the sofa; the wild flap of hair fell forward, and she put it back in place. "I'm sorry I worried you, Martin. I always turn my cell phone off at rehearsal, and then I guess I forgot to turn it back on. I'm still not used to having one, you know? Lenny and I went for drinks after rehearsal. When I got home, I was so exhausted I fell asleep." Martin's worried look dissipated almost entirely as he watched her talk and stroke his head. "I slept a little late this morning and rushed out of here in a hurry to get to the set work session. I didn't even see the message until now when you pointed it out."

"But you're here now, why don't you look at your answering machine every once and awhile?" Martin's worrying energy converted itself into frustration energy. This, after all, wasn't the first time she had failed to check her machine.

Doris let it pass. She hadn't told him how upset she became when she found the messages from her mother, so how could he understand how much his comment hurt? "Martin, you must remember I'm not used to having someone check up on me all the time." She was trying to sound patient and understanding, but a little irritation came through in her tone. She found his concern endearing, but she was feeling a little smothered. Martin must have sensed something because he backed down.

"I'm sorry. Sarah and I always knew where the other one was."

"I'm not Sarah, Martin." He gave her a wounded look. "I'm so happy you had such a great relationship with Sarah and I don't mind you talking about her. But I do mind you comparing us. Also, you are remembering the Sarah you were with for thirty some years—there's no way I can compete with that, and I don't want to."

"I wasn't comparing you and Sarah, Doris, but I guess I was comparing the relationships. I'm sorry. I just haven't had much experience with relationships; Sarah is the only woman I ever loved before meeting you."

"Comparisons are natural, Martin, but you shouldn't judge me because I don't act the same way Sarah did. She was a different person with a very different background and even a different age than I am. I'm very independent, Martin. There are just times I want to be alone, and I don't want to be questioned about everything I do."

Martin sat in thought for a long moment, holding his lips between his teeth. "Ok. I understand what you're saying. I will try to back off some."

"I don't want to force you to change the way you love someone, Martin, but I have to tell you that it's too clingy for me. I've lived alone and taken care of myself all my life."

"You don't need me," he said sadly.

"Maybe. But I do want you," she said softly. "Need and want and love are all different things. I don't have to need you to love you."

Martin looked up with an expression of discovery. "I never thought of it that way, but you're absolutely right."

"You want some coffee? I have a fresh pot." Martin accepted the coffee and asked her about doing something in the evening. "I'll have to see how much work I get done. Lenny called an extra rehearsal for tomorrow afternoon, so I have to get my schoolwork done today. I even left the set work early so I could come home and finish it."

"I have some work to do, too, Doris. Would it be okay if I bring my papers in from the car? We can work awhile and then go out for supper?"

"Now that sounds like a plan," Doris said giving him a big hug. Martin squeezed her extra close, and he didn't let go as quickly as he usually does.

Martin left to retrieve his paperwork, and then they both sat at the dining room table for the entire afternoon, reading and grading. Felix regularly jumped up on the table and plopped himself in the middle of Doris' papers. She petted him, kissed his forehead, and then shooed him away. He sauntered into the kitchen for a bite of food then returned to the table and Doris' papers. At first she laughed, but as time wore on and he kept repeating the performance, she became increasingly irritated.

Occasionally, Martin would freshen Doris' coffee or offer to get her a snack. Around six, Doris leaned back and stretched her arms over her head. "I can't do anymore right now. I need to take a bath to wash the paint off my arms and then we can go eat something, I can get back to it tonight."

Martin looked up, the white flap of hair over his nose. He pushed it away and said, "Sounds good to me. Want me to call Le Petit and get a reservation?" Doris yawned and nodded. "I finished most of my grading; what do you still have left to do?"

Doris took their empty mugs to the sink and ran water in them while she spoke. "I got my papers graded, too, but I need to do a little class prep, and I want to work on my conference paper. The conference is right after the show and I know I won't have any time the last two weeks of rehearsal."

"Can you do it here?"

"Not really, I need to spend some time at the library in the reference section. I want to see if anyone else has published anything interesting on the subject. I know everyone today uses the Internet for everything, but I still like to bury myself in research at a table in the library."

"I feel the same way. Okay, we can go to the library after dinner if you want."

The thought of doing more academic work sickened Doris. "Let's wait and see how we both feel, okay?" Martin nodded and started collecting his papers. Doris headed for the bathroom.

Although she usually takes baths, Doris needed something to help her wake up. She opened a new bar of peppermint soap Avis gave her last Christmas and stepped into the shower. As she was getting dressed, she pulled open her lingerie drawer and spotted the black teddy folded neatly beside her white cotton bras and panties. Something playful seized her, and she reached for it.

Doris looked with some approval at her form in the full-length mirror of her bathroom. The black lace flattered her pale skin and auburn hair. "Not bad," she muttered aloud. She finished dressing, smug with the knowledge Martin was getting a little treat after dinner.

26

Le Petit was crowded when they arrived. Even with reservations, Doris and Martin sat on the small benches near the front for nearly twenty minutes. They chatted about the menu and what to order, then Doris pointed out the new autumn décor around the front arch and windows. As they followed the hostess to their table, Doris noticed the tablecloths were changed from mauve to maroon, a change she liked. They both felt adventurous and wanted something they had never ordered. Martin requested duck, and Doris decided to try blackened fish. When the food came, the fish was too spicy for Doris, so Martin swapped with her.

Doris and Martin conversed about new policies at the college, the last letter Martin received from his son, Cedrick, current offerings at the local art cinema, Doris' rehearsals, and Martin's problem students. *Martin is so interesting,* Doris thought, *he can carry on a conversation about almost anything.* Occasionally, Martin would reach across the table to squeeze Doris' hand or she would push his untamed hair off his glasses. *We look like a happily married couple,* Doris observed at one point, *comfortable and easy with each other—like well-worn pajamas.* The image made her smile, but something tugged at the back of her mind. *Aren't I a little too young to be in a "comfortable" relationship? I haven't even had exciting and passionate yet. How did I miss those?*

Doris and Martin finished their meal and after-dinner coffee as the sky turned to pitch black and heavy cloud cover obscured the stars. A light fall drizzle baptized Martin as he ran for the car. Doris watched him from the little overhang on the front steps of Le Petit. In the bright amber lights of the tiny parking lot his head bobbed between the cars, his glasses were dotted with water droplets, and his hair was in his face. *What a dear, sweet man,* she thought.

Once in the car, Doris suggested they do something fun. She had decided to go to the library after rehearsal on Sunday, and now she wanted some excitement.

"Do you want to go to Cinema Paradiso to see a Fellini film?" Martin offered.

"Sounds good, but we go there so often. I want to do something different." She thought for a moment while Martin wiped the condensation from his windshield. "How would you feel about driving to Chattanooga?"

"Chattanooga?" Martin stopped and looked at her. "What do you want to do there?"

"Well, there are a lot of places to dance there. I'd like to go dancing—what d'ya say?"

Martin opened his mouth and took in a small bit of air. He looked around the parking lot, then at his watch. "We wouldn't get there until around ten," he said wearily.

"Well, that's when the nightclubs get started, anyway, Martin. I've never danced with you. Don't you want to dance with me?" She turned big green eyes his way and playfully batted her lashes. He couldn't help but laugh.

"Okay, okay!" Martin said, "why don't we plan to go to Chattanooga on a Saturday when we can leave in the afternoon, go to dinner, see a show, *maybe* go dancing," he emphasized the maybe, "then spend the night and drive back on Sunday?" Doesn't that sound better than a fly-by-night trip when we're both exhausted and not really prepared for it?"

Doris faced front. She knew he was right, and she hated it. She wanted to do something spontaneous, but she *was* exhausted and she *did* have rehearsal and work to do the next day. "Shoot," was all she could say.

Martin sighed and rubbed her shoulder. "Why don't we go back to Benny's? It wouldn't take long to get there, and we could enjoy a few drinks and listen to some good music. How does that sound?" Martin winced as if he was wondering whether she would slap him or hug him.

Doris turned and looked at Martin. "You are always right, Martin. Don't you ever get tired of it?" Martin stopped breathing. He waited to see if she was angry or grateful. "That sounds wonderful--exactly what I feel like—a good drink and some sexy music." She smiled at him, and his face relaxed. She leaned over and kissed him, and he repaid her with a warm caress.

The rain got heavier as they drove. The jazz club seemed more colorful in the rain, with tiny blue lights along the entrance, which continued into the seating area and up to the stage where a small combo played some standard Doris recognized but couldn't name. They found a table near the middle of the room and settled in with their drink orders. Doris hesitated before ordering anything alcoholic; after her hangover in the morning she promised God she would never drink again. But now, she was feeling better and realized it was the headache talking. Still, she didn't want anything too strong. "I'd like white wine, please," she said.

Martin studied her for a moment and ordered a beer. "Would you like anything else?" Doris shook her head and turned her attention to the stage. The saxophonist took center stage with the melody while Doris racked her brain trying to remember the name of the song. It never came to her.

They nursed their drinks for nearly two hours, talking only occasionally, but cuddling together with her head on his chest and his arm around her shoulders. The server returned intermittently, hoping they might order more drinks so he would get a better tip, but most of the time they sat with eyes closed, nodding to the music. When he came to clean up their empty glasses, Martin handed him a twenty-dollar tip and helped Doris out of her chair. The waiter gave Martin a nod of approval, as if he suddenly changed his opinion of old codgers who come into the bar to nurse one drink and listen to the music. He smiled and said thanks, then started cleaning up the table for the next couple.

Martin wrapped Doris' sweater over her shoulders and then trudged into the muddy parking lot to retrieve the car. The drive back to Doris' house was quiet except for Martin softly humming a favorite tune. Doris leaned her head back, enjoying the afterglow of the music and the wine. She felt sexy in her new lingerie and wondered if Martin would appreciate it. The rain abated, but the roads remained wet and slick. She was looking out the passenger window one moment at the passing scenery, and then suddenly she awoke as they pulled into her driveway. "Oh dear," she said, rubbing her face, "did I fall asleep?"

"Unless you snore when you're awake, yes, you fell asleep," Martin joked. She slapped his arm with the back of her hand. "Just kidding, Honey, you looked like an angel." Doris knew he was being sweet; she gave him a look and pursed her lips together.

Felix greeted them at the door with a meow. Doris picked him up and put him over her shoulder, carrying him around the house while she removed her shoes and hung up her sweater and Martin's jacket and hat. "You want some coffee, Martin?"

"The rain has chilled me to the bone. Do you have any hot cocoa?"

They sat on the sofa sipping their hot chocolates, talking about how much they enjoyed the jazz group. When Martin started yawning, Doris said, "Oh no, you can't go to sleep yet. I have my secrets, too, you know." He gave her a puzzled look as she took his hand and led him into the bedroom. She turned the lights to dim, with enough illumination to keep from bumping into furniture and to make sure Martin could see the black lingerie. Doris sat Martin down on the bed, and he obediently followed her lead. She started kissing him and unbuttoning her blouse. When she peeled off all her clothes, revealing her surprise, Martin looked at her with a smile.

Martin let Doris unbutton his shirt and remove his pants. She didn't like his boxers and tank-top undershirt, they made him look like her father, so she removed them both in a hurry. They crawled under the covers, and Martin asked her to remove the teddy. "Don't you want to do it," she said, teasing him. Martin looked unsure, but swallowed hard and nodded. He pulled gently at the buttons, and they fumbled around trying to remove it gracefully.

Doris began to feel a tingle as he moved the fabric aside and climbed aboard. But Martin did what he always did; he huffed and puffed a bit and then collapsed in ecstasy with his cheek next to Doris' ear. When he finally rolled off her, he kissed her on the cheek and turned over with his back to her.

Doris lay for a few moments absorbing the event. The tingle between her legs subsided, but strangely, she missed it. She wondered if this was what sex was like for everyone. If so, she didn't understand the big deal. She had only known Ethan, one guy in grad school, and now Martin, and they were all disappointingly the same. It was nothing like the sex she had seen in the movies; there was none of the passion, the ripping off clothes, and the obvious hunger to consume each other. Martin started snoring softly beside her as one tear seeped from her eye and trickled down the side of her face and into her ear. Doris didn't bother to wipe it away, she turned over with her back to Martin and studied the way the moonlight cast shadows on her lacy bedroom curtains. Felix, sensing the festivities had settled down, jumped onto the bed and made himself at home on Doris' hip.

Doris dozed off and on through the night. Finally, unable to go back to sleep, she got up around five, took a long bath, then cuddled up in her favorite sweat pants and chenille robe on the sofa. It was still dark outside so she turned on a nearby lamp, retrieved her conference paper, and sat reading and revising. Felix jumped up on the coffee table and gave her a confused look, then nestled next to her on the couch, resting his head on her socked feet. Doris was careful not to wake Martin—not because she wanted him to get his sleep, but because she didn't want to see him or deal with him. She knew she was angry with him, but she wasn't exactly sure why.

When Martin emerged in his boxers and t-shirt around seven, the sun was shining into the little screened-in porch where Doris sat having a cup of coffee and smoking a cigarette. Martin knocked on the French door to say good morning. Doris nodded coldly and gave him a little wave with her cigarette. He turned and disappeared into the bedroom. Doris figured he was disgusted by the cigarette and decided to go back to bed. Apparently, however, he cleaned up, shaved, and dressed, because when he returned, nearly a half-hour later, he looked ready for the day. Doris was enjoying the cold chill ushered in by the rain, especially wrapped up in her robe and slippers. She sat sipping coffee and working on her lines. When the French doors opened, she saw Martin with a tray of food in his hands. He presented a beautiful breakfast of eggs, toast, freshly squeezed juice, and coffee. Without a word, he sat the tray down in front of Doris who moved her feet off a metal chair for Martin to sit. He laid out their napkins, utensils, glasses, and plates, then disposed of the tray beneath his chair. "I thought you might enjoy a good breakfast," he said, kissing her cheek. He didn't notice Doris avoided eye contact with him. He never noticed her nonverbal cues. "Oh, just a minute, I forgot something!" He vanished into the house, but Doris didn't look to see where he was going. She didn't care. The breakfast did look good, though, she was starving, and she knew Martin was a good cook. He came back moments later with his jacket on and the newspaper tucked under his arm. "Here you go, m'lady."

"Thanks, Martin, this looks good."

"Are you okay, Doris? When I woke up you weren't in bed."

"I couldn't sleep, so I got up early and did some work." She was trying to punish him, but the eggs were perfectly prepared.

"Why couldn't you sleep?" He reached out and touched her hand. She didn't respond in kind; she lifted her hand to reach for her orange juice. Doris was torn. Should she tell him what a big disappointment he was in bed? He still hadn't told her he loved her to her face. She was still angry with Martin for not being passionate and ravishing her, but she knew she was being silly. Martin was not that kind of man, and she knew it going into this. Martin is a stable, intelligent, mature, and compassionate man. She loved him; she loved the kind of man he was. She never wanted to hurt him. Here he prepared this marvelous breakfast, brought her the newspaper, and would probably be willing to do whatever she asked him to do today. Why did she want more? How could she when she had so much?

"Doris?" Martin brought her thoughts back to the porch and their breakfast. "Why couldn't you sleep?"

She smiled and looked at him. His face a poster for concern, deep lines in his forehead scrunched down toward his nose, grey eyes full of worry. *I can't bear the thought of hurting him, not now.* "I don't know," she said finally, "I guess I have so much on my mind right now." Martin nodded his understanding. They finished their breakfast in silence, each with their favorite sections of the newspaper. Felix sat on Doris' lap and took a bath. "We have an extra rehearsal today, so I will be meeting Tootsie earlier than originally planned." Martin kindly left after breakfast. She sweetly kissed him goodbye before he drove off.

Doris rushed around getting dressed and met Tootsie a little before noon at the Mexican restaurant. She looked glorious in a soft pink blouse that showed off her blue eyes and flawless complexion. Her soft graying curls framed her sweet face, still as lovely as always, with deep dimples and glossy pink lips. It surprised Doris that she was indeed so glad to see her old friend and disappointed in herself for not making an effort sooner.

"Oh, Tootsie, why have we waited so long to do this" Doris whispered in her ear as they embraced.

"Life," said Tootsie. "We go through every day just taking care of business, making future plans that never materialize because we're so busy with every day. It doesn't matter; we're here now. Tell me everything!" That famous giggle emerged, making Doris feel sixteen again. They ordered lunch and a couple of cocktails and chatted happily about their lives.

"My two sons, Jake and Sam, Jr. are married with two kids each. Jake's in Knoxville, and Sammy is way out in Memphis. My daughter, Hayley, got herself into a bad situation," Tootsie said, pushing her salad around the plate. "She married a man we all liked at first, but we had no idea he was just using Hayley. She's a nurse, a good one, who makes a good living. Richard, or 'Dick', as I like to call him, was happy to live off that and feed his drug habits until Hayley finally wised up and left his ass."

"Oh, Tootsie, it must be so hard to watch your child go through all that."

She smiled. "You always know what to say, Dorie. Yes, it was horrible, but things are getting better now. Sam and I help her out with the kids so she can work to pay off bad credit and other debts that Richard owes."

"Didn't they get divorced? Does she have to honor his debts?"

"They did divorce, but her name was on everything, so when the bank couldn't get money out of Richard, they came after Hayley. Of course, it's not ideal, but she has broken all ties with him, and if she can get out from under this, she has a bright future. The only decent thing Richard did was give her those two beautiful children and then severed his parental rights when they divorced. He wants nothing to do with taking responsibility for any of his actions. He'll probably die in prison." Tootsie looked sadly into the middle distance. Then suddenly, she sprang back to life. "Tell me about your life. I kept up with some of your adventures through your mom, but what about now? The play? How exciting—and are you dating that nice man who was with you at the wake?"

Doris tried to encapsulate the complexities of the past two months for Tootsie. The play, Martin, *Jayson*. "Oh goodness, Dorie, how do you keep your hands off him? He sounds gorgeous!"

Doris took a sip of her drink and smiled. "Well, I haven't told you everything." Tootsie raised one eyebrow, rested her chin on her clasped hands, and smiled, waiting for the rest of the story. Doris had never verbalized her feelings for Martin or Jayson, but she felt completely comfortable sharing with Tootsie. *There are precious few friends in your life that you can go without seeing for years and then pick up a conversation like you saw them yesterday*, Doris thought. *For me, it's Tootsie.* She explained her reluctance to do the show with a student, her struggles to keep Jayson at arm's length, and then Martin, how much she felt for him and how often he disappointed her.

"Oh, God, Dorie, your life is so exciting compared to mine! Whew! I totally understand trying to stay away from Jayson, but lordy, I don't know if I could. Tell me more about Martin. He sounds like a wonderful guy, but I'm not sure he's the right one for you."

"Why?" Doris was shocked. Martin was the perfect man for her, wasn't he? He's mature, educated, kind, and she enjoyed his companionship immensely.

"Well, from what you just told me, he doesn't make you happy. He's inconsiderate in the sack and maybe a little too old for you, a different generation. And he's asked you to marry him but hasn't told you he loves you yet? What is he waiting for?" Doris sat quietly digesting Tootsie's words. Tootsie could see she had taken her friend to an uncomfortable place. "I'm sorry, Dorie, what do I know? It's none of my business; I'm just saying that based on what you're telling me . . .. so, tell me something good about Martin. What do you love about him?"

"He's reliable. He's smart, well-educated, and can talk about almost any subject. And he's loyal, completely devoted to me, I think." Doris' eyebrows were furrowed in worry.

"Why don't you just talk to him Doris? Tell him what you want in bed—he's not a mind reader. If you tell him what you need and he doesn't try to meet your needs, then you might think about looking elsewhere. He's sounds a little old fashioned, maybe he just needs a little prompting?"

Doris looked into Tootsie's sweet face, a true friend, and nodded. "Yes, Tootsie, you're right. How have I lived all these years without you?"

"I was always here, Dorie, just a phone call away. Maybe you didn't really need me until now."

"No, I just didn't know how badly I needed you!" The women continued through dessert and coffee when Doris realized she needed to get to rehearsal. They embraced and promised to be better about staying in touch. This time, Doris really meant it.

The run-through felt different to Doris, but she wasn't sure why. She guessed it was having an audience. The understudies sat watching intently, taking notes for blocking and leaning over occasionally to ask Stacey a question. Being stage manager, she was the understudies' director. Doris thought this arrangement made a lot of sense because it was good training for them and for her.

While she was watching her understudy do her lines, it occurred to her what felt different. She now understood how Martha feels—being drunk, that is. Doris had played intoxicated characters before, but now she realized there was typically an ignorant artificiality to it. She wasn't a method actor to the extent of thinking she needed to be drunk *while* playing the part, but Doris could now appreciate a closer kinship with Martha than before. Jayson was right. Still, she couldn't understand how anyone could become addicted to the feeling of being out of control. She guessed she needed to figure out Martha's pain to know why she prefers drinking to reality.

Doris found it interesting to see the other actors do the play, just as Lenny predicted. She saw a lot of new choices for the role she never noticed before, so she took a few notes. Gail, the woman playing Martha, was a little chubby, which Doris thought was more fitting for the character than her own bony arms and small chest. She knew she didn't want to gain any weight—*Elizabeth Taylor taught everyone a lesson by doing that,* Doris thought, *the most beautiful woman in the world gained all that weight and then couldn't get rid of it.* She wondered if she could do some padding and wear her costume a size smaller. She made a mental note to discuss her ideas with Lenny and Ida. She glanced over at her cast-mates. Jayson and Teri were both watching and taking notes. Although Bill didn't have an understudy, Stacey read his parts so he could observe. He crossed his arms over his chest and stretched out his crossed legs. Just as she looked at him he dozed off to sleep. *How rude*, she thought. *I guess you have nothing to learn here, Mr. "God's gift to theatre."* Doris decided she did not actually like Bill. She didn't dislike him, either, but she certainly didn't like him.

Lenny spent a lot of time after each run-through asking the actors questions and listening to their ideas and discoveries. It was the best rehearsal Doris could remember, but it was also exhausting. The last thing she wanted to do was go to the library and do research. She needed a little down time, and as much as she cared for Martin she was tired of him, too. She stopped for groceries and fast food on her way home and then sequestered herself in her living room with dinner, her cat, and the TV remote. It felt like heaven to be alone again in her own home, with no one calling her name or needing anything from her. She felt like she was breathing for the first time in weeks.

27

Thumbing through her mail on Monday morning Doris found a letter from her real estate agency concerning the estate sale. It was slated for the following Friday through Sunday, and Ms. Grindstaff wanted to know if Doris would like to go through her mother's house one more time prior to the sale. "No, I do not, thank you very much," she said aloud to herself, but she knew she would. She picked up the phone to call the agent and set up an appointment to go through Avis' house one last time.

After her 150 class, Lenny caught her in the hall with some good news. "Dorie, I forgot to tell you yesterday that you have tonight off. Martha is offstage making coffee in the first part of Act 2 so you have a freebie night!"

"Oh, Lenny, you don't know how badly I need this—thanks."

Doris prepared a lecture for her Art Appreciation class and then met Martin at the cafeteria. She told him the good news about rehearsal, but told him she must spend most of the afternoon in the library working on her conference paper. He offered dinner, but she declined. "I'm used to having more time to myself, Martin. I love your company, but sometimes I just need to be at home by myself." He nodded, trying to understand how anyone could actually enjoy being alone.

It felt so good to Doris to just have the space she needed to relax and get her work done. After her afternoon class, she headed to the library to finish up her research; she wanted to get her paper finished and out of the way; there would be no time for extra work after this week.

Doris got to the library and headed toward the reference section. She spread her papers and books around the desk and began taking notes. Doris relished immersing herself in volumes of books. It felt like home to her, being in the library, papers scattered everywhere, open books waiting to give up their treasures. She was grateful for the Internet, how easy it was to locate sources without the cumbersome card catalog, and the time technology saved millions of graduate students and scholars, but hours at a computer were not the same as hours poring over books in the library. The smell of open books, a wooden table, a stack of old volumes, could never be replaced by a computer. She was glad some information remained tucked away in books, unreachable by wires, modems, and megabytes.

She finished her work around six, suddenly realizing she was famished. Foster's made a delicious grilled chicken sandwich so she rushed over to place a go order. While she waited, she noticed several students eyeing her in a suspicious way. They seemed to be gossiping about her, but that was silly, she thought. *I'm tired and hungry. I guess they are not used to seeing a professor in Foster's this late on a Monday night.* She smiled at a few of them cautiously, and they smiled back then turned to their friends and whispered. *Odd*, she thought. Doris paid for her order and took off in Carmen, digging into the bag occasionally to pull out a French fry.

At home, she cleaned, did laundry, finally changed her closet to winter clothes and packed up the summer things, and then did some class prep for the rest of the week.

At rehearsal Tuesday night Lenny explained to Doris she had pre-planned the blocking for Acts 2 and 3. "I will give you the blocking, we will run through it a couple of times and see how it fits. If you have concerns or suggestions, let's talk about it and see what we can come up with—okay?" Then she started dictating moves and positions like a football coach calling plays. The actors wrote furiously in their scripts, looking more like children playing musical chairs than characters in a play. After a few times through, Doris and the others began to see the logic in Lenny's maze.

"We need a break!" Lenny said as she escaped to the porch. Doris stayed in the restroom for most of the time, not wanting to see or talk to anyone. The enormity of this play, the responsibility of playing Martha, the language, the sexuality, began to bear down on her. As people filtered back to the rehearsal room, Doris had a sudden attack of nerves and pulled Lenny over to talk.

"What *ever* made me think I could do this role?" she asked Lenny.

"Nonsense, Doris, what's going on?"

"I don't know. . . well, I don't know if I can kiss a student. The smoking and the flirting I can deal with, but I don't know, Lenny. Jayson is in one of my classes. I mean, I never even touch my students, much less kiss one of them!"

"What can I do to help you, Doris? You're doing a great job with the role, and I think you know Jayson is mature enough to act in a play with you without expecting special favors in class."

"Yes, I know, I know. It's nothing about Jayson, it's all about his classmates. What will *they* think?"

"Well, I don't know, Doris, and we can't control that. I know there was a big controversy last spring when one of the art teachers did a showing of his wife's nude photographs in the gallery, and two years ago one of our faculty members got arrested protesting the destruction of a historic landmark downtown. But it all eventually faded away because it didn't have anything to do with their teaching in the classroom. I guess you need to decide if doing the play the way it should be done is more important than public opinion and gossip. I will tell you I talked with Phyllis before I announced the play and asked you to be in it. She understood the nature of the play and expressed some concern, but she agreed there was so much artistic merit that forbidding it would be tantamount to censorship."

"Yes, I spoke to her after I got cast, and she said she didn't see a problem. Although this was before I knew I would be kissing a current student in the play."

"Well, why don't you go talk to Phyllis again? At least she'll have a heads-up if anyone says anything to her."

Lenny looked at Doris, giving her time to respond. Doris knew she was right. It was a play, and she did many plays before where she was required to kiss other actors. It was part of the job. Doris wondered if she was more afraid of what people might think when they saw her kiss Jayson or what she might feel when she kissed him.

"What would you say if we took some special rehearsal time for you and Jayson to work on this together—with only me there. Would it help?"

Doris smiled and was amazed at how relieved she felt. "Yes, that would be wonderful. It's hard enough to do this, but to do it the first time with an audience, and then lines to worry about . . . it would be so helpful!"

"Okay, then tomorrow night we'll do it," Lenny said and gave Doris a hug. "Don't worry, Doris, we'll work it out."

They ran through the first part of Act 2 up to the part where Martha dances with Nick; it was bumpy, as expected. Lenny announced that

Wednesday's rehearsal would be working difficult blocking such as the attack and the dance, and they'd try to finish the second act on Thursday night. When everyone darted off in every direction, Lenny pulled Jayson aside and explained the special session to him. He nodded and smiled, visibly relieved, and looked over at Doris and winked. She smiled and picked up her sweater and purse to leave.

She was almost to the door when Jayson caught up with her. "Dorie, wait up!" She stopped and took a deep breath. She wanted to escape without notice. "I wanted to tell you how glad I am you asked for the extra rehearsal." Doris nodded and kept walking, Jayson bounding beside her. "I mean I kissed Teri last year when she played Cheri in *Bus Stop*, and we did the same exercise. It's awkward at first, you know?"

Doris pushed her way through the door and stopped on the landing to look at Jayson, those blue eyes, that black hair, the perfect skin. "Jayson, I've done a lot of plays where I had to kiss another actor, but I've never done this with a student. I worry about what your classmates will think about us and how I could possibly explain it if you ended up getting an A in my class."

Jayson started to laugh—those perfect white teeth. "There's not much chance of that!" Doris turned to walk away, he clearly did not understand. "Dorie, wait," Jayson pulled at her arm. She stopped on the first step but didn't turn to face him. "I know what you mean, Dorie, I guess I'm not as worried about it as you are."

"You don't have anything to lose," she said and continued down the steps. Jayson let her go, watching as she climbed into Carmen and pulled out of the parking lot. As she entered the main road, she looked back in her mirror to see Jayson walking with his head down and his hands in his pockets toward the dorms.

Doris barely took time to undress before slipping into bed. She didn't sleep much, though. She tossed and turned most of the night, wrestling with her urge to get out of the show and her sense of loyalty to the cast and to Lenny. She knew she would never drop out of the show—she had never done that before, and she wasn't planning to now. She had been in plays when other actors quit unexpectedly, and it invariably ruined the whole production. Doris had finally made some good friends in this play, and she wasn't going to desert them. But what could she do?

When she did doze off she dreamed of being in bed with Martin on one side and Jayson on the other. They were fully dressed; she was naked. She willed herself to wake up and finally decided it would be better to be sleepy all day Wednesday than to remember another dream like this one. She got up, and Felix looked at her strangely. "Yes, I'm getting up in the middle of the night again—deal with it!"

She made a fresh pot of coffee and took her script and cigarettes to the back porch. Five in the morning in October was chilly as she noticed the first light frost glistening in the moonlight from her azaleas and oleanders. Her breath made little clouds, but Doris didn't mind. She put on her heavy-duty insulated slippers and wrapped her favorite chenille robe tightly around her waist. She lit a candle, propped her feet up on the chair next to her, and cupped her hands around the warm cup of steaming coffee. Felix sat mutely at the French doors, watching his mistress sit on the cold porch. She opened the door a crack to let him join her, but he looked at the door, then at her, and then started washing his left paw. She rolled her eyes and lit a cigarette.

Doris awoke to the sound of Felix pawing at the French doors. The cigarette she was holding had burned completely down to the filter, leaving a long ghostly ash. She was freezing, a rare event for Doris, so she hurried inside to check the time. Thank goodness for Felix or she might have slept through her morning class. She finished the section on dance in her Art Appreciation class and reviewed for Friday's test. When Doris strolled around the campus on her way to lunch she breathed in the aroma of autumn, tugged at the last leaf clinging to a maple tree, and said hello to everyone she passed. The cafeteria was crowded and noisy, as usual, but Doris found it comforting. She spotted Martin at the faculty table with an empty seat beside him. *How quickly the tables have turned,* she mused, *now he is saving a seat for me.* Her Art History class enjoyed a lively discussion about funding the arts during the Renaissance.

Wednesday night, Lenny worked just on the George/Martha attack first. It was intense but good to only focus on the mechanics of the blocking rather than trying to do it with lines at the same time. Then Lenny let everyone go except Jayson and Doris.

"Okay," Lenny said, facing the two of them, "this is a tough play for both of you. The usual roles of teacher and student must be thrown out the window so we can think of each other as actors and friends. Do you both think you can do it?"

Jayson spoke up first. "I don't think that's so much the problem, Lenny. I think it's a little difficult to go from one to the other every day. Dorie has to kiss and dance with me here at night and then walk into class the next day and treat me like all the other students."

"I was wondering how much we can do to suggest a sexual relationship between the two characters and still do as little physicality as possible," Doris chimed in. "I guess I didn't think this through before I committed to the play."

Lenny sighed and clasped her hands together. "Well, Dorie, it's kind of like the smoking. We could pretend she is smoking, but it would certainly take away from the authenticity of the performance. I don't plan on you two doing any more than necessary, but I don't see how Martha can be limited to pretending to seduce Nick. She has to sort of be out there, you know?"

Doris looked at Jayson and nodded. "Well, then," she said, "what can we do to become more comfortable with this?"

Lenny explained they would do a series of intimacy exercises she had used for other actors in a similar situation. Jayson told Doris how much it helped him and Teri, so Doris agreed to try. Lenny asked them first to stare into each other's eyes until they could do it without giggling. This took at least thirty minutes; Lenny stepped outside for a cigarette. When she returned, she found Jayson and Doris staring at each other in complete calm. She then instructed them to hold hands and to explore the contours and surface of each other's fingers while they continued to stare. Eventually she asked them to work their way into a kiss. Lenny sat a good distance from them, allowing them as much time as necessary. After nearly fifty minutes, Doris and Jayson progressed from holding hands to a passionate kiss and lots of hugging.

"Okay," Lenny said gently. Jayson and Doris broke their embrace but smiled at each other and continued to hold hands. "Let's do some improvisations."

She gave them a series of improvisational situations to act out as Nick and Martha to help them get into their characters' physicality together. Around ten, Lenny started blocking their seduction scene in Act 2. Doris was amazed at how effortless it felt to touch and kiss Jayson and to allow him to caress and kiss her. And it didn't feel like Doris and Jayson; it felt like Martha and Nick. Martha with her desperate need to feel attractive and

Nick's agenda to further his career. When they finished rehearsal, Jayson and Doris felt completely comfortable together, and the scene was blocked.

"Good work, people," Lenny said as she wrapped a big coat around her body and donned a knit cap. "I think this helped. You guys are doing great. We should finish the second act tomorrow night and have a few chances to run it on Friday. I'd like to have a run-through of Acts 1 and 2 on Sunday; I'll contact the understudies to see if they can come. Will both of you be able to make it?"

Doris nodded and Jayson said, "Sure, Lenny, no problem."

Lenny strolled out the door and down the hall, boots clicking on the linoleum floor. Jayson and Doris looked at each other in silence as they put on their coats and picked up their scripts. "You okay?" Jayson asked.

"Yeah, I think so," Doris said sincerely. "You?"

"Yeah," Jayson said and smiled. "Let me walk you out to your car."

They headed down the hall and into the chilly night air. "Jayson?" Doris started and then stopped herself.

"Yeah?" Jayson said and stopped. "What is it?"

"Nothing," Doris said and kept walking. Suddenly she stopped, "No, I want to say this." She unlocked her car door and asked Jayson to get in for a moment. "I want to thank you for being so great about all this. A lesser man would try to take advantage of the situation, and you have never been anything but mature and gentlemanly. I want you to know I appreciate it, Jayson. You're something special."

Jayson put his head down, a little embarrassed by her praise. "I think you're special, too, Dorie. I mean, to be so intelligent and scholarly and at the same time fun and creative. And on top of that, you . . ."

Doris started to feel uncomfortable. "Thank you, Jayson. Well, I guess I better get home. Can I drop you by the dorm?"

"No thanks, I like to walk when the weather's this nice." Jayson leaned over to give Doris a big hug and then bounded quickly out of the car and across the street. Doris breathed a heavy sigh and closed her eyes. She remembered his kisses, his crooked smile, and his sweet aroma. "Oh dear," she said aloud and pulled Carmen out of the parking circle, right past the little white car sitting nearby, without noticing either it or the driver.

When she got home, Doris checked her messages. There was only one, and it was from Martin about the weekend. Doris smiled and sighed. *What am I going to do about Martin?* She realized at rehearsal she felt more alive in Jayson's embrace than she ever had in Martin's, albeit as a character. Martin was the perfect man for her in every other way. "Why can't a woman have a bevy of men to meet all kinds of needs," she asked Felix, who blinked and turned his head away. "I could have Jayson for sex, my teaching colleagues for professional friendships, my old friend, Steve, from Tulane for fashion advice, and Martin for everything else." For the first time the idea of a harem made sense to her. She picked up Felix and laughed her way toward the bedroom and into her nightgown. *I can't believe I even said that aloud.*

On Thursday afternoon, after her Visual Arts class, Doris met Sheila Grindstaff on Avis' front porch. She didn't mention this meeting to Martin. She wasn't sure why, but she needed a few moments alone in the house where her earliest memories resided. Doris remained calm and aloof as Ms. Grindstaff showed her how the sale would be run and explained how the items were priced. Once they were finished, Doris told her she wanted to stay in the house for a little while by herself. Ms. Grindstaff eyed her suspiciously, as if she might steal something. "Well, that's a little irregular," she said.

"Irregular or not, I'm staying. This is still my mother's house, Ms. Grindstaff."

Sheila Grindstaff's greatest wisdom was in choosing her battles. "Of course, Dr. Peechum. If you wouldn't mind, however, I will put the lockbox on the front door, so you can exit through the side door in the back. Would that be okay?"

"No problem," Doris nodded without looking at her.

Ms. Grindstaff held out a hand for Doris to shake. "Well, then, I'll be on my way. We have announced the sale in all the usual papers, so we expect a good crowd."

Doris nodded, wishing the agent would leave before she lost control. Ms. Grindstaff picked up her briefcase and purse and headed toward the front door. She stopped before exiting and said, "Dr. Peechum, you can do what you want to this weekend, but I never advise family members to come near the house during the sale. It's usually painful. Once the sale ends, we will clean up the house, repaint, and distribute the remaining furnishings to the women's shelter as you requested." She turned to go and stopped again. "Whatever you need to say to this house, stay here today, as long as you need to, and then never come back." Doris nodded, a tear threatening to escape. Sheila Grindstaff locked the front door and drove off in her shiny black BMW.

Doris sat for a long time on the sofa remembering what it was like to grow up in this beautiful old house. The house smelled the same as always, a mixture of roses and roast beef. Doris couldn't explain it; she knew no other place in the world that smelled like her parents' house. It was the smell that triggered her tears. She realized she would never experience the aroma again, and this chapter of her life was completely over and done with. She would never again see her parents, plop down on the sofa to watch television, sleep in her parents' bed when she was sick, or sit on the front porch swing with a boyfriend. It was time to say good-bye, and Doris was not prepared for the finality of selling the house so soon after losing her mother. She sat and cried until she could cry no longer.

When her breathing finally returned to normal, she was surprised to realize it was nearly five o'clock. *How long have I been here*, she wondered. She walked upstairs to sit in her old room awhile and then did a final tour of the entire house. She needed to get home; staying longer would only postpone the inevitable, so she headed toward the back door. She turned for one long last gaze, told the house she loved it and would miss it, and then left without looking back.

When she returned home, the light on her answering machine was blinking to indicate three messages. She pushed the button and picked up Felix, carrying him around the house while she tidied up and listened to the messages. The first one was from Martin suggesting they go to the Octoberfest in a nearby town on Saturday. He didn't mention the estate sale, but Doris figured he was planning to keep her busy so she wouldn't think about it. The next voice belonged to her old friend, Tootsie. "Doris? This is Toots." There was a long pause, then, "I uh, I heard about the estate sale this weekend. I wanted to say hi and see how you were feeling. Call me if you need anything, anytime, uh, to talk. Well, 'bye." Doris stopped and buried her face into Felix's soft fur. He wriggled in protest. The next voice was Ted calling from work to see if she needed anything. Doris was touched that so many people cared about her.

That evening, Lenny finished the blocking for the second act and let them run through it once. It was particularly difficult since they now had to combine the dance, kissing, and attack into the scene with lines and props. Lenny seemed content that they had the continuity of the scene and told them it would just take repetition to make it come together. "Friday, we'll run through Act 2 at least twice, and then Sunday run the first two acts together. No books and no prompting for Act 1!" That meant no scripts in their hands and they couldn't ask for lines--the actors looked at the ceiling, then each other, picked up their things, and left chatting.

At lunch on Friday she told Martin she would be in rehearsal for the evening and was planning to go in Saturday morning to finish her painting job for the set. He suggested picking her up Saturday night and asked her what she wanted to do. "Surprise me," she said, and finished her salad.

Not even Dr. Peechum stays late on Friday afternoon, so right after her Art History class, she took off to run errands. She resisted the urge to drive by her mother's house and stopped at the green grocers to pick up some fresh vegetables and fruits. Doris made a special effort to look and smell good for rehearsal. She didn't want Jayson to be grossed out by dirty hair and smelly clothes. That's what she told herself, but when she looked in the mirror as she applied the finishing touches to her make-up, she wondered. Do I want him to find me attractive? She searched her face for an answer then finally turned away in disgust. "What is the matter with me," she asked the ceiling.

28

Set work the next morning was productive; Doris finished the painting and headed home before lunch to get all her school work done so she could have the rest of the weekend for everything else she needed to do—laundry, a date with Martin, and Sunday's rehearsal. Lenny contacted everyone, and they could all come except for Teri's understudy, so she decided to go ahead with the rehearsal.

Martin took Doris to a new restaurant near the mall with marvelous Thai cuisine, and then back to Benny's Jazz Club. When they arrived at Doris' house it was after one, and they were both exhausted. Martin asked if he could spend the night, and Doris acquiesced. She begged off on sex, however, because she was so exhausted. She hoped they might watch an old movie together, but Martin fell asleep before the opening credits, so she punched at him to get up and go to bed with her. He slept spoon-fashion against Doris' back. For once, she was too tired to worry about anything so Doris relaxed and dozed off to sleep, too.

They both awoke with Felix walking across the bed meowing in protest that no one remembered to feed the cat the night before. "What a racket!" Martin said, nuzzling his face into Doris' hair. "Okay, okay, Felix, I'll get the kibbles."

Martin sat up, stretched, and shuffled into the kitchen to feed Felix. Doris lay still listening to the sounds of cabinets opening and closing, water pouring, pans clinking, until she dozed off again. When she awoke, Martin was standing over her with a beautiful tray of food and coffee, and the newspaper tucked under his arm. "Rise and shine, darling."

Doris rubbed her eyes and scooted up in bed to accommodate the tray. Martin sat everything in place and laid the newspaper at her side. He scurried back to the kitchen and then appeared with his own plate and slipped under the covers. Doris yawned and tried to wake up, but the stress and increased activity of the last month was starting to take its toll. Still,

Martin prepared yet another perfect breakfast and his coffee was better than anything Foster's offered. They lounged in bed most of the morning, sipping coffee and reading the newspaper. There wasn't much talking, but they felt comfortable enough with each other that conversation wasn't necessary.

Doris finished breakfast and the paper and curled back over on her side with her back to Martin. He snuggled up next to her and started kissing the back of her neck and massaging her arm. She turned over and kissed him and then one thing led to another. Martin was better in the morning, she thought, more energetic and more attentive. But still, once he was on top, the sex happened quickly, and it was all over before Doris could react. She wanted to cuddle with him afterwards, but Martin was up getting dressed and talking about what they would do for lunch. Doris muttered she wasn't hungry, turned back over in bed, and covered her head.

"I have rehearsal today," she said under the sheet. "I have to be there at two, so I probably won't want to eat anything till supper."

"Oh, well, okay. I guess I'll head home then and give you a chance to get ready. Do you want to do anything later?"

"Probably not," she muttered, pulling the sheet off her face. "I need to rework my conference paper after rehearsal. I've finished the research but haven't added anything to the paper. I guess I'll see you tomorrow at lunch, okay?"

Martin sat beside her on the bed. "Okay, honey. Have a nice day." He kissed her forehead and hugged her shoulders then stood up to leave.

"Martin?" Doris said, rising slightly. "I had a great time last night— the restaurant was great."

"Thanks, yes, I read about it in the paper. Glad you liked it." Martin stood for a moment longer and then said, "Well, bye." He rubbed Felix's head, and then Doris heard him go to the foyer, pick up his jacket, and open and close the door. She lay on her back and studied the pattern on her ceiling for a long time. Finally, she got up, took a bath, and got ready for rehearsal.

Doris arrived at the Humanities building a few minutes before rehearsal and realized she needed to go to the bathroom. She pondered the enormity of how her life had changed in a few short weeks as she strolled nearly in a trance to the restroom. Jason came bursting out of the men's room just as Doris reached the women's. Doris had been so preoccupied with her thoughts that Jayson's sudden appearance startled her to the point of a tiny scream. This in turn jolted Jayson into a full-fledged yelp. They looked at each other for a moment—what happened, oh it's you, you scared me to death looks on both their faces—then they collapsed in laughter. Jayson had to lean against the water fountain to stand up, and tears ran down Doris' face.

"Oh, goodness," she could hardly speak, "I'm sorry! Ah . . ." She leaned against the wall wiping her cheeks with the backs of her hands. They looked at each other again, both letting out a long sigh, which sparked another fit of giggles. Jayson, exhausted from laughter, slid down the side of the water fountain and sat on the floor with his legs extended across the hall.

Doris just shook her head, ruffled his hair as she passed, and went into the ladies' room. When she emerged, Jayson had apparently recovered and gone back to the rehearsal room. She took a long sip of water, straightened her slacks, and smiled to herself. Everyone converged at about the same time in room 106, Winnie set out a few final props, and Stacey was in conference with Lenny. Doris suddenly realized she would need a purse to enter with so she would have a place to put her cigarettes. Winnie made a note and promised to have one ready by Monday.

"That's okay, no hurry," Doris said, trying to be helpful, "I can just use mine until you find one." Winnie gave her a grateful smile that said thanks for not talking to me like a servant. So many actors treat crew members like second-class citizens. Doris could never abide it. "Without your hard work on the props, the show just wouldn't work," Doris said for emphasis. Jayson looked up and flashed a smile to Winnie and then to Doris, who just nodded back.

When it came time for her to ask George to light her cigarette, no one, including Doris, realized she had the cigarette backwards in her mouth. Lenny had blocked the scene for Nick to light her cigarette when George refuses. Jayson took the lighter from the table, held it out to Doris' cigarette, and lit the wrong end. The filter spitted and complained almost as much as Doris when she took a big drag of the rancid smoke. Jayson knew that Lenny had a big thing about staying in character during a run-through, but he couldn't help himself. The giggles from earlier erupted again, and Doris couldn't hold back either. They both collapsed on the sofa laughing hysterically while the others looked at them in confused silence.

"I'm sorry, Lenny, ah, ah, ah . . ." Jayson tried to utter through bouts of anguished breaths. He smacked Doris' hand and nodded her attention to Lenny who was sitting at the director's table with a completely not-amused look on her face.

"When you two are ready, I'd really like to run this act." Lenny spoke with a firmness her actors rarely heard from her. She was usually so easy-going, but the stress of a show this massive was starting to take its toll on her sense of humor. Doris gave her a look of horror, a director had never corrected her so harshly, and she found it embarrassing. "I know these kinds of things happen in rehearsal," Lenny said gently, trying to remain calm, "But they also happen in performance. If you don't learn how to get out of this kind of sticky situation in rehearsal, then you won't know how to handle it if it happens on stage."

"We're really sorry, Lenny, and everyone," Doris added, looking around, "Jayson and I literally ran into each other earlier in the hall and got the giggles, I think we just didn't let them all out. It won't happen again." Jayson was nodding but said nothing.

Lenny's face relaxed, and she finally smiled. "Okay, well, I understand. Let's begin again where Martha comes downstairs in her new outfit."

Doris didn't anticipate how difficult it would be to do the seduction scene in front of an audience. Even though these people were in the show or on the crew, it was still hard for her to relax and let go like she had when it was just Lenny and Jayson. Jayson sensed her tension and smiled at her. She gave a half-smile back, but then quickly averted her eyes. *I'm an actor, I'm an actor, I'm an actor*, she kept telling herself.

Despite her nervousness, Doris performed like a trooper. When the act ended, everyone burst into spontaneous applause. Winnie jumped up immediately and said, "Awesome, awesome!"

The cast smiled and took impromptu bows. It felt good to have the approval of her friends and peers. Other than the cigarette outburst, the run-through was a big success—most of the actors knew their Act 1 lines perfectly and did quite well on Act 2. Stacey corrected Bill more than anyone, which Doris found annoying. He wanted to paraphrase the lines to suit himself, but Lenny remained strict about doing Albee's script the way he wrote it. *So much for the "professional" actor*, Doris thought.

After the break, Lenny asked the understudies to go through the second act. Watching her understudy go through the same blocking also helped her put everything into perspective. *It's a play*, she thought, *surely everyone on campus will understand.* They gave the understudies the benefit of applause, also, but it sounded perfunctory and artificial. Doris chatted briefly with Gail, her understudy, about some blocking notes and character tips. Jayson did the same with Moses, and since Bill didn't have an understudy and Teri's was absent, they started to leave.

Lenny spoke up, "Before anyone takes off, I want to ask the principals to do a run-through of the second act tomorrow night before we start blocking Act 3, preferably without scripts. It's just so complex, I think we need another night on it." Everyone nodded. Doris was relieved—she knew they needed more work on the second act before moving on, or at least *she* needed more work.

Everyone walked out together, chatting and conversing about the play. As cast and crew scattered in different directions, Doris found she was once again walking in the same direction as Jayson. *Do I park in that direction on purpose—subconsciously, I mean?* She was wondering about it when Jayson patted her back and told her what a great job she did. She stopped to discuss the rehearsal and noticed little puffs of air coming out of Jayson's mouth as he spoke. "Don't you have a jacket?" she asked.

"Yes, back in the dorm, of course! I thought it would warm up this afternoon, but it seems to be getting colder instead."

"Yes, Jayson, in autumn it gets cold when the sun goes down! And it's gets dark earlier every day; soon the time will change back to Eastern Standard. I hate it being dark at five!" He smiled, shuffled his feet, and tucked his hands into his pockets. "Let me give you a ride to the dorm, okay?"

He nodded, accepting the invitation. They climbed into Carmen and took off toward the row of dormitories. Once she dropped Jayson off, Doris headed home.

Doris felt good; it had been a productive weekend. She booted up the computer on her desk to start work on her conference paper, but she only lasted an hour. "I can't concentrate, Felix." Felix didn't even look at her.

She bathed and put on her pajamas before she put her feet up on the coffee table, watched some television, and ate her dinner. Felix crawled onto her lap for affection as she looked over her school plans for the coming week. She scratched him behind the ear, but soon they both fell asleep. A loud television commercial with some man yelling about great deals on used cars woke Doris. She picked up the remains of dinner and packed up her briefcase for school, then shuffled drowsily to bed. Felix elected to stay on the sofa.

29

Doris made it to school on Monday morning a few minutes before class. She nodded and smiled to several students when she entered, including Jayson, who now sat near the front instead of the dead-head section in the back. Some of the girls giggled but tried to conceal it; Doris considered it part of adolescent silliness. She found it tiresome but learned over the years to overlook it. It annoyed her while she was lecturing, however, so she asked the girls to be quiet. College students usually don't need to be told this, but sometimes it became necessary. They never liked it—they consider themselves adults. Doris figured, however, if they wanted to be treated like adults they needed to act like adults. The giggling continued, and Doris was becoming more and more impatient. Finally, she asked one of the girls if she wanted to share the joke, and she shook her head and looked around the room with her lips hidden between her teeth. Doris finished discussing literature as an art form and gave them their assignment for Wednesday. As she left the classroom, she could hear the girls snickering. *Oh, for goodness sake,* she thought ruefully.

When she returned to her office, Doris settled down to check her email and voicemail. There was a good morning message and a reminder about lunch from Martin, a call from a student regarding a late assignment, and a request from her department head, Phyllis, for Doris to come in sometime today for a chat. *That's curious,* Doris thought, then she remembered she hadn't met with Phyllis to discuss being in the play with a current student. She dialed her number and set up a meeting with Vivian. Doris did some work on her conference paper, adding to the works cited, and printed it out in the Humanities office. She noticed it was almost time for her meeting so after she picked up her paper she told Vivian she would sit and wait until Phyllis was ready. Vivian nodded politely and continued typing something into her computer. Doris took a seat near the faculty mailboxes and started to read through her paper, checking for misspellings or other errors.

Nearly twenty minutes later Phyllis came out and invited Doris into her office. Phyllis was attractive in a 1980s kind of way--she seemed stuck in the period of big hair and shoulder pads. Once they got seated, Phyllis looked down at her hands, adorned with big rings but no wedding band, and then back at Doris, who sat mutely waiting. "Doris," she began, "I don't know exactly how to begin." Doris' eyebrows crinkled toward her nose, and she realized she was holding her breath. When she forced herself to breathe, her lungs sucked in the air in little spurts, like they did when she was crying. Phyllis picked up a piece of paper and then put it back on the desk. "There has been a report, well, a complaint, I guess, from a student, and Dean Rogers has asked me to discuss it with you to see if we can get it cleared up."

"Dean Rogers? A complaint?" Doris said, "No one came to me." In academic circles, everyone knew there was a protocol for student complaints. First, the complainant talks to the instructor. If this doesn't satisfy her then she goes to the instructor's department head who then holds a little conference with the teacher. Most grievances resolve at this level; the department head usually suggests a course of action, which most faculty members comply with. If not, however, the complaint can even go to the dean, the president, or a grievance committee for a hearing. Only a few cases ever reach that level, but it is in place for the times when it's needed.

"Well, the student didn't come to me either, Doris, which makes me think the whole accusation is bogus anyway. The student wrote a letter to the dean, with copies to the president and the board of directors, accusing you of having an affair with a student." Phyllis picked up the paper again and pulled her glasses down to read part of it, Doris felt paralyzed. "The letter also alleges this is not just *a* student, but one of your current students."

"Does she mention any names?" Doris asked, her throat dry, her hands sweaty.

Phyllis lowered her glasses again and peered at the letter. "Yes, a Jayson Jeffries."

"Who wrote the letter?"

"I'm sorry, Doris, you know I can't tell you." Phyllis hesitated. "Dean Rogers and I discussed this late last week, and we both guessed it was someone in one of your classes or former classes trying to get revenge for a bad grade. But we looked over the student's records, and apparently, you never taught this person. That gives the report more credence and makes it something that we should investigate. The president and board members are leaving it up to Dean Rogers, but he wanted me to discuss this with you first." Again, Phyllis looked down, and Doris was surprised to see this appeared painful for her.

Phyllis came to KC from a school in Minnesota, a couple of years after Doris was granted tenure. Although Doris and Phyllis were cordial with each other, she could sense they were two different types of people. But that was okay, as long as they got along professionally, and gratefully, they did.

"I'm sorry, Doris, but I have to ask you some questions." Phyllis' voice snapped Doris to attention, and she realized she had been studying a fern outside Phyllis' window for what seemed like an hour. "First of all, is there any truth to the complaint?"

"No, of course not," Doris responded immediately, and Phyllis appeared visibly relieved. "Jayson and I have become friends—good friends--because we're working in the play together, you know, and we have some steamy scenes together. I guess someone could misinterpret— especially if it's a girl who has a crush on Jayson or someone who has a friend who failed one of my classes." Doris started to say something about Martin, but then thought better of it.

"Good, good," Phyllis said, "Then the rest of these questions won't be so hard to ask. The student alleges he or she has seen you many times alone with Jayson—in your car, in Foster's, sitting on campus together, and even at your home. The complaint claims Jayson picked you up at your house and took you to a party and then came into your house when he brought you home. On another occasion, he came back to your house in the afternoon, and you greeted him at the door in your bathrobe and let him in. The letter also states you were seen being nearly carried into your house, drunk, by Jayson, late one night." Doris took a deep breath; her eyes darted around the room. Phyllis was struggling with her glasses to read the letter and did not notice. "It goes on to say Jayson spent the night at your house, alone with you. You then went to the theatre with him the next morning and did some set work." Phyllis pulled her glasses back up and looked over at Doris, who turned nearly white. "I have to ask you if any of this is true,

Doris."

"Well, yes, Phyllis, but it all has to do with the play." Phyllis'
expression changed from one of confidence to one of concern. "We sit on
campus and at Foster's talking about the play. We sometimes sit in my car
because of the cold. And yes, Lenny gave a show party slash rehearsal to
watch the movie of *Virginia Woolf.* My car broke down and I called Lenny
to tell her I couldn't come, but she sent Jayson to get me. I brought him in
for a short while and offered him tea to thank him for the ride."

"Okay, how about the part about you getting drunk with him and him
spending the night with you?" Phyllis appeared sympathetic, but it made
Doris feel worse.

"I went out to a bar with most of the people from the show. Most of
us drank, and I decided I would experiment with being drunk so I could
better understand how Martha feels in the play. Two girls rode in my car
with Jayson and me, and one of them drove my car back to campus because
she didn't drink any alcohol. I was, well, yes, I was a bit tipsy. We dropped
the girls off at their dorm, and Jayson volunteered to drive me home. When
we got there, he helped me inside, put me on my bed, and then slept on the
sofa. Jayson was a complete gentleman. He ate breakfast with me the next
morning, and then I drove us to the theatre to do set work. I felt bad I hadn't
helped on the set—all the students have to do it, you know—so I did some
painting for him, it, the set, I mean."

"Oh dear, Doris, this is not good." Phyllis was shaking her head and
sighing.

"We didn't do anything inappropriate, Phyllis, I swear on my
mother's grave." Phyllis looked at Doris and realized she was sincere, but
she also knew that sometimes the truth is not enough.

"I believe you, Doris, but I will have to speak to Jayson, as well, and
probably Lenny and some of the others in the play. You know, Doris,
sometimes the *appearance* of impropriety is often enough."

Doris was afraid to ask the next question, but she knew she needed
to. "Enough for what?"

"Well," Phyllis said, taking off her glasses and laying them on top of
the letter on her desk, "Let's cross that bridge when we get to it. Be careful,
okay?" Phyllis stood up, Doris' cue to leave. It took Doris a few moments
to collect herself and stand. She rushed back to her office and closed the
door.

Doris sat in stunned silence in her dark office with only the distant autumn sunlight streaming into her window. She was too much in shock to even cry. She turned her head out the window and for the first time in her life thought about jumping out. She felt like everyone on campus knew her shame, and she should get in Carmen and drive far away and never come back. And yet, she knew she would have to hold her afternoon class. She put her face in her hands and rested her elbows on the edge of her desk. *What am I going to do about the play*, she whispered to herself.

A shadow appeared at her door, a hand knocked, a voice called out "Doris?" It was Martin coming by to escort her to lunch. *Oh god,* she thought, *what will I tell Martin? Will he even believe me?* "Doris?" Martin called again and tried the door. Fortunately, Doris had remembered to lock it; she sat perfectly still until he gave up and turned away. *He'll go look for me in the cafeteria, she thought, and when he doesn't find me, he'll come back. No, he'll eat first, she mused, he is a man, after all. Where can I go until it's time for class? I've missed so much class this semester already, I really shouldn't miss today. But how can I lecture, how can I go out in public, how can I go to rehearsal? Why couldn't this have happened on Friday—at least I'd have the weekend to recover.*

Doris sat for a long time pondering what to do. She finally decided if she disappeared from campus it would give the rumor more power. If she held her head up and carried on with her business, she might convince everyone to recognize the story as nothing more than what it was—vicious, hurtful gossip. *Who hates me this much? And why? I know I've had some conflicts with students, but nothing that would warrant this kind of attack.* She pulled herself together, turned on her lights, and opened her door. By the time Martin came back she was finishing up the plans for her Art History class and had found a viable video on art during the Italian Renaissance to show them so she wouldn't have to lecture.

"Where'd you go, Doris? I came over to look for you and then you weren't at the cafeteria either." Martin looked a little distressed and a little perturbed all at the same time. "Did you have lunch?"

Doris looked up calmly as if this was a normal fall day and said, "I'm so sorry, Martin, I got caught up talking with a student, and then I realized I hadn't gone over my notes for class this afternoon. I went to the cafeteria a little early and ate a snack. We must have missed each other. I'm sorry," she said again. *Stop saying you're sorry, Doris, it makes you sound pathetic.*

"Oh, well, okay, sorry I missed you." Martin pushed the unruly flap of hair from his face. "Do you have plans for supper?"

"Well, I have rehearsal so I was going to eat on the go. I need to be back here by seven, but if you want, we could eat together over at Foster's. Can you meet me there around 6:00?" Doris thought if the students saw her with Martin it might assuage their suspicions. Plus, she guessed she would have to tell Martin some of this, otherwise it would hurt him terribly if he heard it from someone else. This is a small campus, she thought, it won't take long for everyone to hear the allegation.

Martin agreed it was a delightful idea. He planned to work in his office anyway, so he would probably stay here until then. He scurried down the hall with renewed purpose and a spring in his step. Doris picked up her class materials and headed in the other direction.

The class was buzzing when she entered. *Have they already heard? Is that what the girls were giggling about this morning?* Doris tried to put those thoughts out of her head while she called roll and started the dvd player. Once the video began, however, her mind wandered to her time alone with Jayson. She had thought about having an affair with him—was that as bad as having one? *Maybe she deserved this, maybe the student was right.* Maybe.

She dismissed class a few minutes early and headed directly to Lenny's office. Fortunately, she was alone doing some work on the computer. Doris asked if she could spare a few minutes, and Lenny offered her a seat. Before she sat down, however, Doris gently closed the door. Lenny looked at her strangely but didn't speak.

"Lenny, I don't know how to say this because it's something I have never done before. And I have hated people who did it, but . . ." tears threatened to escape so she looked at the ceiling and swallowed, "I have to quit the show."

Lenny didn't say anything at first; she simply stared at Doris. Finally, she leaned forward and said, "Well, Dorie, I can tell this is something you don't want to do, so there must be a good reason behind it. Can you tell me?"

Doris looked down at her hands—*Lenny is wise for one so young,* she thought. "There's a rumor, well, a student complaint, about Jayson and me." Lenny furrowed her eyebrows and leaned back. "Someone has accused us of having an affair. This may jeopardize my job, Lenny. I don't think it's a good idea to add fuel to the fire by kissing him and rubbing around on him on stage for everyone to see. I know this puts you and all the others in a terrible bind, and I am truly sorry. I hope you know I would never do this over something frivolous. I have loved working on the play, getting to know you better, and becoming friends with some of the students, but this is something . . ."

Lenny reached out and took Doris' hand. "I'm so glad I got to know you better too, Dorie, and the students have all made such positive comments about your acting and your work on the set. They all respect you so much, I hope you realize it."

"I hope I don't lose their respect by dropping out. Can you tell them I've had some kind of family emergency?"

"I think it would be better if you told them yourself. If I tell them, they'll carry around the resentment and never resolve it. It may be hard for you, but I think it's best, don't you?"

Doris hated to admit it, but Lenny was right. "Will most of them be there tonight?"

"Yes, we're supposed to run the second act tonight, so, almost everyone will be there even the understudies. It would be a good way to make a clean break. I'll let you talk before we begin. Do you mind staying to help Gail get up to speed on the blocking?"

"Of course not," Doris said, standing. "I'll do anything I can to help. You're being wonderful about this, Lenny, thank you."

"Charley has helped me accept things I cannot change," she said, "remember, we're still friends, okay?"

"Sure, thanks," Doris turned to leave and then stopped and looked back at Lenny. "You never asked. Don't you want to ask?"

"Ask what?" Lenny said, leaning her chair back and lacing her fingers together over her stomach.

"If it's true. Don't you want to know if it's true?"

"It's none of my business, Dorie. And it doesn't make any difference to me either way. I'm your friend, not your judge or your confessor."

"Well, it's not. It's not true, Lenny, but thanks for not asking." Doris turned and walked back to her office with the weight of the world on her shoulders. She put out her notes for Tuesday's classes, took a long look at the office she enjoyed so much, and drove home.

When Doris arrived home, she found Felix sound asleep in his window hammock. She picked him up and nuzzled her face into his fur. Felix squirmed a little but let her hold him. He could somehow sense her need for affection. She carried him to the bed, lay down under the covers, and started to cry. She let herself cry as long and as hard as she wanted. The phone rang, but she let the answering machine pick up.

"Hello, Dr. Peechum? This is Sheila Grindstaff. I wanted to let you know the estate sale was very successful, and we will be spending this week getting the house ready to put on the market. If you have any questions or want to walk through the house again, let me know. Bye!"

She sounded so happy Doris figured they must have made a lot of money on the sale. She turned to look at her alarm clock and realized it was time to get up and take a bath. She arrived at Foster's just before six. Martin was sitting inside with a cup of coffee, reading the newspaper. Doris made a point of giving him a big hug and a longer-than-usual kiss on the mouth. "I'm so glad to see you, Martin," she said. "Have you ordered for me?"

"No, I've been reading the paper and people watching. This is an interesting place, you know?"

"Okay, if you say so. I'm starving, what do you want?" Martin thought for a minute and decided on the poached eggs on toast. Doris made a face but told him she'd get it. He protested, but she insisted. When she came back to the table, Martin put the paper away and gathered the usual accoutrements on the table. Doris brought their drinks first then the "entrees"—his eggs and her grilled chicken salad.

They ate, making casual comments about their classes, the weather, and what to do on the weekend. Martin did most of the talking and finally noticed Doris was being unusually quiet. "I mean I know I usually talk more than you do, but you've barely said a word since you sat down. Are you okay?"

Doris took a deep breath and pushed her salad plate away from her. "No, Martin, I'm not. Phyllis called me into her office today to tell me there has been a student complaint against me."

"Oh, honey, all teachers get those every occasionally—students get angry about a grade and have to blow off some steam. It usually comes to nothing in the end."

Doris listened politely but her expression didn't change. "Well, she wouldn't tell me who it was, but she did say it was not one of *my* students.

He or she wrote a letter directly to the dean, the president, and the board of directors alleging I am having an affair with one of my students."

Martin almost choked on his toast as he burst out laughing. "You're kidding me! Oh, for Pete's sake, Doris, surely no one is taking this seriously." Martin's laughter subsided when he saw Doris' expression. "Well, it's not true, is it?"

"I can't believe you'd even ask me that," Doris said, "of course it's not true."

"Sorry, but it just came out. I didn't mean to imply I didn't trust you. It didn't even occur to me it could be true. I meant . . . oh hell, I don't know. I'm sorry, Doris, what can I do to help?"

"Well, I'm not finished. This person has seen Jayson and me alone together on several occasions—you know, we've been doing some character work, and Jayson gave me a ride to rehearsal when Carmen wouldn't start. We have been together a lot, and I know it looks suspicious, but I swear to you nothing sexual happened between us."

"Well, of course not, Doris, I know that."

Doris wasn't sure if she was glad or offended that he was so confident she wouldn't have an affair. "Except on stage, of course. You've read the play, you know I have to kiss Jayson and rub around on him some."

"Yes, I guess so. But it's acting, right? I mean if I can get over it, surely everyone else can."

"You would think so, but who knows. I'm going over to rehearsal in a few minutes to tell them I have to drop out of the play. I think it would be best for everyone."

"Why? So, they win?" Martin was getting angry, something Doris couldn't remember seeing in him before. "If you quit, isn't that what this person wants? I don't know why someone would go after you in this way, but who knows why half the people in this world do what they do? It seems to me if you drop out of the play then you're letting them have their way."

"But, Martin, what if the president and members of the board come see the play and see me seducing Jayson on stage. He is a student in one of my classes right now. It was a stupid choice to make from the beginning."

"Doris, you didn't cast Jayson. In fact, Lenny asked you to audition. It wasn't even your idea in the beginning. How could anyone say you planned this?"

"I don't know." Doris was silent for a minute. "Do you remember

Ann, the theatre director before Lenny?" Martin nodded, finishing his coffee. "When she didn't get tenure, I asked her if she knew why. She said if they want to keep you they find a reason, and if they don't, they find a reason. I think she was right. I've never been one of Dean Rogers' favorites. This is probably the opportunity he's been waiting for."

"I honestly think you're making too much of this, Doris, but you do whatever you think is best. I'll be right behind you all the way." He leaned over and gave her a kiss. She put her arms around his neck and hugged him for a long time. Doris normally frowned upon public displays of affection, but in these circumstances, she thought it might discourage students from accepting the gossip at face value. "Do you want me to go with you to rehearsal?"

She pulled back and smiled at him. "No thanks, I have to face them myself." She took her hand and gently pushed the wayward flap of hair back into place. She stroked Martin's face and then turned to walk toward the Humanities building. Martin waited until she was out of sight before cleaning up the table and heading home.

30

When she walked into room 106 everyone was milling around getting ready for the run-through. Jayson and Winnie were setting out props, and Lenny was trying to arrange seating areas for everyone to sit and watch. She looked up at Doris and smiled sadly. Doris nodded. Once everything was ready, Lenny clapped her hands a few times to get everyone's attention, asking them to take a seat. She explained what they would be doing in rehearsal, running Act 2 twice, hopefully no books. Then she was silent for a moment and looked at Doris. "But before we begin, Dorie wants to say something."

Doris walked to the set area and looked at everyone's faces. Jayson's eyebrows were furrowed in concern; Winnie's were up in anticipation. Lenny walked to the back of the room and leaned against the wall with her arms folded in front of her. Doris' fingers twisted the birthstone ring on her right hand, and she squeezed her lips in and out of her mouth. "Thanks, Lenny. I wanted to say thank you to everyone for making me feel so welcome here. I know it's hard to be casual with a teacher you don't know well, and you all have been wonderful." Doris felt a burning in her nose that told her tears were not far away; she took a breath and looked down for a moment. "I don't know if you have heard any rumors about me, but there are some circulating around campus. It's not important what those rumors are about because they're not true. What is important to me is how everyone responds to them. So, I wanted you to know if you hear anything about me that you want to ask me about, I hope you will. I promise I will answer your questions as honestly as I can." Teri turned to whisper to Bill; Stacey was studying something in the promptbook while Jayson and Winnie kept their focus completely on Doris.

"Anyway, I have really enjoyed working in this play with all of you. It has given me a chance to stretch my acting skills, and I have made a whole lot of new friends. I want to say thank you by doing something fun, so I want to invite all of you, and your guests, to my house for a Halloween party this Saturday night." Heads turned toward each other, Lenny pulled away from the wall. "We'll have to be in rehearsal on Halloween next week, so we can enjoy some spooky fun over the weekend. You *must* wear a costume, and it would help if you'd bring one item, like a soft drink or chips or cookies, but you don't have to. It will start at seven o'clock, so I, uh, I hope to see you all then! Thanks for the time, Lenny."

Everyone burst into applause and began chatting excitedly about costumes and make-up. Lenny looked at Doris with an odd expression and then clapped her hands again to calm everyone down. "Okay, people, the party's not tonight, so let's take our places and get ready for the rehearsal." Doris picked up her purse and checked to make sure her props were on the set. Jayson looked at her with curiosity, but she just smiled at him.

After notes, several students patted Doris on the arm and said they were looking forward to the party. Lenny pulled Doris to one side and asked her what changed her mind.

"I don't know, Lenny, I really don't. I don't even know if I'm doing the right thing. But when I stood up to announce I was dropping out, I looked at all those faces, and I couldn't do it. I started thinking I should be true to myself and do what's right for me. If I can't do it at this college, then maybe I shouldn't be here."

Lenny raised one eyebrow and nodded. "Well, I'm glad you're staying with us. And I admire your courage."

Doris shook her head. "Only time will tell if it's bravery or stupidity." Lenny smiled, squeezed Doris' arm, and headed for the door.

Jayson, Winnie, and Stacey were finishing up the set and props. Even though no one else would be using the room until this show moved to the stage, the door was never locked, so everything had to be put back in boxes and furniture was shoved into a corner. Stacey and Winnie carried the boxes of props across the hall to the storage closet and locked them up for safekeeping and then waved to Jayson. Doris headed down the hall then she heard Jayson's voice call out her name. She stopped and turned to face him.

"Dorie, are you all right?"

"Yes, Jayson, I'm fine. I guess you need to know this rumor involves you, too. Dr. Hathaway will probably be talking to you in the next few days. She has to ask you some questions about, well, about you and me."

"You and me? What about you and me?"

"I can't say anymore, Jayson, it might be interpreted as trying to influence you in some way. Just tell the truth—whatever she asks you—be honest, okay?"

Jayson nodded, frowning. "Sure," was all he said. "Can I walk you to your car?"

"Thanks, Jayson, but we better not. You go on ahead; I need to stop at the restroom anyway. I'll see you tomorrow night, okay?"

"Okay, if you're sure. Bye." Jayson backed away, his hands in his letter jacket pockets, a black ski cap on his head. He walked backwards until she disappeared into the ladies' room.

Doris leaned against the door and took several deep breaths. She waited a reasonable amount of time for Jayson to be gone and then emerged from the bathroom rubbing her hair. She walked directly to Carmen and drove home. As she was unlocking her front door, her phone started ringing. She started to hurry inside, but then realized she wasn't in the mood to speak to anyone. As she hung her sweater on the hall tree, Martin's voice came on to the answering machine. "Doris? Well, I thought you might be home by now. I was worried about you—thought I might come over and stay with you. Let me know what you need." There was a pause, then, "Love you." Click.

Doris stood looking at the machine; Felix rubbed around her legs. *He tells me he loves me in a phone message but never to my face? He was right, he is not good with romance.* She called Martin back to assure him she would be all right by herself. They made a date for lunch and said goodnight. She didn't tell him she was staying in the play or that she volunteered to host a party on the weekend. She didn't want to talk long enough to explain everything. *I'll tell him tomorrow*, she thought to herself as she entered her bedroom. Neither of them said "I love you." She paused, staring at the phone, checked her watch, and decided to call Tootsie. If she remembered correctly, Tootsie was a night owl and might still be up. She was.

Doris told her the whole story, all the details, including her little crush on Jayson.

"A party?" Tootsie nearly squealed. "Can I help—I love costume parties, but I can't get Sam to go anywhere!"

Doris was flabbergasted. "That's all you have to say after that whole story? Aren't you curious about Jayson or if it's true?"

"Oh, Doris, I know you, remember? I know that it's not in you to be dishonest and cheat on Martin, or carry on like that with a current student. It's just not who you are!" Doris wasn't sure if she felt flattered or insulted. "I'm really sorry to hear you have to go through all this crap, but I can't imagine the faculty giving any credence to this rumor. And IF you WERE going to have an affair with a student it wouldn't be such an obvious and poor choice, and you would break up with Martin first. Right?"

Doris had to admit she was right. *How could I have gone so long without a close girlfriend*, she wondered. Then she knew. Her mother had been her best friend. She frowned, realizing that neither one of them knew it while it was happening. She felt a sharp pain in her chest thinking about her mother.

"Doris?"

"Yes, of course, Tootsie, I'd love your help with the party. I'll call you tomorrow so we can start planning."

Doris' Tuesday morning seminar was a welcome relief from the tension she'd been feeling about interacting with students. If they had heard the rumors they gave her no indication. Valerie asked her how the play was going and mentioned she favored Edward Albee's plays. "I saw the revival of *A Delicate Balance* on Broadway a few years ago—it was wonderful," she said.

The group held a lively discussion about working as an artist in specialty shops, such as the Mardi Gras museum in New Orleans, where Doris had worked briefly while in grad school at Tulane. She reminded them she needed their final paper topics by Thursday and let them go a little early. She met Martin at his office for lunch. "This is a short lunch day for me, Martin, so let's grab something at Foster's and come back here to eat. Is that okay with you?"

Martin grabbed his heavy winter coat from its hook and put on his dark brown fedora. "Sounds good to me," he said and shut the door behind them.

When they got back to Doris' office they spread their sandwiches and chips on her large desk and uncapped their drinks. "So, Doris, you haven't said anything about last night. How did it go at rehearsal—when you told them you planned to drop out of the show?"

Doris chewed a massive wad of turkey on whole wheat and swallowed before answering. "I didn't tell them I was quitting, Martin. I thought about it and decided you were right. If I can't do something I want to do because some malicious *student* tells ugly lies about me, then I don't want to teach here anyway." Martin raised both eyebrows and sniffed, Doris took a sip of tea. "Gerald Rogers will have to make up his mind whether he's going to let some petty gossip from an immature adolescent decide my fate or if he's going to have the balls to do what's right and tell him or her to grow up."

"Doris!" Martin was surprised to hear Doris speak with such venom. Doris surprised herself, as well, but she guessed playing Martha was beginning to take its toll on her vocabulary.

"Sorry, Martin, this all makes me so angry. I haven't done anything wrong, and I don't understand why he is giving this complaint so much attention."

Martin and Doris didn't speak for a long time. They finished their sandwiches, and Doris pushed her chips to Martin, who happily ate them. She finished her tea and picked up her purse. "I need to fix my face a little, Martin, I'll be right back." He nodded, his mouth full of chips. When she returned, he had cleaned up the trash, thoughtfully leaving her tea for her. "Thanks for cleaning up, Martin, I need to get ready for class."

"Yes, me too, Doris. I enjoyed our lunch, and I'm glad to hear you're not giving in to this. But be careful, okay? Academia is more political than a presidential debate."

"Okay," Doris said, laughing a little. "Oh!" She said it so suddenly Martin jumped. "I almost forgot to tell you! I'm giving a Halloween party this Saturday night for the cast and crew. Can you help me with it?"

"A party?"

"Yes, why?"

"Well, it's odd. Here you are going through this, this, whatever it is, and you decide to throw a big party?"

"I didn't plan it, Martin, it came out of my mouth while I was talking to the cast. I'm sorry to spring it on you like this. Don't worry about it, I think I can manage everything. Tootsie wants to help."

"I didn't say I wouldn't help you, Doris. You know I'll be happy to help. We'll discuss it later; I don't want to make you late for class."

Doris pushed up her sleeve to check the time. "Oh dear, yes, I need to be going. Thanks, Martin, you are such a sweetheart." She gave him a quick kiss on the cheek and then rushed down the hall.

Doris' most apathetic class, her afternoon Introduction to Visual Arts, barely gave her a second look when she entered. *Good*, she thought, *maybe it isn't all over campus yet.* She lectured about the major differences between Greek and Roman sculpture technique without even bothering to wake up Thomas who routinely fell asleep on the back row. She reminded them they had to be able to discuss the relief sculpture on the back wall of the Roman stages, called the *scaenae frons*, on Thursday, and that captured their attention enough to make them moan. Doris shook her head as they zipped up backpacks and shuffled out. When she got back to her office she checked her email and voicemail, hoping there was nothing from Phyllis or the dean. There wasn't. "Good!" she said to the phone.

At rehearsal, Lenny began blocking the third act. Doris thought Act 2 had been difficult; she had no idea how hard the final act would be. First, she started the act with a long monologue on stage by herself then segued into a scene with Nick followed by another long, albeit marvelous, monologue. Once again, rehearsal was for Jayson and her. *At least I don't have to seduce him again,* she thought. This is the scene where Martha berates Nick for not performing well in the bedroom. Everyone noticed Martha's anger was a little more intense than expected the first time through. "Doris, I know it's early with this scene," Lenny said during notes, "but you might want to tame her down a little in the beginning—give her somewhere to go. If she starts out ranting and raving then she has nowhere to go, but if she can build the anger, it will be more effective."

Doris smiled. "Thanks, Lenny, that was a gentle way of saying it. I know I need to do that—Martha has so many more colors than red. I think I was using her to let off a little steam."

"Understandable," Lenny said. Jayson was silent, looking at the interplay between the two women, as if he was trying to decide if he could ask what was going on. He never spoke, however, until Lenny turned her notebook toward him and started asking him questions about Nick's feelings in the scene.

Doris made a point of walking out with Lenny; Jayson and Stacey trailed behind them. She got into her car without lingering, waving at everyone and driving off as quickly as possible. In her rearview mirror, she saw Jayson crossing the street toward his dorm. When she arrived home, she cleaned out the refrigerator before going to bed. Cleaning made her feel better—immediate results. Still, she tossed and turned most of the night, trying not to dream.

The rest of the week was grueling for Doris—wondering if or when a bomb would drop about the rumors, struggling to keep her mind on her classes and working on the intensely emotional final act of the play. By Friday, she had not heard anything further from Phyllis, so she hoped Dean Rogers decided to let the whole episode die a natural death. She and Martin talked excitedly at lunch on Friday about the party. Martin did some shopping for decorations and brimmed with all kinds of ideas for games and food. "I don't know if college kids play games, Martin. They might not consider it 'cool'." Doris said.

"Oh, well, I think they'll like these little games. They are theatre people, right? I think they might enjoy Halloween Charades and Murder."

Doris laughed, "Okay, you win, it does sound like fun to me!"

"Have you decided on your costume?" Martin asked.

"Well, I thought about coming as a famous artist, of course, but I didn't like any of those ideas. I think I might dress like Hester Prynne--as an inside joke, you know?" She was referring to the famous fictional woman who was branded an adulterer by her community by being forced to wear a large red "A" on her chest.

"*The Scarlet Letter*? Oh, that's a good one!" She smiled. Martin got the joke; she wondered if anyone else would.

"What are you wearing?"

"What else—the nutty professor! I found some big buckteeth, and I got a black rinse for my hair. I'll look like Jerry Lewis. I still have some old suits Cedrick wore in high school, so they'll be short and show my cuffs and white socks. I'll have to work on keeping my eyes crossed!"

"Martin, I'm glad I thought of having this party. I haven't seen you this excited since, well, I can't remember since when."

"It'll be fun—I'm looking forward to getting to know all your theatre friends better."

Doris tried to get the house cleaned up once she got home. She figured it would take most of Saturday to decorate and get ready for the party. Martin and Tootsie promised to come over early and help her get started. At rehearsal, the cast did a rough run-through of the third act. No one seemed to be in the mood to rehearse. Lenny recognized an off night when she saw it and sent everyone home. Doris handed out flyers with directions to her house and reminded everyone to come to the party.

As she was turning the key in Carmen's lock, Jayson came up behind her. "Dorie?"

"Jayson, I truly have to hurry home—I still have some cleaning up to do to get ready for the party. You are coming, aren't you?"

"Of course. I thought you'd want to know I spoke with Dr. Hathaway this morning."

Doris stopped fumbling with her key and turned to face him. "Well, I guess you know everything."

"Yeah, I guess so. I'm sorry, Dorie. I never meant to cause you any problems. I am really enjoying being your friend."

"Me too," Doris said softly. "I'm sorry you have to be involved in all this, too."

"I think I know who did all this." Doris raised her eyebrows and opened her mouth. "Kayla. She hates you. I don't know if you've seen her around here, but she sometimes waits on me and tries to talk about our 'relationship.'" He makes quotations with his fingers.

"She hates *me*? Why?"

"She told me she thinks you're the reason we broke up. She thinks that the only reason we broke up is because you advised me to do it, and the only reason you did is because you are after me for yourself."

Doris leaned against the car to stand upright. "Do you think she followed us when we were at the bar?"

"I think she follows me all the time. When I came to your house to help you smoke, when we went to the Shipyard, when I picked you up for Lenny's party. I think she's been following me, and well, you and I have been spending a lot of time together because of the play."

"Why would she go to the dean and the president?"

"Surely you can figure it out. She probably thinks if she can get you out of the picture, then we would get back together. Which is *so wrong*! I don't ever want anything to do with her—she's a psycho!"

"I almost dropped out of the play, you know."

"Was that what you were going to say on Monday?" Doris nodded. "Well, I'm glad you didn't. Kayla would just love that!" There was a long pause; Jayson shuffled his feet on the concrete. "Dr. Hathaway asked me if you were drunk that night. She asked me if I spent the night with you."

"I figured she would. She asked me, too. I hope you told her the truth."

"I told her you got drunk in order to do a better job in the play, and I slept on the sofa. I don't know if she believed me. She listened, you know. It was weird."

"I never told you to break up with Kayla, Jayson."

"I know! I've told her that—over and over. When I broke it off with her, I told her that you advised me to be honest with her, it was unfair to her if I didn't."

"Yes, I think I remember saying that."

"So, she claims you put the whole idea into my head."

Doris was still leaning against the car trying to breathe. "Well, it's all out there now," she said, "the problem is it *looks* like we are having an affair—and that may be enough."

"Enough for what?" Jayson was hopping from foot to foot to stay warm.

"Enough to . . . " Doris stopped short, she couldn't bring herself to say the words. As much as she didn't want to cry, tears welled up in her eyes, and she buried her face in her hands. Jayson instinctively put his arms around her and gave her a hug. At first, she buried her face into his warm shoulder; she needed this hug, she needed him. Suddenly she realized what they were doing and shoved him backwards. "Jayson, we can't be hugging like this in public--on the campus! Someone might be watching."

Jayson backed off, his arms outstretched, his hands palms forward—he looked like he was surrendering to the police. "I'm sorry, Dorie, I'm sorry for all of this." He turned and bounded quickly across the campus toward the dorms. Doris turned the key in Carmen's lock and tossed her script and purse into the passenger seat. Before she climbed into the car, however, she looked around the parking lot. Is she up in a tree or sitting in a dark car nearby? Where will Kayla Washington be next?

31

At six o'clock on Saturday night Martin was hanging the last spider web on the front porch, and Doris dropped the dry ice into the orange punch Tootsie had made. They truly outdid themselves in decorating for the party—orange and black streamers hung throughout Doris' living room and onto the screened porch. The fireplace had a large skull that lit up and candy all around it. The front porch was strewn with fake spider webs from banister to gutter, with two huge black Styrofoam spiders lying in wait. A series of orange and black luminaries lined the sidewalk, and lighted jack-o'-lanterns dotted the porch and house. Martin worked on the decorations while Doris prepared the food. Her new dining room table was covered with traditional Halloween treats—candy corn, festive cookies, caramel apples, and molasses popcorn balls. Martin had transported Felix to his house earlier in the day for safety. The door would be opened and closed so many times, Doris feared he would dart outside out of curiosity, and no one would even notice.

Martin came inside to set up the music, which was comprised mostly of classical music on what the students would call "vinyl" plus a few CD's he purchased with Halloween music like "The Monster Mash" and spooky sounds such as screams and creaking doors. It was time for the party, so he put on the CD with Halloween songs and then checked on the food. Doris and Tootsie were in the bedroom putting the finishing touches on their costumes. Tootsie chose to dress like Bette Midler in the movie, *Hocus Pocus*, with a huge red wig and beaver teeth. Martin made a perfectly hilarious Nutty Professor, and Doris had borrowed a costume from the theatre department, something once worn in a production of *The Crucible*, a gray long-sleeved dress with a big white collar and cuffs to which she pressed a bright red A on the chest. She tied on a large white apron and was tucking her hair under the bonnet when the doorbell rang.

When Doris entered, Martin had already opened the door to admit an oversized Dalmatian dog with a collar and leash leading to the hand of Cruella Deville—it took a moment for Doris to realize it was Charley and Lenny. "Oh, my, it's a Disney movie!" Doris laughed as she led them into the living room. "Charley, are you Perdy or Pongo?"

"Perdy's the female, so what do you think?" Charley chuckled then looked at Doris and pointed at the big red A on her chest and laughed.

Lenny came closer and said, "Who the hell *are* you, Dorie?"

"Oh for goodness sake, Lenny," Charley chided her, "Hester Prynne—you know *The Scarlet Letter*? Very funny, Doris, and so appropriate!"

Lenny screwed up her face and said, "Oh yes, I think I read that in high school—what a dreadful book! But oh yes, OH! I get it now!" Everyone laughed at Lenny, and Doris looked over at Martin and Tootsie who were waiting patiently to be introduced.

"Oh dear, I'm sorry, Martin. You know Lenny, of course, but this is her friend, uh partner, Charley. Charley this is Martin Winborn; he teaches American History at the college. Charley's a doctor, Martin."

Charley and Martin shook hands and Charley said, "Oh, I bet I know, you're the Nutty Professor!"

"God, Charley, that was rude!" Lenny scolded her partner.

"Lenny, do you know anything except theatre? *The Nutty Professor* is an old movie with Jerry Lewis. Martin looks like him—it's great to meet you, Martin." Again, they all laughed at Lenny's expense. Then Charley noticed Tootsie. "Oh my god, if it isn't Bette Midler!" They all laughed; even Lenny loved the movie *Hocus Pocus*.

"Well, Perdy, I'm hungry, let's eat. Oh, Dorie, here are some hot and spicy potato chips and French Onion dip. I know it sounds horrible, but it's delicious. Wow, your house is so cool!"

"Thanks, Lenny, I'll put this on the table, make yourselves at home." Doris poured the chips into a nice bowl and put them on the table while Martin served as doorman. A huge influx of students entered in a variety of costumes, ranging from the ridiculous to traditional, but they were all creative. Winnie came as Little Bo Peep, carrying a stuffed lamb, and Stacey was dressed all in black with ghoulish make-up. "I'm a campus Goth," she explained, and Martin nodded and smiled as if he knew what she meant.

Teri came dressed as Cleopatra with her boyfriend as Mark Anthony.

Jayson and Moses came in together as Laurel and Hardy, and Bill entered in his typical sweatshirt and jeans. *Of course*, Doris thought, *he's way too cool to dress up.* He told them his wife came down with the flu and stayed at home. He was followed by a large group of students Doris didn't recognize. She figured they were members of the production class who were doing some technical assignments. She knew there were still several crew members whom she had not seen since the first meeting, and at that time, she was focused her mother.

The party was in full swing within an hour, and everyone seemed to be having a great time. Martin kept the music current—some of the guests brought CD's, and Martin played them. Occasionally a group would get up to dance to a favorite song and then sit down or wander into the dining room. The food was a big hit; Doris and Tootsie continually refilled the punch bowl and cookie trays. Most of the guests had contributed something—mostly soft drinks which she sat up in the kitchen with an ice bucket and plastic cups. As usual, large groups congregated around the food tables in the dining room and in the kitchen. Another group, the smokers mainly, set up camp on the screened porch. Doris provided several ashtrays, cushions, and even a small heater.

Doris was filling up the punch bowl from a large pitcher when she heard a familiar voice over her shoulder. "Where's Felix? I was looking forward to seeing him again." Jayson held his derby over his heart and scratched his head with the other hand. Doris burst out laughing.

"You look so great! You have it down. How do you even know about Laurel and Hardy, anyway? They were even before *my* time."

"Oh, I adore all those old comedy teams—Abbott and Costello, the Marx Brothers—my dad loves them, too. We used to rent the old movies on video—Stan Laurel was my favorite. I think he was a genius."

"I agree; he was. Felix is at Martin's house. I was afraid the party would overwhelm him a little."

"Makes sense. The food is terrific—how did you ever get all this done?"

"Couldn't have done it without Martin and my friend, Tootsie. We went to school together. Martin shopped most of yesterday and then spent the whole day here decorating."

"I'll have to tell him how awesome everything looks," Jayson said, munching on a cookie. "Is Tootsie the *Hocus Pocus* witch? I love that movie! I'll go introduce myself."

"That's a good idea, Jayson," a soft female voice spoke behind him. "It would give me a chance to talk to Dr. Peechum."

Jayson's face became ashen, and Doris looked at him with concern. "Kayla," he said, "what the hell are you doing here?"

They both looked at her dressed as Tinker Bell; she looked beautiful and sweet. Her blonde hair was sprinkled with glitter and her young figure was draped in a form-fitted pastel chiffon outfit, short enough to reveal her bare, and flawless, legs. *What a perfect costume*, Doris thought ruefully. "I was invited by someone in the show," she said demurely, "Why? Is there a problem?"

Doris reminded herself she had no proof Kayla was responsible for the rumors and even if she was, it would not be a good idea to alienate her. "Of course not, Kayla, I'm glad to have you here. Are you enjoying yourself?"

Jayson stood between the women as if he could shield Doris from Kayla's venom, but Kayla was polite and unassuming. "I'm having a great time, thank you," she said, "I wanted to talk to you about taking an art class next semester. Should I come by your office sometime next week?"

Doris looked at Kayla and then at Jayson for a short moment. "Why, Kayla, that would be fine. Are you interested in art?"

"Well, sort of," she said, "I'm interested in interior design, so I need some art training to get into a good school."

"Yes, it's true, you do. I would be happy to talk with you during any of my office hours next week, check the schedule on my door and drop by any time it's convenient for you." Kayla agreed and thanked Doris again for the party. Jayson watched her walk away, breathing loudly through his nose.

"Damn, I can't believe her!" Jayson said under his breath.

"Jayson, there's no proof Kayla is our culprit. I can't be rude to her."

"I know, Dorie, but she shouldn't show her face around here, that's all."

"Forget about it, Jayson, go have some fun. Dance with Stacey, she looks kind of lonely sitting over there by herself." Jayson nodded and smiled. He headed toward Stacey who was sitting on the sofa, and Doris headed back into the kitchen. She hid it from Kayla and Jayson, but Doris was shaking all over. She refilled the pitcher and put it in the fridge to chill then escaped to the front porch for a break. There were only a few people sitting on the front steps sipping the hot chocolate Martin made earlier. She took a seat by herself on the swing and looked up at the ceiling of her porch as she gently rocked herself to and fro. Doris wanted to stay on the swing through the remainder of the party, but she knew, as hostess, she needed to mingle. Near midnight it occurred to her if they didn't stop serving food the college students would never leave, so she told Martin and Tootsie to plug up the supply and let the party wind itself down. Martin nodded, seeming to understand, and put his classical CD's on the stereo.

Sure enough, the wild partygoers started to filter out in groups, which left a small contingency of quiet talkers clustered in corners and in the kitchen. Martin started cleaning up the kitchen while Doris and Tootsie started picking up the trash, urging everyone to stay put and enjoy themselves. "If we don't get some of this picked up, it will take over the house!" Doris teased. Lenny, Charley, Moses, and Jayson pitched in to help, and by the time everything was picked up and washed or thrown out, they were the only ones remaining. They all said goodbye around one, including Tootsie, leaving Doris and Martin in a clean house with a large collection of unopened soft drinks on the kitchen counter. Doris promised Lenny to bring them to the cast party.

Martin said he wanted to take a good shower to get the rinse out of his hair, and Doris gave him clean towels, pointing him toward the guest bath. She took her big robe and headed to her bathroom where she could soak in a warm bath of fragrant jasmine bubbles and let her worries float, however temporarily, from her mind.

She missed Felix terribly, but it was too late to drive over to Martin's to retrieve him. She put on her favorite cotton nightie with a pair of socks and tucked herself into bed next to Martin who was already snoring. *Poor Martin,* she thought, *he's exhausted.* He was so wonderful in getting ready for the party, serving as host, keeping the food and drinks fresh, while still managing to talk to everyone. How nice it must be, she pondered, *to be so self-confident and easy-going with people.* Doris hated small talk and had to force herself to go around and greet everyone equally. It wasn't that she didn't like them; she was a true introvert, and being around people simply exhausted her. She'd much rather be huddled in the corner with some interesting person like Charley discussing some topic of deep concern.

Doris and Martin enjoyed a relaxing day together on Sunday after taking down the spiders and pumpkins. It had been a long time since they'd had a day to do whatever they wanted. First, they drove to Martin's house to get Felix. He clung to Doris' shoulder so tenaciously she didn't even put him in the carrier for the car ride home. Once at Doris', he jumped out of her arms and proceeded to sniff every inch of the house, trying to see if any of the interlopers disturbed his territory. Finally, he climbed into his window hammock and took a thorough bath before falling asleep. Martin suggested they take a trip to Sweetwater to look at antiques and then have a nice supper somewhere new. Doris didn't argue—she wanted someone else to do the thinking for today. She was content to sit in the car and look at the passing scenery. In the evening, she, Martin, and Felix cuddled up on the sofa to watch a TV movie. Martin, of course, fell asleep, and she woke him up to send him home. He gave her an enduring kiss, assuring her that everything would be fine, and took off down the road in his Volvo.

Wow, Doris thought, *if he could just be as good in bed as he is with kissing!*

32

Monday morning seemed to come early for Doris. She wanted to stay in bed and cover her head. But, duty bound as usual, she got out of bed and followed her morning ritual, getting to her office a half hour before class. She was dismayed to find a note taped to her door from Phyllis. She wanted to have a meeting "ASAP", as she put it. Doris held her breath for a long moment, put her books down, and called Phyllis to ask if it was okay to come on over.

When she got to her department chair's office, Vivian greeted her warmly and ushered her right in to see Phyllis. This looks like a well-planned effort, Doris thought, Vivian hardly ever smiles at anyone. Doris took a seat, and Vivian quietly closed the door behind her. "What can I do for you, Phyllis," Doris said, trying to sound upbeat and like she didn't notice the somber expression on Phyllis' face.

"Doris, I don't know where to begin with all this. First, let me say I think the whole business stinks, and I will stand behind you whatever you decide to do. You are a valued member of this faculty and of the department, so if you want to fight this, I will do whatever I can to help." She paused, and Doris once again realized she hadn't been breathing. Phyllis leaned forward, propping an elbow on her desk. "Doris, this student has filed a formal complaint against you. He or she has agreed not to go public with the accusations if you agree to resign and leave the college. If not, he or she will not only go public on campus but in the community. The intention is to ruin your academic reputation, so even if you do stay here, your career will pretty much be over." Phyllis took a deep breath; Doris did not speak. "My advice to you is to find another position as if it is your idea to leave. Nothing will be revealed about your behavior with Jayson, and you can leave at the end of the year like many professors to pursue a better position."

"My behavior with Jayson?"

"Doris, I don't believe the accusation about the affair, but both you and Jayson have admitted you got drunk with him, he did spend the night at your house, and you and he have been spending a lot of other private times together. If you take this to the grievance committee to fight, it will be your and Jayson's word against this student's about the affair, but what you have done already would be viewed with disapproval by your colleagues and certainly the board of directors. This is a Christian college, Doris, many of our alumni and benefactors would find it impossible to support keeping you here—regardless of the reasons behind your behavior or your sterling academic record. And then, of course, you will have to face insults and criticism about the play and how the two of you behave together there. It's not a good situation any way you look at it. I'm so sorry, Doris."

"Me too," Doris said, trying to contain both her tears and her anger. "I think it's a damn shame that supposedly intelligent and reasonable administrators are going to allow the jealous and immature behavior of one student to ruin not only a well-respected professor's career but the reputation of this college."

"Doris, you know the dean and president don't keep me in the loop. But I know Dean Rogers has a file of complaints against you he is planning to bring to your attention if you don't agree to resign. I don't know if I was supposed to tell you, but I think the way you're being blindsided is disgraceful."

"Thanks, Phyllis, I'm sure you've done what you can. I . . . I uh, I think I need some time to think about this. I'll let you know in a few days—okay?" Doris stood up, and Phyllis followed her lead.

"Of course, Doris, take your time. No one can make this kind of decision quickly. I'll tell Dean Rogers you will tell us something by the end of the week. Can I do anything to help you?"

"No, well, you could tell me who this student is—I would really like to know."

"You know I can't reveal that, Doris, unless you decide to stay and fight. If you do, you would have a chance to face your accuser in the grievance committee hearing."

"Okay, I understand," Doris said as she left, although she didn't. She retreated to her office and sat in the dark for a long time. *How can everything change so quickly,* she asked herself. *Two short months ago I could talk to my mother and thought my place at this college would be*

secure until I retired. Should I fight this or go quietly into that good night?
The grievance committee would be the first phase of hashing out the
student's complaint—it was a panel of tenured faculty and upper-class
students who, like a court of judges, listen to both sides of a complaint and
then render a decision. If they couldn't resolve the complaint then it
progresses to the faculty council, and then the administrative council.
Usually campus disputes could be handled at the first level, but Doris
wondered if perhaps she should go directly to civil court, charging the
student with slander. Or perhaps sue the college—but for what? Stupidity?

When the phone rang she nearly jumped out of her chair. It was
Martin asking about lunch. She told him she was skipping it today and
going home early with a headache. He said he hoped she would feel better
soon and that he would call her later. Doris showed a video about
Shakespeare to her Art Appreciation class and a series of slides to her Art
History class, which covered French Neoclassical architecture.

When the class was over, she put everything away in her office and
told Vivian she would not be holding her office hours because of a
headache. Vivian nodded and gave her a smug look. Doris didn't even care
enough to worry about what Vivian was thinking. She stopped by the
market for some cigarettes and Dr. Pepper and then headed home to
ruminate her fate.

Her mail contained a letter from Sheila Grindstaff and Kerryville
Realtors concerning the estate sale. It was an itemized list of all the items
that sold and the amount collected, plus a list of all goods contributed to
the women's shelter. There was also a letter explaining the realty company
would be repainting the interior, cleaning the house and tidying up the
landscaping in an attempt to sell the house for a good price. All she needed
to do was look all this over, sign it, and send it back to them for processing.
They would then take care of selling the house, paying themselves for their
efforts, and putting the remainder of the money into a fund for her to claim
at her convenience. Doris called Ms. Grindstaff explaining she needed to
send a copy of this to Ted, as well, and they would confer by phone and
get back to her as soon as possible. She didn't sound happy, but she agreed
and said she would wait to hear from them.

Doris called Ted at his office to explain what he would soon be
receiving, and he agreed it was a good idea for him to look over it. "Ted,"
Doris began hesitantly—*should I involve my brother in this? Do I want him*

to know I got drunk with a student? "Nothing," she finally said.

"What, Doris? Is it about the house?"

"No, it's about school," Doris began. "Let me ask you about something . . .." Doris explained the basics of the situation to Ted, without revealing the part about her being drunk, to see what his advice would be.

"God, Doris, what did you do to piss a student off this badly?" Ted was never the sympathetic type, Doris thought. "He or she has you between a rock and a hard place. If you fight it, either on campus or in civil court, everyone on campus and the community will find out about it. Believe it or not, most people think that where there's smoke there's probably some kind of fire, so you will be viewed with suspicion and even blamed by some. If you have done *anything* out of line, anything that can be proved, then it will become public knowledge, also. My guess is even if you win, you would become so uncomfortable in Kerryville you would start looking for another job anyway. Of course, the accusation will follow you, which might make it difficult for you to secure a good position." Ted was quiet for a moment; Doris listened to his breathing. "I don't know, Doris, I think you'd be better off in the long run to start looking for something else and get out of that place. You can make them sign some kind of contract, the student included, which states the complaint will never be acknowledged by the college as legitimate, and if the student or the college makes any such revelation, they will be libel for personal damages and your reinstatement."

"Could you draw me up a contract like that?"

"Of course, Doris. Take some time to think about this and let me know what you want to do. I'll help in any way I can."

Doris thanked Ted for his advice. It wasn't what she wanted to hear, but she knew he, like Phyllis, was probably right. *It's so easy for them to advise me to leave and go somewhere else,* she thought, *they're not the ones who have to give up everything they have grown to love and depend on. I'd have to sell my house, find a new job, move to a new place, and leave my friends, my colleagues, and my home. Tootsie and I have just gotten back in touch. And Martin, I'd have to leave Martin, too.* She lay on her bed crying, burying her head in the pillows. Felix sat next to her head, a silent sentinel.

By the time she arrived for rehearsal, Doris was exhausted with worrying and crying. She put forth as much energy as possible, but Lenny could see her heart was not in it. She didn't give Doris any notes, except simple blocking instructions, and let them go with only one run-through of Act 3. She did warn them lines were due the next night, and then they would begin run-throughs of the whole show for polishing. The production was less than two weeks away. Lenny explained they needed to get the show tight before the next weekend when technical rehearsals would start.

Doris picked up her belongings and walked to her car without speaking to anyone—even those who bid her goodnight. She wasn't intending to be rude; she didn't even hear them. Her mind was reeling with the responsibilities of the next three weeks—the show, the conference, her first Thanksgiving without Avis, and, of course, her decision about her job. A hand touched her shoulder, and she looked up to see Lenny's kind face looking at her with concern. "Dorie? You look like a ghost—what's wrong?"

Doris glanced around to make sure none of the students were in hearing range. "I talked with Phyllis today. She's recommending I look for another position."

Lenny stopped walking and hugged Doris, who recoiled quickly. She didn't want to draw any attention to herself or have people asking what was wrong. "Oh Dorie, I am so sorry. I feel like this is my fault. If you weren't in the play, none of this would have happened."

"For goodness sake, Lenny, that never occurred to me--not even once. I'm the one who made the decision to have Jayson over to my house to work on the smoking, and I'm the one who allowed myself to get drunk in front of him and the others. I got myself into this, Lenny, there's no doubt in my mind about it."

"But, Dorie, there are a lot of us on the faculty—myself included—who have been drunk in front of our students. Lots of us have invited them over to our houses, and I even know some faculty members who have *actually* had affairs with students. It's not fair you have to lose your job over something so many of us do."

"The difference, Lenny, is none of you have been caught. No vengeful student has directed the attentions of your department and the administration to your indiscretions. I am the one who got caught. And no matter how you look at it—what I did was bad judgment. I still don't think I did anything *wrong*, but ask the parents of these students if they want teachers who take their kids out drinking at gay bars. No matter what anyone else has done here, I did do that."

"Well, I did it, too. I've done it many times, Dorie. And you know how some of the faculty and especially the alumni and community would feel about me teaching here if they knew I was gay."

"Don't worry, Lenny, no one will ever hear it from me."

The women embraced in friendship and started walking to their cars. "Let me know if I can do anything to help, Dorie. You can call me any time, okay?"

Doris nodded and took off in Carmen. Jayson waved at her as she drove past him and Winnie. Doris felt a sudden urge to keep driving and never come back to Kerryville, take off down the road and start a new life. If not for Felix she may have done it, but she knew she must go home, feed the cat, and go to bed. She wanted to go through her normal day even if her heart was breaking.

The rest of the week was agony for Doris. She began isolating in her office and trying to avoid contact with students and colleagues. She started doing better at rehearsal for the simple reason it was the only place she had any fun. Martin was showing a great amount of concern for her, and she knew she should sit down and tell him what was going on. Lenny wanted to work with the understudies on Wednesday night, so Doris elected not to attend rehearsal. She invited Martin over for dinner and resolved to confess everything to him.

Martin arrived on time, as usual, carrying a bottle of wine and a treat for Felix. Doris managed to appear nonchalant during dinner and even dessert. She served Martin coffee and sat down at the table with her own cup.

"Martin, do you remember the night you were so worried about me— I told you Lenny and I went out for drinks?" Martin nodded and sipped his coffee. "Well, I did go out with Lenny, but I didn't tell you the whole story. I'm not sure why. You were so upset with me already; I didn't want you to get the wrong idea about anything."

Martin stopped sipping coffee and looked at her across the table. "Doris, you look pale—are you all right?"

"Well, Martin, I went to a gay bar in Chattanooga with a group of students *and* Lenny. I, uh, drove Jayson, Stacey, and Winnie. I was getting ready to leave rehearsal, and Lenny asked who wanted to go, so I thought it would be fun."

Martin listened intently. "Okay, I understand. They invited you, right?"

"Yes, they go there all the time, apparently." Doris felt encouraged by Martin's calm demeanor. "Anyway, we were there, and, well, I drank way too much. I was thinking it might be good to have the experience of being drunk at least once in my life, so I could relate better to Martha—she's drunk through most of the play, you know. I have been faking it, pretending I know what it's like."

"Uh-huh," said Martin. "Has it helped you?"

"Yes, it has, a lot, actually. But that's not all, Martin. I need to tell you all of it."

"Okay," Martin said, setting his cup down, his eyebrows furrowed toward his nose. "I'm listening."

"Well, I didn't think I should drive home, so Stacey drove us to the campus—she didn't drink anything. We dropped her and Winnie off at the dorm, and then Jayson said he felt good enough to drive me home. He only drank a couple of beers and wasn't drunk. I know it wasn't the smartest thing I've ever done, but Jayson did fine, and he got me home safely. Apparently, I fell asleep in the car and then again as soon as he got me inside." Martin opened his mouth to ask a question, but Doris forged ahead. "There was no way for Jayson to get home, so he slept on the sofa. We ate breakfast the next morning, and then I drove him to campus and stayed to do some set work."

"I swear to you, Martin, nothing happened. Jayson was a perfect gentleman and took good care of me." She paused. "Are you angry?"

Martin sat with his fingers laced together under his chin, that wild flap of hair hanging over his eye. "Why didn't you tell me all this before if nothing happened?"

"I told you--you were already mad at me, and I didn't want to upset you further. It's not like I did anything wrong. I didn't actually lie to you; I just didn't tell you everything."

"Okay, fair enough. Thanks for telling me now, I appreciate it." She couldn't tell what Martin was feeling, she'd never seen him angry. But she needed to tell him everything—it would be far worse for him to find out from someone else.

"Well, there's more," Doris said, rubbing her forehead. Martin assumed a defensive posture and stared at Doris solemnly. "This complaint—well, it's based mainly on me getting drunk with students and then having Jayson here spending the night. It seems we were being watched the whole time, and this person saw Jayson bring me home and then not come out until the next morning."

"Well," said Martin, "it certainly makes it easier to understand why you are being accused of having an affair with him. I suppose this student has proof?"

"Unfortunately, I told Phyllis the truth when she asked me. If I had lied and told her he didn't spend the night, then it would be my, and Jayson's, word against the student's. But I didn't know that when she asked me."

"Well, great," Martin said in exasperation. "You tell the truth and get punished for it; this student tells lies and gets rewarded for it."

"You're not angry with me?" Doris felt a wave of relief wash over her.

"I'm hurt, Doris, that you didn't tell me all this before. But, no, I'm not angry with you. I believe your story—it's too stupid to make up."

"Well, thanks, I think." Doris was a little offended, but she let it go. Martin was being so tolerant with her she knew she shouldn't bicker.

"Sorry, Doris, but you must've known this was foolish. Why didn't you just get drunk with me? No one would have known, and you wouldn't be in this mess right now."

Doris looked stunned. "I never thought of that, Martin. I don't know why." Doris left the table and sat down on the sofa with her hands covering her face.

Martin sat beside her and stretched his arm around her shoulder. Doris turned and buried her face in his collar. Felix jumped up on Doris' lap and she reached a hand out to pet him. The three of them sat silently for a long time.

"What has happened to college education, Martin?" Doris asked in earnest. "When I started teaching, even as a lowly graduate assistant, my department chair stood up for me."

Martin leaned back on the sofa and looked up at the ceiling. "I remember those days," he said wistfully. "We used to have a department head here in Humanities, Dr. Grazzi, who told complainers they needed to grow up and take responsibility for their lives and their studies. A student complained to him once I was boring in class, and he laughed. 'Do you think you're going to like every boss you have in life—do you think it's going to make any difference as to whether you need to do your work?' The kid couldn't answer him, so that was the end of it.'"

"These days, it's all about money, Doris. The bottom line for colleges is they have to keep students in the seats to operate in the black—there are a lot more colleges competing for the same money."

She told Martin she was heading to bed and got up to lay out her clothes for the morning. Martin followed her into the bedroom and put his arms around her. She pushed him away, "I'm okay, Martin, I need to get some rest for tomorrow. Why don't you come to my office for lunch—I'm brown-bagging it again."

"Your colleagues miss you at lunch, Doris. Don't you want to go to the cafeteria and eat with them? They can support you right now."

"Don't they all know about this? I can't face them."

"I don't know how much they know, but they always ask where you are and how you're doing. I think some of them think you're still upset about your mother's death."

"I *AM* STILL UPSET ABOUT MY MOTHER'S DEATH!" Doris was shouting and not sure why. Martin took a couple of steps back and stared at her. "I'm sorry, Martin, but of course, I'm still upset about my mother, and losing my childhood home, and being accused of something I didn't do, and having to face losing my job because some student has more time to follow me around than to do *his or her* homework." Doris was crying again, and Martin tried once again to embrace her. This time she let him, falling into his arms and crying on his shoulder as he led her to the bed. They sat for a long time with Doris struggling to breathe and stop crying with Martin patting her arm gently, telling her everything would be okay. Finally, Doris lay down on the bed and cried herself to sleep. Martin curled next to her and dozed off, both still fully dressed. In less than two days, Doris would have to give Phyllis her decision.

33

Jayson was good about keeping his distance from Doris in class and at rehearsal. He was friendly, and often she caught him staring at her with a frown on his face and his eyebrows furrowed. She could tell he was worried about her but glad he was leaving her alone. Any "extra" friendliness between them could be so easily misinterpreted by anyone on campus now; Doris couldn't be sure who her enemies were so she tried to keep to herself as much as possible.

At Thursday night's rehearsal, they did the first run-through of the entire show. It was rough, but most of the lines were secure, except for Bill's, and the play was developing into something greater than its parts. Lenny announced she wanted to use Friday night to work on a couple of trouble scenes between George and Honey and George and Nick. Doris' face brightened when she realized this meant she would have the night off. Lenny reminded everyone the cue to cue tech rehearsal would begin Saturday at two, and every student was expected to be at the theatre Saturday morning to finish the light-hang and focus, and get the stage and dressing rooms ready for the coming performance.

Doris waved to everyone and made a hasty exit for her car. She still hadn't made up her mind about the job, so she decided to take a spin around the river road to clear her head and think. It felt so good to have the cold air rushing through her hair and Beethoven's angry fifth symphony playing at full volume. She tried not to go too fast; the last thing she needed was a speeding ticket. But she drove over an hour trying not to think about anything except the music, the air, and the road in front of her.

Friday morning finally arrived, and Doris didn't feel any more prepared to announce her decision today than a few days before. Her stomach was so jumpy she didn't even try to eat breakfast. She lectured about dance in her nine o'clock class for the whole hour. When she took roll, she realized Jayson was not in class. That was unusual. Jayson wasn't much of a scholar, but he practiced good attendance. *I hope he's not ill,* she thought to herself, *he has so much work to do in the coming week.* As she approached her office, she saw him standing outside her locked door. He was kicking his foot against the doorframe, his hands tucked in the pockets of his high school letter jacket.

"Jayson? Are you all right? I wondered why you weren't in class."

"Yeah, I'm fine, Dorie, I need you to sign this drop slip."

"Drop slip? Are you dropping the class, Jayson?"

"Yeah, I realized last night I'm not doing well in the class anyway, and I know I won't have time to study for the big test next week, so I thought it would be best if I dropped now before you have to fail me."

"Jayson, you're not failing, and you know it." She unlocked her door and took a seat at her desk, Jayson sat in the "student chair." Neither of them made any attempt to close the door. "You can definitely pull a C in the class if you continue working hard. If you don't finish the class you won't be able to graduate in May, will you?"

"Well, I have two choices. I can take an overload in the spring or I walk through graduation and pick up the course next summer."

"Jayson, I don't suggest you take an overload. With all your theatre work you don't have much time to study. I'm not sure we'll even offer this class in the summer. It seems to me you'd be better off staying in the class now."

"Dorie, you and I both know it would be better for both of us if you weren't my teacher--especially with the play next week. I think it would be easier for you, and me, of course. Sign the slip, Dorie, please."

It finally dawned on Doris that Jayson wasn't doing this because of bad grades; he was doing this for her, to protect her. She stared at him for a long moment trying to decide if she should let him make this sacrifice. She couldn't deny; however, Jayson was right. It was probably something he should have done a long time ago. After all, Jayson was twenty-one. If he hadn't been in one of her classes, it wouldn't be viewed so badly if they were spending so much time together. It wouldn't be good, but it wouldn't be such a big deal. It might not be threatening her job right now, but then again, maybe it would. Doris didn't know for certain what to do about her current situation, but she certainly wasn't going to let Jayson take the fall for her stupid mistakes.

She stood. "No, Jayson. I won't do it." Jayson stood with her and started to speak. "I won't let you make this sacrifice."

"But Dorie, I can't let you lose your job for something that's my fault."

"Your fault? How do you figure that? I'm the one who made all the poor choices. Now it's time to face the music. Go. I'll see you soon." Jayson stood for a long moment without speaking. Doris tore the paper in half and tossed it in the trash. "Go on, Jayson, this is time you could use to study for that big test." He shook his head, bit his lips between his teeth, and sighed. After he left, Doris closed the door and locked it. Now she wasn't worried about what would happen. Now she was angry.

Doris sat for several minutes, lost in thought. Phyllis' gentle rapping on her door startled her, but she caught her breath and looked up. "Doris? May I come in?" Phyllis try the doorknob. Doris quickly wiped the tears away and grabbed a tissue to dab at her nose.

"Enter at your own risk," she said to Phyllis, "I think I may be coming down with something. I hope it's just allergies. Please, have a seat."

Phyllis closed the door and took the same chair Jayson occupied moments before. "Doris," she began, "I was wondering if you had made any decisions about the, uh, situation."

Doris stared down at her hands, her breathing slow and steady. "Yes, Phyllis, I think I know what I want to do. I'm not going to leave just because one student hates me enough to tell untruths about me."

"But, Doris, you admitted to me you got drunk with Jayson, he stayed in your home overnight, and you've spent a great amount of time alone with him . . ."

"That may be true, but the fact remains Jayson and I are only friends. We might look like lovers onstage, but we have never done anything beyond a friendly hug offstage. He is a twenty-one-year-old man, not a kid. He wanted to drop the class today; I hope everyone is happy. He was willing to give up his chance to graduate with his class just to help a friend. I am not going to let him make this sacrifice so I can sneak out of town with my tail between my legs. I have decided to fight the charge, so you let me know what comes next."

Phyllis stared at Doris with concern and then a small smile cracked the severity of her expression. "Good," she said, standing up to leave. "I'll talk to Dean Rogers sometime today. I'll be in touch."

The door closed behind Phyllis, and Doris took a deep breath and exhaled loudly. *What have I done?*

When Martin came by for lunch she told him about her decision. It brightened his spirits considerably, and he suggested they go out for lunch. Doris' class met at one, though, so she suggested dinner. Martin was surprised she didn't have rehearsal, but he was never one to look a gift horse in the mouth. He told her he'd be by at six to pick her up.

Doris walked down the hall to her Art History class, amazed at how much better she felt. She didn't know if it was an unfortunate decision, but it had lifted a burden from her shoulders. She was feeling more like her old self, not the victim she had seen herself becoming.

When she arrived home, there was a message from Ted on the machine. The real estate papers looked good to him, go ahead and sign so they could get started on the clean-up and sale of Avis' house. At the end of his message, Ted asked about the "college situation."

Doris called Ms. Grindstaff, who was not in. She left a voicemail message telling Sheila the papers would be mailed tomorrow morning, and they could go ahead with their plans. Next, she picked up the phone and caught Ted at his office. "I've decided to fight this, Teddy. I don't know if it's the smartest choice, but I can tell you it *feels* like the right one. If I need a lawyer, could you recommend someone good around here?"

"Well, I don't know if you want to do this, but I can't think of anyone better than Ethan Anderson. His firm has a wonderful reputation, especially for personal injury cases. If you decide not to go with him, let me know. I'll do some research and find someone else."

"No," Doris said, thinking how ironic life is, "Ethan is fine. At least he knows what kind of person I am, right?"

"Right," Ted said. There was a pause.

"Okay, then, I'll call him. Thanks, Ted. Tell Tammy and the kids I say hi."

"Let me know how it all goes, okay? I worry about you, Sis."

He hadn't called her "Sis" in a long time, about as long ago as she had called him "Teddy." Sissy and Teddy were their names for each other growing up. Somewhere along the line, it became Doris and Ted. Ted explained once that having two names for Aunt Doris was too confusing for his kids, and Doris figured Ted wanted her to call him a more adult name. There was tenderness in his voice today, however, that Doris hadn't heard since their father died. *Maybe we should be Sissy and Teddy again,* she thought. She assured him she'd keep in touch and then looked around her house. "I'm not giving all this up," she said aloud to herself. "My home is here, my history is here," she said, "I want to be here."

She picked up the phone to call Ethan who was out; she left a message with his secretary who assured her Mr. Anderson would call her Monday. Doris gave the secretary her office and home phone numbers and the times she would be available for a call and hung up. *There's nothing I can do to stop it now,* she thought to herself.

Martin took Doris to a new restaurant on the east side of town that served Greek food. Doris was impressed that little ole Kerryville was growing enough to sustain a Greek restaurant—the place was packed. They both ordered falafel salads, shrimp saganaki, and agiorgitiko wine, which was so sweet Doris said she might not order the baklava, though she knew she would. They chatted happily about classes, students and world events, carefully dodging all issues concerning the student complaint. They were having such a good time, Doris almost hesitated to bring it up, but she knew she needed to clear things up with Martin. When the baklava was served with authentic Greek coffee brewed in a briki and served in demitasse cups, Doris made her move.

"Martin," she said and he looked up, the wild flap of hair hanging over his eye. "I want to talk to you about something kind of serious." Martin dabbed his mouth with his napkin, pushed his hair back, and nodded.

"Ok," was all he said.

"Martin, you know I feel great affection for you, and I think you feel the same for me."

Martin reached across the table and took Doris' hand in his. "Of course, I do, Doris."

"Well, you never say it, Martin. You say, 'love you' at the end of a phone call, but never to me in person." She paused, he started to speak, but she stopped him. "I can't help but wonder what the problem is, so I've been afraid to say it myself. I . . . I mean . . ."

Martin stood up and moved to sit beside her in the booth. He put his arm around her shoulder and squeezed her to his side. "I'm so sorry, Doris, of course I love you," he kissed her forehead gently and said loudly, "I love you, I love you, I love you."

Doris began to blush as she noticed people from other tables were watching. "Martin, please, don't make a scene!" She scolded him, but everyone could see the smile on her face from across the room.

"I don't care if people know it," he looked around. "I love this woman!" Suddenly the server, a man of about fifty with a heavy Greek accent appeared at their table.

"But does the lady love you?" he asked. By now the whole room had frozen in anticipation of her answer.

Doris truly panicked for a moment when she realized all eyes were on her. Martin took her hand and kissed it. "Doris, do you love me too?"

"Yes, of course, Martin, yes, I love you!" The room exploded into thunderous applause and cheering. Martin gave her a long kiss as the cheering continued.

"Doris?" she heard Martin's voice across the table. "Doris, are you all right?"

She looked at him suddenly realizing what just happened must have been a daydream. *Wait, am I awake, are we here, where are we?* Doris looked around. The other diners were eating and drinking and conversing quietly at their tables. Martin was munching on his dessert; his face showed concern for her. "Doris, are you all right?" he said again.

Doris gave a shallow laugh and assured him all was well. "The wine went to my head, I think. I haven't eaten all day." Martin's face relaxed.

"Do you feel well enough to finish dinner or do you want to leave?"

"Nonsense," she said with as much false bravado as she could muster. "This looks delicious, I love baklava. This place is amazing!" She pushed the wine away and sipped at the strong coffee. *I'll talk to him tonight at the house,* she resolved.

Once home, she and Martin kicked off their shoes and relaxed on her sofa. "You wanna watch some TV, Honey, or maybe read?" Martin asked as he rearranged the sofa cushions.

"Not yet, Martin, I, uh, I have something I want to talk to you about." *Maybe this is also a good time to talk about the lovemaking,* she thought.

He leaned forward and looked at her with concern. "What is it?"

She took one look at his face and realized she couldn't do it; she couldn't bear to hurt him. "Oh, never mind, Martin, it isn't that important."

Martin turned to look at her squarely in the face and took her hands. "Doris, please tell me. I can't stand to think you have something on your mind but don't feel you can discuss it with me. Please? I'm a grown-up, I can take it."

It broke her heart that he was trying so hard. She took his face in her hands and kissed him. "Okay." She explained how it frustrated her that he hadn't told her he loved her. "You say it quickly at the end of phone calls, but never just say it to me. I can't be sure how you feel about me, and it makes me hesitant to say it to you."

He kissed her and said, "I love you, Doris." Then he smothered her with kisses, repeating "I love you!" over and over until before she knew it, Doris was in bed staring at his back again. She looked at the ceiling of her bedroom and wondered how on earth she could explain what she thought of his lovemaking.

34

Doris felt a renewed energy that propelled her through the nightmares of tech rehearsals. Everyone in the theatre knows this is the worst weekend of any production. For weeks, the actors work on the play and the crew works on the set, props, lighting, and costumes. Tech rehearsal is a time when all these elements get put together for the first time, and it is usually long and grueling. One could watch a tech rehearsal and wonder if it will ever look like a production worthy of an audience, but then somehow it magically comes together during the following week of dress rehearsals. And this production was no different.

They worked into the night on Saturday to finish setting the light cues, and Doris dragged herself home around nine. Martin was waiting there with a beautifully prepared dinner. She was grateful for his efforts but would have rather had the time to herself. On Sunday morning, he woke her up with breakfast, which was very sweet, but she would've rather slept in. He brought the paper and coffee in and crawled into bed next to her. They sipped and read for a while, then Doris remembered rehearsal and looked at the clock; it seemed earlier than she had guessed.

"Is it just ten o'clock? It seems so much later."

"Time change," Martin said. "I fixed all your clocks last night after you went to bed."

"Aw, you're so thoughtful, Martin."

Sunday afternoon they added costumes which threw a whole new wrench into the machine. Quick changes are always a challenge so Lenny let Doris practice just the costume changes first since hers is the only character that changes clothes. Eventually, they achieved a rhythm and finished the run-through by supper time. Lenny announced the schedule for the rest of the week would be full dress every night with pictures on Tuesday.

Ethan called Doris Monday afternoon and set up an appointment for a week later. Doris was circumspect on the phone, vaguely telling Ethan she needed some legal advice if he was willing. He was gracious, as always, making Doris feel that calling him was the best thing she could have done.

By final dress on Wednesday night, Lenny had no fingernails left, and she had upped her smoking to two packs a day instead of one. But the play, the set, the music, all combined into such a good production Lenny was still wiping away her tears as she gave her notes after rehearsal. The understudies and crew served as audience and gave everyone resounding applause. Doris wanted to cancel her classes on Thursday and Friday so she could rest for the show, but she planned to cancel the following week for her conference so she knew she needed to at least hold class. She showed videos to all her classes on those two days, so she didn't have to lecture. *Thank goodness I have collected these videos over the years; they're really good and they've saved me more than once!*

Opening night, Doris entered the dressing room with cream on her face and her hair in rollers. Teri was using hot curlers on her hair and smiled at Doris via the mirror as she set her make-up box in her place. A gorgeous arrangement of red roses sat beside Teri, and Doris leaned over to smell them. "My how beautiful! You must have a special admirer, Teri."

"Not me, Dorie, you." Teri said, smiling as she stuck a clip onto a roller.

"Me?" Doris looked genuinely stunned. "Who would send me such beautiful flowers?"

"Well, why don't you open the card and see?" Teri was amused by Doris' surprise.

"Oh, good idea!" Doris pulled the card off its little stand and opened it to read: For Doris with all my love, Martin. "Oh, how sweet," Doris said, tearing up.

"Who is it, Doris? As if I didn't know," Teri grinned.

"Yes, they're from Martin. He is such a dear man."

"And romantic, too," Teri said, finishing up her rolling and heading to the bathroom for water.

Yes, Doris thought, *I guess so.* She didn't answer Teri, she concentrated on getting her table set up and beginning her make-up. "He was so hilarious at the party last weekend!" Teri called from the bathroom.

"You two must have a lot of fun together."

Yes, we do, thought Doris, *don't we?* "He surprises me a lot," she said.

Teri came out of the bathroom with four little bags in her hands. "This is for you, Dorie, you have been so wonderful to work with in this show. Thanks for putting up with us!" Teri gave Doris a big hug and handed her the bag full of candy treats. "I need to find Jayson, Bill, and Lenny. I'll be back in a minute." Teri said and disappeared down the hall.

"What d'ya mean—putting up with you?" Doris called, but Teri was gone on her mission of gift giving. Doris dug into the little bag and found a card that said simply: Break a leg! Love, Teri. Under the card was a wide assortment of candy, some of Doris' favorites. She munched on a Snickers bar as she dug into her purse to find her gifts.

Then, Jayson knocked on the door. "Dorie, are you decent?"

"That's a loaded question these days, Jayson, but if you mean should you come in, then yes, you certainly may."

Jayson peeked in with his hands behind his back. "I wanted to bring you your show gift." He closed the dressing room door behind him, which neither of them thought anything of. This was a safe place; no one here would be spying on them. "Dorie, I can't tell you how great it has been getting to know you as a person and working with you. You are so awesome! This isn't much, but I thought you might like it." He handed her a small box, wrapped in white tissue paper with a ready-made red bow stuck on top.

Doris unwrapped the gift and smiled at Jayson. It was a first edition hardback copy of the play with Edward Albee's signature on the inside front page. "Oh, God, Jayson, this is so special—where in the world did you find it?"

"Aw, you can find anything on E-bay!" He laughed, but she could see the genuine friendship in his face.

She held out her hand and took his, squeezing it tightly. "This means so much to me, Jayson. I have enjoyed getting to know you, too. You are a special young man; I hope you know that. You're going to make some young lady very happy one day." She looked down at the book, rubbing her thumb over the smooth front. Jayson stood quietly, as if trying to decide. "Oh! I almost forgot." Doris jerked her hand away and bent down to dig in her bag. She pulled out a box wrapped in a tasteful blue and black plaid, with a black bow. "Your show present. It's not as special as yours, Jayson, but when I saw it, I thought of you."

Jayson's hands fumbled with the paper and bow until finally it was open. "Ah, an alarm clock," he said, smiling. "I bet you can push a snooze alarm and it will go off again." Doris nodded. "It's great, Dorie, thanks." Jayson was gritting his teeth; Doris couldn't tell if he was angry, wanting to say something, or ready to cry. He pursed his lips, took a breath, and walked out of her dressing room. Doris held onto the back of her chair and looked at herself in the mirror. She stared at her own image for a long time, shaking her head.

The opening night performance was tense but wonderful. Doris tried to push back thoughts of Kayla, Dean Rogers, or President Simpson in the audience, gathering evidence for the hearing. She tried to focus on Lenny and Martin, two people she knew would be supporting her. In the final moments of the show, there wasn't a dry eye in the audience. They rose for a spontaneous standing ovation once the lights dimmed to black. Doris found she was crying, too. It had been so long since she had enjoyed being on stage. She felt exhilarated, despite her concerns.

As soon as the curtain hit the floor after the final bow, Lenny ran onto the stage and hugged and kissed the cast effusively. Doris noticed she and Teri were wearing her show present, a little sterling silver necklace with two little drama masks. Winnie came out to give everyone a high five. Bill gave thumbs up to everyone and disappeared backstage. Jayson picked up Winnie and spun her around and then gave Lenny a meaningful embrace. By the time he got to Doris, she was hugging Lenny. Finally, she reached out for Jayson and they hugged for a long time, weeks of tension melting between them. "Okay, anyone who's up for it can come over to my house," Lenny yelled above the den. "I have some soft drinks and chips, bring anything you want."

Martin peeked around the curtain as Doris was releasing Jayson. "Doris?" he said.

"Oh, Martin!" She ran into his arms and kissed him on the lips.

"You were wonderful," he told her, "You all were— magnificent!" He hugged her again and asked if she wanted to go out for dessert and coffee.

"Lenny has invited us to her place—I think I need to decompress with the cast. Can we go over there?"

"Well, of course! Sounds like fun." Martin offered to help Doris get her things, but she explained she and Teri needed to change clothes, remove make-up, and get her costumes ready for the following night. "All right, I'll run to the store around the corner and pick up some food, then come back. I'll be right outside in the car. Okay?"

"Perfect," Doris said, giving him a quick kiss on the mouth. "See you in about fifteen minutes."

When they arrived at Lenny's house, most of the cast and crew were already there, eating, yelling at the top of their voices, and dancing to some disturbingly loud rap music. Doris wondered if Lenny's neighbors ever complained. "Doris! Martin!" a chorus of voices shouted as they came in carrying a wide variety of chips and dips along with plenty of Dr. Pepper.

Winnie came over and gave her another hug. "You were so awesome, Dorie, just awesome!" She turned quickly and bounced back into the dancing circle with Jayson, Stacey, and Moses. Martin poured Doris a large drink while she picked up a little of everything and put it on their plates. They found an empty spot on the sofa next to Charley.

"Well, you certainly blew me away tonight, Doris. The whole cast was wonderful, but you know the play turns on Martha. You held up your end of the bargain nicely," Charley said then took a sip of her drink.

"Thank you so much, Charley. You remember Martin, don't you?" They made chit-chat for several minutes about the Halloween party, the show, and how cold the weather was getting. Then Charley leaned over and whispered something to Doris. "Thanks, Charley, it means a lot to me to have your support. Lenny has been wonderful, as well." Charley patted Doris' arm and got up to freshen her drink.

"What was she saying, Doris?" Martin asked with his mouth full of potato chips and the unruly flap of hair hanging over his eyes.

"She's sorry about all the nonsense at school." In her euphoria over the show, Doris managed to forget about her problems for a little while, but the sight of Jayson dancing and Charley's comments brought everything back down on her like a load of bricks. Her demeanor darkened considerably, and she sat munching quietly for the rest of the evening. Martin recognized this mood by now and knew all she needed was an arm around her shoulder and a willing ear when she was ready to talk.

Martin took her home while everyone else was still making a lot of noise and playing charades. She explained she had an early class the next day and a performance to rest for. Everyone seemed sad to see her go, but no one argued with her. Lenny walked them out to Martin's car and gave Doris a hug. "You were astounding tonight, Dorie. I'm so proud of how strong you are to face everything that's going on right now and still be able to give that kind of performance."

"It's necessary, Lenny, otherwise the bad people win." Lenny nodded and waved to Martin. They drove home in silence then Martin helped her get all her bags into the house. He said he guessed she needed some alone time and gave her a quick kiss on the cheek. She surprised him by pulling him close for a big hug. She lingered on his shoulder for some time, then pulled away and thanked him for being so understanding.

"Martin, did you see Gerald Rogers or President Simpson there tonight?"

"No, and I looked," he said. "I didn't see Kayla Washington or Phyllis either. But you know most students come on Thursday so they can save Friday and Saturday nights for dates, and the faculty and community come over the weekend."

Doris took a deep breath, realizing she would have to go through another performance wondering if they were out there with their notebooks, keeping score of demerits to bring up in the hearing. Martin kissed her again, told her he loved her, and bid her goodnight. The stress of the past week must have taken its toll on Doris, because for once, she laid her head down on the pillow and fell almost instantly into a dreamless sleep.

She showed videos in her two classes the next day and then hurried home to rest and get ready for the Friday performance. When she arrived at the theatre and saw Martin's beautiful roses, she felt guilty. She completely forgot to thank him, so she resolved to do it as soon as she saw him. Second night jitters cast a pall over everyone, and there was no joking around or yelling from room to room. According to theatrical superstitions, an opening night so spectacular meant tonight's performance could be a little off if the cast didn't stay completely focused. Doris hated second night performances; it was usually a letdown after opening. But still, she was grateful to finally be playing this wonderful role, so she tried to keep her spirits up.

Against all odds, the show held a consistent excellence that even a second night couldn't ruin. The tone of celebration was subdued, but there was still a lot of hugging and kissing going on behind the closed curtain. Doris was pulling away from Lenny when she looked up and saw Martin standing in the wings. She hugged him tightly, thanking him profusely for the roses. He laughed and waved to everyone else on stage. "You all keep getting better!"

A few people said thanks, but many of them were busy talking with parents and friends who drove long distances to see the play. Bill hugged a woman whom Doris presumed was his wife. Later, he introduced her as his sister, Colleen, from Georgia. "Oh really? Where in Georgia?" Doris asked politely. When it turned out to be Atlanta, the two women chatted about Atlanta, since Doris had lived there during her college days at Agnes Scott. And so, the conversation continued until Bill finally pulled Colleen away.

Doris didn't feel like partying tonight, she wanted to go home with Martin and watch television. They were headed toward the dressing room when she heard a familiar voice call out her name. It was Phyllis, standing near a large saw in the shop area. "Phyllis, how nice of you to come," Doris said, trying to pretend this was any other play when her department head would come out and lend her support.

"Well, you were magnificent, Doris. I know you are talented with art, but I had no idea you were such a wonderful actress." Phyllis moved to Doris and took her hands. "I can't imagine having to do such a demanding role—especially with everything else you have on your plate right now."

"Well, frankly, Phyllis, the play is what's kept me sane. It was therapeutic to throw myself into such a complex character who has more troubles than I do!" Doris was trying to make a joke; Phyllis laughed a little, but it rang as false as the joke.

"I wanted to let you know your hearing has been set for the Monday before Thanksgiving at three in the faculty meeting room. I'll give you more details later—you need to enjoy the play right now."

Doris nodded and made a mental note of the date. She would be back from her conference and have a short work week due to the holiday. Perhaps she would recover enough strength to handle whatever the outcome. Phyllis wished her a good run and turned to go. Martin stepped back over and put his arm around Doris' shoulder. They walked quietly into the dressing room to pick up Doris' belongings.

All day Saturday Doris and Martin spent quiet time together grading papers and getting notes ready for the coming week. The weather took a turn for the worse, and it poured a cold rain all day long. It felt good to Doris to curl up on the sofa with Martin and Felix and sip hot chocolate. She didn't even get out of her nightgown.

Around three o'clock the doorbell rang and Doris opened the door to see her brother's smiling face. "Ted? What are you doing here?"

"You think I want to miss my favorite sister in her big performance?" Doris stood for a moment in shock and then lunged out to hug him and pull him into the house.

"Martin! Look who's here!" Martin came over and shook Ted's hand with one hand and took his suitcase from him with another. "I can't believe you came—where are Tammy and the kids?"

"Well, we didn't think teenagers would appreciate it." Doris laughed. "Tammy had a church commitment anyway, so she stayed at home with the kids."

"Gosh, I am so glad you're here." Doris was genuinely touched by Ted's visit and immediately became a gracious hostess. "The guest bedroom is all clean and ready for you, so do whatever you need to get settled and then come on into the living room. The weather is so nasty, Martin and I are being lazy today." Suddenly, she felt uncomfortable in her gown and robe. When Ted disappeared into the hall bath, she made a hasty exit into her bedroom to dress. She put on her favorite corduroy slacks with a black sweater and pulled a brush through her hair. When she emerged, Martin and Ted were sipping coffee in the living room, talking about the play and how good it was.

Martin made a lame excuse to leave so Doris and Ted could have some time together. He agreed to come by later to take Ted to the play. At first Doris tried to maintain an air of casualness, asking about Tammy and the kids and chatting about the mercurial weather in Tennessee. Ted nodded and smiled occasionally, letting his sister go around the block before she came to the point. "And mother's house is being fixed up. I assume so anyway. To tell you the truth, I haven't been out there to check on it. I've been so busy. And, you know, it's hard."

"Well, I doubt if there's any need, Doris. I'm sure it will sell quickly, and you will be able to put it behind you." Doris stared at Ted, licking her lips and wringing her hands. Suddenly she leaned over on the sofa and hugged him tightly.

"I'm so glad you came, Ted." She pulled away, wiping a small tear from her eye. "I have decided to stay and fight the complaint, you know. I'm meeting with Ethan on Monday. My campus hearing is set for the following Monday, before Thanksgiving break. Everything is moving so quickly. I finish the play tonight, then go to my conference on Thursday, then . . . are you and Tammy coming up for Thanksgiving? No, I guess you wouldn't, would you, with Mother gone. I guess you'll go be with Tammy's family? It will be nice for the kids, not to have to travel so far again."

"Doris?"

"Yes?"

"You want to tell me what this whole mess is about?"

Doris looked down at her hands and took a deep breath. She went into the kitchen and poured them glasses of wine. When she came back to the living room, she told him all about Jayson, the smoking lessons, the night at the bar, and his ex-girlfriend. Ted assumed the posture of a concerned lawyer listening to a client, but Doris didn't notice. She was too ashamed to look him in the eye. When she finished, she leaned back on the sofa and covered her face with her hands.

"Is that all?" Ted said in astonishment. "I thought for sure there was some kind of sex going on—I mean, isn't this kid over twenty-one anyway? What's the big deal?"

Doris couldn't believe how insensitive he was being, but she tried to remember how the non-academic or "real" world operates. You're presumed innocent until proven guilty. But at a small liberal arts college, being innocent has little, if anything, to do with it. "Ted," she said evenly, "I know it's hard for anyone not in academia to understand the complex politics of tenure, promotion, and moral codes, but this is a serious allegation. This student has threatened to go public if I don't resign, which will not only hurt me and my career, but it will reflect negatively upon the college to prospective students and their parents, not to mention the board of directors and alumni. The appearance of something improper is sometimes enough to ruin a career. I know it might be best for me to leave, pretending I want to move on to bigger and better things." She paused, took a sip of wine and ran her finger around the rim. "But this is my home.

Martin is here, my house is here, and my life is here. I can't give it all up without a fight." Ted put his arm around her, and they sat for several minutes on the sofa, breathing in unison. "I'm so glad you're here," Doris said again.

35

Everyone knew it was closing night so they gave their best efforts and were rewarded with another standing ovation. Ted came backstage with Martin, his arm full of pink roses. Doris was so overwhelmed she cried on his shoulder. Tootsie came around the corner carrying a bouquet of yellow roses, for friendship, and gushed about her performance. She introduced her to a lovely young woman, maybe thirty, with Tootsie's curly blonde hair, dimples, and bright blue eyes. "You must be Hayley! I'm so glad to finally meet you," Doris said taking her hand.

"You were just amazing Dr. Peechum, I don't have time to go to the theatre often, but I think this is the best thing I've ever seen."

"You are so kind, Hayley, but please, just call me Doris." Doris introduced her to Ted who remembered Tootsie right away.

"I remember you two locking me in a closet one time."

Tootsie laughed. "You were going to tell Mrs. Peechum that we were the ones who broke that picture frame—what did you expect us to do?"

Doris frowned. "I think you're making that one up, Teddy!"

"I remember Mom found me asleep on her shoes, and you were grounded for a week!"

They laughed and recalled childhood memories until Tom started moving furniture off the set. The cast dispersed in different directions, knowing they had to be back early the next day to strike the set, and the big party would follow at Lenny's. Martin drove Ted and Doris to a little bistro in nearby Chattanooga that stayed open until the wee hours serving a full menu. Tootsie and Hayley begged off, saying they had to make sure the kids were in bed.

Once they got settled into their booth, Martin reported to Doris the dean and president were both in the audience and seemed to enjoy the show. "Who could tell for sure," Martin gave a mirthless laugh, "but they were standing with everyone else." He paused, then noted, "I didn't see

Kayla. Of course, that doesn't mean she wasn't there."

"Well, I guess if there's any problem, I'll find out soon enough. Let's enjoy our drinks and my brother's visit," Doris told Martin. He nodded his head and patted her hand.

"You were wonderful, Doris," Ted said, stretching his arms out and resting them on the back of the booth. "I know you've done a lot of acting, but I had no idea you could handle a role like this. Why didn't you go into theatre?"

Doris was flattered, her cheeks turned a rosy pink. "You are so nice to say it, Ted, but first, I couldn't deal with the lifestyle of professional theatre, so much travel and always wondering if there'll be another gig. And I certainly didn't want to teach it. There's no money in it, either! At least with art, you can get a job in layout or graphic design. With my degrees in art history I can teach, be a museum curator, or even do research for a media firm or such. No. I'm happy with it this way, but thanks." Their food came, and Doris soon realized how famished she was. They chatted happily for the next hour; Ted entertained them with stories of raising teenagers. He even told Martin some childhood stories about Doris that made her blush, but she was having fun. *For the first time in so long,* she thought, *I'm having such a good time.* She didn't want the evening to end, but eventually it did. Ted had an early flight back to Baton Rouge, and Martin was struggling to stay awake. Doris was so invigorated she could have stayed up all night. Martin dropped Doris and Ted off at the theatre so she could drive her car home.

Doris tried to make small talk with Ted on the ride home, but her mind kept trying to rewrite history. *If only I hadn't gone to the bar,* she thought. *If only I hadn't gotten drunk. If only, if only . . .*

"Doris? Are you all right?" Ted's voice cleared the fog.

"Fine, why?"

"Because you just drove past your house."

Doris jerked her head around and then back again. "I'm sorry, Ted. I have so much on my mind." She pulled into a nearby road and turned the car around. When she parked in her driveway she rested her forehead on her hands on the steering wheel. "I don't know what to do, Ted. I'm so scared I'm going to go through all the hearings and still end up losing my job. Then I couldn't even pretend I wanted to leave—everyone would know I was forced to. How will I ever get another good position if that happens?" She was sobbing into her hands; Ted started rubbing her back.

"I wish I could tell you what to do, Doris. I think I would leave as soon as I could. If these people consider you this 'disposable', then why would you want to work for them? There are other colleges and other jobs—like you were telling me tonight." He paused, Doris kept sobbing. "But, still, I see your point. This is your home, you haven't done anything wrong, so why should you give it up without a fight? I hope you haven't lost the fight before you even begin."

"That's what I'm afraid of."

"I think you should wait and speak with Ethan. He's much better with these kinds of cases, and because he still lives in Kerryville, he may be better able to gauge public opinion. Why don't you try and put it out of your mind until you talk to him?"

"I'll try."

Doris drove Ted to the airport around eight the next morning and waited with him as long as she could. He kissed her cheek and gave her a warm hug. She squeezed him tightly and thanked him for coming. With both parents gone now, Doris felt closer to Ted. They waved, and Doris stood there watching him and the endless parade of passengers removing shoes and putting their bags and purses on the conveyor for security check. She seriously considered buying a ticket to anywhere and getting on the plane right then and there. But she resisted. Felix was waiting at home, and she had other responsibilities.

She took a long bath, listened to some soothing music, and was finishing a cup of coffee when Martin rang the doorbell to take her to the theatre. The strike ended more quickly than she expected. Jayson did a wonderful job in planning and organizing, despite snide comments from Tom. Lenny stayed at home to get the house ready for the party, so Doris suggested they leave a little early and go help Lenny. By the time they arrived, Lenny had cleaned the house and was beginning to set candles on the porch. Charley was on call at the hospital and had left at the last moment, so Lenny was grateful for the help. Doris and Martin put the soft drinks left over from her Halloween party into the refrigerator and then arranged tables and chairs, set out bowls, and got everything ready in time to sit down and talk for a few minutes before the hurricane hit.

Around five, the doorbell started ringing and the music started playing. They all danced, played charades, ate too much food, and stayed too late, but it was a wonderful celebration. Doris even felt comfortable enough to dance with Jayson while Martin tried to bounce around with Winnie. When Martin walked her to her door, they were both dragging their feet up the steps. He came inside long enough to give her a decent kiss goodnight and feed Felix a bit of cheese he brought home from the party.

Doris finished her classes Monday afternoon and headed to Ethan's office located downtown. Kerryville had one main street with two traffic lights. Since the mall was built in the early eighties the only businesses left downtown were law offices and a few bookstores and cafes. The recently renovated old town area near Le Petit, had blossomed nicely with art studios, boutiques, and coffeehouses, but "official" downtown Kerryville was almost sad. Doris remembered when a large J.C. Penney's store anchored one end of town with a Woolworth's and Miller's on the other end. In-between was a series of small dress and gift shops bustling with activity every Saturday morning when Avis led Doris by the hand on her weekly shopping trips.

Doris stood on the street, looking up and down, remembering Avis in her red wool coat, arms loaded down with bags. Ethan's was the nicest building on its block. Inherited from his father, he left the building much as it has been before, a large red brick edifice, with Doric columns and a white marble foyer. Doris once visited Ethan's father there years ago, but she couldn't remember any details. Someone had apparently updated the decor. His secretary greeted Doris warmly, offering her something to drink and assuring her Mr. Anderson would be with her shortly. Doris accepted a bottled water with a cup of ice and smiled as she remembered her nights on Avis' velvet sofa with Ethan.

"Doris?" Ethan's voice hadn't changed a bit, still deep and smooth. He put on more than a few pounds over the years, but his eyes were still kind and his smile quite special. He led her into his spacious office, and she made some comments about how nice it was and how proud she was of his success.

"Well, thank you, Doris. You haven't done so badly yourself." Doris smiled at first, but then she remembered the mess she was in and turned her gaze toward the floor. Ethan didn't sit behind his desk, like she assumed he would with most clients. He sat in the chair beside her and laced his fingers together, resting his hands on one arm of the chair. "Mother and I came to the show Saturday night, Doris. You were amazing."

"Oh, thank you, Ethan. You should've come backstage to say hi."

He smiled. "I had to get Mother home, you know. But I was really blown away by your performance."

Doris lowered her eyes, shy when receiving compliments. "Thanks, Ethan."

"Now why don't you tell me what I can do to help you?"

Doris explained the whole story to Ethan, who sat listening intently without any comment or appearance of judgment. Ted advised her to tell him everything. "One thing you don't want," he warned, "is Ethan being surprised by something in a hearing or in court."

"I'm so ashamed of myself, Ethan, and I'm especially sorry you have to know all this about me. But Ted says you're the best, and well, I already knew that, anyway."

"Doris, don't be silly. First, you have nothing to be ashamed of. It sounds to me like you are a victim of someone's sick revenge plot. I won't lie to you, Doris, your actions were not, well, not the smartest decisions you've ever made. But, you didn't do anything illegal, and to my mind, nothing immoral. You didn't drive while intoxicated, you didn't sleep with this young man, and you tried to be honest and up-front with your department head. Unfortunately, that may have been your worst mistake. If you and Jayson had simply lied, said he didn't spend the night, then it would be the complainant's word against yours."

"It's not who I am, Ethan." Doris took a deep breath.

"I know, Doris. It's what I always admired about you. That brutal honesty!" He chuckled, perhaps remembering the time she broke up with him. Doris wasn't sure how to respond. "I'm trying to lighten things up a bit, Doris, sorry."

"So, what do you think I should do?"

"Well, that is the question, isn't it?" Ethan looked at her and nodded. "Here's what I advise."

Doris barely had time to digest Ethan's suggestions over the next few days. She needed to cover a lot of material in her classes to get them ready for the two days off for her conference. Over the course of time, Martin's clothes had gradually made their way into Doris' closet, but now she had cleared a drawer for him, as well. He moved some more clothes into Doris' house Wednesday evening so he could stay with Felix during her absence. He spent the night and then drove her to the airport early Thursday morning and saw her off to New York City.

She settled into her spacious room at the Marriott Marquis in Times Square where her conference was being held and then approached the registration desk to get a schedule of events. She wanted to confirm the time for her session and then go find the room so she wouldn't have to hunt for it before her presentation. She looked over the hotel map, located the small room situated on a side hallway on the third floor. She would present her paper the next afternoon at one thirty, right after the lunch break. "Okay," she said to herself, "now I can relax and have some dinner."

After a quiet meal of grilled chicken salad, Doris headed up to her room. She called Martin to let him know she arrived safely and to ask about Felix, then took a hot bath, and napped before dressing up for the opening reception.

Doris noticed on the job postings board a call for applications to head the art department at Agnes Scott. *Dr. Chavatel must be retiring*, she thought. She impulsively signed up for an interview slot; *better keep my options open.*

The conference was good for revitalizing her interest in art history because it made her feel like a graduate student again, but most of the conference was uneventful. On Friday afternoon, Doris presented her paper on a panel with two other presenters who discussed female artists in other periods. They had a good-sized audience who asked relevant questions and seemed to appreciate their efforts. She sat in on several interesting sessions, ran into a few old friends from Agnes Scott, some former colleagues and people she knew only through the conference, and took in one Broadway show on Friday night.

Her interview for the position at her alma mater was set for Saturday afternoon. Doris arrived early and sat outside the hotel room door waiting to be called. The door opened and a young man, possibly thirty-something, was ushered out by Alex Pickrell. "Oh my gosh, Doris! I saw your name on the sign-up sheet and wondered if it was you!" She stepped forward to hug Doris, and they chatted happily as they went into the room. Although there were beds in the next room, this was apparently a suite with a large "living room" that had been reconfigured into an interview space. At a large table sat Georgia Chavatel, Doris' former teacher and advisor who became chair of the department about 15 years ago, Alys Slovinik who headed the studio art program, and Alex, who had started teaching at ASC the same year Doris began as a freshman. There were hugs and chatting all around as Doris greeted her old family from college.

"Doris, or I should say Dr. Peechum, it is so good to see you," began Dr. Chavatel. I hope we can meet for supper or something tonight to catch up on old times, but we do need to try and keep to a schedule today since we have others signed up for interviews."

"Of course," Doris answered. "It is wonderful to see all of you again." As Doris had guessed, Georgia explained that she was retiring after this year.

"In respect to her many years of service, the committee asked her to be a part of the decision-making process in bringing someone in to replace her," Alex explained.

"I know this is not my business, but I would have thought the chair would be chosen from within." Doris knew she had no position to pose this question, but it was awkward knowing them so well.

Alys spoke up first. "Well, Doris, Alex and I are happy in the classroom and really don't want to be in administration. As you know, we have a small department, and we thought it would also be more beneficial to the students to have some new blood. We've all been at ASC since you were there." Doris nodded and they got into the business of the interview, asking her why she was applying, what had she done in the past 25 years in her field, and so on. She wasn't sure why she was applying, but she didn't say that. She explained that in this point in her career, it was time to either move on or stay put, and there was no opportunity for advancement at KC.

Doris thought the interview went well, and everyone maintained a professional deportment. They asked her to join them for dinner, and she left to attend other sessions. When she opened the door, there were two hopefuls sitting in the hallway. *I guess I took up more than one slot*, she thought, but just smiled and nodded at them.

By Sunday she was ready to come home. She missed Martin and Felix and sleeping in her own bed. Martin picked her up at the airport and took her to dinner at Le Petit. When she got home, Doris hugged Felix so hard and for such a long time he started meowing. She and Martin laughed as she placed him gently in his hammock, and then he made her a cup of coffee while she unpacked her bag. Finally, the reality of the next day settled on them like a layer of radioactive dust. The hearing was set for three o'clock in the faculty meeting room. Martin would not be allowed to attend, but he assured her he would be nearby. Doris didn't feel like crying, she felt numb. The realization that the college was going forward with the hearing and making her answer the complaint in such an indiscreet manner, left her with more pain than anger. *Where are my colleagues,* she thought, *where are my champions? Have I done nothing useful here—have I contributed nothing?*

36

Doris did her best to keep up a normal day attitude during her Monday classes, but she didn't think she was succeeding. She wondered if every giggle or sly look indicated her secret was out, and more than once she found herself miles away when someone asked a question. She let both classes go a little early then retreated to her office to hide. An occasional student or colleague knocked at her door, but she kept the light off and the noise down. She didn't want to see anyone—not students, colleagues, no one—not even Martin. At quarter till three, she made her way across campus to Hillman Hall and up the stairs to the faculty meeting room. The tiered seats allowed everyone to see and be seen, which Doris hated. She waited at the door patiently until Ethan showed up. The committee and a few others, such as Dean Rogers and Phyllis Hathaway, came striding down the hall, chatting amicably. *So casual,* Doris thought, *they are all calm and easy-going. I may lose my job today, and they are chatting in the hall like they're on their way to lunch.*

They all greeted Doris warmly, which made her even more apprehensive. She introduced everyone to Ethan, who shook hands politely with the dean and chair of humanities. "You don't need a lawyer today, Doris, this is just a hearing," Dean Rogers commented as he looked Ethan up and down.

"Well," Doris started, "Ethan is an old friend, and he suggested it would be in my best interests to have someone as my advocate." Dean Rogers raised his bushy eyebrows and tilted his head, giving Doris a suspicious look. She didn't care, this was war and all was fair—right?

Everyone filtered into the room, with the dean and Phyllis taking seats near the rear. They were here only for observation. The committee was comprised of two seniors, neither of whom looked familiar to Doris, two tenured full professors, and the president of the faculty, Abigail Johnson. She asked the committee members to take their places at the head table and instructed Doris to sit in the front row of seats. Ethan sat behind her. While everyone was getting situated, Jayson appeared at the door and took a seat near Doris. As she looked up to greet him, Stacey and Winnie appeared at the door behind him. Dr. Johnson invited them to sit in the front row, near but not beside Doris. Doris and Jayson looked at Stacey, who was clearly in charge, and then back at each other in total disbelief, but they didn't speak. Doris closed her eyes and breathed deeply. Winnie took a seat on the other side, away from Stacey.

Dr. Johnson stood at the center of the front table, an attractive, albeit overweight, black woman in her mid-fifties wearing a simple but attractive navy suit. Doris had seen her at faculty meetings, knew she taught sociology, but had never interacted with her except for faculty functions. She introduced herself, the committee members, the complainants, the defendants, and the observers. "We are only here today to determine if Ms. DeBenedetto's complaint holds enough merit to warrant a review by the faculty council. If so, that group would decide if Dr. Peechum has violated the Kerryville College code of ethics to a sufficient degree that further action should be taken. It is important to note the committee members have not been told anything about the details of the complaint. It is our function to listen objectively and render a decision based on evidence brought forth today, not rumor or innuendo.

"Although this is an informal hearing, we will observe a few rules of procedure. Ms. DeBenedetto will speak first, then Dr. Peechum and Mr. Jeffries. Winifred Lawson is here as a witness to events, but she will not be testifying unless someone has a question for her. The committee may ask questions of anyone at any time, but the principals of the hearing are asked to speak only with permission. Observers may not participate in any way. Also, the faculty secretary, Dr. Van Buren, will take the minutes of this meeting. Anything said here today is strictly confidential. I am here only to serve as a facilitator for the hearing and cannot vote unless the committee members reach a tie vote. Are there any questions?" No one spoke. Doris was gritting her teeth so hard Jayson looked over at her and grimaced. She didn't look at him; she couldn't. She promised herself she would not cry—and if she looked at Jayson right now, she knew she would.

Dr. Johnson asked Stacey to state her complaint. She explained she had evidence of an affair between Dr. Peechum and her student, Jayson Jeffries. She testified she saw them alone together on several occasions outside of rehearsals and class, and Jayson visited Dr. Peechum's home, alone, on several occasions. "Probably the worst incident, however, was when she, Dr. Peechum, I mean, took three of us in her car to a gay bar in Chattanooga and then got too drunk to drive us home. I drove her car to campus and then Jayson, I mean Mr. Jeffries, drove her home and spent the night with her." Stacey didn't appear nervous, angry, or in any way upset. She did, Doris noted, look arrogant.

A student committee member asked, "How do you know this, Ms. DeBenedetto? Didn't you say you drove home to campus and Mr. Jeffries took Dr. Peechum home?"

Stacey looked down at her hands. "I got in my car and followed them. I knew Jayson drank a few beers, and I didn't think it was a good idea for him to be driving. I saw him basically carry her into the house and not come out until the morning."

"You stayed there all night?"

"I stayed until the lights were out and there was no sign of any movement."

"So, you don't know for sure Mr. Jeffries spent the whole night—right?"

"Well, they came in together the next morning to set work, so I assumed he spent the night." Stacey was resolute. "Ms. Lawson here was at the bar with us and can testify to Dr. Peechum's condition and that they came in the next morning together."

The Latin professor spoke up and said, "Ms. Lawson, is that true? Did you see Dr. Peechum intoxicated? Do you think Mr. Jeffries spent the night at Dr. Peechum's home?"

Winnie sighed and looked around the room. She was clearly uncomfortable with being at the hearing and having to speak against Dr. Peechum, her new friend with the cool car. Doris wondered what power Stacey had over her. "Dr. Peechum took us to the bar, but we go there all the time. It's not like it was her idea. I have no way of knowing if Jayson spent the night at Dr. Peechum's. If they came in together the next morning, I didn't notice. And frankly, I don't care." Stacey eyed her with a look that promised retaliation, but Winnie crossed her arms over her stomach and looked away.

"Winnie—uh, Ms. Lawson is only nineteen, which means she should not be drinking at a bar, and I saw her drinking a beer. I think Dr. Peechum paid for it," Stacey said, trying to distract from Winnie's comments. Doris looked at her with an open mouth, then turned and looked at Jayson. She wasn't going to cry now; she was too angry.

"Ms. Lawson, you said you have been to that bar before," the Latin professor asked, "Did you ever have a drink when you were not with Dr. Peechum?"

Winnie looked at him and smiled. "Yes, many, many times, Dr. Davis. And I don't remember Dorie buying my beer."

The Latin professor straightened up and nodded. Doris was looking at Leonard Davis, remembering a party she attended at his home. Dr. Johnson asked if Stacey wanted to make any further comments. She looked at Doris and Jayson, then shook her head. "All right then, Dr. Peechum, what would you like to say in response to this complaint?"

Doris stood to speak; she couldn't do this sitting down. "Thank you, Dr. Johnson. First, I would like to say there is nothing of a sexual nature going on between Jayson Jeffries and me. We were cast in a play, which put us together a lot for rehearsals and yes, those scenes are pretty steamy, but I don't think Elizabeth Taylor had an affair with George Segal any more than I did with Mr. Jeffries. That's why they call it acting." Dr. Johnson and other committee members raised their eyebrows at Doris' tone. "I don't mean to be flip, but Ms. DeBenedetto's allegations simply do not hold any merit. The few times Jayson came over were for rehearsals—he taught me how to smoke—and he gave me a ride when my car was broken down." Doris paused and took a slow even breath. *Should I take Ethan's advice*, she wondered. Doris stood for a full minute, which seemed like an eternity, looking at her hands. The panel had just asked her "truth or dare," and she decided to take the dare. She looked at Jayson and then to Ethan; they smiled and nodded. She looked over at Stacey, took a deep breath, then looked at the committee members as she continued. "The incident in question simply didn't happen the way Ms. DeBenedetto remembers. I did go to the bar with the students because they invited me. I drove because Ms. Lawson asked to ride in my car. I didn't eat much for supper that evening, so when I had two drinks at the bar I didn't think it was a good idea to drive. So, I asked Stacey, Ms. DeBenedetto, to drive. I knew she had not had anything to drink. When we dropped the girls off at the dorm, Jayson said he felt all right to drive, so I agreed. He walked me to the front door, came in for a minute to see my cat, and have a cup of coffee. I did turn the lights off in the front of the house, which must be why Ms. DeBenedetto thought we went to sleep, but my living room is in the back of my house. You can be back there with a lamp on and no one would know from the front." Jayson looked up at Doris in surprise, but he maintained a calm expression, Ethan crossed his arms and tried not to grin. "After our coffee, Jayson took my car back to campus and, I assume, went to his dorm. He returned to pick me up for set work the next morning, and I drove us back to campus. That's why we came in together Saturday morning. It was totally innocent, and I'm sorry Ms. DeBenedetto put herself to so much trouble and was so concerned. She had no reason to be. If she had only come to me first, which I believe is the usual protocol, then this whole misunderstanding could have been avoided." Doris sat down; Jayson stared at her. She didn't look back at him, but kept her gaze front, facing the committee with a calm expression.

Phyllis raised her hand from the back of the room, and Dr. Johnson nodded to her.

She stood and said, "I have information pertinent to Dr. Peechum's testimony." She gave Doris a piercing stare and pursed her lips.

Dr. Johnson cleared her throat before speaking. "I'm sorry, Dr. Hathaway, you are not allowed to speak about the incident in question during these procedures because you were not involved. You and Dr. Rogers are only here to observe. I mean no disrespect, but if you interrupt again, I will have to ask you to leave." Phyllis gave her an indignant look and sat back down. She scowled at Dean Rogers who maintained a complacent expression and gave her no eye contact.

Dr. Davis raised his hand slightly off the table and Dr. Johnson nodded for him to speak. "I'd like to ask Ms. DeBenedetto why she didn't speak with Dr. Peechum first."

Dr. Johnson looked toward Stacey and said simply, "Ms. DeBenedetto? Would you like to respond?"

Stacey rubbed her front teeth with her tongue and looked at Dean Rogers and Phyllis. Dr. Johnson spoke again. "Ms. DeBenedetto?"

"I didn't know that's what I was supposed to do. I mean, if you're not happy with a waiter in a restaurant, then you speak to the manager. I figured I should talk to her boss. Besides, we were working on the play together, and I wasn't sure how it might affect that relationship."

Dr. Davis bit his lips together and tapped a pencil on his notebook.

He looked over at Dr. Johnson. "May I ask Phyllis, I mean, Dr. Hathaway a question?"

Dr. Johnson looked at the other committee members, who shrugged their shoulders at her. "Well, Dr. Davis, it's a little unusual, but I don't see any harm. Dr. Hathaway, you'll have to confine your answer to the question asked and not elaborate."

Dr. Davis nodded and looked up at Phyllis. "Dr. Hathaway, I am wondering what you did when Ms. DeBenedetto came to you for advice. When students come to me with complaints about a teacher in my department, I send them back to the teacher to see if the issue can be worked out between them. I'm wondering why you didn't do that first?"

Phyllis stood and smoothed her skirt against her legs. "Well, Dr. Davis, it was mainly because Stacey was so upset. She was clearly concerned about upsetting the members of the cast by bringing this up before the play was over, and well, I was concerned about the situation itself and Dr. Peechum's alleged behavior. I didn't feel qualified to handle something so potentially damaging myself, which is why I advised Stacey to write a letter explaining her concerns so I could take it to the dean and try to decide what should be done."

Dr. Johnson pulled her glasses down and let them dangle on her ample bosom by a thin gold chain. "You mean you're the one who advised Ms. DeBenedetto to write the letter of complaint?"

Phyllis cleared her throat and looked over at Gerald Rogers who was picking at something on his thumbnail. "Well, I asked her to put her concerns in writing so I could take it to the dean. I never told her to write a letter to the dean, the president, and the board."

Stacey turned around quickly and wrapped her arms tightly over her chest, her mouth closed tightly.

"I see," said Dr. Johnson. "Thank you, Dr. Hathaway, you may be seated." She asked if anyone else wanted to ask Dr. Peechum any more questions."

"But I did talk to Dr. Peechum, and she told me . . ."

"Thank you, Dr. Hathaway, you have answered the question. That is the only information you are allowed to present." Once again Phyllis took an even breath, set her jaw, and took her seat.

The members of the panel looked at each other, but none of them asked any questions. They seemed more eager to hear from Jayson, as they all looked his way. Dr. Davis tapped the eraser of his pencil absentmindedly on the table. Dr. Johnson nodded to Jayson. As he stood up, he tucked his hands into his pockets. "Dr. Peechum said it as well as I could. We go to this bar all the time, the theatre students, that is. And for the record," he paused, looking at Stacey who was sitting with her teeth gritted together so tightly Doris thought she might chip a crown, "*I* paid for Winnie's beer. I had eaten a large supper, and two beers did not make me drunk. I was fine to drive, so I took Dr. Peechum home and then came back to campus. I'm sorry she has to go through all this because some busybody," another pause, another glance toward Stacey, "doesn't have a life and must spend her time watching others live theirs. That's all I have to say." He gave Stacey one last and especially cruel look, then took his seat. Stacey looked up at the ceiling, and Doris continued to stare at the committee.

Dr. Johnson waited for a few moments, but there were no questions or comments. She announced the committee would meet before the Thanksgiving holiday to make its decision, which would be announced in the same room, at the same time, on the Monday following. Dr. Johnson reminded everyone that what transpired during the hearing was confidential and not to be discussed outside this room. She then looked around the room to see if anyone wished to comment. When no one spoke, she adjourned the hearing.

Doris and Jayson looked at each other and smiled. Stacey hurried from the room without a word to anyone, but Winnie lingered behind. She didn't speak to either Jayson or Doris, but she smiled at them as she sauntered out the door. Dean Rogers walked out behind Winnie, not looking at Doris, then the committee members began chatting about plans for Thanksgiving as they filtered out.

Doris was holding her breath until Jayson took her hand; he squeezed it gently. "Don't worry, Dorie, I'll make sure everyone in theatre knows what Stacey did. Lenny won't be asking her to direct next year, I guarantee it." Before Doris could say how sweet he was, he gave her a quick kiss on the cheek and ran off to catch up with Winnie.

Doris turned to thank Ethan and gave him a hug. He told her to call if she needed him again and then picked up his coat and gloves and left the room. Doris was gathering her purse and coat and started toward the door as Phyllis came down from the upper level of seats.

"Well, you certainly made me look like a fool," Phyllis said, wrapping her jacket over her arm.

Doris looked up, appearing stunned. "I'm not sure what you mean, Phyllis. It certainly wasn't my intention—this wasn't about you, you know."

"Well, I had already spoken to the dean and the president about what you told me, and now . . .now I guess I will have to either fight you on this or say I misunderstood you."

"I think that's what happened, Phyllis, and it's probably all my fault. When we talked, I guess I was feeling guilty about drinking in front of students. But as I thought about it, I really wasn't drunk, and when I said Jayson spent the night, I meant he stayed with me for a while. Not he spent the *whole* night. I'm sure I confused you. I would be happy to talk to Dean Rogers and President Simpson and straighten this all out."

Phyllis gave Doris a wary gaze. "I guess you will never get over my being hired as department head instead of you, will you?"

Doris was truly flabbergasted. "Is that what this is all about? You think I want your job? You must be kidding!"

"I know you did not recommend me for the job. I can only guess you wanted it for yourself."

"No, Phyllis, you don't know how wrong you are. First, I was offered the position because the board wanted to start with an internal search," Doris was finding she could lie quite easily if the occasion called for it. "I wasn't interested. I'm still not interested; I'm happy in the classroom. And once the committee opened the search to the public, I didn't have anything further to do with it. I wasn't even asked if I endorsed you for the position."

"Well, you certainly didn't support my new curriculum ideas last year."

"The interdisciplinary fine arts major?"

"It was a good idea."

"Maybe in a big university—we don't have the resources, faculty or otherwise, to offer that kind of program here."

"We could have worked it out."

"Yes, perhaps, if everyone worked an extra ten hours a week. Don't you think we're overworked enough as it is?" Doris kept her tone calm and sympathetic.

"You didn't even give it a chance, Doris. It was all I was asking for—

that you would help me develop it into a proposal for the faculty to vote on."

A light was dawning in Doris' mind. "Oh my god, you did all this, didn't you?" Phyllis took a deep breath and looked downward. "You took Stacey's complaint and made it into this huge deal to get rid of me, didn't you?"

"Doris, I don't think our work styles are compatible, but I would never go to these lengths to 'get rid of you', as you say. Stacey came to me, and I thought we owed it to the students to consider the matter and how it might reflect on the image of this college. Dean Rogers agreed with me, so we proceeded. That's all, Doris. You're the one who helped bring it to this point. If you had only lied from the beginning, then we wouldn't be here now, would we?"

"Silly me, I thought telling the truth was the right thing to do. I assumed my colleagues would give me the benefit of the doubt and stand behind me. But I don't know what I was thinking—I mean—it's dog eat dog here, isn't it? Every man for himself, right? This big 'collegial' hype we push to the press is nothing more than window dressing. And I'm the dope who fell for it."

"I don't know what you're talking about, Doris. I think we all get along quite well here."

"Yes, sure, as long as we keep our mouths shut. Thanks, Phyllis, this little talk has been most illuminating." Doris picked up her coat and turned to go.

"I guess you're better than us—is that it? Don't you think most of us start out as idealists and end up as cynics? Who among us hasn't sold his soul for tenure—you included."

"No, I don't think I did, Phyllis," Doris tried to sound confident, but she had lingering doubts about her debt to the devil when she was granted tenure. "At least I didn't consciously do it."

"Well, you did it today, didn't you?" Phyllis brushed past Doris on her way to the door. She left without another look or word to Doris, who stood for a moment staring at the door. She heard the clicking of Phyllis' heels on the hard linoleum floor of the hall and then down the stairs. It wasn't until the clicking faded completely away that Doris started to breathe again and felt a shaking begin in her legs. Her breath caught in little gasps, and she felt her knees sinking beneath her.

In her meeting with Ethan, he suggested she deny the complaint, but she told him she didn't want to lie, she couldn't do it. She came to the hearing with every intention of telling the whole truth and nothing but the truth, but she was so surprised to see Stacey and so angry at the accusations, that something else took over. She felt so betrayed. Doris had treated Stacey like a friend and trusted her as a theatre colleague. It all came pounding down on Doris alone in the meeting room, and she stayed there for a long time trying to calm down enough to leave. The last thing she wanted was to run into a committee member, or worse, Stacey, with tears streaking her cheeks.

It was nearly half an hour before Doris felt composed enough to go into the hall and down the steps of Hillman Hall. She walked to the faculty parking lot near the Humanities building and spotted Martin leaning against Carmen. He was freezing, his fedora on his head and his gloved hands tucked into his coat pockets; he steeled his face against the wind. She got close to him and didn't say a work; he held his arms out, and she fell into his embrace. Finally, she pulled away and unlocked the doors so they could sit in the car and get warm.

"Jayson told me everything," Martin said as he pulled his hat off and shoved the flap of hair off his face.

"Are you disappointed in me?" Doris hated what she did and would not have blamed Martin if he felt he same way.

"Because you saved yourself? Because you stood up to a mealy-mouthed little weasel? No, I'm not disappointed in you, Doris. I'm proud of you."

"You don't think I 'sold out'?"

"Why would I think that?"

"Well, I lied. I mean I told a lie to save my butt. Isn't that the same as selling out?"

"I think selling out is when you do something against your better judgement to get something you want. This little lie you told today is nothing—and what golden prize are you getting for it?"

"I'm getting to keep my job. And maybe I shouldn't. I mean I *was* drunk in public, and Jayson *did* spend the night at my house. I guess I did what they were accusing me of, didn't I?"

Martin leaned back in his seat and rubbed his chin. "Well, I guess it's a matter of degree. What you did was a one-time event. The only reason you got drunk is because you don't drink enough to know your limits. And Jayson stayed the night so he could take care of you. Do you know how many alcoholics we have on this faculty? Or how about the number of faculty members who truly do have affairs with their students? It happens all the time. Everyone looks the other way. You do one little thing, and no one is willing to let it go; I don't get it."

"It's because I don't know how to play the game, Martin. I realize now it has more to do with politics than morality or college mission statements. God, I am so dense!" Doris leaned forward and gently banged her forehead on the steering wheel.

"Well, I guess I am, too. I didn't even know there was a game!"

"Think about it, Martin. Did you ever play a game in college called 'truth or dare'?"

"I don't think so. Of course, I don't even remember half the idiotic things I did in college. Nor do I want to." He chuckled, trying to lighten her mood, but it didn't work.

"The game is simple—it's a way to get to know each other better. Someone asks you whether you want truth or dare. If you say 'dare,' then you must do some silly antic, usually something embarrassing. If you say truth, then you get asked a question and are sworn to tell the absolute truth."

"Sounds like a perfectly horrible game."

"Well, I always said truth. I thought telling the truth was easier than doing a stunt. People who ask for a dare have something to hide. That's what I thought." She paused, staring into the middle distance. "Today, I took the dare." Doris looked down at her hands on the steering wheel and sighed. Martin remained quiet, studying the little puffs of breath from her mouth lingering momentarily in the cold air of the car.

"I thought I could teach college and not be political. Gerald Rogers once told me in a meeting everything in life is political. I didn't know what he meant then, but I think I do now. It's more about who likes you than about doing a good job, teaching important content, or even helping students. I know those things are important, but not as much as the way you win favor with others." Martin gave her a dubious but sympathetic look. "No, Martin, remember when I wanted to remove ancient history from the Art History curriculum? Don't you remember Dr. Goodman, who incidentally teaches the course, raised some 'concerns for the students'?

Well, I thought she was thinking of the students, but I see now she saw it as taking numbers away from her class. Without enough of those in a class, the class will be cancelled. And I did it in one sweeping movement, without little diplomatic conferences with her in advance."

"What d'you mean 'diplomatic conferences'?"

"Well, when Hannah Waters wanted to take my survey of world art out of the film curriculum, she called me to her office and told me about the switch and why she was doing it. I see now she was hoping to circumvent any opposition on my part. She thought I might see it as her stealing students from my class. I guess survival is more about warm bodies in the seats of your classes than anything else. And Phyllis, basically admitted she orchestrated all this because I didn't support changes she wanted to make in the curriculum last year."

"What changes?"

"Well, that's it—it never got far enough for the other faculty to hear about it. Phyllis asked me to help her with it, and I didn't think it would work. That's not the real problem though, I see now. The real problem is I told her what I really thought, instead of going along with it."

Doris was quiet for a moment, then she shook her head and said, "I should have listened to my mother. She told me to pick my battles. I never thought about it until now. Here I am chugging along thinking that if I teach my students well and prepare them for careers in art, then I am doing my job. But I'm not, am I?"

Martin raised his eyebrows, pushed the hair off his face, and sighed heavily. "I guess you can be a little insensitive about people's feelings, Doris. I mean I don't think you do it intentionally, I see your bluntness sometimes puts people off, and they don't understand why you do it."

"I do it because it's the way I am—it's what people say they want, to have someone be honest with them. But you know, I think people usually want you to tell them what they want to hear with the appearance of being honest."

"Sugar-coating."

"Right."

"I think it's the way the world works, Doris. I don't think it's limited to college teachers."

"Maybe." Doris leaned back in the seat of her car and watched her gloved hands rubbing back and forth on the steering wheel. "Well, Martin,

I don't know if I can do it. I don't think I want to do it. Phyllis was furious with me, and I didn't understand it at all. But now, I think I see. I haven't been behind her enough, in policies, in programs. I don't scratch her back, so why should she go out of her way to scratch mine?"

"Oh, I wouldn't worry about it. I assume the committee will have the good sense to dismiss the complaint, and then it will all be over with. You won't have anything to worry about."

"I wish I could be sure, Martin, but even if you're right, I don't think Phyllis will ever forgive me."

"You're tenured, what can she do?"

"You know what she can do. She can assign me four sections of Art Appreciation, ask me to serve on every boring committee, and not endorse me for future promotions. And I dare say Gerald Rogers would stand right behind her."

"You can't be sure. When this is over, they'll get over it, you'll see."

"No, Martin, people with power never get over being slighted. You didn't hear what she said to me, Martin. I can see now I will have to leave; I can't work with these people anymore. Ultimately, I guess she gets her way."

"Leave? You can't leave, Doris. That would be terrible." Martin's face had a pained expression, the unruly flap of hair hung over his eye.

"Martin, I wouldn't be leaving you. I just don't think I can teach here any longer. I'm not sure I want to teach anywhere right now. Surely you understand why."

"Couldn't you wait and see if Phyllis gets over this and comes to her senses? I mean, you don't even know for sure what could happen."

Doris looked into Martin's soft, gray eyes, welling up with tears. Her nose began to tingle, too, so she took his face in her hands. "It doesn't matter, Martin, I have seen what happened this time. Phyllis was ready to hang me out on a limb and then cut it off. And when I stood up for myself, she took it as a personal insult. It doesn't matter now if she got down on her knees to apologize—which, by the way, she is *not* going to do—*I* don't think *I* will ever forgive *her*. Can you understand?"

Martin could, she saw it in his expression, but he didn't want to admit it. If he agreed with her, it gave her even more reason to leave. "Where will you go?"

"Well, I have some time to think about it, but I don't know. There's an opening at my old alma mater, but I don't know if I want to pursue it. I wish I knew, but I don't. I want to go forward, not back. Let's go have supper and stop talking about this okay? I need to take a break."

Martin nodded and leaned his head back on his seat. They both pulled tissues from the box Doris kept on the floor of Carmen's backseat and wiped wetness from eyes and noses. They had driven to school together in her car, so Doris took them both to her favorite fast food place and ordered for them both, and then headed home. Martin was quiet on the ride home. Doris' cell phone rang; Martin searched for it in Doris' purse till it stopped ringing. It was from Tootsie. "I'll call her tomorrow," Doris said.

Felix jumped down from his hammock to greet them as they entered her foyer. Doris put the food on the counter and picked him up. She rocked him like a baby as she waltzed into the bedroom to take her shoes off and change into something more comfortable. Martin took the initiative of getting the food onto plates and pouring Doris a huge glass of Dr. Pepper and milk for himself. Their dinner of cheeseburgers and fries was waiting on the table when she emerged.

"I'll go with you," he said, resolute and calm. "I don't have any ties to Kerryville—except for you. If you want to leave, then we'll both leave . . . if you want me."

Doris gave him a hug and whispered in his ear, "Of course, I want you to come! A wife shouldn't move somewhere without her husband, right?"

Martin looked at her, his face bright, the flap of hair staying in place for once. "Doris—do you mean it?" She nodded and he spun her around so fiercely her feet left the carpet.

They stopped spinning and laughed, the top of each one's forehead resting on the other's. He pulled away and bent slowly down to one knee and pulled the ring box from his pocket. "Doris Peechum, I love you so much. You are the perfect woman for me--smart, beautiful, and funny. Will you please do me the honor of being my wife?"

"You're willing to quit your job to go with me? Martin, you know it will be hard for you to find another job at this stage of your career."

"You mean as an old fart?" He laughed. "I'm close to retirement age, maybe I can just retire early and do research and write that book I keep putting off."

"You'd do that for me?"

"I'd do anything for you, Doris. I love you."

"Anything?" She gave him a wicked smile. He lowered his brows, wondering what mischief she had in mind. She just took his hand.

"Is this a truth or dare moment?"

"I guess you could say that." She helped him to his feet and started walking backwards, leading Martin by the hand, as she started to unbutton her blouse. "Follow me into the bedroom and I'll answer your question."

"The bedroom? Aren't we going to eat dinner out here? I have the table all set." Martin was truly puzzled, but Doris kept walking.

"Hmmm, suddenly, I'm not hungry—how about you?"

"Oh, well, I guess not." Martin wasn't sure how to respond; he had never seen Doris like this. She finished the buttons on her blouse by the time they reached the bedroom door and let it slide off her shoulders onto the floor. Before Martin could catch his breath, her pants were off and she let her hair down. She took him by the shoulders and backed him into the bedroom, where she pushed him gently onto the bed. Martin lay still, watching Doris as she peeled off her undergarments and lay down next to him. When his shirt came off and she started unbuckling his belt, he started to smile.

"Before I can say yes to your proposal, I have one condition," she said, kissing him, leading his hand to important places on her body. Martin smiled and nodded; he was eager to learn, and Doris was grateful to finally have a real lover. Somehow, it seemed all Martin needed was a little encouragement.

In the living room, the phone was ringing, but Doris and Martin didn't even hear it. The answering machine kicked on and the high-pitched voice of Sheila Grindstaff came through. "Dr. Peechum, I wanted to let you know we found a buyer for your mother's house. Call me whenever it's convenient."

Felix looked at the answering machine, tilting his head slightly to listen to the voice. He decided, however, the message wasn't important and continued eating his supper: the cheeseburgers and glass of milk Martin had left on the table.

 **END**

ACKNOWLEDGEMENTS

This book could never have been completed without the support of my loving family and friends. I've had so many wonderful friends willing to read through this manuscript and give me much needed advice. I'd like to thank Thelma Bianco, Ann Killebrew Taddie, Donna Latino, Elly Bolar, and Adrienne Bergeron for their responses and reflections. Special thanks to Christine Landry, Carol Luther, and my husband, Gary, for their in-depth analysis, careful eyes and notice of typos, grammar, syntax, and other content errors, such as plot and character inconsistencies. Any remaining problems with this book are my sole responsibility.

www.ingramcontent.com/pod-product-compliance
Lightning Source LLC
Chambersburg PA
CBHW030022180626

46810CB00001B/173